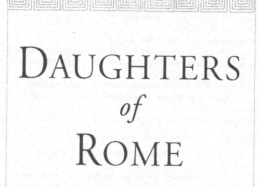

DAUGHTERS

of

ROME

KATE QUINN

BERKLEY BOOKS, NEW YORK

THE BERKLEY PUBLISHING GROUP
Published by the Penguin Group
Penguin Group (USA) Inc.
375 Hudson Street, New York, New York 10014, USA
Penguin Group (Canada), 90 Eglinton Avenue East, Suite 700, Toronto, Ontario M4P 2Y3, Canada
(a division of Pearson Penguin Canada Inc.)
Penguin Books Ltd., 80 Strand, London WC2R 0RL, England
Penguin Group Ireland, 25 St. Stephen's Green, Dublin 2, Ireland (a division of Penguin Books Ltd.)
Penguin Group (Australia), 250 Camberwell Road, Camberwell, Victoria 3124, Australia
(a division of Pearson Australia Group Pty. Ltd.)
Penguin Books India Pvt. Ltd., 11 Community Centre, Panchsheel Park, New Delhi—110 017, India
Penguin Group (NZ), 67 Apollo Drive, Rosedale, North Shore, 0632, New Zealand
(a division of Pearson New Zealand Ltd.)
Penguin Books (South Africa) (Pty.) Ltd., 24 Sturdee Avenue, Rosebank, Johannesburg 2196,
South Africa

Penguin Books Ltd., Registered Offices: 80 Strand, London WC2R 0RL, England

This is a work of fiction. Names, characters, places, and incidents either are the product of the author's imagination or are used fictitiously, and any resemblance to actual persons, living or dead, business establishments, events, or locales is entirely coincidental. The publisher does not have any control over and does not assume any responsibility for author or third-party websites or their content.

PRINTING HISTORY
Berkley trade paperback edition / April 2011

Library of Congress Cataloging-in-Publication Data

Quinn, Kate.
     Daughters of Rome / Kate Quinn.—1st ed.
          p.   cm.
     ISBN 978-0-425-23897-4 (Berkley trade pbk.)   1. Wives—Rome—Fiction.   2. Sisters—Rome—
Fiction.   3. Rome—History—Civil War, 68–69—Fiction.   I. Title.
     PS3617.U578D38 2011
     813'.6—dc22

                                                                                    2010032736

For Stephen
A.F. ∞

DAUGHTERS

of

ROME

Prologue

∽◡◟

A.D. 58

A hand.

Just a little girl's hand like any other, plump-fingered and a little sticky, but for a moment he saw blood all over it.

"Interesting," Nessus gulped. The girl stared up at him, expectant, and he looked at her palm again, hoping it had been a trick of the light. Maybe a shadow. But no, there it was: not a shadow but blood.

You're seeing things, he told himself. *You're seeing things.*

"What?" the child said, curious.

He swallowed a sudden burst of nervous laughter. Wasn't an astrologer supposed to see things when he looked at the stars, or into a palm?

But he never had before, not once since he'd gotten started in this business. Astrology wasn't about truth, after all—it was about pleasing the clients. Telling pregnant women that their stars foretold healthy sons; telling legionaries their futures held medals and glory. What successful astrologer told anybody there was enough blood in their hand to soak all Rome?

I could have run a wine shop. The sun was hot overhead, but Nessus felt chill sweat start to creep down his neck. *I could have become a trader. But no, I had to become an astrologer. Reading stars, reading palms when business gets slow, oh, why didn't I just open a wine shop?* The only blood anybody saw in a wine shop came from drunks giving each other a swollen nose.

And the morning had started with such promise. Nessus had come early to the Forum Romanum, staking himself a place on the shady side where the afternoon sun wouldn't beat down on his head like Vulcan's hammer, and laid out his little display of star charts on threadbare silk. By noon he'd been commissioned for three horoscopes (payment on delivery), read the palm of a grain merchant and spoke mysteriously of fat profits coming on the next harvest; squinted at the hand of a giddy young woman and whispered of a rich husband. Nessus had just been mopping his already balding forehead on his sleeve and contemplating a jug of wine at the nearest tavern when four little girls arrayed themselves expectantly before him.

"We want you to read our futures," the tallest had announced, and the rest promptly collapsed into giggles.

"There's no time," their nursemaid scolded, but Nessus looked them over with a practiced eye. Patrician girls, or he'd eat his straw sun hat: silk dresses, tooled leather sandals, veils over their hair to shield their skin. And patrician girls, even little ones like these, had coins to spend.

"Such futures ahead of you!" he intoned mysteriously. "Your stars sing to me of fame and fortune, beauty and love . . . two sesterces apiece, and cheap at the price. Which of you first?"

"Me, me!" Four hands presented themselves, variously grubby.

"No, me first, I'm the oldest! I'm Cornelia Prima, and that's my sister, she's Cornelia Secunda, and that's Cornelia Tertia and Cornelia Quarta, they're our cousins—"

Definitely patricians—only patricians had such a complete lack of imagination when it came to naming their daughters. Four girls born to one clan—undoubtedly the Cornelii!—and as was traditional, they'd all just been named Cornelia and then numbered in order. Nessus listened to their chatter with half an ear, not bothering to figure out which girl was which. They ranged in age from perhaps thirteen to five or six: a girl with dark hair wound in a crown around her head, a taller girl with the beginnings of a bust, a scabby-kneed towhead and a plump little giggler.

"Yes, what a future!" He put on his most oracular voice, and the first of the girls leaned in with round eyes even as the nursemaid sighed impatiently behind. "A golden-haired man who loves you, and a long journey over water . . . now, for *you*, let's see that hand. A dark stranger who adores you from the shadows, who turns out to be a prince in disguise . . . And for you a rich husband, yes, you'll have six children and dress in silk all your days . . ."

He'd been congratulating himself on a nice fat fee when he got the last palm. His breath stopped in his throat then, and for a moment the whole busy Forum—the housewives bustling past with their baskets, the hoarse-voiced hawkers crying their wares, the stray dogs and noisy children and clouds of white summer dust—seemed to freeze in place.

"What is it?" the girl said again, looking at him quizzically. Nessus felt icy fingers dancing up and down his spine; he had to force himself not to drop her hand like a hot coal and go running around the Forum for a while shrieking. But threadbare young astrologers just getting started in the business of telling the future didn't last long if they went around shrieking in front of the customers, so he forced a bright smile.

"Little mistress, you have a very grand future ahead of you. All little girls dream of wearing a crown, but you're going to be Empress of Rome someday! Wife of the Emperor, with more jewels and slaves and palaces than you can count. Isn't that wonderful?"

"*I* want to be an empress," one of the other little Cornelias objected. "No, me!"

"Horsie," crowed the youngest, waving chubby fingers at a cart horse plodding by.

Nessus dropped the hand of Cornelia Number Three or Two or whichever one she was. *I didn't lie*, he thought queasily. *I just didn't tell . . . all of it.*

He looked at the other girls, the ones to whom he'd promised rich husbands and dark lovers and many children, just as he promised all girls, and now he could feel the sweat pouring down his body. Because he didn't need to look at their hands anymore; he could see futures for all of them.

You're ill, he told himself. *That fish you ate last night. A piece of bad fish, and now you're hallucinating.*

But he wasn't. Clear as day he saw widowhood for three of the four girls; a fair amount of misery for one and fame for another; a total of eleven husbands and eight children between them—and of course, that one little hand spilling over with blood.

The four girls went skipping off into the Forum after some new diversion, veils fluttering behind them. The nursemaid counted a few coins into Nessus's hand, gave a censorious sniff at his threadbare tunic for good measure, and swished off after her charges. Nessus quickly packed up his star charts and headed to the nearest tavern.

He had had his first vision of the future, and he needed a drink.

"I am entering on the history of a period rich in disasters, frightful in its wars, torn by civil strife, and even in peace full of horrors. Four emperors perished by the sword."

—Tacitus

PART ONE

GALBA

June A.D. 68–January A.D. 69

"All pronounced him worthy of the empire,
until he became emperor."

—TACITUS

One

〰〰〰

W E'RE going to a wedding, not a battle." Marcella blinked as her sister came into the bedroom hauling a huge spear. "Or are you planning on killing the bride?"

"Don't tempt me." Cornelia sighed, looking up the length of the spear. "Lollia and her weddings . . . I sent my maid out for just the spearhead, but of course she came back with the whole spear. Put that pen down for once, won't you, and help me get the shaft off."

Marcella shoved her writing tablet to one side and rose from the desk. She and her sister tussled the spear between them, Cornelia yanking at the head and Marcella twisting the long shaft. "It's not coming," Marcella complained, just as the blade came loose and sent them tumbling in opposite directions. Marcella banged her elbow against the tiles and swore. Cornelia began a dignified reproof but started to giggle instead. Her stern, serene face cracked for just a moment into a little girl's, bracketed by those deep dimples she disliked so much. Marcella started to giggle too.

"All this trouble," she said ruefully, "just so you can part Lollia's hair with a dead gladiator's spearhead and give her a happy marriage. Did it work the first two times?"

"I have faith."

"It didn't work at my wedding either—"

"Enough!" Cornelia rose, holding out one elegantly ringed hand. Marcella took it and scrambled up. "Aren't you ready yet? I swore I'd be there early to help Lollia."

"I got wrapped up in chronicling Nero's death," Marcella shrugged. "You know I'm writing up Nero now? It'll make a short account, but not as short as my history of Caligula."

"You and your scribbling!" Cornelia scolded, rummaging through Marcella's dresses. "Here, wear your yellow . . . when did you change bedrooms?"

"When Tullia decided she preferred my view to her own." Marcella made a face at the narrow little corner chamber that had recently become hers, tugging her plain wool robe over her head and dropping it on the narrow bed. "So our dear new sister-in-law got the nice bedchamber with the window over the garden, and I got the view of the kitchens and the mosaic with the cross-eyed nymphs. No, put that yellow dress back, I want the pale blue—"

"Pale blue, too plain," Cornelia disapproved. "Don't you ever want to be noticed?"

"Who's going to be looking at me?" Marcella dived into the pale-blue *stola*, shivering in the November chill that crept into the bedchamber despite the drawn shutters. "For that matter, who's going to be looking at the bride? You're the one they all want to see—the future Empress of Rome."

"Nonsense." Cornelia looped the silver girdle about Marcella's waist, but a little smile hovered at her lips.

"If it's such nonsense, then why did you dress the part?" Marcella surveyed her sister: Cornelia Prima, twenty-four to Marcella's twenty-one; the oldest of the four cousins collectively known as the Cornelias, and the only one of them not to get a nickname. A severely elegant figure in amber-brown silk, a wreath of topaz about her throat and coiled mahogany hair crowning her head like a diadem, her oval face as classic as any statue's. As somber as any statue's too, because when Cornelia smiled a dimple appeared on each side of her mouth, deep enough to sink a finger into, and she'd long since decided that dimples weren't dignified. Smiling, she looked like the sister who had helped Marcella steal sweets from the kitchens when they were little girls. Unsmiling, Cornelia could have been a statue of Juno herself. "You look very queenly."

"Not queenly enough. Oh, why didn't I get your height?" Cornelia mourned, looking into the glass. "And your figure, and your nose—this little snub of mine just isn't dignified."

"Isn't Imperial, you mean?"

"Don't *say* it! You'll spoil Piso's luck."

"Where is he, anyway?" Marcella reclaimed the mirror, coiling her hair quickly on her neck and reaching for the box of silver pins.

"He'll come later, with the Emperor." Cornelia's voice sounded quite casual, but Marcella slanted a brow at her and she blushed. "Maybe the announcement will come today . . . ?"

Marcella didn't bother asking *what* announcement. All Rome knew Emperor Galba needed an heir. And all Rome knew how highly Galba regarded Cornelia's husband, Lucius Calpurnius Piso Licinianus . . .

The November morning had dawned blue and cold. Breath puffed white on the air as Marcella slipped down from the litter at the outdoor shrine of Juno and went to join the wedding guests already waiting. Cornelia had gone to assist the bride, still toting the spearhead. *We'll see if it works any better this time*, Marcella thought as she slipped in with a group of cousins, avoiding her brother and his loathsome new wife. At the shrine stood Lollia's latest betrothed with his own entourage—Marcella had to admit he wasn't an appetizing sight. Fifty-seven, bald, wrinkled, and glaring . . . but he was very eminent; consul and adviser to Emperor Galba. All Lollia's husbands were eminent. *The richest heiress in Rome can afford to choose.*

Strains of music came fading through the crisp air at last, and the guests rustled. The bridal procession: flute players, slaves tossing flowers into the street . . . Lollia's proud grandfather, born a slave and now one of the richest men in Rome, a festival wreath perched atop his wig . . . a curly-haired doll of a little girl, Lollia's daughter from the first of her short marriages, beaming from her great-grandfather's arms . . . Cornelia, regal as any empress, leading the bride by the hand to her newest husband . . . and the bride herself in her long white *tunica*: Cornelia Tertia, known to everyone as Lollia. Not the prettiest of the four cousins, most agreed, but Lollia did have a soft chin, a lush mouth that looked almost bruised, and merry painted eyes. Her mass of curls, dutifully parted by Cornelia with a gladiator's spear to ensure luck for her coming marriage, had this month been dyed a violent red that clashed cheerfully with the flame-colored bridal veil. Lollia's kohl-rimmed eye gave a wink to Marcella as she passed, and Marcella smothered a snort of laughter.

Cornelia put Lollia's hand into that of Senator Flaccus Vinius and took her own place in the crowd of wedding guests. "Don't tell me," Marcella murmured. "You gave Lollia your little speech about how when she put the red veil on she was a carefree girl, and when she takes it off she'll be a married woman with all the attendant duties and responsibilities."

"What makes you say that?" Cornelia whispered back as the priest began to intone a homily on the virtues of marriage.

"You gave me the same speech at my wedding. You really should get some new material, you know."

"Well, I'm her bridal escort. I'm supposed to prepare her for what's coming."

"She's nineteen, and it's her third wedding. Believe me, she knows what's coming."

"Ssshh!"

"Quando tu Gaius, ego Gaia." Lollia joined hands with her senator at the altar, intoning the ritual words.

"At my wedding I was so excited I could hardly stammer the vows," Cornelia whispered, and Marcella heard the smile in her voice.

"At mine I was too busy hoping I'd wake up and find it wasn't real."

Lollia and Senator Vinius shared the ritual cake, sitting on stools inlaid with gold. Lollia's rubies winked—cuffs on both wrists, brooches at both shoulders, shoulder-sweeping earrings, and a collar wrapping her throat. "Lollia gets such nice presents from her grandfather whenever she gets married," Marcella mused. "All Father gave me was a letter of congratulations sent four months late from Gaul. And he couldn't remember who I married."

"Our father was a great man."

"He couldn't even tell us apart! He barely bothered giving us enough of a dowry to marry on, and he didn't come home from his precious legions one year in five—"

"Great men have more important matters to tend to than domestic concerns," Cornelia sniffed. She had mourned their father very properly when Emperor Nero ordered his suicide, observing all the correct rituals, but Marcella hadn't seen any point in pretending grief. She hardly knew her father, after all—he'd been too busy crashing around Gaul during her childhood, racking up victories. *I suppose all those victories made Nero nervous. It just goes to show that too much success is bad for one's health.* That might make a neat little aphorism on ambition, with a bit of rewording. Just the thing to finish up her account of the life and reign of Emperor Nero . . .

A white bull was led forward onto the steps of the altar, and the priest shoved back his sleeves and cut its throat with a practiced double slash. The bull bellowed, but went down easily before the shrine—a good omen for the marriage. Marcella twitched her pale-blue hem away from a creeping trickle of blood and heard a careless voice at her shoulder.

"Am I late?"

"*Yes,*" Marcella and her sister said in unison. Diana, of course—late for everything. The bull might be dead on the altar and Lollia fidgeting, but the priest was fussing with the bloodied knife and consecrating it to the goddess of marriage, so Diana slid into place behind them.

"I saw the most marvelous race in one of the little circuses! Four Arab stallions and a Greek running for the Whites beat Perseus and the Greens—gods' wheels, Cornelia, what are you fussing about? Lollia won't care if I'm late. Can you imagine the Whites beating the Greens? They've already sworn the Greek can't do it in the Circus Maximus, but I think he might. Good hands, a nice sense of timing, driven eight months for the Whites so of course he hardly has any victories because Helios the Sun God couldn't get many wins driving those mules the Whites call horses—Marcella, what are you rolling your eyes at me for?"

"Because you're drowning out the priest and everybody's shushing you, that's why."

The wedding was over. The priest finished his prayers, and Senator Vinius offered Lollia his arm. Marcella and her sister fell in behind with the rest of the guests, making a slow procession back toward the house of Lollia's grandfather. Everyone with a spring in their step now, as they looked forward to the wedding banquet. Lollia's new husband was already engrossed with a gaggle of balding well-wishers, and Lollia beckoned her cousins up on her other side. "Come keep me company! Gods, that was a dull wedding. Is it just me, or do they get more boring every time?"

"It's marriage, Lollia," Cornelia sighed. "Your third or not, *try* to be serious."

"I think of it as less of a marriage than a lease agreement." Lollia lowered her voice so her new husband wouldn't hear. "Senator Vinius gets conditional use of me and my dowry for a period of time not to exceed his usefulness to my grandfather."

"Fair enough," Marcella conceded.

"Sorry I'm late." Diana sauntered up to link her arm with Lollia's, not sounding at all sorry. Half a dozen charioteer medals clanked around her neck, a sprinkle of freckles gleamed like powdered gold across her nose, and her red silk dress was knotted so carelessly it looked ready to slide right off her shoulders. All the men present were probably hoping it would. "I saw the best race!"

"Oh, don't go on again," Marcella groaned. "You're more boring than the whole Senate house put together." But a beauty, of course, could get away with being boring: Cornelia Quarta, the youngest of the four of them at sixteen and certainly the most lovely, all white-gold hair and blooming skin and cloudy blue-green eyes. But Diana didn't care a fig for any of the suitors panting on her doorstep. The only thing that made her eyes shine was horses, horses and chariots wheeling around the hairpin turn at the Circus Maximus. As far as she was concerned everything else could go to Hades, including all the men begging to marry her. The spurned suitors were the ones to nickname her Diana: the virgin huntress who scorned all men.

"I adore Diana," Lollia had said many times. "But I don't understand her. If I were that beautiful, the last thing I'd be was a virgin *anything*."

Marcella envied Diana too, but not for the beauty or the suitors.

"Diana, your hair looks like a bird's nest," Cornelia was scolding. "And couldn't you have worn something besides red? You know only the bride wears red at a wedding. A nice blue to bring out those eyes—"

Diana bristled. "You think I'd wear blue after the way that Blues charioteer fouled us at Lupercalia?" There were four racing factions at the Circus Maximus—the Reds, the Blues, the Greens, and the Whites—but to Marcella's youngest cousin there was only one, and that was the Reds. She went to the circus every other day, cheering her Reds and cursing all the others like a pleb girl on a festival day. It should never have been allowed, but her father was another odd bird in the family Cornelii, and he let his daughter do as she pleased.

So lucky, Marcella thought enviously, *and she doesn't even realize it.*

"Enjoy those races while you can, my honey," Lollia was telling Diana. "Galba disapproves of horse races—'frivolous waste of funds,' he calls it. If you think festivals and chariot racing won't be first in line for budget cuts—"

"Where did you hear that?" Marcella asked over Diana's groan. "I'm usually the one with all the news."

"I had myself a Praetorian guard a few months back when Galba was first acclaimed," Lollia explained, swirling her scarlet bridal veil over her head. "There, am I ready for the banquet?"

"In all ways but modesty." Cornelia gave a quelling stare as they came forward into the atrium, Marcella laughed, the slaves rushed forward to place festival wreaths on Lollia and her balding husband, and everyone trooped in for the feast.

* * *

CORNELIA couldn't help a weary little exhalation as the wedding banquet swept into full swing. Lollia's doting grandfather had put on his usual spectacle: silver dining couches heaped with Indian silk cushions, musicians plucking harps in hidden alcoves, jasmine and roses twining every column of the vast blue-marbled triclinium that overlooked the whole of the Palatine Hill. A golden-haired slave in silver tissue stood at every guest's elbow, and a stream of servitors scurried in and out with a series of exotic dishes: sow's udders stuffed with soft milky eggs, flamingo boiled with dates, a roast boar stuffed with a roast sheep that was in turn stuffed with game hens . . .

Such pomp and spectacle, Cornelia thought, *and for what?* She sipped her wine—ancient, expensive, and in exquisite taste, like everything else in this house. So much expense for a marriage that probably wouldn't last the year. Well, Lollia's grandfather *was* just a freed slave, even if he had managed to get rich and marry into an ancient patrician family. No matter how good his taste was, slave blood showed. Cornelia's own wedding had been a modest thing by comparison—her father would never have countenanced such expense—but she had at least managed to stay married to the same man for eight years.

Entertainers streamed out between courses: dancers in thin gauzes, poets with hymns to married love, jugglers with gilded balls. An orator in a Greek robe was just preparing a recitation when a sudden blare of trumpets drowned the plucking of harps. Cornelia looked up to see a line of red-and-gold-clad soldiers filing into the triclinium. The Praetorian Guard, personal army and bodyguards of the Pontifex Maximus and ruler of the world. Whispers ran across the throng: "The Emperor!"

A hunched figure in Imperial purple stumped in. As one, all the guests in the room, from host to bride, rose from their couches.

"So that's him?" Marcella managed to cast her glance upward even when she bowed with the rest of the guests. "Oh, good. My first close look."

"Sshh!" Cornelia had seen Emperor Galba many times before—he was a distant cousin of her husband's, after all, and a guest at her table long before he'd taken the purple. A man of seventy-one, hawk-nosed, wrinkled as a tortoise but still sturdy. Emperor for five months now, appointed by the Senate upon Nero's suicide. The Imperial mouth turned down in a frown as Galba looked around at the wreaths of flowers, the silver dishes, the flagons of wine. Everyone knew the Emperor had frugal tastes. "Some might even say cheap," Marcella murmured whenever the latest money-saving decree passed through the Senate.

Galba made greetings in his barking voice, waving irritably for the guests to resume, and Cornelia rose from her bow and threaded breathlessly through the throng to the only figure in the crowd of Imperial arrivals who mattered. "Piso!"

"My dear." He smiled down at her: Lucius Calpurnius Piso Licinianus, her husband of eight years. Chosen for her at sixteen, and she had never wanted another. "How lovely you look."

"Did he say anything?" Cornelia lowered her voice as Galba stood barking orders at his Praetorians, and a troop of dancers in bells and beads undulated in to entertain the guests. "The Emperor?"

"Not yet."

"I'm sure it will come soon."

Neither of them elaborated. It rang loud enough unspoken: *The day when Galba chooses you as heir.*

Who else could the Emperor choose, after all? A man of seventy-one needed an heir, the sooner the better, and who would be more suitable than his distinguished and serious young cousin? Lucius Calpurnius Piso Licinianus, with his distinguished bloodlines and impeccable record of service to the Imperium? Everyone knew it would be Piso.

Certainly no man in Rome would make a handsomer Emperor. Cornelia looked at her husband: tall and lean, his features somber but lightening when he smiled, his eyes that always looked straight at the world where other men looked for shadows. Emperor Nero had once mistrusted that straight gaze and threatened to exile her husband to Capri or even Pandetaria, where few men survived—but Piso had never looked away, and Nero had found a new fancy for his fears.

"You look very serious," Piso smiled.

Cornelia reached up to smooth back a strand of his dark hair. "Just thinking of our own wedding day."

"Was that such a serious occasion?" His dark eyes twinkled.

"Well, I took it seriously." Cornelia shook her head at Lollia, who was pealing laughter from her dining couch and utterly ignoring her new husband. "Piso, do let me introduce you to the new Praetorian Prefect. Be sure to ask about his son's appointment in the legions; he's very proud of that—"

Cornelia was very proud herself, watching her husband from the corner of her eye as they made their way through the throng. A smile here and a nod there, a wine cup ready in one hand for a toast, the other hand ready to clap the shoulder of a colleague or press the fingers of a new acquaintance. Reserved, courteous, gracious . . . *regal* . . .

She made the introduction to the new Prefect, smiled, and bowed out as a proper wife should once the conversation turned to politics. Emperor Galba stayed at the banquet only a few moments more, casting another disapproving glare around the lavish room and stumping out as abruptly as he'd arrived. "Thank goodness," Lollia tittered all too audibly as the Praetorians filed after him. "That sour face! Nero may have been crazy but at least he had *glamour.*"

"And Lollia may be an idiot, but she's right," Marcella murmured in Cornelia's ear.

"She is not. Galba had a very distinguished career."

"He's a sour, cheap old man." Marcella spoke under cover of the white-bearded orator who had just come out for the second time to launch into sonorous Greek verse. "All those money-skimping policies—"

"Nero emptied out the treasury. We should be glad someone's trying to refill it."

"Well, it won't make him popular. That will work in your favor, of course—by the time Galba dies, and at his age *that* can't be long, everyone will be cheering your Piso like a god."

"Marcella, hush!"

"It's truth, Cornelia. And I always speak truth, at least to my sister." Marcella lifted her goblet. "Or should I say, my future Empress?"

"You should not say." *Empress* . . .

Marcella's knowing smile curled Cornelia's toes. She never could fool her little sister—though half the time people assumed Marcella was the older: half a hand taller and as statuesque as a temple pillar; a column of cool blue ice topped with leaf-brown hair and a calm carved face. *Much more regal-looking than me. Oh, why didn't I get her nose?* "You should go talk to Caesonius Frugi, Marcella. He spoke very fondly of your husband, I believe they were tribunes together in the Twelfth. I'm sure you could do something for Lucius there, advance his career—"

"Lucius can take care of his own career," Marcella said. "I'm having much more fun watching you work the room."

"I don't see why you're always so dismissive of Lucius. He's perfectly pleasant."

"You aren't married to him. We weren't all lucky enough to fall madly in love with the man our father picked for us, you know." Marcella's eyes drifted over Cornelia's shoulder. "Dear Fortuna. Is that the ghastly Tullia headed straight for us? Hide me."

"You always do that!" Cornelia accused. "Ever since we were little! Disappearing to let me face the worst—Tullia, how delightful to see you!"

"I can't say the same for you, Cornelia—I understand you've had the Emperor to dine last week, and you didn't invite me! Your own sister-in-law—"

Eventually the sun fell, the wine sank in everyone's goblets, and soon the guests were drifting out for the final procession. Cornelia took her husband's arm and joined the throng, Lollia and Senator Vinius in the lead, the slaves darting ahead to throw walnuts for fertility and silver coins for prosperity. Cornelia applauded with the rest as Lollia was carried over the threshold of her new home and knelt for the first time to light the fire in her new hearth. Squealing girls lined up for the bridal torch, and Lollia tossed it straight at Diana. Diana poked the business end of the torch at a young tribune begging her for a kiss.

"—must come with me," Lollia was groaning to Marcella and Diana as Cornelia approached. The last of the guests were trailing out of Senator Vinius's house with tipsy congratulations. "It's sure to be dull as Hades—Cornelia, Vinius is dragging me to dinner at the palace with sour old Galba next week. Tell me you'll come and glare at me for drinking too much wine—"

"Of course I'll come," Cornelia smiled. "Piso and I were already invited. I thought I'd wear my blue—"

"Not blue," Diana said at once. "I hate blue, and we all have to dress in the same color when we sally out in force."

"Why?" Marcella met her sister's eyes over Diana's head, and they traded familiar amused glances.

"Because we're like a chariot team," Diana explained. "Cornelia on the inside—slow, but like a rock around the turns. Marcella next, steady on the inner pair. Then Lollia, fast but wild. And on the outside, me. Fastest of anybody."

"Why am I the slow one?" Cornelia wondered, and they all started giggling. Vinius frowned.

"Better go, my loves." Lollia caught his expression, groaning. "And pity me, because the worst part of the day is yet to come."

"Don't be crude," Cornelia chided.

"He smells like sour milk," Marcella said, "and I imagine he'll last about as long."

"Is he a Reds fan?" Diana asked.

Lollia kissed them out the door, and Cornelia took her husband's arm. She turned to wave her sister and cousin into the dark and saw Diana toss the wedding torch into the gutter.

"A very good wedding." Piso raised a hand, and one of the hovering slaves dashed forward to beckon their litter. "An older man will steady Lollia, I'm sure."

"He won't have her long enough to steady her." The litter approached; Cornelia accepted her husband's hand in and drew the rose-silk curtains against the garish yellow glow of the streetlamps. "Lollia's grandfather will have her divorced and married to someone else the minute Senator Vinius ceases to be of use."

Piso gave the litter a tap, and it rose swaying on the backs of six Gauls and went trotting into the night. The curtains fluttered, and a wedge of yellow lamplight cut across his aquiline nose and square jaw.

Cornelia smiled. Her husband smiled back, moving from one side of the litter to the other to settle his arm about her, and she could feel the litter-bearers hitching below to accommodate the shifted weight.

"I went to the temple of Juno today," Cornelia found herself saying against Piso's shoulder as the litter jogged into the night.

"You did?" Had he tensed?

"Yes. I had a sow sacrificed. I think it will do better than a goose."

"You know best, my dear." Eight years of marriage, and he had never uttered one word of reproach for her failure to provide him with children.

Sometimes I wish he would.

"So Diana caught the bridal torch," Cornelia said brightly. "She'll be our next bride."

"They'll have a job forcing that one into a red veil," Piso laughed. "Lollia will be on her fourth husband before they get Diana to her first."

"Lollia thinks husbands are like new gowns." The litter jolted to a halt; Cornelia saw the flickering torches before their front gate and gathered her skirts as Piso stepped down. "Just get a new one every season, and throw out the old."

"She's one of the new wives." Piso gave his arm to hand her out of the litter. "There are not so many of the classic sort, my dear."

He smiled. Cornelia squeezed his hand as he lighted her to the courtyard, and they passed under the guttering torches. In most houses the slaves would have all been dozing against the walls, but Cornelia's slaves were alert and waiting, whisking the cloaks away and bringing drinks of warmed wine. Torchlight flickered on the long line of ancestral busts lining the hall in niches; Piso's taking one wall, stretching back to Pompey Magnus and Marcus Crassus; Cornelia's taking the other wall, starting with the first of the Cornelii who had come from the Etruscans. The last of the busts was Piso's own aquiline face, carved by Diana's odd sculptor father and presented on their wedding day. *He made the mouth too pinched*, Cornelia thought.

"Lollia is one of the new model of wives," Piso repeated, putting an arm about her waist now that the slaves had retreated from their bedchamber. "I am pleased to have my Cornelia."

Cornelia smiled a little, feebly. So Lollia was a fickle wife, vain and giggly and frivolous. She'd still been rewarded with a child: Little Flavia Domitilla, three years old and pretty as a sunbeam, whom Cornelia had carried upstairs to her bedchamber in the middle of the wedding banquet when she fell fast asleep in the middle of all the excitement.

And her cousin hadn't even wanted Flavia. "I was so careful," Lollia had complained when she found herself pregnant. "How in the name of all gods did this happen? Who even knows if she's Titus's or not. I hope she looks like him . . ." Cornelia had had to bite her tongue savagely at that.

Many years ago, another Cornelia of their family had famously been asked why she wore no jewels, and she had gathered her children about her to say that her sons were her jewels.

I'm modest enough about jewels. Cornelia unfastened the wreath of topazes from her throat as she began undressing for bed. *So why do I have no sons?*

M ARCELLA," her sister-in-law, Tullia, snapped as they entered the house. "You really must not daydream at parties. Senator Lentulus's wife had to address you three times before you noticed her—"

"Senator Lentulus is very useful to me," Marcella's brother, Gaius, interjected, reproving. "He supports my proposal about the new aqueduct—"

"—and you have *duties* to your family at functions like this." Tullia shed her *palla* into the hands of a hovering slave, ordered the lamps lit, and frowned at Gaius for calling for wine, all without interrupting her flow of complaints. "There are a great many important people at such parties, people who could benefit your brother's career and you owe it to him—*Gaius*, no more wine!—to advance him at every opportunity. Not to mention your own husband. He may be in Judaea, but you can still work on his behalf. Perhaps host a party in his name. Lollia's

grandfather hosts Piso's parties often enough in return for a little consideration on trade laws in the Senate—"

"In return for which you all look down on him," Marcella said.
"How genteel of you."

"Now, now—" Gaius began, but he never got to finish a sentence
since marrying Tullia.

"Don't be pert, Marcella." Tullia's sandals clicked across the mosaics. "I have only the family's best interests at heart."

"You've only been a member of the family for ten months," Marcella pointed out. "Of course it feels like ten years. Or ten centuries—"

She drifted out before her odious sister-in-law could think of an
answer.

The Cornelii family home: dim, gracious, considerably improved
in the past few years by the flow of money from Lollia's grandfather.
Though most of the family manages to ignore that fact. A beautiful house,
its every vase and ornament whispering of gracious years passing and
the many Cornelii who had passed serenely through these same halls.
Tullia had managed to ruin the gardens by planting rigid clumps
of delphiniums in loud primary colors, and she insisted on putting
insipid nymph statues everywhere, but it was still a lovely house.

But it's not my house. Not anymore, anyway. Married or not, Marcella
had never had a household of her own. "I'm hardly in Rome four months
of the year," her husband Lucius Aelius Lamia had shrugged when they
first married. "Why keep the expense of a household? We'll just stay
with your family for the time being, until I get a proper post in the city."
But somehow, in four years of marriage, the post in the city had not
materialized, and Marcella had never left the house where she grew up.

Not that it had mattered, back in the days when her father had
still been alive. He'd been too busy marching his legions around Gaul
to take an interest in her life, and Gaius had been too busy trying
to live up to his example, so Marcella had ordered the household to
suit herself. But then Nero had disposed of her father, and the family
fortunes had plunged for a while—until Gaius, now paterfamilias of
the Cornelii in his own right, had married the rich and well-connected
Tullia. And after that . . .

"Marcella must conduct herself properly while under our roof," Gaius's new wife had been quick to decree in that voice of hers that sounded like a cart grating over flagstones. "A young wife with her husband gone so long is a swarm for butterfly boys and rakes. And since that incident a few months ago with Emperor Nero—!"

"Tullia," Gaius had given a quick glance at his sister's face. "Perhaps we shouldn't—"

"*Gaius*, of course we should. It is your duty to guard the reputation of your sisters, and Marcella's duty to obey you!"

"I'm a married woman," Marcella protested. "My only duty is to my husband."

"Who isn't here. So who else should step in for his authority but your brother?"

Absolutely no one. That had been the beauty of it, all those days when Lucius was traveling and her father waging wars. No one had been around to object to the hours Marcella spent writing and making notes at her desk. For months at a time, Marcella had managed to forget she had a husband or a father at all . . . but here was Tullia, giving her a beady predator's stare. "Lucius Aelius Lamia trusted you to our care. And in *my* house, when you're eating *my* food, you'll follow *my* rules!"

"Your house?" Marcella shot back. "Gaius is master here, not you."

Tullia smirked. "And if husband and wife speak together as one?"

"I've hardly heard Gaius speak at all since you married, Tullia. Is he even capable of speech anymore?"

If it had just been Gaius, Marcella knew she could have beaten down any arguments in ten minutes flat. *Paterfamilias or not, legal rights or not, he's no match for me.* But if Gaius was the silk glove, Tullia was definitely the iron fist, and together they had the laws of Rome on their side. Money, duty, tradition: the trifold clamp forcing Marcella into whatever role they chose.

"When Lucius gets back from Judaea, I'm going to *make* him get a house of his own," she'd told Cornelia wrathfully, just last week. "I'll nag until I get what I want this time. That stingy stick owes me!"

"Try honey instead of vinegar," her sister advised. "Much more effective when it comes to wheedling husbands. If you'd just apply yourself to Lucius a little—set yourself to advancing his career, have a child or two—"

"You're the one who wants babies, not me. I'd rather get the pox than get pregnant."

Cornelia dropped the subject then, and so did Marcella. She might tweak her sister about her dimples, her lectures, the particular queenly tone she got when she was angry, but *never* about children. Not when Cornelia spent more hours praying for a child with every year that passed.

Not me, Marcella thought. *But I'll even promise Lucius a baby, if he'll just get me my own household.*

Well, until he got back to Rome, all she had was her *tablinum*: cluttered, scattered with pens and ink pots, shelves of scrolls and a bust of Clio, the muse of history, that Diana's odd sculptor father had astutely given Marcella on her nineteenth birthday. The *tablinum* might be small and dusty, but it was still all hers.

She banished Tullia's carping from mind and pulled out the stool, reaching for a tablet. Clio gazed serenely overhead with blank marble eyes as Marcella wrote a fresh heading: *Servius Sulpicius Galba, sixth Emperor of Rome. A man of great lineage and long service. A high forehead, indicating intelligence; an upright bearing, indicating discipline. A bark of a voice, better suited to a parade ground than a dinner table.* Unyielding eyes—that was good; Rome liked her Emperors unyielding. Tight lips—cheapness; not so good. Emperors might be wicked or even insane, but they had to be generous. Marcella had heard whispers that Galba was even refusing to pay his Praetorians their usual bounty. "So he should," Cornelia had said approvingly when she heard that particular rumor. "Galba wants greater discipline in the ranks, higher standards."

"Admirable," Marcella agreed. "And the ranks love being disciplined, don't they?"

They did look sullen, the guards I saw at the wedding banquet tonight . . .

Marcella put her pen down, looking at the shelf where a few modest scrolls were immaculately stored. A woman might not be able to influence history, but she could certainly watch it—analyze it—record it. Marcella had already written histories of Rome's past Emperors, from Augustus the God to Nero the mad. *What a descent.* Galba could hardly be anything but an improvement on Nero. Nero's history was the newest on her shelf, still not quite finished—she had just this morning penned his death, with a pleasant sense of impartiality. A historian must never allow personal opinion to color her writings, after all. *Cornelia Secunda, known as Marcella,* she had enjoyed jotting down in the mental portrait of herself. *A profoundly disinterested and impartial observer of history.*

Being impartial to Nero had been . . . difficult.

"That *incident* at the palace." Tullia had accosted Marcella that spring, shortly after it happened. "It must have been terrible, my dear. *Do* tell me."

"Should I?"

"Everyone needs a listening ear at such times."

"Do they?"

"Marcella," Tullia snapped, dropping the cozy coyness, "don't be difficult!"

"You want to hear all the details about Emperor Nero, Tullia? How his breath smells? What pomade he uses on his hair?"

"I don't—"

"I'm sure you're panting to hear every last sweaty detail, but I'm not going to oblige."

Off Tullia went. *"Gaius, you will not believe how your sister spoke to me!"*

Well, no use thinking now of Nero with Galba on the throne. An old man, but it seemed certain enough he'd adopt Cornelia's husband Piso as Imperial heir. Marcella smiled, thinking of her older sister's regal command of Lollia's wedding guests as she moved through the crowd. Piso, on her arm, had been dwarfed by all that majestic poise. *If he does become Emperor, he'll be the dullest one we've ever had.*

"Marcella?" A peevish voice broke her reverie. "The slaves aren't cleaning the mosaics properly. Have a word with them?"

"That's not my job anymore, Gaius." Marcella didn't bother looking up as her brother came into the *tablinum,* stooping his height under the lintel.

"Yes, but Tullia will have the slaves lashed for it, and they don't mean any harm."

"You really could have done better for a wife, Gaius."

"None of that," he answered severely. "Our father selected her for me himself, before he died."

"And our father was perfect?" Marcella raised her eyebrows. Certainly Cornelia and Gaius seemed determined to remember him that way.

"He was a great man!"

"And are any of us the happier for all that greatness?" Marcella said tartly. "Personally, I think great men are overrated."

Gaius shifted, uncomfortable. "A Roman's true duty isn't happiness. It's—well, duty."

"Martial would have said that better. You never were any good at epigrams, Gaius." Nor good at much else, truth be told. Marcella looked at her brother: tall, handsome, broad of forehead and sloped of nose, but somehow forgettable. He hadn't even tried to match their father's career in the legions, and now the Senate didn't seem very impressed with him either.

"Maybe you could write me a few epigrams," Gaius was hedging. "I could trot them out at parties and look clever."

"Only if you pass me all the gossip from the Senate," Marcella relented. "You know how I love news."

"Here's a bit for you." He raised the eyebrows that Tullia had decreed he begin plucking lest he look like a caterpillar. "There's rumors Governor Vitellius in Lower Germania will revolt. Even declare himself Emperor along with Galba."

"Vitellius?" Marcella shook her head. "He's a drunk. I saw him once at a faction party, and he could hardly keep upright after the first hour."

"Well, it's what they say. Not that it matters. Everyone knows Piso will be Galba's heir." Gaius brightened. "What a thing for our family, eh? I wonder if—"

Marcella looked down at the tablet on Emperor Galba as her brother chattered. It was hardly written on, but she put it away. Better to wait for another day, another month, when she knew more of Galba's character. Besides, sitting on a throne changed a man. Who knew what Galba might become in another year or two?

Who knows what I'll become in another year or two? Marcella thought. *Mistress of my own household? Published historian? Owner of just the occasional hour or two of privacy?*

No. *That* was too much to hope for.

Two

~⌒⌒~

SHOULDN'T we be going?" Piso retied the lace of his sandal, frowning. "The races will have started by now."

"But we aren't going to the circus for the races." Cornelia shuffled a dozen different lists as a bevy of anxious slave girls hovered at her elbow. Their atrium was a hive of activity: litter-bearers waiting outside to carry them to the Circus Maximus, maids with Cornelia's sunshade and fan, freedmen with Piso's correspondence and cloak. "We're going to the circus to let people see us, and we're going to make an *entrance*. You're a public figure now, and public figures have a duty to make an impression on the populace. The right impression—here, take these."

Piso shuffled through the armload of tablets and scrolls. "The household accounts?"

"Just shuffle them importantly between races." Cornelia smiled at him over her lists. "The responsible Imperial heir, tending to matters of state even on a festival day."

"I'm not Imperial heir yet," he said reprovingly, but his eyes smiled at her as he took the accounts.

November was passing in a storm of winds and blown leaves, and with it the Ludi Plebii, the games of the people. Cornelia didn't care for the games, but Diana had spoken of nothing else for days. "It won't be a proper festival," she complained. "Galba is too tightfisted to give any good purses, which means all the charioteers will save their horses for the races at Saturnalia instead."

"Even your precious Reds?" Cornelia couldn't help teasing her.

"The Reds don't run for a purse," Diana flashed back. "They run for glory. You will come, won't you?"

"Better the races than watching the gladiators die in the arena." Cornelia detested the gladiatorial festivals. It made her sick to see so many people—from good families too! Not just plebeians—stand there shrieking for blood. The races, now, they had turned into something quite different from the staid laps of her childhood. Emperor Nero had been mad for racing—or perhaps just mad—and Cornelia might deplore the money he had spent, but there was no denying that the result was impressive. The Circus Maximus was now a proper arena with a central *spina* thick in carvings, golden dolphins dropping their noses for each of the seven laps, sprays of victory palm for the winning charioteers. A place to see and be seen . . . and who better to be seen by all Rome than her husband?

"Domina," a maid said breathlessly, tumbling into the blue-tiled atrium, "the wine has been delivered to your box at the Circus Maximus."

"Was it properly warmed? Last time the steward had it boiling— Lollia's grandfather gave me the pick of his own cellars for the occasion," Cornelia explained to Piso. "Falernian, Aminean, Nomentan—"

"With his breeding, you'd think he'd drink common beer." Piso made a face. "He's vulgar as Hades."

"Oh, surely not. He has exquisite taste. Not one of our friends or relations has anything to match his house, or his collection of statues, or his wine cellar."

"Yes, and that's my point. Freed slaves should live modestly, not flaunt themselves higher than their birth."

"Well, he has been very helpful to us," Cornelia murmured. More than helpful, really—Lollia's grandfather was extremely generous with gifts, and there was no denying that his assistance in other areas had been invaluable. Piso's family had been hard hit under Nero's suspicious eye, and even Claudius's before that—she and Piso would never have kept their house and assets if not for a few timely loans. . . .

"It's still not fitting." Piso frowned, and Cornelia tactfully changed the subject. Her husband, she knew, liked things in their place—patricians of good blood and family in the Senate, equites to serve them, plebs to serve *them,* and freed slaves who showed proper appreciation for their station in life. Freedmen as rich as Midas who had to be applied to for loans had no place in Piso's orderly vision of Rome. Cornelia patted his arm brightly and turned to the maids. "Leda, Zoe, did you arrange the ivy and the larkspur in the box as I showed you?"

"Yes, Domina—"

Cornelia had been up by dawn, flitting to the Circus Maximus to set her slave girls to work on the Cornelii family box: an enclosed marble space perched high in the tiers with a breathtaking view of the track's hairpin turn below. The arena attendants had been raking the sand of the track, and pale fingers of sunlight stretching over the top of the tiers, when Cornelia set the slaves to work. Flowers, swags of ivy, silver platters and gold wine cups—she'd give her guests more than just a good view. She'd give them a bower, a last breath of summer in the pale blue coolness of autumn. The slaves had been flying about the box like bees by the time she raced back to the house, her hair coming down and her cheeks pink with excitement, to prepare herself and her husband for their grand entrance.

"What a general you are, my dear," Piso said as she rearranged the folds of his toga over the shoulder. Of course he didn't lean down and kiss her, not with slaves present, but his eyes crinkled approvingly. "And a beautiful general at that."

"I wish I didn't have to wear red," Cornelia said ruefully, looking down at her dark-red gown with the jet beads at the hem. "Diana swore she'd behave herself today if I just wore red for her precious team. Not my best color—*why* couldn't she support the Greens instead?"

"Nonsense, red suits you. Do sit down, my dear, you've been sprinting about since dawn."

"I want everything just right. The Emperor may drop by, after all."

"Doubtful. He dislikes festivals."

"But he likes *you*." Cornelia reached up to smooth a stray strand of her husband's hair. "Perhaps he'll make the announcement today."

"Why today?"

"He's made himself very unpopular lately with all the new tax levies, that's all." All Rome knew that Galba's stern-faced accountants had swept up the jeweled butterflies of Nero's court and were squeezing them for every sesterce they had ever sucked away from the treasury. There was a great deal of complaining, of course, as people watched their houses, their jewels, their slaves and estates flowing into Galba's eager, wrinkled hands—but Cornelia approved. Everyone knew Nero had spent the treasury empty. Had no one thought the account would ever come due?

But still, people were inclined to mutter resentfully now when they heard Galba's name. He'd want to soothe the crowds, give them something new to talk about.

Like an Imperial heir. A young, handsome, able, and vigorous heir.

"You look very handsome, Piso. Very distinguished." Very *Imperial.* "Shall we go?"

They came from the atrium to the brilliant sunlight of the steps outside. Piso lifted a hand for the litter, and Cornelia raised the sunshade over her face.

A man's voice came from the glitter of sun. "Senator Lucius Calpurnius Piso Licinianus?"

Cornelia blinked and saw a soldier at the foot of the steps before their house. A soldier in full armor and red-plumed helmet, a half-dozen guards behind him.

"Yes?" Piso's voice sharpened.

"Centurion Drusus Sempronius Densus of the Praetorian Guard." The man stepped forward into a crisp salute. "I have the honor of serving as your escort and bodyguard, by order of the Emperor. I am yours to command, Senator."

The Praetorian Guard. Second only to the Emperor . . . or to members of the Imperial family.

Yours to command.

Cornelia felt a smile breaking over her face, but suppressed it with as much nonchalance as she could muster. Piso looked cool as cream—like he'd had Imperial bodyguards at his heels all his life. She all but burst with pride. "Thank you, Centurion," she heard Piso say. "We would be pleased if you would escort us to the Circus Maximus."

"Senator." Another salute, and the Praetorians fell in behind the litter. Piso nodded dismissal to the centurion, but Cornelia came forward down the steps.

"Drusus Sempronius Densus, you said?"

"Yes, Lady." He removed his helmet, bowing, and Cornelia saw a younger man than she would have anticipated, chestnut-brown hair curling vigorously despite the close cut. He stood stocky and broad-chested in his armor, not tall—she had grown used to tilting her head back to meet her husband's eyes, but this centurion was scarcely taller than she was.

Cornelia offered her hand with a smile. "I welcome you to our service, Centurion. And I charge you with my husband's care."

"My life for his, Lady." The centurion bowed over her hand, his own fingers rough. An Imperial sword had roughened them—an Imperial sword that now belonged to her, and to Piso.

Cornelia saw the looks on the faces of her guests when she and Piso made their entrance to the box, just late enough for the second heat. She saw the eyes evaluating her flowers, her wines, her Praetorians . . . her husband.

The bows were deeper now. The smiles more ingratiating. The voices tinged with respect.

It's going to happen, Cornelia thought wonderingly as she nodded and smiled through the rounds of well-wishers. *It really is. My husband is going to be Imperial heir.*

She gestured her maid forward with a sunshade. Even less than a snub nose and dimples, the wife of a prince of Rome could not have a sunburn.

* * *

THE family was out in full ghastly force. Cousins Marcella hadn't seen for years had come scurrying to the Cornelii box now that Piso stood in such high favor. He stood looking pleased and a little dazed, and of course Cornelia looked as serene as if she'd had Praetorians at her beck and call all her life. Tullia cast a resentful eye over the inlaid chairs and garlanded tables, and gave a sniff. "All this larkspur—I could have told her roses would make a better display for fall—"

"Only if she asked your advice," Marcella said to her sister-in-law. "And why would Cornelia need to do that? She managed to outshine you without any help at all."

Marcella left Tullia sulking into her wine cup, turning to smile at the nearest relative. "Marcus! How lovely to see you again, it's been an age."

"Lady Marcella." He bowed over her hand: Senator Marcus Vibius Augustus Norbanus, Tullia's former husband and a distant cousin in his own right. Grandson of old Emperor Augustus through some illicit love affair, and Marcella thought she could see the resemblance in Marcus, who looked so noble and senatorial in his snowy toga that he should have been carved in marble and stuck on top of the Senate house. For all that, he wasn't boring—in fact, he was one of the few cousins Marcella could stand.

She smiled again, and his eyes swept over her in pleasant appreciation. Marcella was glad she'd worn her pale-pink *stola*, fluted in dozens of intricate folds like the pillars of a temple. No jewelry—Lucius had sold her last string of pearls to bribe the governor of Lower Germania last year—but Marcella knew she didn't need jewelry to be noticed. Who cared if her olive skin wasn't much next to Lollia's vivid complexion, if her hair was dead-leaf brown to Cornelia's rich dark coils, and if her features didn't have nearly the beauty and delicacy of Diana's? Marcella counted herself the proud owner of the best breasts in the entire family. "Possibly all Rome," Lollia often sighed, enviously. "What I'd give for a figure like yours!" Even a scholarly man like Marcus Norbanus, Marcella was glad to see, wasn't above a glance of appreciation.

"I was sorry to hear about your recent misfortunes, Senator." Marcus's descent from Emperor Augustus had clearly made Galba nervous, because one of his first actions after taking the purple had been to strip Marcus of most of his lands and estates. "I think it very unfair."

"Emperors have disliked me before," Marcus said dryly. "I expect I'll survive."

"On the other hand, you've had some good fortune as well."

"Such as?" He raised graying brows—he was only thirty-five or so, but he'd already begun to gray rather devastatingly around the edges.

"On getting rid of Tullia, of course." Marcella lowered her voice. "That certainly deserves congratulations."

He smiled—too polite, of course, to disparage a woman. Even a woman who richly deserved it. Why did the nicest men always end up with the nastiest wives?

At least Tullia and Marcus's three-year-old son took after his father. Little Paulinus stood round-eyed and well behaved at Marcus's side, ignored by his mother, and when Marcus unpacked the paperwork he usually took to the races, Marcella bent down and whispered into the little ear. Paulinus nodded happily, trotting off, and five minutes later there was a shriek as Tullia discovered a beetle in her wine goblet.

"Marcella, can you find Diana for me? She's already disappeared into the stables." Cornelia cast her eyes to the heavens. *She might not be a mother yet,* Marcella thought, *but she has the exasperated sigh down to perfection.* "And of course Lollia's flirting with my new centurion. I swear, if I didn't have you, the other two would drive me stark raving mad!"

"Then be glad you have me."

The stables of the Circus Maximus: a different world, Marcella often thought. The whisper of straw and the swearing of stable boys, the creak of wheels, the grooms rushing back and forth with armloads of harness. The roars of the crowd filtering down distantly from the tiers, the charioteers muttering their prayers and fingering their good-luck charms, the stallions giving their full-throated whinnies.

A different world—certainly not Marcella's world, as the grooms and charioteers and even the horses seemed to know, looking at her dubiously as she picked through the straw and manure. But oddly enough, it was Diana's world.

Marcella found her youngest cousin in the Reds quarter beside the Reds faction director, a squat bald man named Xerxes who looked like a scarred frog. They stared with equal concentration at a quartet of gray stallions tied to the grooming posts.

"They're getting old," Diana was saying. "We need a new team for backup."

"They have a few victories left in them."

Diana walked behind the stallions, too close as she trailed her hand down a glossy flank, but horses never seemed to kick Diana. She should have been as out-of-place as Marcella—a pretty little thing with her scarlet silks and pale hair—but no one gave her a second glance. The faction director for the Reds had given up trying to boot her out by the time she was eight, when he found her playing unconcerned under the belly of a stallion who had kicked in the heads of no less than four grooms. What a ruckus in the family *that* had been.

Diana stepped back, chewing absently on a piece of straw. "Who's driving, Xerxes?"

"A Greek boy. Won a few races at the Circus Flaminius. Got good hands."

"The bays run too?" More than one team of horses could run for each color faction.

"Aye. Under Tarquin."

"He'll win, if those buggardly Blues don't foul him."

"Diana!" Marcella broke into the litany. Uninterrupted, Diana would go on all day. "Cornelia sent me down for you. She's going mad trying to make everything perfect."

"Go on with her, Lady," Xerxes grunted at Diana. "Take your pretty sandals out of the muck."

Diana came forward, catching one of the gray stallions by the nose and dragging his head down. Her arms looked too slim to hold a big horse, but the stallion's broad nose dropped under her hand, and the baleful gaze was caught by a pair of cloudy blue-green eyes that had half the men in Rome stammering like schoolboys. "Keep steady out there," Diana told the horse. "It's a wild time once the flag drops."

The stallion chuffed against her hand, scarlet ribbons fluttering in his braided mane just like the red ribbons plaited into Diana's hair. Marcella tugged at her elbow again, and the grooms ran forward with the red-dyed harness. Behind stood the racing chariot, slung light between two gilded wheels, crested by a fire god's head with writhing scarlet snakes for hair. The charioteer stood ready, a skinny dark-eyed boy barely older than Diana, and she stared over her shoulder at him as Marcella hauled her out through the stable doors.

"Your eyes are about to fall out of your head." Stopping to pluck a few wisps of straw from Diana's hair. "Have you finally fallen in love? Lollia will be so pleased."

"I'm not in love with him." Diana brushed that thought away just as she brushed away Marcella's hands. "I want to *be* him."

No doubt. Plenty of people liked to hiss rumors about Diana's reputation, but Marcella didn't believe that her youngest cousin haunted the stables for the charioteers. Plenty of fine ladies might flop on their backs for a famous driver, but not Diana. At a Lupercalia faction party last year, Marcella had watched the star charioteer for the Blues trail his fingers along Diana's neck and ask her if she wouldn't like a walk in the moonlit gardens—and Diana had fixed him with a blank blue-green stare and said, "I wouldn't walk out of a burning house with a man who steered a turn as badly as you." Not a girl with hayrick tumbles on her mind.

If Diana *had* a mind. Marcella had never been entirely sure. How much did horses think?

Diana glared at her as they started up the broad path away from the faction stables. "You didn't wear red."

"It's pink. Sort of red."

"But there's no pink faction!"

No, not much of a mind there.

They returned to the Cornelii box, where Diana dropped a kiss on the head of her absentminded father. As beautiful as his daughter, Marcella thought, and just as crazy. Nicknamed Paris by the besotted women of Rome, after the prince whose pretty face won him Helen of Troy. Diana's father wasn't so interested in causing trouble as *that* Paris, though. In fact, he wasn't interested in anything but sculpting marble. *What really annoys the family is how good he is.* Even now he sat ignoring anyone who tried to talk to him and making sketches for his statues. "Good face," he told Cornelia's startled centurion, Densus or whatever his name was. "You might make me a good Vulcan. Maybe a Neptune if you had a beard. How long would it take you to grow a beard? Profile, please."

"Um," the centurion stammered. "I'm on duty."

"You can be on duty in profile, can't you? Turn around."

Diana was looking at the centurion and the row of silent Praetorians at the wall behind him. "What are they doing here?" she asked Marcella. "Arresting us?"

"No, they're Cornelia's new toys." Marcella took a handful of grapes from a silver bowl. "Piso's bound to be announced heir any day now."

"Piso likes the races," Diana said, hopeful. "He won't cancel festivals if he becomes Emperor, will he?"

"He likes everything and will cancel nothing. It would be too much of a decision for him." Marcella looked over at her sister's husband where he stood with a wine cup and several senators. He was nodding seriously at something, but then he was always nodding seriously. *Lucius is bad enough*, Marcella thought, *but eight years of Piso would have me dead from boredom.* "Your precious Reds will be safe."

"Don't joke. It's looking like a lean winter for the charioteers, with Galba canceling celebrations left and right. 'Frivolous waste of funds,' he calls them." Diana flopped her folded arms on the marble balustrade, contemplating the circus with its fantastic carved *spina* and golden dolphins, shut up and shrouded for the long Galban winter. "The horses will go stale."

"Cheer up. Galba's sure to die soon."

Diana looked at her. "And they all think I'm the shocking one."

"I run around with parchment and pens, not charioteers," Marcella said cheerfully, reaching for more grapes. "Much more respectable."

Diana cast her eyes back to the circus. Marcella turned to take a goblet from a slave and noted Lollia and her new husband hissing at each other in low voices, almost nose to nose.

"—disgracing me! No wife of mine paints herself in public like a whore."

"Your last wife *was* a whore, Vinius. You divorced her for humping half of Gaul, or did you think we hadn't all heard about *that* here in Rome?" Lollia looked very bright and pretty in violent magenta silk checkered in silver around the hem and a pearl-and-silver necklace, but the glare she aimed at her new husband was ferocious.

He glared back. "Wipe your face, or I will send you home."

"I'll speak to my grandfather about this." Scrubbing at her cheeks in angry little jerks.

"Do. That vulgar old freedman will never—"

"*What* did you call him? After he paid your debts and funded your campaign for—"

Cornelia's voice broke through the hissing. "Flavia, be careful!"

Lollia's little daughter had escaped her mother's lap and was trying to climb up the railing of the box. Cornelia started forward, but the centurion at her back had moved first. He swooped the little girl up capably, his professional hardness cracking into a friendly grin as he returned her to Lollia's lap. Lollia gave a last scowl to her new husband and hugged her daughter absently.

"Thank you, Centurion." Cornelia touched his arm in thanks and rounded on Lollia. "You couldn't keep a closer eye on her? Three years old, you know she's climbing into everything—she could have fallen!"

"With your gallant centurion standing guard?" Lollia fluttered her lashes at the chestnut-haired Praetorian. Senator Vinius glared again.

"I see you'd rather flirt than watch your own daughter." Cornelia looked as if she'd like to say more—a great deal more—but she just gave Lollia one last heartfelt glare and glided away to join Piso. Lollia just shrugged, gave a final narrow-eyed look to her husband, and moved pointedly away to join Marcella. Little Flavia wriggled in her arms, crowing, and Lollia set her down and gave her a diamond bracelet to play with. Flavia cooed, twirling the bracelet around her chubby wrist.

"Definitely your daughter," Marcella said.

"Old Flaccid over there has her so cowed she hardly speaks anymore. I'm divorcing him if it's the last thing I do."

"Your shortest marriage yet," said Marcella. "Three weeks! If only mine were that short—"

A dutiful cheer started, and Marcella looked up to see Emperor Galba making his way into the Imperial box. He looked sour, doubtless counting the cost of everything. The chariots came out to much louder cheers. The warm surge of applause rose tier by tier, the plebs surging to their feet and screaming for their favorite faction, the patricians putting their palms together in more restrained approval. Seven teams: three for the Green, all twelve horses tossing the tall green plumes on their heads; one for the Blues with their famous blood bays; one for the Whites—and two for the Reds.

With all the cheers for the chariots and the bustle of guests, no one should have noticed the entrance of one more man in the Cornelii box. But everyone did, Marcella saw—everyone. A shorter man than Piso, with glossy dark curls and teeth that gleamed, his lawn synthesis flamboyantly patterned in gold, a ring on each hand and a gold chain about his neck. He paused in the entrance of the box to let everyone look at him, his smile embracing the crowd, lighting it as if a torch had been carried before him.

"I know I'm late," the newcomer said airily, "but surely you all forgive me?" Most of the guests smiled involuntarily, Marcella noted. All but her sister, whose brows creased in a faint frown.

"Senator Otho?" Lollia whispered. "Gods, what's *he* doing here?"

"Do you know him?" Marcella asked.

"Oh, we bounced the bed a few times back in the old days, when he and Nero were such good friends. Do you know him, my honey?" Lollia gave a reminiscent smile. "He's well worth knowing, believe me."

Marcella knew *of* Senator Marcus Salvius Otho, of course—one of Emperor Nero's boon companions, at least until the minor problem arose when Nero fell in love with Otho's wife, married her, then kicked her to death. *But did I ever meet him before?* The narrow, clever face looked familiar somehow.

Familiar or not, Senator Otho had a pair of red-and-gold Praetorians at his back, just like Piso's.

Well, well, Marcella thought. *Does Piso have a rival?* Perhaps her brother-in-law's ascension to Imperial heir wasn't so certain as everyone assumed. Given Cornelia's suddenly neutral expression, she was thinking exactly the same thing.

"My dear Lollia!" Otho paused before them, his black eyes sparkling amusement. "It's been an age. You're newly married? Congratulations, Senator Vinius," he called across the box. "You have caught Rome's most charming woman for a wife. And you, Lollia, have snared Rome's wisest statesman!"

Vinius preened, mollified. Otho smiled again dazzlingly, and Marcella noted how many of the guests whispered behind their hands as they looked at him. Piso was looking decidedly nonplussed now.

"Reds!" Diana jumped up with a raucous cheer as the Reds chariots paraded past on the track below. *"Reds!"*

Otho's amused gaze transferred to Diana. "There's a young lady who likes the races." A titter rippled through his party—like Nero, he traveled in a party of sculpted women and gleaming men; everyone young, everyone handsome, everyone amusing. He had taken over the Cornelii box like it was his own. "So this is the charming little Cornelia Quarta, for whom half my friends are perishing of love! Or I hear you are called Diana? How very fitting—"

"Sshh!" Diana hushed him impatiently, leaning forward over the railing, and let out a cry with the rest of the crowd as the cloth dropped and twenty-eight horses surged forward over the sand, noses straining and colored plumes blowing. Emperor Galba sat hunched in his box reviewing his accounts, but the plebs were all on their feet, shouting, waving colored pennants, clutching their medallions as the chariots flew into the hairpin turn at lunatic speeds. Even Marcella had to admit it was a stirring sight. Where else could you find two hundred fifty thousand people all going mad at once? *Perhaps a war . . .*

"Stir them up!" Diana shouted down at the first Reds charioteer as he got rattled out of the turn and dropped into fourth. *"Gods' wheels, stir them up!"*

"You'll have to excuse my cousin, Senator Otho." Cornelia approached with outstretched hands, her smile serene and warm—but Marcella knew her sister and saw the unease at the back of her eyes as she looked at Otho's Praetorians. "Diana lives for the Reds, and nothing we can say will quell her."

"Don't quell her," Otho said. "She's an original, and I like originals. I see you are an original as well, my very great lady." He captured Cornelia's hand, which she withdrew when he pressed too warmly.

"Lady Statilia, how lovely to see you—" Cornelia moved on to the ladies and praetors and tribunes in Otho's party, each of whom she knew by name and family, and Piso, who had been hanging awkwardly in the background, was now hanging on his wife's arm, making himself known to all, and Otho frowned. Especially when he noted the Praetorians at Cornelia's back too, who scurried to her lifted finger like obedient slaves.

"Pity Cornelia can't be Emperor," Marcella mused aloud to no one in particular, and Otho's sharp ear caught it.

"Very true, Lady." He gave a bow, eyes raking her face. "Cornelia Secunda, isn't it? I believe I know you already."

"We've never been formally introduced, Senator." Marcella tilted her head quizzically.

"No, but I remember that Emperor Nero once found you beautiful. I am not surprised to find him right."

A cry from Diana as the Blues pulled ahead in the fourth lap. "I'll die if they win," she whispered, eyes following the storm of sand. "I'll *die*—" Half of Otho's tribunes were clustered about her, shouting down at the arena, but Marcella's ears had blocked out the din.

"I don't care to discuss that night, Senator," she said finally. "What's done is done."

"Then you are a courageous lady—and one who holds my admiration."

Marcella sipped at her wine, not tasting it. She had seen the former Emperor often enough, from a distance: waving to the cheering plebs with a gold wreath perched on his false curls, reciting his own poetry to properly respectful courtiers, whispering in the ears of beautiful women who were not his various ill-fated Empresses. But up close? That warm night at Lollia's party this spring, she had seen a man with ruddy, pleasant features . . . and eyes that gleamed at all times, as if with a fever.

Marcella blinked as one of the Green teams went down on a hairpin turn, and the crash penetrated the buzzing in her ears. Even Piso, who had found someone important to bore at the back of the box, turned around. The horses staggered clear, dragging the charioteer behind them, still strapped to the reins, and a team of arena slaves rushed out behind to clear the wreckage of the chariot. The charioteer finally cut himself loose from the maddened horses, rolling limp and bloodied in the sand as they careened away, and the arena slaves rushed to pull him to the sidelines.

"Good," Diana blew out a relieved breath. "If the Reds ran over him, they'd foul their wheels and lose half a lap."

"Little savage," Marcella said, still feeling Otho's watching eyes as he twirled the gold stem of a wine cup between his fingers.

"I'm sorry, you know," he said unexpectedly. "I wish I could have said something, that night."

"At least you didn't laugh," Marcella found herself saying. Most of the guests at the party had laughed—tittered, really, when Nero had looked her over on introduction and said in his offhand high-pitched voice, *"You'll dine alone with me tomorrow."* Marcella looked up at him, startled out of her internal musing, and Nero's gilded guests had found it all very funny. Just another Imperial whim. Everyone knew Nero's whims; even with the Senate rumbling fire at his back, he yielded to every fancy that touched him. Whether it was a goblet of wine, a golden palace—or a general's daughter.

"No, I didn't laugh." Otho's eyes crinkled in a smile. "You were too brave for that."

"I'm not sure if it's bravery if you don't have a choice, Senator."

"I assure you, it is. Courage is defined by how we meet unfortunate circumstances—inevitable or not."

Last lap of the race. Marcella forced her harried attention down on it. Diana was on her feet now, shouting as the Reds darted up to fight for the lead with sixteen legs blurring and the charioteer flapping his reins. The crowd surged up and Marcella found herself surging with them, palms sweaty from nerves that had nothing to do with the race. Otho and his sophisticated crowd never showed excitement; they just murmured and arched their plucked brows, but Lollia shouted encouragement and Diana was shouting right along with her as the Reds and the Blues battled neck and neck, eight horses strong across the track. The last turn, and Marcella gasped along with everyone else as they took it at deadly pace, but the Reds somehow squeaked clear, the charioteer white-eyed and lashing his team all the way.

Marcella looked down and saw that she was banging her hands against the rail. *Fortuna*, she thought in some amusement, *the race got me too.* Vinius looked as sour as ever, and Tullia was tight-lipped to see anyone having fun, but decent boring Piso stood muttering under his breath and Cornelia clung to his arm in excitement, and behind them the impassive centurion named Densus was swearing like a stable hand and clenching his fists as he urged the Reds on. Even Senator Marcus Norbanus looked up from his paperwork in mild interest. The pounding of hooves thudded like a heartbeat.

No conversation now as the teams pulled into the straightaway. Just Blue and Red battling it out, axles clashing, the outside horses snapping at each, both charioteers laying their whips on. Every soul in the circus was on their feet, shrieking, screaming, begging for a victory. Sour-faced Emperor Galba was busy shuffling his lists and counting his sesterces when the Reds pulled ahead, confounding all the odds to beat the Blues in the climactic race of the Ludi Plebii.

The circus exploded.

Diana yelled in triumph and flung her arms around the nearest person, who happened to be Marcella. She laughed and hugged her craziest cousin back, ruffling the mess of untidy hair. Cornelia and Piso were hugging each other too, Lollia was tossing little Flavia up in the air, and Otho looked amused. Below, the Reds charioteer blinked as he was presented with his victory palm. The Blues charioteer snapped his whip spitefully over the heads of the exhausted Reds team, making them jump and making every Reds fan in the circus from Diana to the lowest pleb leap up shrieking obscenities.

"By Jove," Otho said as Diana shouted down at the Blues charioteer, "I've not heard such fine cursing since my days in the legions."

The party was spilling outward now, and Lollia bubbled invitations to everyone to come to her house, where the winning charioteer would be hosted. "I will not have racing riffraff in my home!" Old Flaccid sniffed.

"Then I'll throw a party for him at my grandfather's house," Lollia said sweetly, and Marcella laughed behind her hand to see how Otho's entourage of beautiful glossy people brightened at the prospect of a free meal from the table of such a famous host. Senator Vinius kept hissing imprecations, flapping his wrinkled hands, and Lollia rolled her eyes openly. Marcella gave Old Flaccid another month before Lollia wangled herself a divorce.

"I thank this is my cue to go." Otho bowed over Marcella's hand. "I'll be at the party later, of course—when do I ever miss a good party?—but for the time being I should go apply myself to all the dullards so they'll all think I'm capable and well informed."

"You *are* capable and well-informed, Senator," Marcella said. "I hear you did a very good work as Governor of Hispania last year."

"Really? I didn't think anyone noticed." He wandered off, calling greetings.

Cornelia and Piso had been summoned to the palace to dine with the Emperor, but the rest of the family flooded back toward the house of Lollia's grandfather, Diana leading the charge with her arm slung companionably about the victorious charioteer. Wine at once began to flow and music to soar, and Marcella collapsed in a corner with a cup of wine to watch everything. *Because that's what I do best*, she thought. *Marcella, keeper of history and watcher of emperors.*

She laughed aloud, mocking herself. Such purple language from a historian!

Lollia's grandfather beamed in the atrium, welcoming senators and charioteers and giggling ladies alike with open arms, happy in everybody's success because he owned shares in the Reds. Also, Marcella knew, in the Blues, the Greens, and the Whites, because he was careful to back *all* sides. *No wonder he's the richest man in Rome.* He'd gone from an ex-slave running the low-rent district in the Caelian Hill to a trader with so many tentacles of business that he could marry into the patrician class and deal with emperors . . . Lollia was already pleading prettily with him in a corner, doubtless angling to get rid of Old Flaccid. Of course she'd succeed—her grandfather might be hard-nosed in business, but he was clay in the hands of his only grandchild, whom he'd raised as his own when her mother and father died in that boating accident. If Lollia wanted a new husband, a new husband her grandfather would get for her—just as he'd gotten his jewel the ponies, the dolls, the dresses, and the pearls when she was little. *She had all the best toys back then,* Marcella thought. *I suppose she still does.*

At the center of the raucous crowd was Otho, leading the guests in a toast to the Reds, cheering the return of good times in the cold onset of December. Marcella saw his brilliant smile as a Praetorian approached to whisper in his ear. "Apologies to all!" he called gaily. "But Emperor Galba summons me to the palace. Dear gods, I wonder what I've done wrong?"

"Why did Galba invite him?" Cornelia wailed to Marcella the next day.

"Because he's handsome?" Marcella suggested. "Galba does like a strapping handsome man, one hears. I always thought that might be why he likes your Piso so much, but if Otho is more to his tastes . . ."

Her sister wasn't listening. "—Piso and I were supposed to be the only guests! Otho just lay there all through dinner making jokes at Piso's expense. And why Otho got assigned Praetorians too, I'll never understand—"

Marcella slanted a brow. "I think you do understand, Cornelia."

"Never mind." Cornelia smoothed her hair with both hands, and her expression with it. "It doesn't change anything. Piso is Galba's cousin, after all. He's descended from Pompey and Crassus, and he's a *serious* man, not some frivolous perfumed sophisticate. Those are the things that matter."

"Maybe so. But guess who has more money to sprinkle around in bribes? Guess who can charm the birds out of trees? And guess whose name the crowd was screaming after the races?"

Three

☙❧

CORNELIA always hated the public slave market. The pushing, the shoving, the auctioneers shouting like cattle drovers, the jeers of the men who just came to see the female slaves stripped naked. So off-putting—she always attended private showings for her slaves.

"My dear ladies." An unctuous little man bowed before Lollia and Cornelia. "You honor me with your patronage. Only the finest slaves to be seen here, all healthy and docile—"

"You know what I find depressing?" Lollia complained. "That a trip to the slave auction is the highlight of my month."

"You have only yourself to blame," Cornelia pointed out, filing slowly past the long row of slaves on their display pedestals. "Kissing a charioteer at a party—Juno's mercy, most husbands would object to that!"

"Oh, it's not kissing a charioteer that he objects to. It's the *indiscretion*. 'I will not have my wife known as a whore,'" Lollia mimicked savagely. "'Since you seem unable to behave yourself in public, you are henceforth confined to the house. Properly supervised, you may go to the Forum, to the bathhouse, to visit your family, and to such entertainments as I deem appropriate.' And believe me, there isn't much he deems appropriate."

Cornelia perused the line of slaves, absently accepting a cup of barley water from the hovering slave dealer. Male and female slaves alike were dressed in crisp white tunics, limbs oiled and gleaming in the lamplight, a discreet plaque hanging about each neck to advertise names and skills. Servitors, secretaries, scribes . . . a proper cook, that was what Cornelia needed. Her current cook would be quite defeated by the prospect of a forty-course banquet. Not that her own tastes were so elaborate, of course—or Piso's—but an emperor's heir had to keep up certain standards when he entertained . . .

If Galba chooses him. But she squelched that thought firmly. Of course the Emperor would choose Piso. There were no other possible candidates. *Some* people might appear more popular and charming, *some* people might be sprinkling money about like spring rain, but that didn't matter in the long run. Men of character and integrity would always win over men of charm and money.

"I thought I'd buy a new maid to replace that harpy Old Flaccid set to spy on me," Lollia was saying meditatively. "But perhaps I need something else too. Something large and handsome and male to help me pass the time."

"Lollia, really."

"Well, who else is supposed to keep me occupied while I'm under house arrest? Unless you're willing to lend me that stalwart centurion of yours on your next visit. He can show me what he can do with his spear, and you can talk all you want about Piso being Emperor."

"I hope you're just trying to be funny, because if you sincerely think I would ever—"

"Oh, don't ruffle your feathers," Lollia sighed.

Pushing down her irritation, Cornelia paused before a plump slave with a bald head. She leaned closer to read the plaque at his neck: *Varro, Greek, forty-three years, cook.* "What kind of cook, Varro? For an *equite* household, or for a senatorial family?"

"I have cooked for governors and consuls and emperors, Lady. Emperor Nero himself admired my boiled ostrich."

"Did he? Tell me, what sauce would you use to cook a fallow deer?"

"Onion sauce," the slave said promptly. "With Jericho dates, raisins, and honey."

"And what menu would you set if Emperor Galba were to eat at your table?"

"Jellyfish and eggs, boiled mushrooms with a sauce of pepper and fish fat, roast parrot—"

"If only husbands came with plaques." Lollia held out her goblet to be refilled—wine, Cornelia noticed, not barley water. "*Vinius, Roman, fifty-seven years, windbag.* I'm divorcing him if it's the last thing I do. I'd have done it already, but he said he'd turn the Emperor on my grandfather—confiscate all his assets, just like they did with poor Marcus Norbanus."

"He shouldn't have said that," Cornelia admitted. "Varro, what would you say is the best stuffing for roast dormice?"

"Pork and pine kernels, Lady."

"Old Flaccid certainly won't get away with threatening my grandfather," Lollia said ominously, and wandered farther down the line of slaves. "*Masseuse—hairdresser—litter-bearer—*"

"He comes with five more, Lady," the slave dealer interjected. "A matched set—"

"I'll take this one on a trial basis," Cornelia decided, and smiled at the plump little cook. "Welcome to my household, Varro."

"Thank you, Domina." He bowed over her hand.

"Hmmm . . ." Lollia paused before the last slave in line. "Who's this?"

Cornelia read the plaque about the slave's neck. "*Thrax, Gaul, twenty-eight years, body slave.*" Now there was a polite euphemism. One look at the slave—tall, broad-shouldered, with wheat-blond hair and muscles like a statue—and anyone would know what his skills were.

Lollia was looking him up and down. "You're called Thrax?"

"Yes, Lady." He had a deep voice, vaguely accented.

"And you're from Gaul? That's a long way away."

"I hardly remember it, Lady."

"I'm sorry, do you mind if—?" Lollia arched her eyebrows at the slave with an appealing smile. Thrax pulled his tunic up over his head and drew his naked body up for examination. Cornelia looked away, feeling another flash of disapproval. There was absolutely no reason to strip a slave for inspection—if they had defects they could always be returned, so why bother stripping them naked at the auction unless it was simply to gape? And even a slave had his pride. The big Gaul was flushing slightly, but he smiled at Lollia in genuine if abashed friendliness.

Lollia turned to the dealer. "I'll take him."

"You don't buy a slave just for beauty," Cornelia said as Thrax was led away shouldering back into his tunic. "That Gaul will distract all the female slaves in your house, and half the male."

"I don't care, as long as he's distracting *me*."

"Do you even need a body slave?"

"I certainly need a body like that." Lollia eyed her new acquisition where he waited by the end of the hall. He brushed the fair hair out of his eyes, and the muscles of his arms moved under the skin. "Just the thing to liven up house arrest!"

Cornelia stopped. "Lollia, lovers from your own class are one thing, but bedding a slave? It—well, it demeans you. And them too."

"You wouldn't say that if I were a man." Her cousin tucked a red curl behind her ear. "Every husband I ever had took a roll with the slave girls now and then. Slave boys, too."

"That doesn't make it right."

"Any slave who looks like Thrax over there knows he'll be bought for a bedmate," Lollia said, exasperated. "He's probably thanking whatever gods he worships that *I* bought him and not some middle-aged hag or nasty old senator."

"I'm glad you think so well of yourself," Cornelia said, disgusted.

"Your purchases will be delivered direct to your door in an hour." The little dealer bowed. "Perhaps you ladies wish to look further? A new maid to make you even more beautiful, or perhaps—"

"I think I've seen enough." Cornelia lifted a hand for her steward so he could haggle the price.

"That's new." Lollia captured her hand, looking at the wrist. "That bracelet—it looks Egyptian."

"Just a trinket." Cornelia pulled her sleeve down hastily over the little bronze amulet tied around her wrist.

"Looks like a charm to me." Lollia winked as they left the long hall for the atrium. "Let me guess—a good-luck charm for Piso? Or a fertility charm for you?"

Cornelia blushed. "Piso doesn't like charms—just magical superstition for plebs, he says."

Which was why she'd felt so guilty giving over a handful of coins at the Temple of Isis. The priestess had assured her that if she wore it for a month and sewed a matching charm to her husband's pillow . . . Cornelia had stitched the charm as directed but hidden it from Piso. He didn't approve of foreign gods. Neither did she, really, but she'd heard such encouraging things about Isis and her fertility rituals—

"It's none of your business, Lollia."

"Don't snap at me, my honey. I don't see why you're so keen for babies, really. Flavia's a darling, of course, but my waist has *never* been the same."

"How is Flavia?" Cornelia said hastily. The atrium was cold, the winter skies leaden through the open roof, but she felt her cheeks flaming.

"She's ill," Lollia said. "Anybody would be, living in Old Flaccid's house. I plan to be sick myself as soon as Thrax arrives—lots of headaches to keep me in bed, but I won't be alone there—"

"Flavia's ill?" Cornelia halted. "What's wrong with her? Have you summoned the doctor?"

"Oh, she just has a cough. My maids are watching her every minute."

"Why aren't you watching her yourself?"

"I read to her every morning. What else can I do?" Lollia blinked. "The slaves know how to look after her much better than I do."

"If Flavia were my child, I wouldn't leave her to the care of slaves! A child should be raised by her mother—"

Lollia laughed. "Not one of us was raised by our mother, Cornelia. You, Marcella, Diana, me—all of us were brought up by slaves. And we turned out well enough."

"Our mothers all died *young*, Lollia. I don't see why Flavia should have to—"

"And I don't see why it's any of your business. Flavia isn't your child."

"Maybe she should be!" All at once Cornelia's temper snapped. "Your daughter lies ill, and you're out buying a pet stud!"

"And maybe if I loan him to you, you might *get* a child instead of envying me mine," Lollia flared. "Because your husband clearly isn't getting it done."

"Don't you dare say a word about my husband!" Cornelia rounded on her cousin in the middle of the atrium.

"Oh, he's such a catch?" Lollia's voice turned acid. "He turns up his nose at my grandfather every time they meet, and so do you! Just because he's slave-born and believes in *working* for a living, making all that nasty money the whole family likes to borrow. Your Piso certainly doesn't turn up his nose at *that*."

"You're jealous," Cornelia snapped. "Just because my husband will be Galba's heir—"

"Yes, and you can look down on me even more once you're the Empress." Lollia planted fists on hips, glaring. "Don't think I never see you and Marcella smiling behind my back when I talk! You two always looked down on me, and Diana too—"

"Well, why not?" Cornelia demanded. "Why shouldn't we look down on the pair of you? A girl who runs around like a common slave, and a girl who sleeps with them!"

"Maybe you should try it. Have you *ever* had a good screw?"

"My husband adores me!"

"Well, that's certainly fatal. Adoration doesn't make for good lovers, Cornelia. Why don't you go back into that auction room and buy yourself some hulking Greek with a cock like an ox, just to see what you're missing?"

"And you wonder why I look down on you? A mouth like a common dockside whore; anyone can see you've got slave blood! Someday you'll realize what a slut you are."

The slave dealer stared cautiously from his door. Two patrician women shrieking at each other like fishwives in the middle of his atrium.

"You'd better hope that fertility charm works, Cornelia." Lollia's eyes narrowed. "No emperor wants a barren wife, you know. Your precious husband will divorce you for some pretty little thing who will pump him out lots of sons, and then the most perfect wife in Rome won't be looking down at *me* anymore."

Cornelia slapped her. Lollia slapped her back.

They stood a moment, glaring at each other.

Cornelia stamped away, before Lollia could see the tears spill out onto her stinging face.

W*ELL*, Diana thought, *it finally happened.*
      She twirled a lunatic circle in the grass, smiling a new and dreamy smile: utterly, madly, and completely in love at long last.

"So, who's this Briton you keep talking about?" Diana had asked the faction director for the Reds as the hired litter turned down a smaller lane. "I thought I knew every horse breeder in Rome."

"Used to be a rebel in Britannia somewhere, now he breeds horses. Doesn't sell many, but they're good. He might have something that will do for the Reds." Xerxes looked at her irritably as the litter swayed down the muddy lane. "Why did I bring you, anyway?"

"Because I'm getting my noble relatives to help pay for this new team of yours." Diana twined a finger through one of the racing medallions about her neck. Two horses lost in the first race of the year, before the running had even begun—the Reds team had tangled badly when the hateful Derricus snapped his blue-beaded whip over their heads, and two horses had panicked in their traces. Both inside runners had walked away hobbling. "And if I'm helping to pay, I'm helping to pick."

Xerxes grumbled. Diana knew he didn't like her, but that didn't bother her a bit. He had just enough respect for her family's patronage to keep from kicking her out of the Reds stable, and that was all that mattered.

The farm where they finally disembarked was broad and sprawling, orderly pastures running down a long slope crowned at the top with a small, columned villa. All the best breeding farms lay outside city walls. Diana climbed out of the litter, sniffing delightedly at the cold clean air. So different from the smoke and stench inside Rome's city walls. If not for the Circus Maximus, she'd quit the city altogether and stay out here where the air smelled clean to the nose.

A portly steward came out of the villa in greeting, and he and Xerxes lapsed into business. Diana looked down the hill instead, where a man stood leaning on a rail and watching two colts frisking in the field, a big black dog of no particular breed sitting at his feet. She looped her red *palla* up out of the mud and came to stand beside him. The colts were too young for racing, but she liked the look of them. "Good legs," she said. "Do you have anything older?"

The man turned. She was used to surprise when men looked at her, but he didn't look as if he was surprised by much. "Horses to run, or breed?"

"To run." Diana leaned down and scratched the black dog's head. "For the Reds."

"I don't think much of your charioteer this year." The Briton's voice was low and mild. "Doesn't cut close enough on the turn."

"No," Diana allowed. "I'd do better, but no one's offering to let *me* drive."

A smile twitched the Briton's mouth. No one would ever mistake him for a Roman, Diana thought—his hair was too long, iron gray and shaggy; a bronze torc clasped his neck, and he wore breeches instead of a tunic. He wasn't old, despite the gray hair—thirty-five or forty, tall and broadly built with a cleft chin and a calm face.

Xerxes came down from the villa then, trailed by the steward, and brusquely introduced himself. The Briton grasped his wrist in greeting rather than bowing. "I am Llyn ap Caradoc."

"Caradoc?" said Diana. "I've heard that name."

"Some have," the Briton replied, and set off up the slope where the sprawling stables began. His breech-clad legs ate the ground, and she loped to keep up.

He brought out four gray stallions and put them through their paces. Xerxes began to haggle, but Diana turned away restlessly. The grays ran well, but it would take something better to beat the Blues with their team of savage blood bays. It would take something extraordinary.

Another large paddock stood, divided into four by rails. Four stallions penned beside each other—Diana leaned against the rail.

One of the stallions nipped at another, and they lunged over the rail, manes flying. An older stallion in the next pen squealed at them with pinned ears and they went streaking off along the fence instead, racing each other. They passed Diana in a storm of red: chestnuts all, red as a setting sun.

"Wait," Diana called to the faction director.

She was already swinging under the rail and striding into the grass as he and the Briton came to the fence. "This one," she called, looking at the stallion who squealed at the other two. "He's older than these other three?"

"Their sire," said the Briton. "He keeps them in order. Careful, he doesn't like people."

The stallion swiped at Diana, but she ducked the slash of teeth and seized the long nose, looking him over. He glared at her, stamping.

"Too old for the circus," Xerxes said disapprovingly.

"No, he isn't. He'll steady them." She released the stallion's nose, turning back to the tall Briton. "Let's see them run." Her stomach trembled and her mouth was dry.

The Briton brought the chestnut stallions in, and she fell in beside him to help with the harnessing. He gave her a long look, but she proceeded matter-of-factly among the buckles and straps, and after a moment he passed her the outside runner's bridle without comment. The horses stood eager in the traces, red manes falling like flames along the crests of their necks.

The Briton vaulted up into the chariot, and for a moment Diana hated him—she'd have given anything on earth to have those reins in her own hands. She fell in beside the chariot as he reined toward the rough track.

"You know horses, Lady," the Briton observed.

"These chestnuts are marvelous." She shifted into a trot to keep up with the rattling wheels. "Have they raced? Do you breed from those big Gallic horses, or—"

"From chariot ponies out of Britannia."

"Ponies? Too small."

"I bred the size up, once I got what I wanted. Briton chariot ponies are bred for battle, so racing's nothing to them." He gave a nod of professional pride as he turned the chariot onto the rough makeshift track. "These four will keep calm even in the last lap."

He lined them up, poised light as a breath. Diana flung herself against the rail, chewing the inside of her lip, and they leaped down the track: four horses, moving as one like a red wind.

The Briton took them on four circuits, but Diana had seen enough by the end of the first and so had Xerxes. "That *turn*—!" The old stallion leaned into his harness like a bull, bringing the other three leaning with him, and the chariot hairpinned around the turn with an inch of clearance.

Diana vaulted up onto the rail as the chestnuts at last eased to a halt. Her palms were sweating, her eyes swimming, and butterflies had turned her stomach into knots. Lollia always told her she'd feel like this when she finally fell in love—and she finally had.

She grinned at the Briton as he came down from his chariots, grinned too wide to play calm. "We'll take them," she said radiantly. "And if you don't sell them to the Reds, I'll *steal* them."

The Briton laughed. Standing on the lowest rail of the fence put Diana level with his eyes. "They'll run well for you," he approved.

The faction director was jotting on a slate, working figures. Diana swung over the fence to greet the chestnuts—they were barely winded, tossing their heads as if they'd just cantered to the end of the paddock and back.

"Oh, my beauties, you're going to make mincemeat of the Blues."
She ran her hands over the warm silk of the outside runner's neck.
"What are their names?"

"I don't name horses." The Briton ran a horn-hard hand down the
old stallion's nose. "Makes it harder when you lose them in battles."

"You've fought many battles?"

"A few." The Briton turned to start wrangling with the faction
director over price. Diana unharnessed the chestnuts, taking the two
outside runners and walking between them back to the field. The
horse on Diana's left shied at a gust of wind, lifting her off her feet
for a moment. She clung to his reins, clucking under her breath till he
quieted and followed her again.

"They don't usually follow along like that," the Briton said from
behind, following with the second pair of horses. "They like to kick
anyone they don't know."

"Horses never kick me." Reaching up to tug the bridle over the
curved ears, she released first one stallion and then the other into the
field with a slap on the rump. The Briton released his pair, and they
leaned on the fence watching the chestnuts take off snorting across the
grass.

"What will you name them, Lady?"

"That's easy." Watching their red manes catch fire in the noon sun.
"I'll call them the Anemoi. After the Four Winds."

HIDE me," Marcella greeted her sister. "I am fleeing Tullia. She
was going on and on about a chipped tile in the atrium, and it
was either flight or murder."

"Of course you're welcome here." Cornelia kissed her cheek, composed as ever, but the hand that gripped Marcella's was damp.

"I was hoping we could have a good gossip," Marcella confessed,
unwinding the *palla* from her hair. "Kick off our shoes and curl up
with a flagon of wine, the way we used to do in the old days?" *Before
husbands and politics came along.*

"Not today, Marcella." Cornelia cast a glance over one shoulder to her thronged atrium, noisy with slaves and guards and hangers-on. "Piso's gone to the palace. The Emperor so relies on him, he went to Galba's side the minute he heard the news—"

"What, the news from Germania? The legions going about smashing Galba's statues—"

"Sshh." Cornelia took her sister's arm, moving serenely back through the room. A nod to Galba's chamberlain; a word to the slaves to bring more wine; a warm greeting for a senator who had taken thousands of sesterces from Otho to speak against Piso in the Senate . . . "Everything got tense as soon as the news filtered to the soldiers," Cornelia said in a low voice, her bright social smile never faltering. "If the German legions don't acknowledge Galba as Emperor, the Praetorians may revolt—"

"Well, they have enough reasons. Galba's still refusing to pay them their bounty."

"Why should he bribe them? They're honorable soldiers of Rome, not common thugs."

"Yes, but honor doesn't pay your dicing debts or buy you a drink at a tavern, does it?" Otho was doing quite a lot of that these days, or so Marcella heard.

"It's only the miscontents who are grumbling." Cornelia paused to exclaim over the new wife of a very old enemy, smiled, moved on. "Centurion Densus assures me all *his* men are loyal—Densus, that's the centurion assigned to our protection. He's a gem. If they were all like him—!"

Marcella smiled. "Isn't he the one Lollia asked to borrow?"

"I've given up even talking to Lollia," Cornelia sniffed.

"Don't let it go on too long. Life is very dull without Lollia."

Several overdressed matrons came forward to gush over Cornelia, who kissed cheeks and asked after children. Neither of the matrons had a word for Marcella—her husband wasn't terribly important, after all. Shedding the matrons, the sisters reached the long hall where the busts of Piso's ancestors faced a long row of dead Cornelii, and

Cornelia dragged Marcella behind a stern bust of their barely remembered mother. "The Emperor will announce his heir today," Cornelia whispered, fingers digging into her sister's arm in open excitement. "He'll have to, to pacify the legions—they'll calm down if they realize there's another man coming behind him, someone young and energetic and generous—"

"So Piso is at the palace, pressing his claim?"

"Of course not, he's just—there. Steady, reliable, ready for anything. Of course Otho is there too—" Cornelia began chewing her varnished nails.

"Stop that." Marcella rapped her knuckles. "Would an empress have ragged nails?"

"Of course not." With something of an effort, Cornelia smoothed herself back into the picture of serenity: a dark violet *stola* suggesting Imperial purple (but not too blatantly); a collar of amethysts and pearls on silver wire enclosing her neck; a calm expression. "I should attend my guests. We should be hearing from Piso soon."

"Domina?" Her centurion appeared in the door of the hall. "The slaves want to know if they should keep circulating the wine."

"Of course." Cornelia glided back to the throng, her Praetorian at her back like a pillar. Marcella thought she'd never seen her sister look more regal.

Still . . . Marcella had to admit that she might have chosen Otho as Imperial heir over Piso, had it been up to her. He was much more interesting, for one thing; at the endless round of dinner parties over the past few weeks, Otho ignored the rising tension and just stretched himself out lazily talking of the new production of *Thyestes* and the latest gossip from Egypt, while Piso droned on in the background about coinage. *Ever since Nero, Rome wants her emperors witty and intelligent, not just worthy.* Not that Nero himself had been much of a wit—or a poet, or a musician, or an emperor for that matter—but he did have a talent for collecting witty people. Like Otho.

Well, witty or not, in the end Marcella had to cast her hopes with her sister's husband. *The moment my sister becomes Empress and Tullia tries to boss me . . . !*

Another hour. Marcella watched as faces grew more taut, voices more shrill. All but Cornelia, moving like a goddess among the throng.

An insistent hand tugged at her elbow. "I got you more wine."

"Thank you." Marcella took a goblet from an admirer she had somehow acquired, a stocky boy of eighteen with staring black eyes and abrupt manners. The younger son of the brilliant Vespasian, Governor of Judaea . . . who might have been Emperor himself if he hadn't been common born and also a thousand miles away.

"I've seen you before," Vespasian's son said, still staring. Domitian, that was his name. "Lucius Aelius Lamia's wife, aren't you?"

"Yes, unfortunately." Marcella looked about the crowded room for her cousins. Diana had gone utterly mad lately, so consumed with her new Reds team she wouldn't notice if Galba appointed a horse as his heir. But it wasn't like Lollia to miss such a fraught gathering, no matter what kind of tiff she'd had with Cornelia. Well, she'd been housebound lately with a great many headaches.

I'd have them too, married to sour Old Flaccid.

"General Gnaeus Corbulo was your father," Domitian was saying. "I admired him."

"Did you?" Marcella sipped her wine.

"I'm going to be a general. My brother is. Titus—he was married to your cousin for a while, the rich stupid one. Lollia. Titus is very good—a good general, I mean—but I'll be better. Nessus says so."

"Who is Nessus?"

"An astrologer I found. He's very skilled."

"I've never heard of him."

"Well, he's always right!" The boy sounded defensive. "He says I'm going to be a general someday, and after that—"

Marcella stifled a yawn. "Of course."

For such an important announcement, it came quietly. Two men entered from the atrium. Senator Otho, his black curls glossy and perfumed, his smile so brilliant it warmed the room. Piso, pushing the folds of his toga off his head, looking weary and dazed. Marcella saw her sister freeze, saw the ripples spread outward through the guests as Otho moved into the room exclaiming greetings and an exhausted

Piso trailed in his wake. Marcella was already framing sympathies before she realized what they were saying.

"Congratulations to Senator Piso!" Otho threw back his head, smiling. "Our future Emperor!"

A roar of applause swept through the chamber, and Piso looked even more dazed, and Cornelia was somehow at his side, turning him away a little so his first smile came for her. She murmured something, and his smile finally broadened. His dark hair gleamed in the lamplight and he looked rather taller.

Who would have thought it? Marcella mused. Galba had weighed his two possibilities for Imperial heir, and in the end chosen lineage and respectability over charm and popularity. *Emperor Lucius Calpurnius Piso Licinianus.*

The party spilled out into the night. Lollia arrived very late, looking rather hastily put together in a great many emeralds, but she poured congratulations on Cornelia. "I was beastly to you." Her remorseful whisper carried to Marcella's ears, and Cornelia hugged her with no stiffness at all. Diana came, still babbling on about her wretched new Reds team until Marcella hoped they'd all break a leg. Dull as Diana was, two more senators proposed marriage to her. Why not? She was no longer just a beautiful little bore, but a beautiful little bore related to the future Empress of Rome.

As am I. Strange thought. Still, Marcella couldn't see that it would make much difference to her life. History would always march on regardless of what man wore the purple, and historians would always be there to watch.

Though perhaps she could leverage Cornelia's influence to get Lucius a post here in Rome. So she could have her own household at last, and finally get herself out of Tullia's . . .

"Allow me to present my congratulations, Senator." Otho pressed Piso's hand. Surely his cheeks ached, Marcella thought, with holding that smile. "You are fortunate in the Emperor's favor."

"Fortunate?" Piso's voice was lordly, already Imperial. Marcella wondered if he might be remembering the day at the races when Otho outshone him so effortlessly at his own party. "Fortuna favors the worthy. Not the fools."

A ripple of laughter spread across the room: a hundred guests all eager to find the Imperial heir a wit. For just an instant, Otho's smile froze. Then he threw back his head and laughed as heartily as anyone else.

"A good jest, Senator. I do hope it gave you pleasure. In future there will be so little time for baiting us poor fools."

Piso had already moved on to the next well-wisher. Otho stood alone; impulsively, Marcella shook off the Governor of Judaea's stubborn black-eyed son and moved to his side. "Senator?"

He looked up at once, still maintaining his bright smile. "Cornelia Secunda! Though I prefer Marcella, as you do. Your sister does rather take possession of the name, doesn't she, and someone as special as yourself deserves a name of her own."

He'd have gone on chattering airily, but Marcella tilted her head to one side and stood observing the wide berth the other guests now gave Otho as they flooded to Piso's side. "I see no one's lost any time worshipping the rising sun, rather than the setting."

"You think my sun has set?" Otho's smile never faltered.

"Hasn't it? You've lost. And there are plenty of people here—including Piso—who are dying to see you squirm."

"I suppose you'll congratulate me on how well I'm taking it? If I do say so myself, I'm being quite splendid about it all."

"Well, what's your alternative?" Marcella said briskly. "Beating your head against the floor and wailing? Slipping the priest a bribe tomorrow, so he reads Piso's omens badly and all those superstitious soldiers come rushing back to you?"

Otho looked startled. "My dear Marcella, I can't imagine—"

"Oh, don't be polite. Just admit that you'd like to wring Piso's neck. You'll feel better."

Otho laughed.

"I want to wring Piso's neck too, sometimes. Especially when he tells those long pointless jokes . . ." Marcella smiled at Otho in farewell and moved back to the party. Perhaps it was time she went home—Gaius and Tullia didn't have the good news yet, after all, and she'd enjoy bringing it to them herself while it was still fresh.

Besides, I want to see the look on that curled cow's face when she tries to order me about, and I tell her I would rather follow the advice of my sister. The future Empress of Rome.

Four

ᔕ◯ᑕ

CORNELIA put her lips very close to her husband's ear. "Good morning, Caesar."

"Don't call me that!"

"Why not?" Cornelia kissed him. "You're going to be Emperor someday."

He laughed again, pulling her against him, and Cornelia felt a happy shiver down her spine. Winter sunlight splashed through the windows of the bedchamber—they had gone to bed only hours before, when the last of their entourage—*we have an entourage, now!*—stumbled from the house.

"Just because I've been appointed heir doesn't mean I'll be Emperor, you know," Piso was pointing out. "As that sharp sister of yours said to me, think of all those other heirs who never got to take the purple. All those grandsons and nephews of Augustus. . . . One shouldn't take these things for granted. It would be tempting the gods."

"Oh, I know." Cornelia smoothed a hand over his chest. "And I'll be entirely cautious and respectful in public. But in here, where it's just us—well, can't we gloat just a little?"

"Maybe a little." Piso laughed, and tilted his head down to give her a long, lingering kiss.

"You'll be late," Cornelia murmured between more kisses. "Galba wants to present you to the troops this morning." Of course she couldn't go to the Praetorian barracks; that wouldn't be fitting for a woman.

Piso twined his hand through her hair. "They can wait."

"Mmm . . ." She kissed him drowsily. "Really?"

She hoped he'd stay, but he groaned and sat up. "No, you're right. I should go."

Cornelia robed him herself, brushing the slaves away as she brought out his finest toga. "Lift your arm—no, the other one—hold *still*—"

"I really am late," Piso moaned.

"Blame it all on your lascivious wife." She aligned the pleats along his shoulder.

"I intend to," he said, mock stern. "And afterward I shall make you Augusta."

Cornelia smiled demurely, hiding her excitement. Augusta, the title given to Emperor Augustus's wife Livia in mark of her virtue and intelligence, giving her the power of sitting alongside her husband in political matters. "The Senate might not approve. I'm very young to be Augusta."

"They'll approve. It will be one of my first decrees." Piso pulled a fold of his toga up over his head. "Though first, my dear, I shall see if I can persuade Galba to pay the Praetorians their bounty. They do expect it, and we don't want them grumbling."

"Who could grumble at you?"

His lips found hers and they kissed again until footsteps sounded outside. Piso immediately broke away, and Cornelia felt a little wistful urge that he would just keep kissing her—although of course, the heir to an empire must maintain the decorum due his station. She turned with a smile to see Centurion Drusus Densus in the door, helmet beneath his arm, two Praetorians in red and gold behind him. "We stand ready to escort you to the palace, Senator. Another detail has been assigned to your use."

Cornelia felt a moment's embarrassment at having been caught in a loose bed robe with her hair still hanging down her back but couldn't repress a radiant smile. "I am pleased to put the safety of Rome's next Emperor in your hands, Centurion."

Densus smiled. "The pleasure is mine, Lady."

"Stay with Lady Cornelia today, Centurion," Piso ordered. "I'll take the other detail to the barracks."

"Yes, Senator." Densus gave a crisp salute.

Piso did not kiss her good-bye, but he did squeeze her hand under cover of his toga's folds. *"Augusta,"* he mouthed, and was gone: every inch an emperor. Even if it wasn't proper to think so just yet.

Cornelia waited until he was out of earshot, then couldn't resist giving a little squeal and whirling in a circle. A stifled laugh, and she realized the centurion was still standing in the doorway. She giggled at him, unable to stop herself. "I'm sorry, Centurion. I shall be more dignified soon, I promise."

"I won't tell, Lady." He bowed. "Where shall I escort you this morning?"

"The Temple of Fortuna." A sacrifice to the goddess of luck seemed very much in order. "And the Temple of Juno." For a more personal sacrifice. "After that, I can rejoin my husband at the palace to hear the augurs give a pronouncement. And there's sure to be a banquet this evening."

Cornelia took more pains with her appearance than usual. Her hair went up into a more elaborate coil, she chose a *stola* in deep-green silk clasped with gold brooches at the shoulders, and she unhesitatingly took out the necklace Piso had given her at Lupercalia last year: a massive square-cut emerald on a slender gold chain, with square chunks of emerald for her ears. A simple matron might not wear jewels during the day, but the wife of an Imperial heir had to look the part. Galba would expect them to keep up appearances now (though Piso had already noted, dryly, that the Emperor had offered them no increase in allowance to help pay for an Imperial lifestyle). And even though Piso wouldn't be Emperor until Galba died, Cornelia's own duties as first lady of Rome would begin much sooner. Galba had no wife, no mother, no sisters—he would certainly call on Cornelia now to act as Imperial hostess!

Centurion Densus bowed very low when she finally appeared, pulling up a gold veil to cover her hair. "Empress," he said.

"Not yet, Centurion," Cornelia chided.

"Empress in spirit, Lady." His eyes went over her admiringly. "Every inch."

She could feel people whispering as she alighted from the litter before the shrine of Fortuna. "She's to be Empress," the whispers flew. "Her husband's been named heir!" They made way even without the Praetorians clearing a path, and Cornelia knelt alone, center of all eyes, before the statue of Fortuna. The goddess of luck, carved in pink marble with her feet upon the wheel with which she turned the fortunes of men. The wheel that had spun Piso and Cornelia so high. She closed her eyes in heartfelt thanks, and the priests did not hesitate to bring out their best bullock to be sacrificed.

Cornelia rose, careful to avoid the spatters of blood. "She's to be Empress," the whisper went up again as she descended the steps.

"Those *emeralds*—"

Definitely, she had been right to wear the emeralds. Plebs were pleased by a bit of display.

The centurion beckoned for the litter, and Cornelia accepted the rough hand that helped her in. "Centurion," she said impulsively as he made to fall back. "Speak with me a moment."

"As you wish, Lady." He fell into step beside the litter as it rose swaying, his eyes now level with Cornelia's shoulder.

"What do you hear from the Praetorian barracks?" No better source of information than a bodyguard, Cornelia knew, and an empress should have her own sources. "Are they pleased with Galba's choice of heir?"

"Well enough, Lady." Guardedly.

"Speak freely, Densus."

He hesitated, walking along sturdily, hand never far from his short *gladius*, scarlet plumes nodding over his head. Morning hawkers cried their wares on either side of the street, and the other litters, seeing the Praetorians, fell back to give Cornelia's litter precedence. "They'd not care if the Emperor chose a mule, Lady, as long as he paid them their bounty."

"And he hasn't, yet."

"No. Senator Otho, he passed out plenty of coin among the Praetorians—there's those that liked him. My lot are better than that," Densus hastened to say. "I don't take any but the best. But most soldiers are greedy bastards, Lady." He flushed. "I'm sorry—"

"No, you only speak truth." Even the first lady of Rome could unbend a trifle, now and then—it would only encourage loyalty. "What do you hear of the legions in Germania—are they being, ah, greedy bastards too?"

"There's a whisper they proclaimed Governor Vitellius as Emperor. But it's just a whisper, Lady."

"I can't believe they'd be such fools," Cornelia said dismissively. Senator Vitellius, well, he was a fat drunk who cared for nothing but feasts and chariot racing. "He'd never make a real emperor."

"Senator Piso will." The words surprised her. "He'll be a fine one, Lady. Good and steady."

Cornelia smiled behind her fan. "I'm sure he is glad to have your approval."

"No disrespect, Lady." Densus swatted a swarm of shouting urchins away from the litter. "But Praetorians see everything. Yesterday it was Nero, today it's Galba, tomorrow it will be Senator Piso. I know emperors. He'll do us fine."

Better not to underestimate a common soldier's eyes, Cornelia decided. "I'm glad you think so, Densus."

He smiled up at her, chestnut eyes friendly under the helmet's crest of plumes, and Cornelia allowed him to take her arm when she alighted in the crowd before the shrine of Juno. A grand place in the Capitoline Temple, her statue as goddess of wives and mothers towering sternly beside the shrine of Jupiter. The steps thronged, as always, with women: young girls praying for luck in their forthcoming marriages, women far gone in pregnancy praying for an easy birth, matrons praying for grown sons and unruly daughters. Juno heard all.

Cornelia paid no attention to the murmurs this time, the ripple of speculation that greeted her emeralds and Praetorians. She just knelt, one among many, bowing her head.

Great Juno, an emperor must have a son and heir. Give me a son. Surely with Fortuna's wheel spinning herself and Piso so high, they would find good luck in this as well?

Eight years married, and never a sign of a child. Never a miscarriage. Never even one week's lateness with her monthly bleeding.

Cornelia stared up at the stern marble face. *Oh, Juno. Just hear me.*

The crush was thicker as the Praetorians beat a path back to the litter—curious women crowding close to see every detail of their future Empress: what she wore, how she carried myself, what she looked like. Cornelia did not find it quite so comforting as she had before. She sighed a little as Densus assisted her back into the litter.

He spoke unexpectedly. "Juno will answer your prayers, Lady."

"Prayers?" Cornelia blinked.

"For—whatever you pray for. She'll hear you." He fell back before Cornelia could wonder if he knew what it was she prayed for so hard.

"—so big and *golden*, Marcella, you can't imagine! And so strong—he can hump me while standing up and holding me in the air, it's absolutely divine. He was shy at first, but I just kept asking for massages until he got the idea—"

"—settled in well to the Reds stables, though there was a bout of bad grain. I'm not ruling out poison, those Blues will try anything—"

"Both of you hurry up," Marcella said, not troubling to hide her annoyance. Lollia on one arm droning about her pet stud, Diana on the other droning about her blasted Reds—between the two of them, it was a wonder she wasn't dead from boredom. Dear Fortuna, didn't her cousins have *any* unexpressed thoughts? "Hurry up! I want to get to the Domus Aurea."

"—don't know why you had to drag us away from the Campus Martius," Diana complained. "I was watching the tribunes race their teams. Not one of them fit to drive a real race, of course—"

"—to put it in words Diana can understand, Thrax is an absolute *stallion!*" Lollia was bubbling, oblivious. "I suppose I shouldn't be saying such things, Diana being unmarried and all, but surely you know the facts of life, my honey. Horses are always humping each other."

"Maybe so," Marcella snapped, "but at least they don't talk about it."

On this cold and breezy winter day, the sun lay hidden behind blustery gray clouds. Somewhere Marcella heard thunder. *Not a good omen.* But all the omens had been bad since the turn of the year this past week, starting with the day when Piso had been presented at the Praetorian barracks. The bull sacrificed by the priests had been diseased, the liver malformed, and the soldiers had muttered that it meant grave ill fortune. But Galba had shouted at them, and they'd quieted.

Or had they?

The anteroom of the Domus Aurea was filled, anxious, jammed: armored guards, courtiers in fine lawn and jewels, slaves looking edgy. Despite the uneasy quiver in her stomach, Marcella couldn't help looking around at Nero's famous golden house. A sumptuous palace with three hundred feasting rooms and a hundred sculpted acres of pleasure gardens; a place for intrigue, for beauty, for trysts and secrets while Emperor Nero had sat toying with his silver lute and watching over all: a genial and not entirely sane god.

"Is this the first time you've been here?" Lollia whispered as they were ushered into the triclinium. "Since . . . ?"

"Yes." Marcella looked up at the fanciful ceiling: carved ivory with hidden shutters, built to revolve slowly and send a mist of perfume and rose petals down over the guests. Now it was still and unlit. "At least I'm not the only guest this time." That night last spring she *had* been alone, and the slaves had gotten confused and loaded the ceiling with not one but three different kinds of perfume. Marcella left not only feeling like a whore, but smelling like one.

"Don't go," her sister had advised her, hearing of Nero's invitation. "You can't let him dishonor you, even if he is Emperor!"

"Just tell him you're sick," Lollia had said.

But what real options had those been? Marcella's father had been dead by then, and Lucius had been gone on one of his many journeys. Gaius had been oblivious to everything except his new duties as pater-familias. Tullia, for all her carping about womanly virtue, would have shoved any of her sisters-in-law into the Emperor's bed with her own hands to secure Imperial favor. Marcella had seen no option but to grit her teeth, dress in her finest, and go to the palace.

A very different palace now. Dusty and cold, the mosaics and frescoes unlit by lamps, half the furniture stripped away and sold for Galba's greedy economies, and the smell on the air was sweat rather than rose petals. *Nero's Golden House, golden no longer.*

Even Lollia's dreamy happiness evaporated as she looked at the forced smiles and tense eyes of the crowd around them. "What's wrong with everyone?" she whispered.

"I imagine they already know what I noticed at the Campus Martius just now," Marcella said. "That there are Praetorians massing." She hadn't liked the look of them: tight-bunched in their red-and-gold breastplates, gesturing fiercely at each other under the low gray sky.

"The Praetorians are always grumbling. What of it?"

"Perhaps they're grumbling a little worse than usual." Marcella thought of the latest rumor—that Piso had tried once again to get Galba to pay his soldiers their bounty, and been refused.

And then there were the slaves she'd seen at the Campus Martius. Wearing, Marcella was certain, Senator Otho's badge.

The air was stifled from so many bodies in one room. Marcella cleared a path back to a niche where a jade-and-silver lamp had somehow avoided Galba's auctioneers. The crowd swirled, and for a moment she saw Galba himself, wrinkled as a tortoise in his toga, Old Flaccid at one elbow and Piso at the other. Piso looked worried but stalwart; Cornelia clung to his arm with a crease showing between her dark brows—then the crowd swirled again and hid them.

Marcella felt a little tendril uncoil in her stomach—excitement this time, rather than unease. "Isn't it rather thrilling?" she couldn't help saying. "To be right in the thick of it all like this?" *Not just forever stuck in the background, waiting for news.*

"If I want thrills, I go to the races." Diana looked out over the nervous crowd. "I think it's Senator Otho."

"Otho isn't here, Diana."

"No, but he's somewhere else. Causing trouble."

Of course Marcella had long since arrived at *that* conclusion. *Diana never sees anything unless it's waved under her nose.* They found a slave to bring some wine—passed a few more idle speculations—waited an agonizing, finger-tapping hour before the hysterical messenger brought the news.

The Praetorian Guard had proclaimed Otho as Emperor and were carrying him shoulder-high through the streets.

It was all a great confusion after that. Marcella tried to see everything, take note of everything, but for once her mental pen was overwhelmed. Too much was happening for notes.

She heard Galba's voice snapping orders but couldn't make out what he was saying. She saw Piso's chalk-white face as he squared himself to go address the cohort of guards still here in the palace; he stumbled on the threshold, and his sturdy chestnut-haired centurion had to steady him. She saw a pair of young courtiers playing dice in the corner, calling for wine and laying loud wagers on how soon it would be before someone brought Otho's head in on a spear. Clearest of all, she saw an old slave woman unconcernedly refilling the wine cups. *And why not?* Marcella thought, bemused. *All this hysterical swapping of emperors has nothing to do with her, not when there are wine cups to be filled.* Marcella stared at the woman until she placidly took herself out.

Cornelia came then, pressing through the crowd. She looked calm as a pillar in her fluted *stola* of smoke blue, lapis lazuli banding her throat and wrists, but her hand was moist and cold when she blindly found Marcella's and grasped it tight. *When did she last do that?* Marcella thought. *When she was ten years old, maybe, and Father came back from Gaul after two years and didn't even bother trying to tell us apart.*

"You shouldn't be here," Cornelia was saying. "It could be dangerous—nothing to fear from Otho, of course, he'll be in chains as soon as the Praetorians come to their senses. But with so much confusion in the palace, it isn't proper for you to be here." She gave a disapproving glance—even now, Marcella thought, her sister cared about the proprieties. "Marcella, did you even bring a slave for a chaperone? Considering that people still whisper about you and Nero—"

"Never mind the chaperone," Marcella said impatiently. "You shouldn't be here either." The lamps were flickering now as purple twilight began to fall outside. She glanced through the window and saw lights at the gates of the Domus Aurea—torches, as the curious citizens of Rome came to watch. *Two emperors at once*, she thought. *Better than a play! Come one, come all, come early, and get your seats for the show!*

"They've sent emissaries to our other forces in the city." Cornelia spoke rapidly, twisting her wedding ring around and around her finger. "And Piso spoke to the guards—they received him well, Centurion Densus told me," she continued, pride in her voice. "He reminded them of the honor of the guards, how they have never betrayed their lawful Emperor for a usurper—"

"Well," Marcella murmured, "you could call Galba a usurper too, you know."

But Cornelia rushed on, unhearing. "—and he talked about shame, too, reminding them of their duty. I wish he hadn't done that, but Galba thought it best if he *shamed* the guards into doing the right thing—and it doesn't matter, Densus assured me the men received him well enough—"

"Cornelia—"

"And now some people are urging Galba to reinforce the palace and arm the slaves, in case there's a fight, and others are urging him to go out and meet Otho head-on—"

"Cornelia, come home." Lollia cut off her babbling. "Wait with us until it's all safely over."

"My place is with my husband." Cornelia's cold hand flinched in Marcella's, and then she drew herself visibly together. "But truly, you should all—"

"*Lollia!*" Old Flaccid caught sight of his wife for the first time and started flapping his hands. "Go home at once—the *idea* of coming here now—"

"Oh, don't hiss at me." Lollia rolled her eyes. "It's like being married to a gander—"

"I've just fetched a litter," Cornelia said soothingly. The slaves were starting to get excited now, whispering in corners behind their hands, and none of them wanted to listen to her. But she was the Empress of Rome, or something very near to it, and when she clapped her hands they scattered obediently. Marcella had never felt prouder of her sister.

A gap in the babble drew Marcella's eyes as Cornelia hastened them all out. Galba was tossing his toga aside, snarling at the hovering courtiers as his breastplate and greaves were brought forward.

"It looks like he'll go out to meet them," Marcella said.

"Yes." Cornelia was pale now, but her voice was still composed.

"Do I have to leave?" Marcella begged. "Just when all the excitement is beginning? I may have written about history, but I've never *seen* it happen—"

"*Out,*" Cornelia ordered in the big-sister voice she had not used since they were small, and bundled Marcella into the hired litter after her cousins.

The bearers jolted below as they swung away from the palace, but none of them called down for a smoother pace. Lollia nibbled her nails anxiously, but Marcella couldn't help peeking through the curtains and Diana peered over her shoulder. The light was purple with dusk, and after a while Marcella began seeing people—bakers, brewers, old soldiers, beggars and urchins, women with children clinging to their skirts—gathered along the street. Saying nothing, just watching silently. Though there was shouting in the distance.

"Turn ahead," Marcella called down to the litter-bearers as the surge of shouting grew louder. "Avoid the Forum."

But the crowds were pressing thicker, and they couldn't turn anywhere. The litter lurched, lurched again, and then one end fell and Marcella spilled out, hip smacking painfully against the stones. Lollia fell against her legs with a sharp little scream, Diana scrambled more nimbly to her feet, and Marcella looked up to see the litter-bearers dashing away into the night. Several street urchins let out a cheer and leaped into the litter for a game, but the rest of the crowd was silent.

Marcella saw eyes glittering like pieces of jet, assessing her, and fear leaped suddenly in her throat. She wore one of her plain pale gowns, and Diana had a dusty smock fit only for grubbing in a stable, but Lollia's silks and pearls . . .

"Forget about trying to reach the house." Diana hauled them both up with rough little hands. "We need shelter, and we need it now."

"Yes," Marcella agreed faintly. "Maybe this is enough excitement."

But there was more shouting ahead, and torches being waved in the air, and the crowd was murmuring now, not words so much as a low ominous rumble. Marcella felt herself pushed forward, Lollia's fingers latched to her elbow, and then Diana managed to yank them all up a rough step into a vestibule.

"Can you see?" Lollia craned her neck, eyes wide and white.

"Yes." Marcella, far taller than either of her cousins, could see everything—she had a clear line of sight down into the end of the Forum, where a bald head bobbed over a hired chair in the torchlight. Galba's wrinkled tortoise neck turned this way and that, and Marcella could even see his mouth opening as he shouted orders, but the crowd bore him along hysterically, hearing nothing. She saw Old Flaccid close at his side and looked for Piso, for Cornelia—but there was only Galba in his useless breastplate.

Hoofbeats. Marcella couldn't hear where they were coming from, but suddenly mounted Praetorians were spilling into the square and surrounding Galba in his chair, and short swords waved overhead and the red plumes of crested helmets looked like smears of blood in the twilight. Galba's arm thrashed as his chair overturned, and then the swords were rising and falling.

"Marcella!" Lollia was screaming, pulling at her arm. The crowd's silence shattered; half of them were screaming and buffeting to get away, and half were screaming and pushing forward to see an emperor get hacked to pieces. Marcella saw Lollia's husband dragged from behind Galba's fallen chair and stabbed through the gut as he shrieked for mercy.

Lollia gave a strangled whimper.

"*Run!*" Diana snarled, and gave such a yank to both their elbows that Lollia staggered halfway to her knees. Marcella steadied her, and suddenly they were all running. "The temple," Marcella gasped, and suddenly the crowds were behind them and the round curve of the Temple of Vesta loomed ahead, impossibly serene, as they lunged up the steps to the sanctuary.

Silence inside, incredible silence. The flame crackled quietly in its eternal hearth, and the marble coolness of the temple was empty. Marcella skidded to a halt, feeling the breath burn in her lungs, and Lollia collapsed at the base of the nearest pillar. "He's not dead," she kept saying blankly. "He's not dead." Marcella didn't bother answering her. The word kept throbbing in her own mind—*dead, dead, the Emperor dead.*

Oh, Fortuna, where was Cornelia?

Diana went to hammer on the inner sanctum and came back with a string of curses, flinging the hair out of her eyes with a savage hand. "We're locked out. It looks like the Vestal Virgins have fled."

"Wise," Lollia said with blank calm. "They won't stay virgins long if the Praetorians find their way in."

"Nor will we," Marcella said, looking around the temple. Just a few pillars to hide behind—no doors to bar and close.

"You can't be much of a virgin by this time, unless your husband doesn't know his job." Lollia managed to stand, her red curls sticking to her temples with sweat although she still shivered violently.

"Well, I still don't fancy being ravished by half a cohort of Praetorians," Marcella retorted. "Does any of us have a knife, in case it gets to that?"

"I have one," Diana volunteered, producing a neat little blade.

"You would," Marcella said, somehow feeling irritated.

More shouting, and they all froze. The street below was empty, the crowd long scattered into the side alleys or gorging itself on the Forum's hysteria, but there was shouting, and suddenly torches. A knot of Praetorians, and two figures before them, running and stumbling. It wasn't dark yet—plenty of light to see who they were.

Marcella lunged from behind the pillar, and Diana caught her just in time. "You can't!"

Cornelia was gasping and limping—she'd lost one of her sandals, and her dark hair unraveled down her back. Piso helped her along, wild-eyed, his toga in shreds around him. Behind them, whooping, grinning, fanning out in a leisurely pack, spread half a dozen Praetorian guards.

No, Marcella thought wildly, *only five.* The one in the lead wasn't with the rest. He pushed Piso ahead, up the steps of the Temple of Vesta, and he whirled around with his *gladius* drawn. Cornelia's centurion, Densus. He'd lost his plumed helmet, and a gash beside one eye masked his face in blood, but his teeth bared in a snarl as he flung himself on the guards.

One went down as Densus's short sword plunged through his neck and out again, but Cornelia went down too, tripping over the first of the temple steps. A guard lunged at her, and Piso gave a cry and flung himself at the man. Blood bloomed on his sleeve.

Densus booted the first man off his sword and turned on the second, slashing his knee out from behind. The man shouted, crumpling, and Piso staggered back, staring in disbelief at the blood on his arm. Cornelia seized his hand, screaming something, dragging him up the stairs. Densus half-turned, pushing at them both and shouting, and then they took him from behind.

A tall tribune with an ugly stub of a knife found the gap between Densus's breastplate and back plate and drove the blade in deep. Densus doubled over gasping, but he lunged at the tribune and they tangled drunkenly on the steps. Two more Praetorians lunged around them, grabbing for Piso. One missed, but the other caught the bloody trailing end of Piso's toga.

Whooping, they yanked him back, reeling him in like a fish, and his last motion was to shove Cornelia ahead of him up the steps. Marcella caught a glimpse of her brother-in-law's terrified white face, his mouth opening in a square hole to say something—to beg or plead, or maybe just scream. Because even though a patrician was supposed to die proudly, there wasn't much pride in being an emperor's heir for five days and then being butchered on a staircase like a stray dog.

The blades slid into his chest and out again. Unhurriedly, they hacked at him until he looked like a bundle of red cloth.

Cornelia shrieked on a rising note that cored Marcella's ears. She wrenched loose of Diana's grip, stumbling out from behind the pillars and running down the steps toward her sister. She hauled Cornelia back desperately and saw the two remaining Praetorians turning with grins. A strangled sob sounded behind, and suddenly Lollia was there, wide-eyed and terrified, lunging forward with a bronze bowl in her hands, a sacred vessel of some kind. She emptied it with a wild swing, and a cloud of burning ash gathered from Vesta's eternal hearth scattered down the temple steps toward the Praetorians. Glowing embers scattered everywhere; the two soldiers fell back a moment, shielding their eyes, and one collapsed with a gurgling shriek as Densus came lurching and bloody up the temple steps and buried a knife to the hilt in the nape of the Praetorian's neck.

Marcella felt rather than heard her sister screaming, fighting inside the band of her arms to get at the bundle of bloody rags that was Piso. Densus fell, dragged down with the Praetorian's body, and he tried to get to his feet again but couldn't. He gave a dogged shake of his head, his bloody hair dripping, and he tried to lever off his knees but he collapsed. He dragged himself in front of Cornelia and managed to raise his short sword halfway. He couldn't get it any higher than that, but he knelt shaking on the step, the blade half-raised and trembling in his hand, and Marcella saw the knife hilt still wedged in his side.

Diana slipped down from the pillars with her little knife in hand, lunging to stand beside him, teeth bared in a feral hiss. Marcella hoped she wasn't planning some desperate attack—the knife would be far better employed slitting Densus's throat before his fellow Praetorians took him down. The only loyal soldier in Rome didn't deserve to be torn slowly to pieces by his former friends.

Marcella, trying frantically to soothe her screaming sister, found herself making disjointed calculations. Lollia certainly couldn't be counted on to stab herself with any degree of competence, but perhaps Diana would take care of that before tending to herself? Just as Marcella would take care of her sister. *So I'm the last one who gets the knife; well, at least a blade through the heart tends to be quick.* The Cornelii women would die on their feet and by their own hands, not on their backs after being ravaged by a band of thugs. "Hush, Cornelia, hush—"

Dimly Marcella heard Densus's breath sawing in and out, heard her sister's screams, heard Lollia's low moans behind, and over that was the sound of shouting men and breaking glass coming from the Forum—but here before the Temple of Vesta, all was somehow muffled.

The Praetorian before them shrugged, and Marcella realized in a jolt of shock that he was the last one. Three bodies at the foot of the steps, another beside Piso—and the last one, grimy and chuckling as he lowered his *gladius*.

"You're lucky I've got better things to do," he said, and the sound of his voice cut Cornelia's screaming off like a knife blade. Marcella gazed at him as he turned to squat down by Piso's silent body. A few sawing strokes of the *gladius* and Piso's head rolled free, but Cornelia didn't make a sound.

"Reckon Emperor Otho will want to see this," the soldier said. "Might make my fortune for me."

The short hair was too slippery with blood to hold, so he hooked a thumb through Piso's gaping mouth and carried the head that way. Densus blinked, still struggling to hold his blade up halfway, and the Praetorian chuckled again as he sauntered past the still bodies at the foot of the stairs. "You're a tough bastard, Densus," he said over one shoulder. "But I knew five of us could do for you."

He jogged up the street, whistling.

Marcella felt air start to flow into her frozen lungs again. She became aware that she was still crooning to her sister, but the woman who had nearly become an empress just stood staring at her husband's truncated body, still as marble.

"Tell me this is a dream," Lollia said behind them. "Please tell me this is a dream." She turned and vomited over the stone steps. Diana put an arm around her, sheathing the little knife.

Densus gave a quiet cough. The *gladius* clattered unnoticed down the steps, and he reached around and tugged the knife from his own side. He looked at it a moment, gray-faced under all the gore, and he collapsed, breathing harshly up at the purple sky. One bloody hand found Cornelia's ankle, and he gripped it. "They turned on me," he muttered thickly. "They turned on me." He spat out a basinful of blood, but he never let go of Cornelia.

Marcella found herself staring back up at the Temple of Vesta. The roof no longer vented its usual plume of smoke—the eternal hearth must have died. She hoped the Vestals wouldn't be punished for letting the sacred flame die out.

Five

∽⚬∾

IF you've had four weddings by the age of nineteen, Lollia reflected, you have to do something to tell them apart.

Initially, of course, came the First Wedding, when the red veil and bridal wreath still seemed terribly fresh and exciting. *Little did I know.* Then there was the Drunk Wedding, when Lollia's second husband-to-be had swilled down so much wine at the feast that he had to be carried to their new house and laid out on the bridal couch like a corpse. *The longest wedding night on earth, getting waked every hour by snores.* Then there was the Ancient Wedding, just a few months back, with Flaccus Vinius and all his wrinkled, balding friends hissing disapproval at anybody younger, which was everybody. *Not that it stopped us having a good time.*

But this wedding, Lollia thought, looked like it was destined to be the Quiet Wedding.

"Scandalous," Tullia sniffed when she heard the news that Lollia was to marry again barely ten days after being widowed. "Before poor Senator Vinius's ashes are even cold!"

Scandalous. For once Lollia found herself agreeing with Tullia. It wasn't right, though she couldn't think what else she could possibly do.

"M'dear," her grandfather had said not four days after Otho had been made Emperor by the sword. "I wish I didn't have to rush you, but—well, that marriage to Vinius tied you strongly with the Galban faction. We must consider a new alliance."

"Yes." *But—*

"An heiress like you won't be allowed to remain single, after all. If I start casting my nets now, I can find you the best match possible, someone to protect you." He patted her hand. "I just want my jewel to be safe."

"Yes." *But—*

"And surely you aren't grieving too hard? I know you weren't terribly fond of poor Senator Vinius."

"No." *But . . .*

Lollia felt a queasy pang in her stomach every time she thought of Old Flaccid. He'd been an old stick and she'd hated him passionately . . . or at least found him very irritating . . . but he hadn't deserved to be torn to pieces by maddened guardsmen. *And it wasn't very kind of me, calling him Old Flaccid to everyone I knew. Even if it was perfectly true.*

The fact was, Lollia concluded, she might be used to getting divorced but she wasn't at all used to being widowed. It didn't feel the same at all. She felt *guilty*, of all things, and why was that? All Vinius wanted was her money, and he'd gotten that—no one could say she cheated him out of anything. Maybe it was the way she'd reacted when she finally went home and announced to a house full of pop-eyed slaves and hangers-on that their master was dead. No one had said a word.

"Don't just stand there like sheep," Lollia had snapped, still splashed in blood—Piso's blood, Centurion Densus's blood, who knew. But they still kept staring, just like a herd of stupid sheep, and suddenly that was funny, *sheep*, how hilarious. "Sheep," Lollia giggled, and couldn't stop giggling. They stared at her, horrified, and she'd been giggling too hard to explain that it was horror and not laughter.

I'm a widow. Was that why she felt so strange now, on the eve of another wedding? Cornelia was a widow too, but at least she looked the part—lying blank-eyed in her black-draped bed, devoured by grief. Lollia looked at herself in the mirror and just saw a bride in a red veil: trussed, varnished, painted, and perfect.

"You look lovely," Marcella said as the maid took the veil off for brushing, but her voice was halfhearted. She looked the same as ever in a pale-green *stola*, bare-armed, unjeweled, and calm in the wash of winter sunshine through the window of the bedchamber, but she'd been very quiet lately. Lollia didn't press her—with Marcella, it was better not to. She'd learned that the day she'd asked a few too many questions about the incident with Emperor Nero. Marcella could cut you up and down with that tongue of hers as good as any *gladius*, if she was in the mood.

"Which one?" Lollia said brightly, holding up two different eye pencils, but Marcella just shook an indifferent head. The cosmetician came forward, and Lollia closed her eyes for the application of kohl. It *was* nice being back in her grandfather's house again: the airy lofty spaces, the jewel-like rooms, the slaves who had known Lollia since childhood and now clucked over her like a baby. But something still felt different, like a shadow at the corner of her eye that faded away whenever she turned to look at it. Something felt *off*. Maybe it was just the feeling in the streets of Rome, as the plebs slunk through their days looking half excited at Otho's gleaming future and half ashamed of Galba's bloody past. Lollia had never seen anything like it.

"Uncle Paris promises you a bust of your new husband soon," Marcella said, fiddling with the beaded fringe on a cushion. "Salvius Titianus."

"Is that his name?" Lollia sighed. "I keep forgetting."

"What do you think of him?"

"He seems decent enough." She'd met him twice: a tall elegant man of forty, graying at the temples, with a lean handsome face very like his brother's. "He has this habit of cracking his knuckles, though . . ."

"An emperor's brother can have all the faults he wants," said Marcella. "Your grandfather certainly has friends in high places, if he can bag an Imperial husband for you."

Lollia's latest betrothed: one Lucius Salvius Otho Titianus, who had divorced his wife in record time when he learned that Lollia was available. *Along with my dowry*, Lollia thought. *The villa in Baiae and the villa in Capri and the villa in Brundisium, the two marble mines in Carrara, the blocks of tenement flats on the Aventine, the shares in the docks of Ostia, the six merchant ships, the estates in Apulia and Praeneste and Toscana and Tarracina and Misenum, the vineyards in Ravenna and Pompeii, the olive groves in Greece, the shares in the racing factions and the gladiator school on Mars Street, the percentage in the Egyptian grain fleets, the rents from the land in Gaul and Hispania and Germania and Syria . . .* Oh yes, the new Emperor's brother had been more than eager for a new wife. He hadn't looked at Lollia at all, but they rarely did. They just looked at the pile of gold shining invisibly around her.

"So you'll be first lady of Rome now, instead of Cornelia." Marcella sounded more animated at that.

"So?" Lollia shrugged.

"Haven't you even thought about what that means? It's power, Lollia. Prestige. Position."

"It means I have to host all those endless Imperial dinner parties now, instead of going as a guest. Much more work."

"And we all know you'd do anything to avoid that. You and your parties!"

I don't ever want to go to another party, Lollia thought. *Not even my own wedding party.* Not even *this* wedding party, which was bound to be even more spectacular than the last one since she was marrying into the Imperial family. *Why can't I seem to care?* Lollia wondered. It wasn't like she did anything *but* go to parties—why couldn't she enjoy it now? She was just longing for it all to be over, longing for wine, longing with all her heart that Cornelia would bustle in to give her trite little speech about the world looking different once the red veil came off. But she wouldn't.

"How is Cornelia?" Lollia asked as the maids began dressing her hair in the traditional six locks across her head. Soon there'd be a lock for every husband . . .

"She's moved in to live with Gaius and Tullia and me." Marcella wandered to the window. "Tullia said it wasn't fitting for a young widow to live alone."

"Who *cares* what Tullia thinks?"

"What she thinks, Gaius thinks, and he *can* make Cornelia come home. He has charge of her, now Piso's dead. And besides, Cornelia doesn't have anywhere else to go. Otho made sure to confiscate Piso's house and all his assets for the Imperium." A sigh. "At least she's at home with me now, and I can look after her."

Lollia wondered if Marcella was really the person to look after anybody. "Is she speaking again? Cornelia, I mean. I know it's too much to hope for that Tullia would ever shut up."

"Not much. She just sits in her room, staring at walls. We had to fight her to get Piso's body properly burned. Cornelia kept saying she wouldn't burn him without his head. But it's been more than a week and we haven't found any sign . . ." Marcella trailed off.

"I had my grandfather's slaves out looking for—" Lollia faltered. "For Piso's head. I told them to pay anything."

"So did I." Marcella shook her head a little. "How is that centurion? Whatever his name is."

"Drusus Sempronius Densus. The doctors are saying he may recover." Lollia had had the centurion brought to her grandfather's house, tended day and night by the best physicians in Rome. Surely it was the least they all owed him. *He couldn't save Piso, but he'd saved us four.* "What about Diana? She was already half mad before; I suppose now she's gone completely crazy—"

"Fortuna knows." Marcella traced her finger along a little ivory statue on an exquisite ebony table by the window. "She keeps disappearing these days."

"At least Otho will restore the races. That will make her happy." Lollia held her head steady as the maids draped her red bridal veil. Properly her hair should have been parted first with the spear of a dead gladiator, to ensure a happy marriage. Cornelia had always insisted on it. Lollia didn't think a spear or anything else could help *this* marriage.

A black shape moved in the mirror over Lollia's shoulder, and she twisted to see Cornelia in the door. She wore mourning black, her arms bare, her hair bound tight to her head. She'd look wonderful in black if her face didn't look like a frozen scream.

"Congratulations," she said. "Marrying the Emperor's brother, how grand. Did he give the order for my husband's death?"

Lollia opened her mouth, not knowing what to say, but Marcella moved swiftly to her sister, murmuring. The slaves looked worried, but the one bitter phrase seemed to have taken all the words out of Cornelia. She let Marcella lead her to a window seat and sat there, staring out into the atrium. Lollia thought of how they had all giggled at the end of her wedding to Vinius . . . she felt her eyes prick, but blinked hard and willed the tears away. Cornelia might weep and grieve, but someone else had to make an alliance that would keep the family safe. *I've got slave blood as well as patrician, and patricians may not bend but slaves endure.*

Her grandfather met them all at the bedchamber door, large and anxious, and Lollia rested a moment against his pillowy soft shoulder, loving him dearly enough to marry a hundred husbands. "My little jewel," he said, as he'd called her ever since she was small. Maybe her cousins didn't understand her unhesitating allegiance to her grandfather, why she never had even the slightest grumble when he chose a new husband for her. They didn't understand that it was an alliance, her grandfather and herself against the world, for all time. An ex-slave with such a fortune had enemies; his lands and monies could be confiscated at any time if he didn't have powerful connections. Marrying Otho's brother would shield her grandfather as well as little Flavia and herself. That was worth anything.

More guests pressed close, cooing congratulations, their faces all blurs. Lollia dropped her saffron bridal cloak and Thrax refastened it about her throat. She couldn't meet his eyes somehow. He'd been so sweet the day Vinius died—when she started giggling and couldn't stop he'd just picked her up and carried her to bed. But he didn't try to make love to her. He just held her close until the giggles turned into tears, and then he rocked and sang soft lullabies as if she'd been about as big as Flavia. "How do you know how to be so comforting, Thrax?" she asked.

"I sang to my sister," he'd replied unexpectedly. "When she was little. When she is four, she goes to the slave market—dry-eyed. Because I sing to her first."

Lollia wondered what had happened to his sister—what happened to the rest of his family. He shared her bed, and she knew so little about him . . . but he was a slave. Why *should* she know anything about him?

"I don't know how you can be so calm." Lollia had pulled away, scrubbing at her wet cheeks. "The world is ending."

"Maybe." He dried her eyes deftly. "Then I end with it."

"That doesn't trouble you?"

"My Lord died. That turned out all right." He smiled, touching the rough little wooden cross hanging about his neck. It was something to do with his god—a carpenter or maybe the god of carpenters; Lollia wasn't sure. "You turn out all right too, Domina."

How could he say that? How could he know that?

Ever since, Lollia found it hard to meet Thrax's eyes. Somehow, looking at him was just one more thing that made her feel uneasy.

Emperor Otho and his brother and their wedding party of guests were already waiting when Lollia stepped out into the gardens: grouped as artistically as statues, laughing among themselves and making graceful jokes. Beautiful as any Greek frieze, but her unease just increased. For the first time in Rome's history, an emperor had gained his throne by the sword. Could so many people really just laugh at a party afterward as if everything were exactly the same?

Perhaps it *was* the same. If they could laugh, then so could she: Lady Cornelia Tertia again, known as Lollia the scandalous, who did nothing but go to parties and *enjoyed* them too.

She gulped a goblet of strong wine under the red veil before proceeding out, and her fourth wedding went much the same as the others. The ritual cake, the words *"Quando tu Gaius, ego Gaia,"* the procession to the altar of Juno for the sacrifice. Emperor Otho was there only for a brief blessing at the temple before slipping off—of course he was far too busy establishing himself as Emperor with the Senate to waste much time on weddings. She swallowed another goblet of wine as she saw Cornelia's dry hating gaze follow him out.

Lollia took her bland and handsome new husband's hand, kneeling before Juno's statue. She tried to pray, but the prayer trailed off before it even began. Venus had always been her goddess, not Juno—beauty and love, rather than marriage and children. Besides, Lollia didn't know if she trusted Juno. *She certainly never answered any of Cornelia's prayers.*

The priest was just leading a white bull out for sacrifice when the guests stirred. Twisting, Lollia saw a slight figure winding through the crowd: Diana, her plain wool robe not at all suitable for a wedding. She had something in her hand, wrapped in a sack, and she went straight to Cornelia.

"I brought you something," she said. "I'm sorry it took me so long."

She held out the sack, and Lollia saw that it was bloodstained. It couldn't be heavy, but Cornelia staggered.

"I had to go all over the city," Diana said sturdily, sunlight slanting on her pale hair. "I must have visited every Praetorian in the barracks before I found the right one. But I got it for you."

"Oh, Fortuna," said Marcella, quicker on the uptake than the priest who started fussing, or Lollia's new husband who just looked bewildered. Lollia quieted them both as Cornelia looked into the sack.

She looked for a long moment.

She looked back up at Diana: so stalwart, so anxious to please.

Then Cornelia's face broke into pieces.

"No," Lollia whispered as ripples fluttered through the wedding guests. Horror stirred in their eyes, panic still close to the surface after last week's storm of murders. "No," Lollia said again, stupidly, as her new husband looked into the sack that fell from Cornelia's trembling hand. He leaped back swearing, as Cornelia sobbed into Diana's shoulder.

"No," Lollia whimpered, but it was too late. An emperor was murdered, and she'd never be able to laugh giddy and unaware at a party again.

Looking back, Lollia thought she was the first to see it—even before Marcella, who saw everything. The first to see that Rome had tilted on its axis, and that the coming year would bring nothing good. She clutched after herself—Cornelia Tertia, known as Lollia, who could have been a better mother, who could have been a kinder wife, who could have treated the slave in her bed like a man instead of a stud.

A strong hand covered hers. "Domina?" whispered Thrax.

She gave his hand a fierce squeeze. "Call me Lollia."

The wedding resumed, but everyone was stilted, awkward, cut short. Lollia sleepwalked through it all. So much for the Quiet Wedding. Thanks to her dear, darling, savage little cousin, this would forever be known as the Wedding with the Head.

Enough said.

PART TWO

OTHO

January A.D. 69–April A.D. 69

"By two actions, one utterly appalling, one heroic,
he earned just as much renown
as disgrace in the eyes of posterity."

—TACITUS

Six

～⌒～

"WHY am I doing this for you again?" Lollia whispered.

"Because Gaius wouldn't let me go alone," Marcella whispered back. "Which really means Tullia won't let me go alone, that curled cow."

At the front of the long room, a man in the stiff pleats of his best toga was declaiming in a nasal voice. He had a good turnout for his reading, Marcella thought—the long hall had been filled with rows of chairs, and every chair was occupied by an attentive listener. Or at least, they'd been attentive at the beginning. Now everyone was beginning to yawn and fidget.

"What's he going on about now?" Lollia whispered. "Whatever his name is."

"Quintus Numerius, and it's his latest work." Marcella made dutiful notes on her tablet. "'The Administrative Problem of Cisalpine Gaul during the Consulship of Cornelius Maluginensis.'"

"Fascinating," Lollia sighed.

"He was an ancestor of ours."

"He was a crashing bore, and so is Cisalpine Gaul."

"You owe me, Lollia! All the times I've listened to you rave on about your pet stud—"

Lollia's eyes flicked toward the big blond Gaul who stood beside her, gently waving a fan. "Don't call him that."

Quintus Numerius concluded the latest quotation and bowed. A bored ripple of applause crossed his audience. "A brief pause," he said, and everyone broke into a buzz of conversation.

"Thank the gods," Lollia groaned, and peered around the throng of guests: senators, scholars, and historians all. "There's not a one under sixty besides us!"

"Not your kind of party, perhaps," Marcella agreed. Certainly not like the glittering parties Emperor Otho threw every night now to light up the Domus Aurea. Here the room was undecorated, the buzz of conversation was sober and sprinkled with Greek quotations, and there were far more togas and bald heads than silk dresses and painted faces. "Don't yawn! At least not openly."

"You should have taken Cornelia. She never yawns in public."

"She's still in her bedroom, slinging vases at the door if anyone knocks." Marcella didn't know what to do about her sister, but there didn't seem to be anything she *could* do until Cornelia unlocked her door.

"I wish she'd let me visit," Lollia fretted.

"I'd leave it a while. She still won't speak your name, since you married Otho's brother."

"Oh, dear. I don't even like him all that much. He's handsome enough, but he cracks his knuckles all the time . . ."

"Well, it's not just him. You're first lady of Rome now, since Otho doesn't have any wife or sisters. You got Cornelia's place."

"Like I wanted it to begin with. It's not as grand as it sounds, you know—Otho doesn't need me to host his parties or manage his guests. He does that himself, and I just pay for everything. That's what being the first lady in Rome is." Lollia shook her head, half weary and half angry. "Even if it were different—Marcella, I'm not like you and Cornelia. I don't want to be important. I just want a few pretty dresses, and nice parties with people who tell good jokes, and a handsome man to come home to. Does an empress ever really get that?" Lollia shook her head again. "I don't think so."

Marcella eyed her cousin a moment—was everyone in the family turning moody now? *She's been quieter since her last wedding. Quieter for her, anyway.* "Lollia—"

"I thought you'd come," a voice interrupted them. Marcella looked up from her chair to see a stocky boy in a tunic, perhaps eighteen, staring down at her. He looked vaguely familiar. "I asked about you, and they said you liked histories and readings—this kind of thing. So I came to see you."

He was the younger son of the Governor of Judaea—Marcella vaguely remembered meeting him the night Piso had been acclaimed heir. Awkward, black-eyed, eighteen-year-old Titus Flavius Domitianus. "How nice of you."

"I like histories too," the boy continued abruptly. "I'll visit you, and we can talk about them." He continued to stare at her, hands clasped behind his back. *Like a child looking at a toy he wants to take home.*

"Yes, do visit someday," Marcella murmured. "If you will excuse me—Marcus Norbanus, I did hope I'd see you here." Rising, she skirted Domitian and cut swiftly across the room toward the first acquaintance who caught her eye.

"Lady Marcella." Senator Marcus Norbanus bowed his dark head in greeting. "Delighted to see you, of course."

"And you." Marcella smiled at him, giving her hand to be kissed. Domitian was staring after her blackly and Lollia was talking to her big Gaul, so Marcella took Marcus's arm and steered him in the other direction. "Though I'd rather hear a reading of *your* works, Marcus. I hear you've written a treatise on the reorganization of religion under Augustus?"

"Not finished yet, I'm afraid. I've had very little time to work on it, with the recent . . . unrest."

"Unrest?" Marcella laughed. "How tactful. Yes, watching a city stab its emperor to death in the middle of a mob can be quite unrestful."

"At least things are now quieter." Marcus gave one of his quiet, encompassing gestures back to the flock of white-robed men now flooding back toward their rows of chairs. "Any city where scholars can meet to debate the past in safety . . . a good sign, shall we say."

"Come sit by me for the second half," Marcella said impulsively.

"I'd like that."

Domitian scowled as Marcus's quiet authority displaced him to the second row. Their host rose again, and Lollia was already fidgeting as he launched again into the declamation with a quotation by Seneca.

Diagrams. Gestures. More quotes. "You could write better in your sleep," Marcella whispered to Marcus. He choked off a laugh but was silent. Marcella smiled too but felt irritation rising like a bubble. *I could write better than this in my sleep, too,* she thought resentfully as their host droned on—more Seneca! How original! *But Quintus Numerius is the one who gets an audience for his works, and a publisher too. Who would come to hear me read from my histories?*

Well, Marcus might. She had once showed him a passage from her study of Emperor Augustus, his Imperial grandfather, and he'd offered thoughtful praise. "Your style is a trifle florid," he'd said as judiciously as if talking to a colleague in the Senate, "but your research is sound." And she'd flushed pink at the praise.

She took a sidelong glance at Marcus, who appeared to be yawning with his mouth closed. An invaluable talent, he had once told her, for any senator. He wasn't precisely handsome, but he had a certain gray-edged distinction and a face as carved and noble as a statue . . . *I wonder if he admires me.* Surely he must, or young Domitian wouldn't be casting such dark looks from the chair behind them. Marcella felt sure she could manage a discreet affair without Gaius and Tullia being any the wiser—far stupider women than she managed every day. Look at Lollia, even now leaning her curled head and drooping lids toward her Gaul.

Still, Marcella had never been one for lovers. Oh, she'd had one or two back in the early days of her marriage—Lucius was gone most of the time, and even when he was home he never had much interest in her bed. But the best breasts in Rome had their share of other admirers, even if Marcella's husband wasn't among them—a tall broad-shouldered tribune, for one, and an aedile with a gift for epigrams. But the tribune hadn't had much to recommend him besides the shoulders, and it turned out the aedile paid a poet under the table to write his epigrams for him. And it had all felt so grubby somehow, sneaking out of the house to meet a man at some tawdry inn. Bored wives who dallied with lovers whenever their husbands left town—was there anything more commonplace? *Far better to dedicate yourself to books and writing*, Marcella had decided, *than to turn into a stale joke.*

Only now, books and writing were beginning to feel rather flat, too.

A sudden burst of chatter interrupted the latest quote, and Marcella twisted her head. A throng of latecomers had just fluttered into the study, and far more glamorous ones. Curled and painted women in bright silks, handsome men in embroidered tunics and gold chains, a languid actress from the Theatre of Marcellus, a few star charioteers—and one man who outshone them all.

"So sorry to be late," Emperor Otho said airily. "I couldn't bear to miss the presentation of such an interesting work. Cisalpine Gaul, so fascinating."

The audience murmured, and flustered slaves ran for more chairs. Marcella tilted her head, watching as Otho drifted expertly through the room—the first time she'd had to observe him up close since his ascension to the purple. Everything about him dazzled: his smile, his black curls, his gold-embroidered synthesis and gold bracelets. He trailed a wake of charm and chatter behind him in the staid crowd, perfectly calculated against the memory of sour old Galba. No wonder Otho was cheered wherever he went.

"Since when did he care a jot for scholarly readings?" she whispered to Marcus.

"What makes you think he cares a jot for them now?" Marcus whispered back.

"My dear new sister!" Otho raised Lollia from her curtsy and kissed

her on both cheeks. "I feel you've been part of the family forever. And
Senator Norbanus, yes—wasn't your father one of old Augustus's little indiscretions? We shall have to talk about that someday soon."
Another smile, just as dazzling, but somehow it held a cue for Marcus
to bow and take his leave. Young Domitian, Marcella noticed, gave
another black scowl as Otho turned and kissed her hand extravagantly.
"Delightful as ever, my dear."

"Caesar." Marcella curtsied but lost her grip on the writing tablet.

"Taking notes?" He retrieved it for her. "How studious."

"I have a love for histories, Caesar—I even write my own."

"Do you?" He looked faintly surprised.

"Contrary to popular belief," Marcella said tartly, "breasts do not
preclude a brain."

Otho burst out laughing. "You have a tongue on you," he said as
he slid into the seat at her side. "But I like it. Carry on," he called to
the flustered Quintus Numerius, still clutching his notes uncertainly
at the head of the room. "I've been fearfully rude, interrupting you this
way. Do carry on!"

Numerius cleared his throat, faltered over a few lines as the Emper-
or's glittering party flopped into chairs all around the study and called
for wine, and at last stuttered back into his presentation. The Emperor
listened a few moments, nodding at intervals. "Very interesting," he
said, and held his goblet to be refilled.

"Not really," Marcella replied. "I could do better."

"Could you, by Jove!" His smile encompassed her with warm inti-
macy, shutting out the rest of the room. "I'd like to see that."

He can look at anyone like that, Marcella thought, amused. *Like they're
the only person in a roomful of guests whom he really wants to see. I suppose
it's as useful for an emperor as yawning with a closed mouth is to a senator.*

"Though I am disconcerted to see you outside your customary band
of four," Otho continued. "I just left the little Diana at the races—she
won a bet for me this morning on those red stallions she loves so
much. A charming little thing, that one."

"She's a child," Marcella said. "No matter how many suitors pant
over her."

"Never fear," Otho laughed, and his entourage tittered with him, though they could not possibly have overheard the joke. "I don't fancy children, no matter how pretty."

"Nero would have wanted her."

"Indeed he would have. Fortunate I'm not Nero, isn't it?" Otho applauded the latest stammering quotation, and Numerius gave a timid smile. The reading had certainly livened up; the Emperor's entourage had brought their own wine, flowing freely between courtiers and scholars alike, and more than one solemn-faced historian was drinking appreciatively.

"And when am I to see the fourth of your quartet again?" Otho was saying. "Your poor sister, I would so like to offer my regrets for what befell her husband. You must know I never intended Piso Licinianus's death."

"Oh, come now," said Marcella. *We'll see if he really likes my tongue.* "You gave the order yourself."

The Emperor blinked at that, his expression neutralizing as if he were deciding whether to be angry or amused. But he settled on amused. "Perhaps I did, you clever girl. Though I am sorry for your sister. I intend to find her a noble husband, to replace the one I cost her."

Marcella wondered just how well Cornelia would take *that* idea. At least if she turned down some proposed suitor of Otho's, Tullia would die in a fit of rage . . .

"Something's made you smile," Otho exclaimed. "I do hope it was me. I'm a witty fellow, or so they keep telling me since I became Emperor. You know, I owe you my thanks."

"For what, Caesar?"

"For offering your sympathy when I lost the position of Imperial heir to your sister's husband." A gold bracelet glinted around Otho's lean brown wrist as he beckoned a slave for more wine. From the merry flush on the slave's face, some of the Emperor's wine was finding its way to the back quarters as well. "I've wondered how I could repay you, now that I'm in a position to do so."

Any number of quotes sprang to Marcella's mind about the two-edged gratitude of powerful men. "I need no repayment, Caesar."

"But I owe you for more than thanks for your sympathy, little Marcella. You made some joke about bribing a priest to say the omens were bad, so all those superstitious soldiers would intervene in my favor. Shall we say it gave me an idea?"

Marcella's thoughts froze entirely.

Otho grinned at her expression. "Don't feel too guilty," he said, as the room roared laughter at some timid joke from the reading that couldn't have been very funny. "I probably would have had the idea myself, anyway."

Marcella brought her wine cup to her lips again, more of a gulp this time than a sip.

"Is it entertaining, my dear, to know that you've meddled with the succession of emperors?"

"Yes." She managed to keep her voice light. "It is rather entertaining."

"I do like a woman who speaks her mind! And as you see, my dear lady, I *do* owe you. So what do you wish from me?"

"A post here in the city for my husband, Lucius Aelius Lamia," Marcella said at once, shaking off her momentary paralysis.

"Is that all?" Otho made a face. "I'd hoped you'd come up with something more interesting. What kind of post?"

"Anything. So long as he has to stay in Rome for a change."

"You're so fond of him?" The Emperor raised skeptical brows at Marcella. Meanwhile, the languid actress from the Theatre of Marcellus rose to tell the now-beaming Quintus Numerius that she would declaim the last portion of his marvelous treatise herself.

"I don't care for my husband in the slightest," Marcella said frankly. "But I care even less for living with my sister-in-law. Make Lucius the Imperial Manure-Shoveler in your stables if you like—just so long as he has a house of his own and can move me into it before I murder my brother's wife."

Otho burst out laughing again, drawing eager glances from his cronies, who were always on the lookout for the Emperor's new whim. "There are easier ways to escape a meddling sister-in-law. Not to mention a boring husband."

Marcella looked at him. He leaned negligently in his chair, black curls carelessly tousled, his arm just brushing hers. "Such as?"

"I could find you another husband easily enough."

"As long as he comes with a household of his own, the one I have suits me well enough." Lucius at least allowed her to lead her own life—better that than some new man who expected a domestic goddess or tireless hostess.

"Perhaps your husband might be persuaded to share?" Otho drew a finger down Marcella's cheek to the curve of her neck. "Nero spoke highly of you, and whatever you say of Nero, you can't say he didn't have exquisite taste. He fancied my own wife once, and all Rome knows *that* didn't end well, but I could hardly blame him for thinking her lovely. You are lovely too, my dear—and I must say, as much as I admire that clever brain, your breasts could bring whole legions to revolt."

Marcella smiled but moved back. "I've already been one emperor's whim, Caesar. It didn't suit me."

The reading was over now, their host standing smug and smiling amid a circle of well-wishers who had not listened to a word he said and were now mostly tipsy.

"Don't judge by the purple cloak, my dear." Otho trailed two fingers along her wrist—to the evident fury of Domitian in the seat behind, Marcella noticed. "Judge by the man inside it."

"One Emperor was enough for me."

"Perhaps I can change your mind someday." But the Emperor withdrew his hand from her wrist, rising with a good-natured nod. "Lovely to speak with you this afternoon, Lady Marcella."

"Is that why you came here, Caesar? I doubt it was the pleasure of the reading."

"I find my pleasure wherever I can."

"A pity you had to find it here." Marcella adopted his light tones. "Since you showed up to applaud this very dull treatise, it's sure to be a huge success. And Rome has quite enough bad literature already."

* * *

"CORNELIA, you must come to dinner." Tullia's aggrieved voice came clearly through the door.

"I'm not hungry." Cornelia huddled deeper into her shawls.

"But Lollia and her husband are coming to visit—"

"I will not speak to that man. And I will *never* speak to Lollia."

"Salvius Titianus is the Emperor's brother! It would be very unwise to keep shunning him now that he's family—"

Cornelia erupted out of her nest of shawls and cushions, seized a little copper bowl from the dressing table, and flung it across the room at the door. From the other side of the door she heard Tullia's huff of indignation.

"How is she?" Marcella's low voice, almost inaudible.

"Impossible, that's how she is!" Tullia shrilled. "Utterly impossible. She'd do better to let Emperor Otho give her another husband, one of his own supporters, for the family's sake—"

"I wouldn't tell her that if I were you."

"I have only our own best interests at heart."

"Since when are you one of *us*, Tullia? You might have run down my fool of a brother in one of his many weak moments, but that does not make you one of the Cornelii. Our family outlasted Nero, and we'll outlast you too. And given a choice between you and that despotic lunatic, I'm not sure we wouldn't choose—"

"*Gaius!*" Offended sandals clicked away.

Cornelia turned over, pulling her shawl close as the voices faded down the hall. She hadn't left her bed in days. Her own lilac-draped bed in the room she'd had when she was sixteen, before she married. Far too young for her now, with its little silver ornaments and white-on-mauve embroideries. *But Tullia still sent me back to it like a little girl, now that I no longer have a husband.*

Cornelia stretched out a hand, not opening her eyes, and trailed her fingers over the marble bust beside the bed. The bust of Piso that Uncle Paris had carved for her wedding; the one thing she'd been able to bring from home. Even without looking, her fingers knew the arch of his nose, the curve of his ear, his smiling lips.

She couldn't imagine her husband smiling now. All she could see was his dull glazed eyes above the hacked stump of his neck, the mouth distorted into a snarl where the Praetorian had hooked a thumb for easy carrying.

It wasn't him. Surely it wasn't him. That mouth had never laughed, had never kissed her, had never smiled at a crowd while his name was acclaimed as future Emperor. Impossible.

"I wish I could join you," she whispered to her husband. But he was cold marble now; he was white ash—and either way, he couldn't hear.

"At least it's all been properly taken care of now." Tullia had been vastly relieved once the funeral rites were over and Piso's dreadful staring head had been reduced along with the rest of his body to a tidy urn. "I suppose we should thank Diana for that, although I can't imagine what she was thinking, tramping through the Praetorian barracks! She couldn't have just sent a slave, like a normal person?"

"Terrible," Cornelia had managed to say, right before vomiting all over Tullia's mosaics. She'd thrown up over and over—into vases, into the *lavatorium*, into a basin by the bed. She'd felt so ill, she was sure . . . the charm she'd bought from the Temple of Isis was still firmly tied about her wrist, after all. Surely it had worked? *Surely if Fortuna took my husband away, she'll leave me with his child to raise.* She had been so certain, lying desperately still with her hands cupped about her belly, imagining a little boy with his father's name and his father's dark hair.

But her blood came a week later, not a day late, and Cornelia tore the Egyptian charm off and flung it out the window before crawling back into bed, wanting to die or at least to scream and scream and scream. But the women of the Cornelii did not scream. It was not fitting.

"Talk to me," Marcella had pleaded. "I'm your sister; let me help you." But Cornelia slammed the door in her face. What did Marcella know? *She* didn't want children; *she* used pastes and tinctures to keep herself from conceiving on the rare occasions she and Lucius shared a bed—and secretly that had always been a relief to Cornelia, because what would people have whispered if her sister had had a clutch of babies and she'd had none?

Shame on you, Cornelia Prima, she told herself. Marcella was only trying to be kind.

A bright chatter of voices outside. Cornelia heard Tullia's twittering and Gaius's rolling tones—he had been practicing his "important" voice in the bathhouse, where it echoed. Lollia's husky giggle sounded, and Cornelia felt a bright green spurt of hatred. Lollia had been widowed too, though no one would ever think it to look at her. But Lollia was a shallow, brainless little tart who never felt anything deeply in her life. Already remarried, and did she even seem to care?

Cornelia dragged herself off the bed and over to the window that overlooked the atrium. The evening still had a wintry chill, puckering the flesh on her arms, but the sun was radiant over the rooftop and the guests lingered in their *pallas* to exclaim over Tullia's delphiniums. Lollia was easy to pick out in her *stola* of bright-purple silk. *Imperial purple.* Her new husband stood beside her, tall and handsome, looking very much like his Imperial brother in onyx brooches and a saffron-colored synthesis hardly long enough for decency.

Cornelia's stomach twisted violently. She swallowed bile, trying not to vomit again, and when the sour taste lingered she knew she couldn't stay one *minute* under a roof where any Othonian was visiting.

She grabbed her *palla* and stumbled out of her bedroom, avoiding the bright laughter from the atrium and leaving through the slave gate. She reached the street corner, blind and stumbling, before she realized she hadn't even ordered the litter. *Does it matter? I have nowhere to go.* And besides, who would notice her if she walked? Three weeks ago she had been the future Empress, watched by all, parting crowds with her mere presence. Now she was nothing.

A party of legionaries marched past in smart step, intent on some errand for their centurion. A cluster of girls in ribbons and silk dresses giggled as they sashayed down the other side of the street. Children pounded past in some raucous game, shouting at each other, pursued by scolding nurses. *Whores*, Cornelia wanted to cry out to them, girls and soldiers and children alike. *You're all whores!* A few weeks ago they were Galba's subjects, Roman citizens. Now they were just Otho's whores. Otho, who had poured honeyed regrets but been quick to confiscate the house that had been Cornelia's and Piso's, so she had nowhere to go but the lilac bedroom of childhood.

One man hadn't turned traitor—he'd stayed loyal when everything else had crumbled. "Haven't you paid your thanks yet to Centurion Densus?" Marcella had asked a few days ago. "Diana and I did, and Lollia's putting him up at her grandfather's house with the best doctors in Rome. He did save all our lives, you know."

Yes. Cornelia pulled the *palla* up over her hair, realizing she'd been tramping through the streets with her head uncovered like a common woman. Yes, Marcella was right. Thanks must be paid to Centurion Drusus Sempronius Densus.

The vast marble mansion of Lollia's grandfather wasn't far—Cornelia saw the lights, brilliant against the dusk. No doubt entertaining a slew of Othonians himself. She felt another surge of hatred. After all his fervent support of Galba and Piso, Lollia's grandfather had certainly wasted no time arranging Lollia's marriage. Rumor had it too that he'd made himself another fortune selling off the houses emptied by Galba's auctioneers to Emperor Otho's newly rich friends. But he'd been born a slave—how could he possibly know anything about loyalty? *I should have known that Lollia with her slave blood would be no better.*

Still, Cornelia was glad they were playing host to her former bodyguard. She didn't have to toil up to the Praetorian barracks to pay her thanks—not that she could have set foot there anyway, remembering their betrayal.

"Shall I tell Dominus you're here, Lady Cornelia?" The steward bowed. "He has guests, but I know he would wish to see you—"

"No, don't trouble him." She slipped through the slave gate. "Just take me to the wounded centurion."

A lavish room, of course, like every room in the whole overdone house. Blue-marbled and sumptuously draped, with an arching western view of the Palatine Hill and the last dusky streaks of the sunset. Centurion Drusus Densus looked uncomfortable in it, and even more uncomfortable when Cornelia was ushered in.

"Lady—" He tried to rise, then looked down at his bare, bandaged chest and froze. The cut beside his eye had been sewn shut, the line of black stitches climbing his face like a millipede.

"Don't disturb yourself," Cornelia said as he looked around desperately for his tunic. "The slaves say you're still weak."

"I'm recovering, Lady." He sank back against the mounds of down-stuffed pillows, flushing red.

Cornelia averted her gaze, looking for a seat before deciding to remain standing. No need to stay longer than necessary, after all. She suddenly remembered that her hair was still a tangle down her back, and her old brown wool gown was crumpled from two nights' restless sleep. "I wish to thank you for your efforts on behalf of my husband's safety."

Densus looked down at the blue-embroidered coverlet, which he was slowly twisting between square hands. "I failed, Lady."

"You did your best." She meant to say the words brightly, but they came out flat. "You were loyal," she tried again. "No one else was that day."

Densus continued twisting the coverlet.

"And you saved my life." Where, oh where were the gracious words she used to be able to summon to any occasion? *Gone with my chance of being Empress, maybe.* "My husband would be grateful to you."

Densus looked through the window, avoiding her eyes.

"It wasn't your fault your men turned." Cornelia fiddled with a lock of loose hair, feeling a splinter of ice gouge her throat. "You didn't know . . ."

She and Piso had been riding in a litter close behind Galba, a little frightened at the crowds of citizens who surged alongside, but calm. Cornelia had been elevated high, looking over the heads of the crowd, but Densus had seen Galba's killers first. He'd jerked her from the litter so hard her arm bore the mark of his hand for a week, shouting for Piso to get down too. His men had snapped around them with a shouted word, moving out of the Forum before Galba had even been spilled from his chair. They would have gotten away clean if his own men hadn't lunged at Piso themselves, yelling that Otho would make them rich if they brought him the heir's head, and then the chase had begun that ended so bloodily on the steps before the Temple of Vesta.

But that part hadn't been Densus's fault. Of course not.

"You saved my sister and cousins." She looked past Densus's shoulder at the pillow. "My family will see you rewarded for it."

"I don't need a reward, Lady." Mumbling. "You don't become a Praetorian for riches."

"Most of your friends did," Cornelia snapped. Densus looked down at the bedclothes again, and she looked at the floor. "I'm sorry, Centurion." Flatly. "I should not have said that. I'll go now."

She turned toward the door, and he looked up at her for the first time. "Lady—"

"You swore they were loyal!" It burst out all on its own, and Cornelia swung around on him. "I knew them all by name, and my husband paid them from his own purse, and you *swore* to me they were good loyal men!"

"I thought they were—" He was very brown against the bulky white bandages that still swathed his chest, but his eyes were stricken holes looking up from a gray face. "Lady, they were my *friends*—"

"Then you're a poor judge of friends." Cornelia couldn't stop the words coming around the terrible splinter in her throat. "You told me you'd keep my husband safe—'My life for his,' you said—"

"I meant every word—"

"*Then why are you alive?*" she shrieked. "*Why?*"

She fell across the room, hammering at him. He caught her by the wrists.

"*Why am I alive?*" Struggling to hit him. "*Why didn't you let them have me?*"

"Lady—" His voice was hoarse, and he still held her fast by the arms. "I'm so sorry."

"I don't want your apologies, Centurion!" Cornelia screamed. *"I want my husband back!"*

She thought she heard him begin to weep as she tore herself out of his hands and rushed out of the room. Her own eyes burned dry as bone.

The time for crying was done.

Seven

〜◯〜

"A Roman matron should always do her own weaving," Marcella had often heard her sister say. "It's a sign of industry and virtue in women. Even the goddesses in the heavens sit at their looms."

"Even the goddesses of heaven need a way to look busy while they scheme," Marcella agreed.

"That wasn't what I meant!"

It wasn't what Marcella's suitor meant either, as he sat gazing at her with unabashed admiration. "You don't see many Roman matrons sitting at their looms anymore." Governor Vespasian's younger son, Domitian, fiddled with his wine cup, edging closer to her. "I approve."

"I live for your approval."

"Do you really?" he said hungrily.

Irony. So wasted on the young. Marcella felt very worldly under the burden of her twenty-one years, passing her shuttle back and forth. She didn't sit at her loom much, not unless she had some problem to untangle—a good stretch of weaving always seemed to get the knots in her head smoothed out. She had a great many knots to think about today.

Did Otho mean it—that I gave him the idea to . . .

"Are you listening to me?" Domitian's voice came insistently, and Marcella gave her shuttle a yank. Its use as a mental aid aside, weaving was usually a very good way to look busy and thus be shed of annoying visitors, but Domitian didn't seem to be taking the hint. He'd already stayed an hour that morning.

"You'll be happy to know I have a suitor," Marcella had told Lollia. "Your former brother-in-law. Ever since that dreadful reading, Titus Flavius Domitianus has decided he wants to carry me away from Lucius on a white horse and marry me."

"*Domitian?*" Lollia was startled out of her apathy. "I don't think I've seen him since Titus and I divorced. Beastly boy. Always lurking around corners like a spider, eavesdropping on people."

"Yes, well, now he's in love with me. We first met the night of Piso's short-lived accession to Imperial heir. Not a memorable meeting, but clearly Domitian thinks differently."

"Why did you talk to the Emperor so long at the reading?" Domitian was demanding now. "He's not so interesting—he writes down his jokes in advance, you know. And all that curly hair of his is a wig."

"He wanted to thank me."

"For what?" Domitian said suspiciously. "What did you do for him?"

Marcella smiled. "You're very young, aren't you?"

"Not so young," he bristled. "Just a year younger than you."

"Three years younger. And I really am very busy, so—"

"Good," said Domitian, not taking the hint. "A wife should be busy. Idle wives get up to mischief."

Marcella laughed. "According to your vast experience of wives?"

"*Give* me some experience," he shot back. "Marry me."

"My husband might object," Marcella said, amused, and got a scowl.

"He won't be your husband forever. I had Nessus read your stars—"

"Yes, yes, your pet astrologer. Forgive me if I doubt him." Marcella knew the names of a handful of famous astrologers, but none were named Nessus. *Some charlatan getting his money's worth out of a boy's dreams.*

"Nessus is never wrong!" Domitian launched into some speech about his plans to stand for election soon, and how Nessus had guaranteed he would be made praetor. Marcella worked her shuttle back and forth without listening. She was still trying to write an account of Galba's death to finish the scroll of his too-short reign, wondering if she would ever be able to describe the air of peculiar, lascivious hysteria that had overcome the crowd when Galba was killed before their eyes. A strange mood, difficult to convey on the page, and she was meditating on a choice of words while Domitian droned on in the background, when a familiar voice came from the archway.

"My dear, how industrious you look."

"Lucius." Marcella offered an unenthusiastic cheek for a kiss as her husband, Lucius Aelius Lamia, tossed his cloak at a slave and came across the chamber. "I had no idea you were returning from Judaea so soon."

"Neither did I. Governor Vespasian wanted a messenger—"

"How is my father?" Domitian interrupted, scowling.

"Very well," Lucius said. "Young Domitian, isn't it? Your father and brother sent letters for you. I'll call on you later to deliver them."

He waved a dismissive hand, and Domitian had no choice but to rise. "I'll see you again soon," he informed Marcella, ignoring her husband, and stalked out.

"I see you have an admirer," Lucius observed.

"He's a pest," Marcella shrugged. "How are you, Lucius?"

"Well enough." He settled himself in Domitian's chair, gesturing for wine and refreshments. Marcella picked up her shuttle again as he began complaining about the roads and the length of his journey. A tall man of thirty-four, a handsome face with a receding chin and dark hair thinning on top, which displeased him. Married four years, and Marcella doubted they'd spent more than four months at once under the same roof. "It would be shocking if you weren't so casual about it," Cornelia had always disapproved, though these days she was too sunk in grief to disapprove of anything much.

"So what brings you back to Rome so suddenly, Lucius?" Marcella paused to untangle a strand of knotted wool.

"Vespasian has decided to declare his support for Otho." Lucius reached for the dish of oysters in herbed sauce that a slave had just brought in. *Always eating heartily from other people's tables,* Marcella thought. "And I have been sent to convey Vespasian's oath of loyalty."

"Otho will be relieved. There's enough trouble from Germania without adding Judaea into the mix."

"More trouble than you know."

"Well? Tell me!"

Lucius paused, savoring the moment. He didn't normally waste dramatic news on Marcella, but apparently even a wife was better than no audience at all. "Governor Vitellius of Lower Germania was proclaimed Emperor by his legions—and now he's marching on Rome."

"No!" Marcella dropped her shuttle, turning with brows raised. Lucius so rarely managed to surprise her with anything. "Otho's only been Emperor a month—"

"Yes, Vespasian had quite a time deciding which claimant to support." Lucius popped an oyster into his mouth. "But on the whole, he thought he'd be better off with Otho. Otho's quite clever, after all. And Vitellius . . ."

"Is a drunk." Marcella conjured up the mental picture she'd drawn of fat Vitellius, the few times she'd ever seen him. Drunk, yes, that was fair. She'd seen him at a faction party where he'd roared out slogans for the Blues, whom he adored, and then passed out face first in a planter. Had he ever shown ambition for anything more than food, wine, and chariot racing? A detailed study of his previous appointments might reveal something . . . "He must have been *very* drunk when the legions proclaimed him Emperor, or he'd never have had the nerve to go through with it."

"And now he's being propped up by a pair of scoundrels." Lucius attacked the oysters again. "Tullia should use more spices on these. Pass me that dish, will you?"

"Scoundrels?" Marcella prompted impatiently.

"Yes, two of Vitellius's army commanders. Fabius Valens and Caecina Alienus. They're riding him along, stealing everything in sight and filling him with wine whenever he starts getting doubts."

"Fabius Valens and Caecina Alienus." Marcella stored the names away, refilling her husband's plate in the hopes he'd keep talking. "I'm surprised Vitellius is coming south with an army. If I planned on becoming an Emperor, I'd just pay someone here in Rome to put a knife in Otho's back. Much simpler."

"My dear, he hasn't a chance in the world of becoming emperor. He's just another usurper."

"One of those has already succeeded this year—I'm not surprised someone else decided to give it a try." Marcella picked up her shuttle again. "I'm sure Vitellius is being very official about it all, dating his reign from the day he first woke up with a laurel circlet on his head and a blistering hangover. And he does have a few legions backing him up . . . really, what's an emperor besides a man with a laurel circlet and a few legions?" She set the loom going again. "Perhaps I'll write an account of Vitellius too, as long as he lasts. It used to be so simple when there was only one at a time. But perhaps not as interesting . . ."

"Still scribbling, I see." Lucius looked amused.

"Why shouldn't I write?"

"My dear, you'll never publish."

"I could publish under a man's name."

"The idea!" Lucius guffawed. "Anyone would know a woman's point of view."

"I don't write silly tittle-tattle, and you know it," Marcella said coolly. "I give faithful, impartial accounting of Rome's rulers."

"Well, perhaps I'll read a bit someday." Tolerant.

"What a pity you didn't go into politics, Lucius. You have a great talent for making promises you have no intention of keeping."

"One needs supporters to enter the Senate, my dear." The amusement was starting to strip off his voice. "Clients . . . funds . . . a wife who advances her husband's career through *useful* means . . ."

"Perhaps you should start with funds," Marcella said sweetly. "I'm sure Lollia's grandfather could give you a loan. Or should I say *another* loan? Did you ever pay off the first one, Lucius?"

An irate glance. Perhaps this wasn't the best way to get what she wanted . . . One of Cornelia's little marital platitudes flashed through her head, something about honey being more effective on husbands than vinegar. "You'll have heard about my sister's bereavement, of course." Marcella leaned forward to refill her husband's goblet, now conciliatory. "I know she would appreciate your condolences."

"Of course, poor Piso. Such a bore. Your sister should marry again. Otho has plenty of followers who will be wanting a wife."

"Cornelia can't even hear Otho's name without spitting." Marcella put away the decanter. "She'd open her throat with her fingernails before she married any of his cronies."

"How dramatic." Lucius rotated his goblet between manicured fingertips—as much as he was on the road, he always managed to keep himself immaculate. He was forever tut-tutting Marcella for her ink spots.

"So you serve Vespasian now." Marcella called for the slaves to take away the empty dishes and bring fruit. "Is he anything like his tiresome son?"

"I don't know Domitian, but his father is *very* shrewd. The legions wanted to proclaim him Emperor too, you know."

"Fortuna's sake, not four," Marcella sighed. "There's trouble enough with three. Why did he refuse?"

"Better to be a live Governor of Judaea than a dead Emperor of Rome."

"He *is* shrewd. But he still has a tiresome son."

"I can hardly blame the boy for admiring you, my dear. He has excellent taste."

Marcella smiled rather thinly at the compliment. She knew perfectly well that her husband's tastes ran to boyish women, the younger and skinnier the better. *Most husbands would be glad to have access to breasts like these, but oh no, not Lucius.* Not that she really wanted him in her bed, but still . . .

"Gods, I'm tired." He yawned, stretching. "I've been hanging about Otho's halls waiting for an audience since dawn."

"Of course you'll stay here with us tonight." Marcella hitched a smile onto her face, abandoning her loom and its three-inch band of new cloth. "I'll have a bedchamber made up." She ushered him upstairs, disposed of his baggage, and had the slaves turn down the bedclothes.

"Thank you, my dear." He turned away, and Marcella put her hand on his arm.

"Is that all the greeting you have for me, Lucius?" She gave a little squeeze. "It's been a long time, after all. And I *have* missed you."

He turned back, brows raised. Marcella gestured for the slaves to shut the door. He smiled and shrugged, flicking the strap of her dress down her arm.

"By the way," Marcella murmured after a polite lovemaking during which she'd faked a little more enthusiasm than usual, "I spoke with Emperor Otho not long ago, and he said something about a post for you here in the city. Isn't that wonderful?"

"I don't imagine anything will come of it." Lucius tugged the sheets up. "Otho has plenty of his own favorites to reward first."

"*I'm* one of his favorites, Lucius. He mentioned it as a favor to me." Marcella leaned her head against her husband's bare shoulder—she'd seen Lollia use the exact same gesture whenever she was wheedling something out of a man. "You always said you wanted a post here in Rome someday. We can have our own household at last—I thought I'd look for a suitable house this month."

"I wouldn't bother," Lucius yawned. "Finances are tight."

"Lucius, we've been married four years." With an effort, Marcella kept her voice sweet. "Isn't it time we had a house of our own? I really can't impose on my family forever."

"I'm sure they'll put up with you a little longer." Lucius linked his arms behind his head, displacing Marcella from his shoulder. "Otho won't give me a post in the city till after this business with Vitellius plays out, so why bother with the expense of a house? I doubt I'll be here in Rome more than a few weeks."

"But if we could have a place to call our own, even just a modest apartment—"

"I said no, Marcella."

"Lucius, I can't keep living here!" Marcella sat up in bed,

abandoning tact. "Do you have any idea how loathsome my sister-in-law is? She snoops in my desk! She waters my wine! She plants flowers in primary colors!"

"Well, you'll have to make the best of it." He yawned again. "Wake me in time for dinner, will you?"

"You can wake up now, Lucius Aelius Lamia." Marcella shook his shoulder till his eyes opened. "Listen to me. I am trying to be a *wife* to you! You want someone to see that your togas are starched, to talk to your colleagues, to help advance your career? Give me a household of my own, and I can do all that. I'm a clever woman—I could be an asset to you, so why won't you make use of me?"

"Later." Lucius waved a hand vaguely. "When things are more settled."

"You've been saying that for four years." Disgusted. "You don't have any intention of giving me a home, do you? Are you that stingy, or is my company that unpleasant?"

"Sometimes it is," Lucius grumbled, turning over.

"You might find yourself in the minority with that opinion." Marcella addressed her husband's back, her fingers throbbing with the urge to sink themselves into the soft flesh of her husband's throat and just *squeeze*. "You may not have the sense to appreciate me, Lucius, but plenty of other men do. Including Emperor Otho."

"Is that how you got that promise out of him?" Lucius glanced back over his shoulder at her, amused. "I hope you got some decent jewelry out of it too. He's had everyone's wives, you know—more than he can remember. Don't think you're special."

"That's it," Marcella hissed, scrambling out of bed. Her naked skin was burning so fiercely it was a wonder the sheets didn't ignite. "I'd rather have a *snail* for a husband, Lucius. I'm divorcing you."

"Your brother won't allow it." Maddeningly, Lucius's eyes were still closed. "He finds me very useful—the contacts I've made in my Judaean travels this year are keeping him in support for the Senate."

"Then I'll go to the Emperor for permission!"

"Yes, and he'll marry you off right away to one of his own supporters. Who knows which?" Lucius yawned again. "Let me sleep, won't you?"

Marcella felt her hair lifting off her scalp like a handful of red-hot wires. Childishly, she yanked all the sheets off Lucius onto the floor, giving a wordless snarl at his yelp as she picked up her gown from the chair and stalked out of the bedroom.

"Marcella." Tullia accosted her as she stamped across the atrium. "The slaves tell me your husband is home? How nice to have him back in Rome after such a long journey. We'll have a dinner party in his honor—"

"Do that." Marcella yanked the sash of her dress tight with such a snap that she nearly cut herself in half at the waist. "I'll provide the hemlock."

Tullia didn't hear. "—and I'm sure he's a little threadbare after so much time on the road, so you should drop a word in Lollia's ear and arrange a loan from that appalling grandfather of hers—"

"Oh, should I? Lollia's grandfather usually likes a return on his investments. What has Lucius ever done for him?"

"Why, the honor of associating with such a distinguished—"

"Tullia"—Marcella bared all her teeth in a smile—"Lucius is a common mooch. He sticks his wife on her relatives, he sticks his debts on anyone who will take them—"

"I won't hear another word against a fine man—"

"Of course you and Lucius get along, one mooch to another. As far as I'm concerned you can both go jump in the Tiber—"

"—more than forbearing about your faults!" Tullia flared, her silk frills vibrating. "No reproaches from him about your stupid writings! Not one word about the fact that you were one of Nero's *whores*—"

"And what really bothers you about that, Tullia?" Marcella asked. Slaves were gathering round-eyed at the door of the atrium now, but she couldn't stop herself. "That I whored for Nero, or that I didn't get a province out of it for Gaius to govern?"

"You insolent slut, how dare you—"

"*She's* the slut?" Cornelia's screech cut them all off abruptly as she appeared at the doorway, a dark cormorant in her mourning black with her hair wild about her white face. "Marcella's the whore? You're all whores. Gaius hosted a party for Piso's accession as heir, Tullia was

happy to claim him as her brother-in-law, Marcella stood with me
on the steps of the Temple of Vesta when he died—and now you all
drink wine with his murderers. Whores!" Cornelia shrieked. "You're
all *whores*—"

"Now you're being repetitive." Marcella had hardly seen her sister
for weeks, she was always cooped up in her bedchamber weeping—
and now all she felt was irritation. "Fortuna's sake, Cornelia, at least
think of a new insult."

Tullia bristled. "I'll not be called a whore in my own house!"

"Would you rather be called a whore in someone else's house?"
Marcella snapped. "I'm sure it could be arranged—"

"—let her speak to me like this! *Gaius!*" Tullia shrieked, as Marcella's brother tiptoed into the atrium. "What are you going to say to
your sister?"

"Now, now," Gaius said nervously. "I'm sure she didn't mean—"

"*Gaius*, you never support me—"

"I hate you all!" Cornelia sobbed, slamming back out of the atrium.

"Can't we all just get along?" Gaius stood wringing his hands.

Marcella fled upstairs to her *tablinum*, taking the steps two at a
time, and tried to compose a good epigram on the absolute horror of
family life, but for once her pen failed her. She took out her unfin-
ished account of Galba's reign instead and penned his death in a few
vicious paragraphs. Rage made the words come easily: every drop of
blood that fell, every cry of terror and roar of the mob. *Purple prose.*
She mocked herself savagely. *Where's the impartiality you bragged about
to Lucius?* But Marcella wasn't in the mood for impartiality anymore.
Or for subtlety, or for decorum, or for good behavior. Where had it
gotten her?

Where had it gotten anyone this year?

IT was some days before her fury subsided enough to give cool consideration to the news Lucius had brought her: the news about Vitellius. The city had already seen two emperors within two months—and
now, these rumblings about a third.

No one, Marcella thought, knew exactly which way to turn. Galba had been sober, frugal, distinguished and suitable; Otho was madcap, extravagant, charming, and shrewd. *Women who walked the streets with their heads covered under Galba's eye bare their hair and their shoulders too under Otho's rules,* Marcella wrote on a new tablet, shoving the scroll on Galba aside. *Senators who struggled to look serious and well informed for Galba now hire poets to make up epigrams so Otho will think them witty and entertaining. Rome is . . .*

What? Dazed? Spinning? Staggering?

Whatever it was, Marcella didn't know if her pen could ever capture the strange febrile excitement that now gripped the streets. The fever that gripped them all—Cornelia, who kept hurling vases at her bedroom door if anyone dared knock on it; Diana, who ranted on about her damned Reds until they all wanted to throttle her; Lollia, whose laughter at every party got shriller and whose eyes behind the painted lines of kohl got sadder. The tide was rising, catching them all in its restless grip.

Even me, Marcella thought.

"Don't you feel it?" she asked Lollia the next day as they were being fitted for new gowns. "Like the whole city is on edge, and everyone in it?"

"Oh, I've felt it." Lollia stirred restlessly. "Don't we all? Except Cornelia, maybe. She's the lucky one."

"I'd hardly call her lucky." The bedchamber was a riot of color: bolts of silk unrolled everywhere, maids dashing here and there with pins and needles and reels of thread. Marcella brushed away the coral silk the maid held up for her approval. "No, too bright. Let me see the pale yellow—"

"Well, I'd call Cornelia lucky. She didn't get to be Empress, but at least she has a tragic love." Lollia twisted before the glass, surveying a new *stola* in oyster silk hemmed with pearls. "Too plain . . ."

"What do you mean, a tragic love?" Marcella held out her arms so the maids could drape the pale yellow silk about her. "Nothing tragic about it, except the ending. She and Piso were very happy."

"I'm sure they were. But an emperor needs heirs." Lollia stepped out of the oyster silk, strolling naked over to her dressing table. "Mark my words, a year or two after taking the purple, Piso would have divorced Cornelia and married some fresh-faced little thing who could push out plenty of sons."

"No, he wouldn't. He could have adopted an heir, like Galba. None of our Emperors have passed their throne to their sons."

"Yes, and look where that's getting us. Murders and coups everywhere." Lollia frowned in the mirror at her naked self: pink and smooth-skinned as ever, her riotous red curls standing out in wiry disarray. Marcella saw her own reflection in the glass over Lollia's shoulder, a tall column in yellow silk, a line showing between her brows. *A line placed there by Lucius and Tullia,* she thought resentfully.

"I tell you," Lollia was saying, oblivious, "Cornelia might have been a perfect empress, but she wouldn't have kept the position for long. A year or two of senators whispering how an emperor with sons brings stability to the Empire, droning about all the jostling that goes on when an emperor adopts an heir, intoning platitudes about the sacrifices an emperor must make for the good of Rome—do you think Piso would have refused?"

"Well, we'll never know." Marcella looked down at the seamstress tacking up her pale-yellow hem. "A little white embroidery around the bottom, I think—"

"Oh, Cornelia knows," said Lollia. "But now Piso's dead, so she can pretend it never would have happened; that Piso would have been an emperor to rival Augustus and she would have been his Augusta for all time. When really he was just a bland bore, and she had all the ambition for both of them." Lollia gave a hard shrug as the maids came forward and began draping her in bright-green silk embroidered in tiny golden flowers and vines. "What she needs is a good hump."

Marcella looked at her cousin as another maid pinched the yellow silk folds into place at the shoulders. "You're very hard on Cornelia."

"Well, I don't like being called a whore just because I married Otho's brother," Lollia said shortly. "We lost your father to Nero's whims. You know how easy it would be to lose the rest? For Otho to confiscate the family estates and exile the lot of us? He's a charmer, but don't think he wouldn't do it if the mood took him. I'm on my knees to his brother every other night, asserting the family loyalty, but that doesn't make me a whore. I keep all of us in food and roofs and silk dresses." Lollia plucked at her airy green draperies. "I keep my grandfather alive and making money that the rest of you are only too happy to borrow, as long as you don't have to acknowledge where I came from. I keep my *daughter* safe."

"Lollia, I'm sure Cornelia doesn't think you're a whore—"

"Oh, she does. But I don't mind. Someone has to do it, after all. It's what women are for: whoring themselves out to useful men. And who will do it in this family, if not me?" Lollia's lush curving mouth was set in a straight line. "Cornelia isn't much use, carrying on like a pleb who lost her man in a tavern fight. Diana could have her pick of important suitors, but she'd rather run around with her horses all day. And frankly, Marcella, you aren't much use either. Keeping to your loom and your scrolls, watching us all, keeping above everything. I don't know what Nero did to you, because you won't tell anyone, but you've certainly milked it for all it's worth. Any excuse to stay locked in your *tablinum*."

"*Lollia*—"

Little Flavia ran in at that moment, dripping wet, a scolding nurse behind her as she dumped a soggy handful of water lilies into her mother's hands. Lollia bent and exclaimed over them, her voice brittle, and Marcella looked away, clamping down hot words as the maids busied themselves with the yellow silk *stola*. "Lollia," she said finally. "I wish you hadn't said those things."

"I wish I hadn't either." The words were muffled in Flavia's curls. "I think I'm done fitting dresses today." Lollia picked up her daughter and held her tight, moving off in a flutter of half-pinned silk with maids fluttering behind.

"I think I'm done too." Marcella unpicked the yellow silk, slipped into her own *stola* again, and climbed slowly into her litter. She didn't go home, though. She ordered the bearers to the Gardens of Asiaticus. "Leave me," she snapped as the litter came down, and set off alone down one of the wide curving paths.

A beautiful place, the Gardens of Asiaticus. A vast spread of sculptured green acres along the southern flank of the Pincian Hill, in summertime all soft mounds of roses and silky grass and mossed statues. Cold in February but still beautiful, the groves of poplar trees spiking a violet twilight sky, the fountains murmuring, the chain of pleasure lakes like mirrors reflecting the ornamental bridges. Marcella saw lamps flickering ahead on the paths and among the trees too—no better place in Rome to meet a lover than the Gardens of Asiaticus. Lollia had met her share in the laurel groves and behind the banks of violets. *Though she looks too tense and snappish nowadays for trysting.* Marcella had never seen Lollia lose her temper at anyone, not even at the slave who stole her favorite pearls or the tribune who deserted her for an Egyptian dancer. Just a few weeks ago at the reading she had been melancholy, and now she was losing her temper—the city's strange hysteria had even infected Lollia.

"*I don't know what Nero did to you, because you won't tell anyone . . .*"

Marcella shivered, wrapping her *palla* tighter. She left the path, brushing through the winter-dry grass to a sculpted grove of poplars. They waved black branches gently overhead. An empress had died under these poplars, fleeing in terror from the Praetorian guards. Emperor Claudius's third wife. But they'd caught up to her in the end and chopped her pretty, adulterous little head right off.

Would Lollia laugh, if she knew the truth? Marcella thought. Would Cornelia and Diana, Gaius and Tullia? Would Lucius?

Nero never laid a finger on me.

M Y dear." He had looked up at Marcella as the steward ushered her in, and even though she felt frozen with dread, her inner historian scratched away, taking notes on her surroundings. The ceiling revolving overhead, showering rose petals down on the Emperor of Rome, who sat posed like a musician in Greek tunic and sandals with a golden lyre on his lap.

"Caesar." She knelt before him, already feeling sticky in a *stola* of lilac silk draped to show as little of her breasts as possible. Nero waved her up with a beautifully manicured hand.

"No, my dear, I am no Caesar tonight. We eat alone, like any common fellow and his beloved. I have often wished I could be a common musician, playing for my supper. Or perhaps an actor; you've heard me recite, of course—"

A hot night, spring fading into summer. The slaves, all matched blue-eyed blondes chosen for beauty, brought one meal after another in a graceful ballet. Every dish an aphrodisiac selected to enhance a night of love: sea urchins in almond milk, blue-black oysters from Britannia, cakes sheeted with a haze of edible flowers. Marcella stuffed herself. *I'll need all the aphrodisiacs I can get to keep from being queasy when he finally stops babbling and gets on with it.* Nero was tall but pot-bellied, his legs spindly, his chin spotted; he wore a wig of auburn curls over a flaking scalp. And his eyes burned too bright, as if he had a fever. *Or the pox.*

"Or perhaps I should have been a poet—you've heard my poetry, of course? My verse on the love of Adonis and Aphrodite was so much admired in Athens—"

She wished he'd hurry up. He'd set her aside with a casual invitation at the end of a party the night before, hardly bothering to talk to her. Why should he? She was just a passing fancy, hardly likely to last a night. *The sooner he climbs on top of me, the sooner it will all be over and the sooner I can go home.*

He pushed his golden plate aside, stroking her arm with damp fingers. Marcella tensed despite herself, but he wasn't looking at her. Those bright eyes were fixed somewhere between a tall vase of lilies and a reclining marble Leda with her amorous swan. "I'll play for you," he said, calling for his lute. "A private performance from your Emperor, eh?"

"I would be honored, Caesar."

He struck a pose with his lyre, false auburn curls gleaming in the lamplight. A little ditty about spring—"my own work! Do tell me what you think?"

"Brilliant, Caesar."

A long heroic epic about the deeds of Hercules. His voice was shrill and tuneless.

"Incomparable, Caesar."

He called for wine in between songs, but Marcella pushed her cup away. She didn't dare get sleepy—Nero had executed senators before for dozing during his recitals. But he drank cup after cup, in frantic haste. "And this one—a little ditty about spring. My own work, of course. Do tell me what you think?"

The same song he'd begun with. "Brilliant, Caesar."

More songs. His voice grew shriller, his words slurred. The feverish eyes darted everywhere. He sang the epic of Hercules twice more, rapidly. "I do like to write little verses about heroic deeds now and then, as much as I prefer the deeds of love. You know the Senate's plotting against me?"

Marcella started to say, "Incomparable, Caesar," before she realized what he'd said. "Um. Caesar?"

"They think I don't know. But I hear everything." He cast his lyre aside abruptly. "They'll vote me a public enemy. They'll even vote a new emperor."

". . . Surely not, Caesar."

"They'll try. I'll fool them. I have spies." Jerkily. "They'll be sorry. I'll make the Senate steps run with blood—"

He paced to the end of the couch and back again, running his fingers along the chased edge. His nails were varnished pink. "They think you can vote on an emperor," he said to the tiles. "I am a god. You think I attained divinity by *vote*?"

"Of course not, Caesar," she said cautiously.

"They'll look to name some tight-fisted prune like Galba or Sabinus. Break my statues—I have so many statues—my mother always said I had the prettiest profile in marble . . ." He blinked. "I killed my mother. Did you know that? I don't remember why."

Sweet Fortuna, just get me out of here alive. Marcella stayed frozen on her couch, skin crawling. Nero drank another cup of wine, held the goblet out blindly, drank another.

"They'll strip my pretty palace." He looked around his beautiful, sumptuous triclinium. "My golden house. I never really lived until I built this palace. They'll strip it bare, all those stingy old senators— sell off my pretty slaves, and my chorus boys, and the gold plate I ordered in Corinth . . . but I won't live to see that. They'll kill me first. Hack me to death with spears in my own bathhouse, or on the privy—it's no way for a god to die—"

Marcella groped for words, any words. Her ready mental pen had fallen silent. "The world would lose a great artist in you, Caesar."

His fever-bright eyes wandered back to her, surprised. *Does he even remember why I'm here?* Or had he even wanted her at all? Perhaps he'd just set her aside to show his cronies that the Senate's grumbling hadn't made him afraid. "Yes, a great artist." He nodded vigorously. "I must remember that. There was never another artist like me, was there?"

"No," Marcella agreed.

"No," he echoed, and suddenly he stumbled across the room, crawling onto the dining couch and laying his head in her lap. "No," he said again, shivering, and under the perfumes of amber and myrrh and lilies there was the sharp, malodorous stink of terror.

They said he'd laid his head in his mother's lap and cried, after her murdered body was brought back for his inspection.

"No one will hack you to death with spears, Caesar. You'll defeat them." Marcella felt herself sweating. He could still have her strangled and thrown down the Gemonian Stairs if she displeased him—this was a man who had kicked his pregnant wife to death when he was in a bad mood. Marcella forced herself to stroke his hair, though her fingertips itched as if fire ants were devouring them. "You'll defeat them."

"If I don't?" His voice rose, a thin edge higher and higher. His bright eyes snapped open and held hers. "If I *don't?*"

"You will fall on your own sword," she found herself saying. "Like the kings of old. You'll never see them strip your palace or deface your statues. You'll stab yourself and then you'll sit at Jove's right hand. You'll escape it all."

"Yes," he said, voice spiraling down again. "I'll escape it all. I'll escape it all."

He fell asleep, still muttering. Marcella would have sat all night with the Emperor's head on her lap, too frozen to move, but the slaves descended and bore him skillfully off without waking him, more used to this than she was. She'd staggered home, reeking of scent from that horrible revolving ceiling, to a family that wouldn't quite look her in the eye. In two days' time Nero was pronounced a public enemy of Rome by the Senate. Galba was proclaimed Emperor and Nero fled, committing suicide long before the Praetorians could imprison him— escaping it all. His last words, so they said, were "What an artist dies in me!"

I think I did it, you see, Marcella thought. The one thing she had not put in her history of Nero. *I think that in my way, I killed an emperor.*

Eight

～◡～

A slave dropped a dish outside the bedroom door with a crash and burst into tears. "Stow that," Cornelia heard another slave hiss. "Or Domina will have the skin off your back!"

Feet pattered. She listened at the door, alert for every sound.

Sandals clicked sharply. "Oh, this rain," Tullia moaned somewhere down the hall, rapidly coming closer. "Such bad timing; our guests will have to swim to get to the front door." She and Gaius were hosting a dinner party and the whole house was in an uproar, but that hardly concerned Cornelia. She wasn't going.

That is, she was going somewhere, but not their wretched dinner party.

"Sea urchins and turbot, is it ostentatious?" Tullia's voice again, hectoring the steward. "Perhaps turtle doves boiled in their plumage instead. Perhaps both. Yes, both. *Gaius*—"

Cornelia left the door and went to her window, pushing the shutter aside and looking down at the street outside. Gray waves of rain beat down in gusts, and passersby scurried like mice wrapped in wet wool, wading ankle deep in the gutters. The winter rains had finally arrived last week, and arrived with a vengeance. The Pons Silica had come crashing down just yesterday when the Tiber overflowed. The oldest bridge in the city—Cornelia had heard the slaves whispering about it, saying it was a bad omen for Otho's reign. Surely Tullia would cancel the party? That would have ruined everything, but no, Tullia hadn't canceled her party. "Why should we? Nobody we know lives on the other side of the Pons Silica!"

Just half an hour ago Cornelia had watched her sister dashing into the wetness, chivvied off on some errand of Tullia's. She'd been gone in an instant behind shifting curtains of rain, and Cornelia's heart squeezed. *The last time I'll ever see my sister.* If she could have just said good-bye . . . but no. Marcella would ruin everything if she knew. Better to get it all finished and done with while she and her sharp all-seeing eyes were safely out of the house. The rest of the household was busy, after all, running itself ragged for the upcoming party. Tullia wouldn't come looking for hours, or Gaius, or the harried slaves.

It was time.

"Zoe." Cornelia turned to her maid. "Get out my black *stola*, please. And make up the bed." Perhaps a little dusting too . . . Cornelia ran a finger through the dust on the bedside table, frowning. She was certainly not going to commit suicide in an untidy room.

"Gaius, did you confirm Otho's chamberlain for this evening?" Tullia's hectoring voice, floating up the stairs. "*Gaius*, I asked you to invite him a week ago!"

Cornelia reached under the bed for the black basalt urn she'd stored so carefully. Piso's ashes, which she'd had brought up from the mausoleum yesterday. He'd be with her at the end. Perhaps his shade was waiting even now, smiling. *Not much longer, my love*, Cornelia thought as her maid tidied the bed. *Not much longer.* What else was there for her? A near-empress, a beloved wife, turned into an obscure unwanted widow. She might as well put a knife in this endless pain in her chest, and have done.

"Tullia, can you squeeze one more guest in tonight?" Marcella's husband Lucius's voice came from the other end of the hall. "Pomponius Ollius, he's very useful to me—"

"Another guest? Another guest at this late notice? *Lucius*—"

Why couldn't Marcella have been the one to be widowed? Cornelia didn't think her sister would have cared at all—Lucius was such a bombastic drone, he hadn't even troubled to present his sympathies on Piso's death now that Cornelia was no longer important. *Why not Lucius instead of Piso? Why not Marcella instead of me?* Cornelia scrubbed at her eyes a moment and then made an effort to smile at her maid. "A goblet of wine, please, Zoe. And then you're free to go."

She waited until Zoe slipped out, then drew out the dagger she'd hidden beneath her cushions. No use involving the slaves, after all. Either they'd run tattling to Tullia, or they wouldn't and would then get a beating for it once Cornelia was dead.

She drew a finger down the dagger's edge, sharpened to a whisper, and laid it on the table beside the black basalt urn. No emotional haste here; nothing messy, nothing squalid; all done properly. There were forms to be observed for suicide, after all.

Cornelia slipped into her black *stola*, binding her hair tight and glossy about her head. No jewelry; that would be ostentatious. Another Cornelia had become famous long ago for saying that her sons were her jewels—well, *this* Cornelia might have no sons, but her name would be known too, as a good and loyal wife who had followed her husband into death once honor became impossible. She'd already written out a scroll with instructions for her funeral, as well as good-byes for each of the family. Quite beautiful, really. She'd spent hours on them.

She went to close the shutter and saw Diana splashing through the mud toward the door, her pale head sleek as a seal's in the rain. Not even taking a litter in this storm, never mind a chaperone. *Perhaps my example of wifely duty will inspire her to better behavior in future.*

Cornelia poured herself a cup of wine and sat on the edge of the bed, arranging the dagger across her knees. Properly there should be music playing, preferably a harp—she'd always liked the sound of a harp. Surely drifting away into death would be much easier to the sound of good music. But for a harp you had to have a harpist—and Juno's mercy, what was that racket coming from downstairs? *Can't I get any peace to commit suicide in?*

"—holding you personally responsible if they drown, Gaius!" Diana was yelling downstairs.

"Diana, my dear, be reasonable—I'm sure the Reds faction director has any number of places he can send his horses if the stables flood—"

"Yes, on the other side of the city, and hours away now that the Pons Silica is down! I'm just asking if I could put up my Anemoi here a few days if the rains get harder; Father doesn't have the room—"

Cornelia closed her eyes, draining the wine, but all her peace was shattered. A whole roomful of harpists couldn't have drowned out Diana's voice.

More flapping of wet cloaks outside, and feet tramping up the stairs. "By Jove"—Cornelia heard Lucius's voice outside her door, admiringly—"Is that little Diana down there? I haven't seen her since she was fourteen. She's certainly grown up . . ."

"If you're not four-legged, Lucius," Marcella's voice sounded crisply, coming up the stairs, "then Diana isn't interested."

Cornelia's heart knocked. Marcella was supposed to be gone at least another hour. *Juno's mercy, did I take too long?*

"—family lackey, that's what I am." Cornelia could hear her sister muttering to herself as she thumped upstairs. "Don't send a slave out in this weather, oh no, they might get sick and die and there goes fifteen thousand denarii. Send Marcella, she's expendable—"

Oh, why didn't I just stab myself without all the trimmings? Cornelia wailed inside. *Dead is dead!*

A knock came at the door, and Marcella's voice sounded. "Cornelia?" She dived across the room to hide the urn.

"Cornelia, you can't be sleeping. Nobody could sleep through that racket downstairs." Marcella struck open the door. "One Emperor murdered this year and another one crowned, but none of it with a quarter of the hysteria that descends on this house every time Tullia hosts—" Marcella stopped. Too late, Cornelia remembered to hold the dagger behind her back.

Marcella's eyebrows rose, gaze traveling around the room from her sister's black dress to the cup of wine to the basalt urn Cornelia hadn't quite managed to hide. "Goodness," Marcella said at last. "I know you'd do anything to avoid Tullia's dinner party, but suicide seems a little extreme."

Outside in the hall came the sound of a slap, a slave bursting into tears, the steward scolding. Below, Diana was still roaring at Gaius. Suddenly Cornelia couldn't help a smile, as she brought the dagger out from behind her back and turned it over in her hands. "All houses sound alike when they're preparing for a dinner party, don't they?"

"Not as much shrieking as ours," Marcella said.

"Piso and I gave so many parties." The memory was suddenly vivid, and Cornelia felt her throat tighten. "He was always wandering in asking where I'd put his best synthesis, just when everything was the most chaotic. That annoyed me so much . . . but afterward we'd sit in the triclinium sharing a cup of wine while the slaves cleared up, and we'd laugh about the things our guests said." Her smile wobbled, and she put it away before it could turn to tears. "I can't imagine him laughing now."

"All right, that's enough." Marcella marched in, calling over one shoulder for Cornelia's maid.

"Go away." Cornelia tested the edge of the dagger, eyes still blurring. "I'm going to join my husband."

"Oh, no, you're not," Marcella said. "Though it's a pity to dismantle such a beautiful scene. Really, you have all the details just perfect, and if this were a history and you were an empress, I'd commend your sense of the proprieties."

"Marcella, I've made up my mind, so please don't—what are you doing?"

"Bringing you back to your senses, that's what I'm doing. Please take this back to the mausoleum," Marcella instructed the maid, plunking the urn of Piso's ashes into her startled hands.

"You can't stop me!" Cornelia cried.

"I certainly can." Marcella plucked the dagger away before Cornelia could think to poise it at her wrist or under her breast. "You're being absurd. What's this? Another funeral urn? You ordered one for *your-self*?" Looking at the engraving. " 'Together in death'—Cornelia, how morbid. I wonder if the engraver will take it back? Might as well try, I suppose."

Cornelia suddenly felt very small and silly, sitting on the edge of the bed in her black dress. As if she were the little sister now, and Marcella the older and wiser. "You don't understand. I just want to be with my husband again."

"Well, Piso wanted you to live," Marcella said shortly. "His last act in life was to shove you toward safety. Why don't you take his wishes into account?"

"I don't want to live," Cornelia said wretchedly. "I just want *him*."

"Well, think about that poor centurion who saved you. Are you going to waste all his effort?"

"I don't care!"

Marcella eyed her a moment. "Come with me."

"I'm not going anywhere." Cornelia collapsed back on the bed, but Marcella hauled her up by one arm.

"Yes, you are."

"Where? Where are we supposed to go?"

"A good question. I'd suggest visiting Lollia but you aren't speaking to her, and anyway she sent me word she's gone to her grandfather's house to help feed the huddled refugees from the floods. Which probably means she's in bed with her Gaul—can you imagine Lollia getting her shoes muddy?" Marcella rummaged for a cloak. "You'd better realize what a sacrifice I'm making. I've been trying all day to start my account of Vitellius—the newest Emperor up north, or hadn't you heard?—and between Tullia's errands and your ridiculous suicide attempt, I've written exactly six words."

"Vitellius?" Cornelia cried as her sister bundled her into a cloak. "My life is over, and all you can talk about is your wretched political accounts?"

"It's what I *have*, Cornelia. At least you're a grieving widow; there's stature in that. I'm just an unnecessary sister and an unwanted wife, and I'm at everyone's beck and call. Including yours, and really I could feel quite resentful about that, but I don't want to stamp off in a huff and come back to find you dead. Come *on*."

She pushed Cornelia along, down the stairs toward the quarrel that was still raging: Diana, standing wet and truculent as Tullia berated her.

"Such language! You should have your mouth washed out—"

Diana stuck her chin out. "Father says worse when he chips a mallet."

"I don't care what your father says, you'll behave like a decent well-raised girl in my house!"

"Then I guess I won't be staying for your dinner party." Diana headed for the atrium. "Shame."

"Wait," said Marcella. "We're coming too."

"Don't you dare walk away from me, you insolent little slut!" Tullia screamed after Diana.

"Oh, we're not walking, Tullia," Diana called back over her spiky shoulder. "We're running. Fast as we can."

"Mind if we run along with you?" Marcella caught up, still towing Cornelia behind her. Rain poured in a sheet through the square opening of the atrium. "Cornelia needs sanctuary. She was trying to commit suicide. So will I, if I stay in this house any longer."

"Where are you going?" Tullia cried behind them. "My party—"

"I don't want sanctuary." Cornelia burst suddenly into tears, hot drops mixing with the cold rain already blowing into her face from the open roof. "Oh, why did you have to come home early? *Why?*"

"—finally get some work done today," Marcella added in a mutter, ignoring her. "Six *words*—"

"What a fuss, eh?" Lucius wandered past, looking idly at the rain. "Marcella, will you have a word with the slaves about my togas? Too much starch."

Marcella looked her husband in the eye. "Lucius," she said levelly, ignoring Cornelia's tears and Diana's tapping foot and Tullia still fuming at the other end of the atrium. "You made it perfectly clear the other day that you are never going to make me mistress of my own household. So I am a guest here, just like you, and if you don't like how your togas are being pressed then you can damn well talk to the slaves yourself."

And she dragged Cornelia out into the rain.

D EAR gods, not those blankets—I wouldn't give them to a dog." Lollia wrinkled her nose. "Do we have anything in the storerooms?"

"They were given out yesterday, Domina."

"Horse blankets, then. If they're clean and warm, no one will care if they smell like horse." Lollia wheeled around, back toward the *culina*, and the stewards and the slaves wheeled after her like a trail of ducklings. Flavia trotted at her heels, curly and unconcerned, but everyone else wore frowns.

"Domina," the pastry cook began in aggrieved tones as Lollia swept into the *culina*, "this is beneath my position! I have made pastry for emperors, for kings—and now you have me making flatbread for plebs?"

"Pastry isn't much use in a flood." Lollia peered through a crack in the shutter to the courtyard outside. Nothing but huddled, patient shapes waiting in line, heads bowed under the rain. "Heavens, it isn't letting up at all, is it?"

"But Domina—"

"Oppius, I know you've probably never even *seen* anything as awful as barley flour before, but this is an emergency. You're providing a great service to our tenants, and I'll see you get a bonus for it." She patted his flour-dusted shoulder. "Flatbread, please—and as much as you can turn out."

She scooped Flavia up, set her on the nearest table with a kiss and a bowl of flour to play in, and reversed out of the *culina* with the steward at one elbow and Thrax solid and golden on the other. "Better open the gates. The line looks even longer today."

What a mess. The rains coming far too late in the season, and the Tiber overflowing its banks, and then the Pons Silica crashing down. Entire blocks of crumbling tenement collapsed in a shower of old bricks and mortar; several granaries flooded and the grain turned moldy; shops closed everywhere as shopkeepers fled for higher ground. The fashionable house Lollia shared with her new husband, Salvius, had water lapping over its doorstep, so she had retreated with Flavia to her grandfather's vast house clinging to the higher side of the Palatine Hill. Still, even her grandfather had been robbed by the flooding—two tenement buildings belonging to him had come down, and four streets' worth of client shopkeepers had been forced to close their doors.

"No pushing—you'll all be served, so please line up." The crowd filed into the courtyard, ten days ago a vista of winter lilies and early spring moss, and now just a sea of mud. Lollia had the slaves well drilled now; a calm and orderly line meeting the human tide with baskets of flatbread, cauldrons of barley soup, armfuls of coarse blankets.

"Domina," the steward complained, "some of these people are common plebs from across town. We have an obligation only to feed our own clients."

"Feed them all, Aelius. We can afford it." Slaves, plebs, tenants, they all held out their hands, drenched and shivering, and Lollia's job was to stand to one side with a hefty bag of coppers, distributing money and soothing words. She knew how to do it, too, no matter what her cousins might say about how she never got her hands dirty. *They're ones to talk. I might like my parties and pleasures when times are good, but at least I know how to roll up my sleeves when necessary.* Her grandfather had taught her that—he had been a slave, after all, and slaves didn't forget where they came from.

"There's plenty for all," Lollia soothed. "Yes, you can take another blanket if you need one. Goodness, madam, you shouldn't be out in this rain in your condition. When is the baby due? Go to the kitchens and warm yourself by the fire before you go. No, sir, my grandfather has suspended all rents until business resumes. Open the bakery when you can and don't worry about the rents. Madam, you may talk to my steward about the damage to your roof, all necessary repairs will be made—"

"Domina," Thrax said softly at her elbow in his vague Gallic accent. "You should not be here. You make yourself ill."

"Don't be ridiculous." Passing a blanket over to a wide-eyed woman with two bedraggled children clinging to each hip. "It's my job."

"The steward, he can take care of it."

"He'll pocket all the coppers and sell the grain."

"Not when I watch," Thrax said. He'd already caught one of the grooms hoarding blankets to sell out the back of the stables to desperate beggars. He'd lifted the man up with one hand, cracked him a few times against a roof beam, and tossed him into an overflowing gutter full of stinking refuse. *I do like a man of action!*

Thrax stuck at Lollia's elbow all afternoon, passing new bags of coppers when she'd given out the last coins in her hands, scowling at a butcher who raved too loudly about the damages done to his shop. When Flavia escaped her nurse and came running down to the courtyard, it was Thrax who saw her first and swung her up to sit on his shoulders before her feet could even get muddy. He took a moment to run her through the rain, her little hands stretched out to catch the falling drops, then swung her down and returned her squealing to her nurse. His golden hair was just as bright in the rain as in the sunlight, Lollia thought. And he did look wonderful wet! Tunic clinging to wide shoulders and long flanks, muscles moving under a rainy gleam of skin . . .

"That's the end of the flatbread, Domina," the steward reported.

"Close the gates until tomorrow, then."

The maids dispensed the last blankets; Lollia divvied up her remaining coppers and allowed the shivering children to dip a second bowl into the soup cauldron to take away with them. Thrax and the grooms herded the rest out through the gates. There were a few grumbles, but Lollia had had the grooms armed with stout cudgels, and no one put up much of a fuss. More than one house in this city had been overrun by desperate plebs looking for shelter, and there would probably be more—but none of them would belong to *her.*

"There you are, m'dear." Her grandfather came in from the atrium, shaking out his wet cloak. "All in hand?"

"All in hand."

"That's my jewel." He patted her cheek. "I've just arranged for an extra wagonload of grain barrels—delivery tomorrow, you can take care of that?"

"Of course." Lollia sneezed. "Any more buildings come crashing down in this rain?"

"No, but that tenement I just bought near the Pincian Hill needs shoring up—the roof looks shaky. I'll supervise the workers tomorrow myself." Lollia's grandfather put a plump hand on her damp hair, frowning. "Get warm, m'dear, get warm at once. I won't have you sick. Thrax, put her to bed, if you please."

"Yes, Dominus." Thrax dropped the last blanket over Lollia's shoulders. Lollia kissed her grandfather's cheek again and trudged upstairs to the lavish pink-and-silver bedchamber that was always hers whenever she came back to her grandfather's house—between husbands, in other words. Half the lamps in the halls were unlit, and the statues turned their blank jeweled eyes dully into the shadows as if they were downcast by the weather too. The bedchamber smelled musty, the pink frills muted, every shutter closed against the rain.

"I'll bet all my dresses are moldy," Lollia said, and sneezed again.

"I told you to stay out from the rain, Domina." Thrax rubbed her arms through the coarse wool of the blanket, then stripped it away. "Arms out."

Lollia smiled as he dismissed her maids and then proceeded to undress her like a baby, rub her down with warmed oils until her skin tingled, and wrap her up in a thick robe. He began stroking a comb through her damp curls, and Lollia kept sneezing.

"Better not stay." She wiped her nose as Thrax tucked her into bed. "I'll get you sick too." But he climbed in, wrapping his big golden body around hers, and Lollia was warm to the core in no time. "You're a god," she sighed, cuddling against his chest.

"Thank you, Domina."

"I've told you to quit calling me that, at least when you're in here. It's absurd."

"Yes, Domina." There was a smile in his deep voice, and she smiled back against his shoulder. How nice to relax for once—she'd been uneasy ever since Otho took the purple. Not because of her new husband—Salvius might be handsome enough, agreeable enough, but he didn't make much of an impression on her life. They ate breakfast figs together in agreeable silence, and Lollia went on his arm in equally agreeable splendor to every party where Otho wanted them, but in between breakfast and parties there wasn't much else. Not much between parties and breakfast either; Salvius kept a temperamental young actress in a spacious apartment on Pomegranate Street, and she kept him far too busy to bother Lollia much. He hadn't paid her bed more than two or three visits since the wedding.

No, it wasn't the newest husband who made Lollia uneasy. It was the *omens*. She'd always preferred to read all omens with an optimistic eye, but she couldn't think of any positive twist to put on the current set. Otho talked of marching north to fight Vitellius, and the Tiber promptly threw a tantrum and overran her banks, and the skies went mad. She said as much to Thrax, drawing circles on his broad chest with one finger. "I don't think Rome wants her Emperor to leave."

"So Rome is a woman," Thrax asked.

"Maybe. The Emperor's her husband, and she wants him to stay home."

"Maybe she does not mind." He grinned. "You do all right, Domina."

"True enough." Lollia tilted her head back on the pillow to kiss him. Salvius had cast a sharp look at her when he first set eyes on Thrax, but on the whole he didn't care. As long as she was careful with her Egyptian tricks and there weren't any embarrassing bumps in her belly, Salvius wouldn't fuss. *If I have a lover in-house, after all, I won't be running about town embarrassing him with men of his own class.* "Still," Lollia kept musing, "you can't deny the omens are bad. Everyone's feeling it. This whole city is tense and edgy. Not to mention damp. And that's if they aren't hungry, homeless, or crushed by bricks too."

"Sshh," Thrax said against her belly.

Lollia giggled, running her fingers through his golden hair as his hand stroked her breast. *Who cares if all Rome is uneasy with bad omens?* she thought. *Here, I'm safe.*

Nine

∽◌◌

"Mʏ Cornelias!" Emperor Otho greeted them with a press for every hand. "Dear girls, how wonderful to see you all." He raised his goblet. "To war!"

"I don't see why war is something to celebrate," Marcella observed. "It's simply a necessary evil."

"*Necessary* being the key word." Otho laughed. "And it's become necessary to march north and deal with that fat oaf Vitellius, so lift your goblet and have a toast with me."

"To war," they all echoed, though Marcella reflected that altogether the assembling of Otho's army seemed to be much less cause for celebration than the fact that the sun was finally out again. The flood waters in Rome's lower slums had subsided, shops had reopened, and moldy clothes had aired out, so Otho had ordered gladiators from Gaul and Britannia and a wild beast hunt in the arena and a subsequent banquet in the Domus Aurea to celebrate both clear skies and Vitellius's anticipated downfall. *If that drunkard in the north could be defeated by celebration here in Rome, he'd be dead already.*

"We will all be required to attend," Gaius had said nervously, eyes flicking to Cornelia when the festivities were announced. "All of us—you cannot snub the Emperor this time—"

"I'll go," Cornelia had said unexpectedly. The failed suicide attempt, Marcella was glad to see, had taken something out of her sister. She'd had a wet afternoon of crying quietly as Uncle Paris sketched her. "You can make me the Muse of Tragedy," she sniffled.

"Oh no." He shook his head. "The Muse of Tragedy would be very gentle and misty, not all puffy-eyed and blubbering. Manage a smile for me, will you? With those dimples, I can make you the Muse of Comedy in a heartbeat. Tragedy and comedy are very closely linked, you know . . ."

"I'm glad somebody thinks this is funny," Cornelia said waspishly as Marcella laughed—and there was no doubt she'd been better since. She still didn't eat much, but at least she sat at her loom now and then, or curled up in the atrium with bitter eyes and a cup of warmed wine.

"I'll go to Otho's games," she warned now as Gaius beamed. "But I'm wearing black. I may have to eat that usurping murderer's food, but I won't put off my mourning."

Lollia stepped in fast before anyone could bristle. "A wonderful idea," she said very brightly. "We'll make a statement of it, all of us in shades of black and white and gray. Very striking!"

Lollia outdid herself, and Emperor Otho raised his goblet in appreciation of the picture they made as they entered his box at the gladiatorial arena: Cornelia in narrow black silk with bands of ebony and gold circling her arms above and below the elbow; Lollia in a black pearl diadem and a pleated robe of dark-silver tissue that gave back every ray of the sun; Diana in yards of airy billowing white that wafted on every breeze, her pale hair piled on top of her head with gold combs. "You can't wear that plain thing," Lollia had scolded Marcella, looking at her pale pearl-gray *stola* hemmed in silver. "Don't you at least have a necklace or some earrings?"

"You think I have any jewelry left after Lucius and his never-ending travel expenses?"

"Oh, that's nothing, I'll lend you some. Here, some moonstones—"

"I don't want your borrowed bracelets, Lollia!" Really, it was just like when they were little and Lollia always had the new dresses, the pearl necklaces, the pony and the puppy. She might be lavish in sharing, but she was still the one who *had* everything.

"My lovely quartet of Cornelias," Otho beamed, lowering his goblet after they all drank a toast to war. "Little Diana, I assure you we will have races later this week—and I will cheer privately for your Reds, even though an emperor has to remain impartial—"

"Does not," said Diana. "Emperor Caligula was a great fan of the Greens."

"And look where Emperor Caligula ended up!" Otho chucked Diana's chin, which didn't please her, and looked past to Cornelia. "Ah, Cornelia Prima. So lovely to see you at last, my dear." As the Emperor addressed his former rival's widow in her mourning black, a little glint came into his eye that made Marcella suddenly wary. "You should have come sooner."

Maybe the glint made Cornelia wary too, because she managed a stiff little bow.

They had missed the beginning ceremonies: the priests chanting, the guards in red and gold, the white bulls led in ceremonial parade around the arena with little gilded boys dancing on their backs. The gladiators were parading past, their faces set and withdrawn under their helmets, and they saluted the Emperor as one. Half would die later that afternoon, unless the crowd was in a benevolent mood. Otho acknowledged them with a casual wave, never ceasing in his airy conversation with a dozen hangers-on.

Eager suitors towed Diana off, and Cornelia fell back against the farthest wall with tight lips. Marcella knew her sister didn't approve of the games, but then none of them did. Diana hated the slaughter of animals, Lollia had a slave-blood sympathy for the captives in the arena, and Cornelia thought the whole thing in bad taste. Marcella simply couldn't see the point of it all. *Such petty power, making a few desperate men hack each other to death for a mob's pleasure.* Real power was something bigger, grander . . . but the plebs still packed into the arena in their thousands, screaming over the gladiators as if they were gods before they died like dogs.

Marcella found herself a seat beside Diana where fluttering suitors could be counted on to block the view, and Lollia courted oblivion her own way, drinking wine freely and offering token smiles to the Emperor's jokes. Lollia still looked moody these days, and she did a great deal of gloomy muttering about the omens. "Rome's like a woman," she declared. "Thrax told me that, and he's right. Rome is a woman, the Emperor is her husband, and she doesn't want him to leave."

Or maybe Rome wants a new husband, Marcella thought, looking over at Lucius, where he honked laughter with Otho's officers. *I certainly wouldn't mind.* She'd had to accost Lucius again that morning, and it hadn't gone well. "So you don't want to set up a household—but I really will need some money of my own, you know."

"Why?" He blinked. "Your brother feeds you. What else do you need?"

"What *else*? You mean I have to go hat in hand to Tullia every time I want a coin to go to the bathhouse or the theatre or to buy new pens?"

"Just ask Lollia nicely, she'll buy you anything you want." He waved a hand in dismissal.

"Maybe I'll just find a lover to pay my bills, Lucius!" Marcella snarled.

"Do that. I'm sure you can keep someone interested for a week or two." He'd wandered away, yawning, and Marcella stamped after him.

"How dare you, you can't just brush me off—" But he did exactly that, and as he disappeared into his borrowed study, Marcella caught a wavery glimpse of herself reflected in a window. Her cheeks had flared pink with fury, her eyes glittered, her breasts heaved rage. *I may not be a beauty, but there are plenty who would find me handsome,* she thought savagely, stamping away from Lucius's shut door. *Plenty!*

Senator Marcus Norbanus certainly seemed to think so, claiming the seat beside her and speaking with his usual grave courtesy. And Marcus was a grandson of the divine Augustus, so respected in the Senate that he had been appointed to his first consulship the minute he turned thirty. *If you won't appreciate your wife, Lucius, there are plenty of better men who will.* "How is your little boy, Marcus?" Marcella asked, and turned on her most dazzling smile.

"He's well. For the moment."

"The moment? He's not getting ill, is he?"

"I wish he were. One can call the physician for a fever, but there is no cure for being a Norbanus." Marcus's voice was quiet and his face, Marcella noticed with a start, very drawn. "My father was invited to commit suicide."

"*What*? By whom?"

"Who do you think?"

Marcella's eyes traveled to Otho, laughing with his head thrown back. "Why?"

Marcus shrugged. "Best prune a god's descendants before they get ideas."

"And has your father . . ."

"Oh, yes. A Norbanus is always punctual. Even to the end."

"I'm so sorry." Not everyone, then, found Otho an improvement over Galba. Marcella stored that thought away for future consideration. "Surely you need not be here today, Marcus. Under the circumstances—"

"Oh, but my attendance here is *required*. How else am I to show my loyalty? And I have a son to consider." A flash of bitter grief went through Marcus Norbanus's gaze, but it was gone in another moment. He might only be thirty-three, but he had been reared to an older, stricter school. To show grief in public would be a disgrace.

Marcella admired him more than ever for it. *Surely a love affair would get his mind off his troubles.* And as a choice of lover, he would definitely tweak Lucius's nose—her husband might be at ease with politicians, but scholars made him uncomfortable. "Do let me call on you, Marcus." She squeezed his fingers, just as ink-stained as her own. "Perhaps tomorrow evening?"

"I fear I am not good company these days." He withdrew his hand with a brief bow. "Pray excuse me. Once I make my greetings, I am free to go home. I find I have no stomach for the games today."

Marcella blinked as he made his exit from the Imperial box but decided not to be annoyed. He was distraught, after all—later he'd be glad of a shoulder to lean on.

She turned as trumpets announced the beginning of the wild beast hunt and rose petals showered down on the stands. *How long will it all take?* A tall man blocked her view, his head tilted down toward Diana at his side. Of course, Diana had no difficulty getting any man's attention if she wanted it.

"—still don't know what a horse trainer is doing in the Emperor's box," Diana was saying frankly.

"Why shouldn't I be?"

His voice was low and even, whoever he was, and Marcella took a closer look. Not in the usual mode for Diana's suitors—a tall man of thirty-five or forty, with broad arms and iron-gray hair he'd let grow shaggy. And *breeches*, of all things. "A new suitor, Diana?" Marcella broke in, curious.

"What? Oh, not him." Diana waved a casual hand at the man in breeches. "This is Llyn. Llyn ap Caradoc."

Marcella burst out laughing. "You're not serious?"

Diana blinked. "What? He breeds horses."

The gray-haired man took a swallow from his cup, noncommittal. Common beer in the cup instead of wine, Marcella noted—and a scar on his neck that might have been a graze from a spear or arrow, and a torc of wrought bronze about his neck, in the tribal fashion. "Llyn ap Caradoc—you mean Caratacus? *The* Caratacus?"

"My father," he said. Below, a trained leopard had been released into the arena by his handler: the opening display.

"I remember seeing your father about the city now and then," Marcella said. Time was, every hostess in Rome counted it a coup to have Rome's greatest enemy at her table: the man who had united the tribes of Britannia, fought Rome to a gallant standstill for nearly a decade, and was finally captured and brought to Rome to be paraded through the city in chains—only to be given an Imperial pardon in reward for his bravery, allowed to live in luxury within Rome's walls with his remaining family, under oath and under guard never to try to escape. "I wish I'd had the pleasure of meeting him."

"He died last year, Lady."

"Yes, I think I heard that somewhere. I'm sorry for it—Llyn, you said your name was?"

"Yes."

He looked very much like his father, from what Marcella could remember: the same quiet carved face and silent way of moving.

Diana still looked baffled, and Marcella finally leaned forward to whisper briefly into her ear. Diana listened, then cocked her head up at Llyn. "You were a rebel too?"

"As most would define it. Killing Romans since before I was your age, at any rate."

Diana grinned. Rabbits had been released into the arena below, bounding in all directions, and the leopard chased them down one by one to return them unharmed to his handler in soft jaws. "You know, I thought when we met that your name sounded familiar. My nurse used to tell me the great Caratacus would eat me if I was bad."

"He had that effect on people."

Marcella felt a prickle of excitement in her fingertips. Her history of Emperor Claudius had a few lines about the rebellion in Britannia, but she'd gleaned all her facts from books. If she could get a first-hand account . . . surely the great Caratacus's son would have seen his father's rebellion at very close range, perhaps even led raids and battles himself. Marcella smiled. "How interesting, meeting a legend. My name—"

"My father was a legend," he said, bland. "I breed horses."

"Well," Diana consoled, "they're very *good* horses."

Llyn laughed. A praetor squeezed Diana's arm from the other side—"Come place a bet for me, Lady Diana, you'll bring me luck for the next bout!"

Yes, go, Marcella thought at her cousin as the tame leopard padded out, *let me see if I can get the Briton talking.* A new source, now that was even better entertainment than a love affair. But Diana shook off the praetor and turned back to Llyn, pushing a strand of hair behind her ear. "My question stands," she said. "Why *are* you here? I doubt I'd want to sit with Roman emperors after growing up trying to overthrow them."

"I have nothing against Roman emperors in Rome, Lady," he said mildly. "It's Roman emperors in Britannia I never liked. And I'm here because I'm an oddity. I'm not quite as good value as my father when it comes to shocking guests, but I'm the only one left from my family, and Emperor Otho likes oddities."

"He says the same about me," said Diana. A fleet herd of gazelles had been released into the arena below, galloping in panicked circles. Four lions came roaring one by one from a trapdoor in the sand.

"How long have you lived in Rome now?" Marcella pondered what to call an ex-rebel without family name or title, and substituted a friendly smile for a salutation.

"Eighteen years," he said briefly, and turned back to Diana. "How are your Anemoi, Lady? The chestnuts I sold to the Red faction."

"They won at Equirria. Did you see?"

"I avoid the races." The gazelles were running in panicked circles now, the lions chasing them down one by one.

"Well, Equirria was thrilling. Those wretched Blues scratched, but my Anemoi took the Greens and the Whites as easy as anything. The Whites came up from behind, but—"

"He's not interested, Diana," Marcella said. Too late: a platter of fruit had already been converted into a circus track, a ripe strawberry had become the Reds, a cube of cheese the Whites, a cluster of grapes the Greens. The Briton listened inscrutably, but Marcella thought she caught a flash of amusement in the dark eyes. Well, Diana could be rather amusing in her childlike way. *Still, I'd better rescue him.* "So you were the one to sell her that team of chestnuts?" Marcella smiled, trying to draw his gaze. "You may regret it—she has no other topic of conversation now."

"—three lengths ahead in the last lap—" Diana droned on.

"I don't mind talking horses," Llyn said. "What else does an old savage like me have to offer?"

"Since you mention it," Marcella jumped in quickly, "I'm something of an amateur historian, and I'm always interested in the truth. A view of your father's rebellion from your own perspective—I could do justice to his reputation, if I knew what really happened."

"—and now the Reds are favorites for the Cerealia races, and we're going to *crush* the Blues." Finally finishing, Diana popped the defeated cube of cheese that was the Whites into her mouth and grinned at Llyn.

The last gazelle lay dead in the arena. A lioness tore ravenous at its fallen carcass while a black-maned male stalked the sand and roared. Another trapdoor opened and a team of *bestiarii* trooped out with nets, tridents, short bows. They fanned out toward the black-maned male, blades glittering in the sunlight.

"Perhaps we could speak sometime," Marcella persisted. "I'd be greatly interested in anything you could tell me."

The Briton gave a slow blink and looked at Diana instead. "Why do you care so much for the races, Lady?"

Diana tossed a grape into the air, catching it neatly between her teeth as she considered. The black-maned lion went down snarling in the arena below, taking an archer with him. The man screamed, his belly opened clear through his back by a swipe of claws, and the crowd howled. "I love the speed," Diana said at last, reflectively—or at least as reflectively as Diana ever spoke about anything. "And the danger. The horses running their hearts out and the drivers killing themselves for a win. Don't you enjoy it?"

"No, I've seen real danger."

Marcella drew in a breath to ask him about that, but Diana answered first. "I haven't. Nobody lets me. So I watch the races instead. I'd kill myself for wins too, if I could drive properly."

"Driving a chariot's not as hard as you Romans make it out to be—a knack for the reins, a sense of timing. The turn's tricky, but all that needs is practice."

"Really?" Diana hooked an elbow around the back of her chair, cocking her head at him, and Marcella felt a familiar tingle of anger at being shut out. *Why do the most interesting men always end up talking to Diana—the* least *interesting girl in Rome?*

"You've been a long time in Rome now," Marcella put in to Llyn, quickly counting the years. Eighteen years' captivity—he must not have been much older than Marcella herself when he'd been brought to Rome in chains. "How much do you remember of Britannia?"

Llyn looked at her coolly. "I'm not so old my memory's gone dim, Lady."

"I didn't say you *couldn't* remember it," she shot back. "I merely wondered if you still choose to."

"Every day."

The last two lionesses banded together, snarling and clawing, but the *bestiarii* worked in a team and brought them down. They vaulted atop the fallen tawny bodies, holding their sweaty arms up to the cheering crowd, and Emperor Otho leaned forward to toss silver coins into the arena.

"I hate animal hunts." Diana grimaced.

"They fought bravely," Llyn judged as the *bestiarii* danced off victorious through the Gate of Life and the dead lions were raked away by arena attendants.

"The lions or the gladiators?" Marcella smiled.

"Oh, the lions."

"Can an animal be brave?"

"Of course they can," said Diana at once.

"But how would a lion know the meaning of courage?"

"Why does one have to know the meaning of courage to be brave?" Llyn ap Caradoc countered.

"Does it count as courage if you're just cornered?"

"Yes," Diana and the Briton said in unison.

"You'd know better than I, Diana." Marcella couldn't resist aiming a little jab at her cousin. "You do spend half your life with animals, after all. Quaint."

"Whatever you say." Diana took a swallow of wine as the Gate of Life rumbled open again and the purple-cloaked gladiators came out for their fight. "I just don't like to watch animals die."

Llyn watched the gladiators fling their cloaks aside, pairing off. "I don't like to watch men die, Lady."

"Oh, gods' wheels, call me Diana. Everyone does."

"Briton!" Emperor Otho's beaming voice cut across the cheerful tumult of the box to Llyn. "Come, bend that savage expertise my way and choose a fighter for me to back. I've lost the last two wagers to Salvius here, and I'm determined to fleece him."

"Of course, Caesar." Llyn rose, bowing politely, and came forward to lean on the rail beside the Emperor. He might be taller than Otho, Marcella noted, and broader too—but he was still outshone by the Emperor's dazzling presence. Half a moment's scrutiny of the fighters in the arena below, and he pointed out a Briton with a wiry beard. "That one."

"He's half the size of the others! Why did you pick him out?"

"I always bet on Britons, Caesar."

"Rather sentimental of you," Marcella noted.

Otho wasn't listening. "A hundred *denarii*, Salvius!" And he threw down a handful of coins.

The gladiators fell on each other. Marcella wrinkled her nose, turning her head away before the blood could start to fly, but the great Caratacus's son watched intently, hands locked around the rail as his eyes tracked the fighters back and forth across the sand. Diana wandered up beside him, a cup of wine in hand. "I thought you didn't like watching men die."

"I don't." Following the wiry-haired Briton as he jabbed savagely at a nimble Greek with a trident. "But I'm used to it."

The Briton went down on a quick strike from the Greek, dying slowly with a blade through his lung. The Emperor turned ruefully back to Llyn. "Not a very good choice."

"I didn't say he was a good choice, Caesar," Llyn said. "I said I always bet on Britons."

The glint came back into Otho's eye—the glint that always reminded Marcella of the hard streak behind his charm. The hard streak that had successfully pulled off a coup over the bodies of Fortuna knew how many rivals . . . But Otho at last decided to laugh, and flipped a coin at Llyn. "Well said."

Llyn's arm flashed up and he backhanded the coin spinning over the railing into the arena. A gladiator darted to scrabble it out of the sand, and Llyn saluted him.

"I suppose you don't have gladiators in your own country," Marcella said. "Perhaps you might tell me—"

"No," Llyn ap Caradoc cut her off. "I don't care to discuss those days, Lady. With anyone."

"Don't blame you," said Diana. "Look, the elephants—I think they just dance to pipes and don't get killed."

Absently she passed Llyn her wine cup. Just as absently he took a swallow and handed it back. Diana's hovering suitors looked at the Briton, resentful, and Marcella felt her own lips flattening into a sour line. *I try to start up an intelligent conversation with a man, just for information's sake, and Diana still has to grab all the attention. If she'd been the one to bat her eyes at Marcus Norbanus earlier, I'll bet he wouldn't have excused himself so early.*

The Emperor soon declared the day's festivities at an end, a flashing god in an entourage of mortals as he led the procession back toward the palace. The praetor with moist hands descended on Diana—"My dear young lady, I do hope you will look favorably on my suit! When can I speak with your father?" Marcella enjoyed Diana's protests as the praetor bore her off. She turned to claim Llyn ap Caradoc's attention now that he was free, but he had already seized his cloak and was taking the opportunity to disappear into the throng of guests.

Lollia beat her way through the crowd in her flashing silver tissue and claimed Marcella's arm. "For once, my honey, I'm the one with the news." She was smiling, their last quarrel during the dress fittings apparently forgotten. "Ride with me and I'll torture you with it."

"What news?" They settled into Lollia's litter—much bigger and more ornate, now that she had married into the Imperial family.

"It's your husband," Lollia said as the litter rose swaying and the bearers swung down the street. Marcella couldn't help but remember the last time they'd ridden in a litter together, when they'd been spilled out by a mob and had to run for their lives. "I heard Lucius backslapping with the Emperor's officers. The Emperor offered him a post here in the city, but he angled for one in the upcoming campaign instead."

"As what?" Marcella snorted. "Paid mooch?"

"As observer to the battle." Lollia waved a vague hand as the litter joined the slow procession crawling back through the palace grounds. "Message running and so forth. Whatever it is that observers do during battles."

"Knowing Lucius, it won't involve getting his hands dirty."

"At least this gets him out of your hair, doesn't it? I thought you'd be happy."

"I suppose." Observer to the battle, though . . . *much more my line than Lucius's*. He only bothered observing anything that would boost him up the ladder to a higher post.

"Thank the gods war is men's business." Lollia shuddered as their litter was set down at last, at the marble steps mounting toward the gardens of the Domus Aurea. Lamps glowed like golden bubbles and slaves were already streaming out with rosewater foot baths in silver ewers. "All the mud, the legionaries, the danger—"

"And the chance to see history," Marcella mused. "The clash of an emperor and a usurping emperor, armies deciding the fate of Rome—how wonderful to see all that."

"Wonderful?" Lollia eyed her a little oddly. "It'll be men dying, thousands of men on both sides. It will be *horrible*."

"At least it will be real." Suddenly irritated, Marcella cast a glance over Lollia's jewels, her powdered skin, the wine cup in her hand. "Some of us prefer real life to parties and wine."

"I wasn't the one who didn't want to get my hands dirty helping plebs during the flooding," Lollia said tartly.

"Yes, you were very keen on that as long as you could get away from your husband for a few hours and take your pet Gaul with you. Very admirable, Lollia."

"*He is not a pet!*" Lollia tugged her hand out of Marcella's arm and flounced off as they were ushered into the vast triclinium. Marcella felt no urge to call after her. The mere sight of her cousins exasperated her these days. Even her sister—there was Cornelia now, lurking long-faced by a column. Couldn't she even try to smile?

Marcella took a goblet of wine from the nearest slave, trying to stifle her sourness. It was a beautiful night, after all. Emperor Otho's usual exotic crowd: senators, praetors, consuls, and their wives all mixed together with actresses, astrologers, charioteers, courtesans, even a star gladiator or two from the day's games. Too many guests for formal dining, and they all mixed in the gardens where gilded braziers kept away the chill of early spring and half-naked slaves in gold tissue circulated with cups of warmed wine and trays of dainties.

"These Imperial parties are all the same." Diana's voice came unexpectedly at Marcella's elbow. "Ever notice that?"

"It's rather beautiful."

"Yes, but it's always the *same*." Diana rubbed a hand down the marble nose of a horse rearing, massive and statue-carved, out of a bank of jasmine. "The food is delicious, the wine is expensive, the people are beautiful, and the conversation is witty."

"They aren't all beautiful." Marcella watched a portly senator wheeze past in one of the short embroidered tunics Otho had made fashionable—not a forgiving fashion to the elderly. "And they aren't all witty, either," she added as she heard the tail end of a particularly labored epigram from another guest.

"So what's the point of it all?" Diana turned to the statue of the horse and scrambled lithely up, seating herself sideways on its marble back. Her airy white skirts caught the cool evening breeze and billowed about her knees, and she swung her feet freely, ignoring the stares.

"Diana," Marcella said crossly, "get down from there. Do you always have to be the center of attention?"

"Don't care if I am or not." Diana leaned down to accept a cup of wine from an Imperial slave too sophisticated to look startled. "I just do what I want."

"How nice for you."

"Diana!" Tullia hissed, bustling over with curls bobbing. "Get down! Do you realize how people are staring?"

"Let them," Diana grinned.

"Showing your bare legs in public like a slave girl—the *idea*!"

Diana reached down and peeled off her gold-strapped sandals, hanging them over the horse's marble ear. "Go away," she advised Tullia, "or I peel off the rest."

"Oh, Domina," a half-drunk tribune chortled, draping an arm over Tullia. "Please stay!" A drunken chorus went up.

"*Gaius!*" Tullia slapped the tribune away and huffed off. Diana lay back against the horse's marble neck, her pointed face tilted up at the stars. "Are you making wishes?" Marcella couldn't help but ask. A wild little thing perched on a statue—so beautiful. *So beautiful she can get away with anything.*

"I'm wishing things would change."

"They *have* changed. The moment Piso and Galba died, things started to shift. Didn't you feel it?"

"Things changed for Cornelia, maybe." Diana's eyes were still fixed on the sky overhead. "For Lollia. Not for me."

"Then change them," Marcella said over one shoulder, wandering off. "At least you can." Nothing had changed for her either, but it never did. *No matter what I try to do about it.*

"I just heard Lucius is to accompany the army north as an observer!" Cornelia came to grip Marcella's arm. "Is it true?"

"Yes." Marcella shrugged. "And don't bother being angry at me just because Lucius works for Otho now—you know he'll toady up to anyone who can advance his career."

Cornelia brushed that aside. "It could be terribly dangerous. Aren't you worried?"

"Oh, it won't be so dangerous as all that. Lucius never puts himself in harm's way if he can help it. Besides, Otho won't have far to march, since Vitellius got farther south than anyone anticipated. The two armies will meet somewhere up north, and there will be a battle, and that will be that. Otho's taking eight thousand men, so I imagine he'll win."

"So many?" Cornelia sounded sharp. "I didn't realize."

"This is Nessus!" Domitian dragged up the plump young astrologer in his symbol-spangled robe, oblivious to Marcella and Cornelia's frowns. "I recommended him to the Imperial steward when the Emperor was looking for astrologers to tell fortunes for his guests— Nessus, my Marcella here doesn't believe me when I say you're never wrong! Tell her fortune for her, that will do it—"

The young astrologer had quick bright eyes and a ready professional smile—a smile that blinked a little as he bowed over Cornelia and Marcella's hands. "Ah, my good ladies. Always a privilege to read such lovely palms." A certain amount of mystical chanting ensued, to Marcella's amusement. "Lady Marcella, you should prepare for a long journey, and very soon! And Lady Cornelia," Nessus continued, taking Cornelia's unwilling hand. "Your heart may now be broken, but rest easy! A man comes to heal it. Now, if you will excuse me, I hear the fates calling." His eyes flickered over Marcella and Cornelia for just an instant, and then he disappeared speedily into the throng.

"You see?" Marcella smiled at Domitian. "Charlatans always know a cynic like me when they see one. 'A long journey'—couldn't he have come up with something a little more original?"

"Nessus isn't a charlatan! He said I'd be a great general and a prince of Rome and—"

"I've had my stars read a dozen times," Cornelia broke in, bitter. "Not one of them ever told me I'd be a widow. And now I'm supposed to rejoice because supposedly a new man is coming along?"

"If you were a widow, I could have you." Domitian's fingers dug hungrily into Marcella's arm again as Cornelia gave a blind shake of her head and moved off. "All to myself."

"I doubt there's room in your cradle for me," said Marcella.

"I'm not a child!" he flared. "Don't ever call me that!"

More wine as night fell; more golden globes of light being lit under the sculpted trees. Otho still held court, a brilliant sun surrounded by lesser moons. Nessus read more palms, making plump rouged matrons giggle. Lollia stood dutifully with her new husband, and Diana still sat high above everyone on her marble horse, rather like the goddess in her moon chariot up in the sky overhead. Gaius came to squawk at her for a while, but a troop of acrobats had just begun performing in the atrium to the rhythm of a dozen drums, and Diana cupped a hand to her ear as if she couldn't hear Gaius's complaining. He went off muttering.

"You're always watching everyone," Domitian scowled at Marcella. "It's what I do."

Cornelia had returned to her pillar, taut and fierce in her black, rigidly rotating a gold-and-ebony bracelet around one wrist. A Praetorian paused to square his shoulders before approaching her—Centurion Drusus Densus, apparently restored to health at last, though he still looked drawn. He said something to Cornelia, or tried to before she brushed past him. *So Otho restores the gallant centurion to duty in the Praetorian Guard,* Marcella thought. *Nice to know that loyalty is sometimes rewarded.* "Centurion," she called cordially as he stumbled past. "I'm glad to see you recovered from your wounds."

He looked puzzled. "I'm sorry, Lady—do I know you?"

"You saved my life." He looked blank. Marcella had been to thank him on his sickbed, but he'd been half asleep from a poppy draught and clearly didn't remember her visit. "I am Cornelia Secunda," she enlarged as Domitian scowled to see her talking to any handsome man who wasn't him. "Lady Cornelia's sister? There are four of us—you saved us on the steps before the Temple of Vesta. My cousin Lollia over there too, and Diana. The one on the statue."

Recognition then. "I remember Lady Diana—the hair." He gestured at the white-blond locks slipping Diana's gold combs and tumbling over the horse's marble mane. "Only it was bloody."

Of course he remembers Diana. Marcella stamped down her irritation again, seeing how stiffly the centurion moved as he bowed. "Are you on duty already?" He wore his red-and-gold Praetorian armor, awkwardly formal for a party.

"No, I'm a guest."

"Since when do guests come armed?" Domitian blurted.

"If I'm in armor, they know how to look at me." Densus nodded out over his wine cup at Otho's beautiful butterfly crowd. "I put on a tunic and perfume, and they laugh at me for trying to be like them. Armor's safe."

So the centurion was another of Otho's oddities. *A former rebel who breeds horses, a girl who loves racing, and the only loyal soldier in Rome*, Marcella thought. *All just curiosities for the Emperor's parties.* "Do you march with the army against Vitellius?"

"Yes. After that—" A restless movement of the burly armored shoulders. "Perhaps I'll retire from the Praetorians."

"Why? You've no cause for shame."

"I *failed*, Lady. Your sister, Lady Cornelia—she made that clear."

"The Imperium needs men like you."

"What good is it? Every friend I had in the Guard turned traitor for Otho's coin. I don't blame him for buying them—but they weren't supposed to be for sale. And now they ask me to play dice with them and go to the bathhouse and get whores at taverns. Like nothing happened." He drained his wine cup—not the first he'd drunk tonight, Marcella saw. He looked at her, not seeing her at all, and his eyes were full of tears. "Gods, what a mess."

"It is, isn't it?" Marcella agreed.

"Go away," Domitian said rudely. "She doesn't talk to drunks."

Densus moved off unsteadily. "Did you have to do that?" Marcella demanded.

"Why were you talking to him? He's just a common soldier!"

"Well, he did save my life."

"I'd have saved your life if I'd been there," Domitian muttered.

The highlight of my evening, Marcella thought. *Being panted over by an eighteen-year-old boy.*

She couldn't help looking at Lollia, laughing with her friends; Diana, swinging her feet from the back of her marble horse; Cornelia, standing in rigid dignity by her pillar and looking icily past any Othonian who attempted an introduction. *They can get away with anything, all of them. But not me.* "The Cornelia in limbo," Marcella said aloud. Not a privileged wife like Lollia, not a pampered daughter like Diana, not even a weeping widow like Cornelia—just an unwanted wife living on her brother's charity. Of course, things would be different if she were as beautiful as Diana, or as rich as Lollia, or as grief-stricken as Cornelia—money and beauty and unhappiness bought exceptions to anything. *But if I started bedding slaves or throwing vases at the door or climbing on statues at parties, I'd be raked over the fire.*

"What a fierce face," Emperor Otho said in amusement as Marcella bowed before him. "You haven't come to chide me about your husband's post, have you? I offered him one in the city—"

"And he turned it down." Marcella straightened, looking the Emperor of Rome in the eye. "So, Caesar—do I still have a favor to claim?"

Ten

⌐○⌐

THE hardest part about having a lover was getting out of the house.
Cornelia had heard that over and over, from Roman wives of the
lesser sort. There were women who took hired litters through tortur-
ous backtracking paths to hidden rendezvous, women who dressed as
their own slaves to slip out of the house unnoticed, women who rented
rooms in brothels to meet their lovers, women who spent small fortunes annually on bribes to keep their maids quiet.

And really, how easy it was.

"I'm going to the bathhouse," Cornelia announced that afternoon.
The nearest bathhouse was a mere block away, close enough for walking on a fine day, and no one looked askance when she took only a slave
to walk at her back rather than a litter. She passed through the bathhouse doors, instructing her maid to wait; passed through the *apodyte-
rium* where half a dozen gossiping women were disrobing, and passed
directly out again through the bathhouse's rear doors. She walked
briskly for another four blocks, knocked once at a side door of a gracious house, and was admitted at once.

"My dear lady!" A man with a broad senatorial stripe on his toga rose to clasp her hands: the younger brother of that same Vitellius, who had so recently been proclaimed Emperor by his legions in Germania and was now marching south. "I am so very glad to see you again. May I introduce—"

Half a dozen men nodded around the circular library, but no one rose or offered wine, and Cornelia took a seat without removing her *palla*. This wasn't a social call, after all, and it wasn't any rendezvous with a lover either.

It was war.

"Otho has enlisted Marius Celsus as another of his generals," Cornelia said crisply. "He's also sent word to the Danube legions, but they may not be able to join his campaign in time." She gave all the details gleaned from casual questions to Marcella. Her sister had been such a font of useful information—she seemed to have a talent for putting together one bit of overheard gossip with another, until it formed a complete picture. Of course she was only interested in the complete picture for her scrolls and notes, but she was more than happy to speculate with Cornelia about everything from the size of Otho's army to the character flaws of his generals.

"Otho also means to launch a maritime expedition," another senator added. "Though we don't know where. If we could find out—" Further details. Cornelia drank in every word, nodding slowly. All her limbs felt heavy these days; marble-carved, a statue half-turned from stone to living flesh. Like the legend of Galatea, the statue brought to life by a sculptor's love. Did anyone ask Galatea if she wanted to be alive, moving marble-slow and bewildered through a world going far too fast?

Be marble. Be stone. Far easier that way.

"My brother has crossed the Alps in two columns," Vitellius's brother added. "Moving fast—"

"Otho will move fast too," Cornelia cut in. "He means to catch Vitellius north of Placentia."

"You're sure?"

"I had it from my cousin Cornelia Tertia, who married Otho's brother."

"Thank you, Lady Cornelia. Anything else you hear—"

A terse nod. She heard a great deal, and now she knew to keep her ears open. No more grief, no more attempts to join Piso in the underworld. She'd found a far better way to help him—found it the night of Otho's banquet after the games, when Marcella had chattered on about the army's plans to march north. Information. Information about Otho's troops, about the orders he gave to his generals, about departure dates and supply lists and road conditions . . .

Cornelia had known Vitellius's brother for years; he'd been a mild acquaintance of Piso's and an occasional guest at her table. "Are you communicating with your brother?" she'd asked him baldly, stalking into his airy hall.

Caution had bloomed in his eyes. "Of course not, my dear Lady Cornelia. I am a loyal supporter of Emperor Otho—"

"If you're not, then I have information for you."

"Ah . . ." And of course he *was* in communication with his brother, along with half a dozen notable men in Rome who reckoned their fortunes better with an Emperor Vitellius than with an Emperor Otho.

And a few like Cornelia, who just wanted Otho's head in a jar.

A few more swift words traded back and forth, and they were done. They never met at the same house twice, and never lingered. Vitellius's brother pressed every hand as his illicit guests dispersed. "Lady Cornelia, your contributions have been invaluable—that bit of news about the marching routes alone!" A squeeze of her fingers. "My brother will see your husband avenged, and you rewarded. He'll make you a splendid marriage with one of his own supporters—"

"I don't want another husband." She jerked her hand away. "I want Otho dead."

Cornelia made her way back to the bathhouse, disrobing hastily and ducking into the *caldarium*. The air was hot and steamy, and a dozen women lay on marble slabs in the sweating heat, talking languidly of disobedient children and thieving slaves while being pummeled by bathhouse attendants. Cornelia stayed long enough to bring a sweat to her face before ducking out again, wetting her hair hastily in the *natatio* pool. She returned home in time for dinner, hair damp, face flushed from steam, and not even the sharp-eyed Tullia gave her a second look.

I could be bedding half of Rome, Cornelia thought, moving statue-slow through dinner, *and my family would be the last to know. Fools.*

She kept her ears pricked, and when Marcella mentioned going to the Campus Martius the following afternoon, Cornelia steeled herself and volunteered to go too. She wouldn't gather any information hiding in her bedchamber, after all.

"I'm glad to see you getting out again." Gaius patted her hand. Only Marcella looked curious at the sudden eagerness.

"You'll need someone to accompany you properly." Cornelia summoned a tart note to her voice with an effort. "With your husband in town again you owe it to him not to traipse about unescorted like an actress."

"So nice to see you caring about the proprieties," Tullia said. "Perhaps you can talk your sister out of this mad idea of accompanying the army north!"

That news had burst on the family like a storm: Marcella had somehow talked the Emperor into letting her accompany the army when they marched to meet Vitellius. "Lucius is livid," Marcella had chuckled in Cornelia's ear. "But what can he do? I told Otho I'd write a glowing account of his glorious victory, and he was amused enough to order me along, no matter how much Lucius sputters."

The family was in an uproar, but they couldn't do anything either. Cornelia felt certain her sister had planned it that way.

"Don't even try to talk me out of going," Marcella warned as they strolled along the edge of the Campus Martius.

"I wouldn't dream of it." Cornelia smiled and put an arm through her sister's as they used to walk in the old days. Now that Marcella was going with the army, she was ravenous to know everything about it—she had become Cornelia's best source. Lollia should have been better, being married to the Emperor's brother, but Lollia had a head like a sieve. The only information she retained was what senator was hosting the next banquet, and what praetor's wife had a lover behind her husband's back. Movements of armies and details of supply wagons passed through her mind like water. But Marcella remembered *everything.*

She chattered on about the army, the difficulties Otho was having in setting up supplies, the insistence of so many of his entourage on bringing their barbers and their servants and their silver plate with them. Cornelia asked leading questions, stored away answers. The Campus Martius was a bustle of movement around them: clusters of swaggering Praetorians, young tribunes dashing their little low-slung chariots back and forth, giggling girls making eyes at the soldiers. It was a gray overcast day with a brisk wind flapping through and setting everyone's cloaks alight on the air, but nothing could damp the giddy sense of a party.

"Lady Cornelia!" A braying voice came behind them, and Cornelia turned. A man leaned out of a lavish gold-trimmed litter with aqua silk curtains, waving a beringed hand. Proculus, the new Praetorian Prefect—and now one of Otho's generals.

Her smile came effortlessly this time. "Prefect!" Bestowing a warm hand. "Congratulations upon your new rank."

"Proculus, Lady Cornelia, make it Proculus. And thank you. Wine?"

Cornelia accepted a cup. Marcella paused, brows raised, but another acquaintance called to her and Cornelia waved her on. Prefect Proculus splashed a cup for himself, spattering the slave holding the flagon. "Been a long while since I've seen *you* at the Campus Martius, Lady Cornelia."

"With the army to leave so soon, everyone is here." She sipped her wine. "Tell me, when *do* you leave?"

"Oh, two days. Three days." Wine dribbled down his chin as he drank. "Been pushed back twice, you know. Fortuna knows if we'll be ready in time. The legions are dragging their heels up north, and I can't see rushing to meet them if they're going to be late, eh?"

"Late?" Another smile. "How late?"

"Late enough. Come sit." He patted the litter cushions beside him. Cornelia settled herself, feeling as if she were moving through deep water.

"Surely you Praetorians can handle Vitellius on your own?" She tried for Lollia's artlessness.

"Of course we can!" he said indignantly. "That fat drunk—feasts four times daily, you know; it's a wonder he hasn't burst from eating by now. My lads will whip him any day of the week—"

Your lads killed my husband. Of course this fool was too drunk to remember that.

"Always admired you, y'know." He squinted at her with a lazy smile. "Give me that pretty hand of yours. Let's see if you taste as good as you smell—"

Cornelia managed another smile, allowing him to draw her farther into the litter. "What about the Emperor's maritime forces?" she murmured. "Shouldn't that make a difference to your fight?"

"Of course it will." He nibbled the inside of her wrist, twitching the litter curtains shut. "The Emperor wants us to attack Narbonensis."

"Narbonensis?" Cornelia managed not to jerk away as Proculus nibbled his way up her arm to her neck. The light filtered dim and aqueous through the blue silk curtains of the litter. *Perhaps I really am underwater.* "Really? When?"

"Jove knows—give us a kiss, will you?"

Cornelia turned her face away just enough so his lips latched onto her throat instead of her mouth. "Why Narbonensis?" Stroking the back of his neck.

"To stir up a ruckus in Gaul, of course. Delay Vitellius's army when they start marching south—slide down a bit, will you?"

She made herself lie still, letting him suck on her neck a while and breathe wine fumes in her ear. She slid away with a little laugh when he began fumbling at her breasts. "Not here—my sister will be looking for me."

"You'll be at the theatre tonight, then? Perhaps meet me after in the Gardens of Asiaticus?" Proculus flopped on his back, capturing her hand and sliding it up his leg under his tunic. "You wouldn't send a man off to die without a proper good-bye."

"We'll see." Cornelia gave him as promising a smile as she could manage over her crawling throat, pulling her hand away from his thigh before it could touch—anything. *Marble. Be marble.* "A widow in my position, you understand . . ."

"Of course, of course. Centurion!" Proculus reached outside the silk curtains, snapping his fingers. "See this lady safely home."

The aqua curtains snapped open. Cornelia met the chestnut eyes of Centurion Drusus Densus for an instant, and looked away again.

"Prefect." He saluted rigidly. Proculus waved off the salute, already calling in a slurred voice for more wine. Drusus Densus extended a hand, helping Cornelia out of the litter, and the little knot of nausea resurfaced in her throat.

"Marcella!" she called, but Marcella was busy watching a company of Praetorians wheel through their parade drills. No doubt taking notes for the next volume of her wretched history. "Marcella, I want to go home."

"Go on," she called absently, the wind rippling her light brown hair. "I'll be back soon."

Cornelia turned an aloof smile on Densus. As aloof as she could manage, anyway. "No need to accompany me, Centurion."

"I have orders from my Prefect, Lady. And the streets are full of soldiers. It wouldn't be safe." He hailed for a hired litter, but the Campus Martius was already jammed with litters. "It will be faster to walk."

"As you wish."

"You should—" He fixed his gaze over her head, gesturing wordlessly at her shoulder. Cornelia looked down to see the clasp of her black dress pulled askew, a red mark from the Prefect's leechlike mouth on her shoulder. She pulled up her black-woven *palla*, breasts still tingling unpleasantly from the Prefect's pawing. *It's worth it*, she reminded herself. *Any information that will help bring down Otho is worth it.*

Densus cleared a path through the Campus Martius to the quieter street beyond. It had rained again that morning, and muddy puddles pooled everywhere. Cornelia hoped he would walk behind her, but he fell in at her side, the wind tugging at his red cloak.

"Looks like more rain." Densus looked up at the sky as they crossed into the Forum Romanum. The thunderheads were piling in the west, gray as charcoal. "Maybe the floods aren't done yet."

"Centurion," Cornelia said abruptly. "I owe you an apology."

His profile was rigid. "Your dealings with Prefect Proculus are none of my concern, Lady."

"No, they are not!" She came to a halt before the pillars of the Basilica Aemilia. "How dare you? That is *not* what I meant."

"Lady, I—"

A cart came rattling past, the driver swearing at his mules. The wheels sent out a splash of mud, and they both leaped back. Densus let out a few soldier oaths before remembering himself. "I'm sorry, Lady."

"It's nothing." She brushed a spatter of mud off her sleeve.

They continued through the Forum Romanum, past the Basilica Aemilia. A pair of prostitutes in saffron wigs and dark robes called giggling to Densus, but he glared them into silence.

"I owe you an apology for the way I spoke to you when I visited your sickbed." Cornelia kept her eyes trained on the street ahead. "I should not have screamed like that. And I shouldn't have ignored you at Otho's banquet after the games, when you tried to address me. It was very wrong."

"I failed to protect your husband."

"That was not your fault." Cornelia felt her cheeks heat, remembering how she'd screamed at him in his sickroom. She'd been *shrill*, shrill and graceless as any fishwife. In a way it was worse than having him see her get pawed by that drunken lout of a prefect. She had an excuse for that, even if Drusus Densus didn't know it. But there was no excuse at all for a member of the Cornelii to behave like a pleb.

"You have no need to apologize, Lady."

"Then we won't speak of it again."

They walked in silence. Densus offered his hand as help across a wide gutter. Cornelia dropped it as soon as she could. The sight of his red cloak and crested Praetorian helmet sickened her. She still couldn't see a Praetorian without a pang of nausea rising in her throat.

That's not his fault either.

The words meant nothing. She might have owed him the apology, but she couldn't mean it.

"You've recovered from your wounds?" She kept her voice cordial, formal.

"Yes, Lady."

"I am glad the Emperor rewarded your faithfulness." She avoided his helping hand at her elbow as they crossed an overflowing gutter.

"I wish he hadn't."

"Centurion?"

"The Praetorian Guard isn't much these days," he said shortly. "You know what my duties are, Lady? Mostly I fetch women for Prefect Proculus."

Cornelia flushed. They had turned onto the lower slope of the Palatine Hill—the house was only a few short blocks away—

"He's a bad one," said Densus. "Hope you know that."

Cornelia walked faster. A few short blocks were not short enough. "I'll thank you not to—"

"I'll say it plain, Lady." He swung around, jaw set. "Maybe you're looking to protect your family. Maybe you're needing another husband. Maybe you're lonely. Not my business."

"It is *not*—" Cornelia started furiously, but Densus's voice had a parade-ground crack that overran hers.

"Prefect Proculus has a new woman every night, common whores and patrician ladies alike—"

Cornelia clamped her teeth on the nausea in her throat, feeling those rubbery lips sucking on her neck.

"He doesn't remember their *names* in the morning, Lady, never mind whatever he's promised them," Densus went on doggedly. "And he never wants the same one twice, no matter how much they beg. He just laughs and says they're persistent bitches, if you'll pardon me, and calls for another—"

No. Cornelia felt the nausea rising like a tide. *No. Be marble.*

"So whatever you're looking for, safety or company or status, find a better man than that. I'd tell my own sister the same thing, and I got to know Senator Piso well enough so I reckon he'd want me telling you too—"

Hearing that name did it—her husband's name in her ears, with another man's marks on her neck. Cornelia turned and vomited into the gutter, throwing up over and over, clawing feverishly at her neck. She staggered, and Densus's hand touched her shoulder.

"Lady—"

"No! Stop telling me you're *sorry!*" Cornelia wrenched away from his hand, dragging a hand across her mouth. She felt foul and soiled, shaking and useless. Only pieces of marble left, and she clutched after them. *Don't judge me*, she thought disjointedly toward Piso. *Don't judge me, I do it for you*—but she wouldn't say that to this common soldier. *You don't speak for my husband, Densus.*

"I can find my own way from here." Cornelia drew herself up, meeting the steady chestnut eyes level with her own. "Good afternoon, Centurion."

She turned and toiled up the paved slope, past a mansion with vulgar blue marble columns, toward the ornate house of the Cornelii, which she'd left as a bride and reentered as a widow. *I do this for you, Piso.* She dragged in deep breaths of cold air as the heaviness returned to her limbs. Galatea in reverse, trembling flesh willing itself back into cold marble.

She turned just once at the gate of the Cornelii house as the slaves opened the door, seeing Densus back at the foot of the slope, waiting to make sure she got home safely. His concern meant nothing, nothing at all.

Cornelia looked down at her stained dress and back up at the steward. "An accident with the gutters," she told him. "Please inform Lady Tullia I am going to the bathhouse at once."

Vitellius's brother would want to hear the latest news that she had gotten from the Prefect.

Y OU'RE late," Llyn ap Caradoc greeted Diana.

"You said midday." She blinked.

"Midday yesterday."

"It was raining yesterday."

"Chariots run in the rain."

"Yes. Sorry."

She made the journey every day, learning to bless the rain that had once more descended on Rome. With the skies opening again, though much more gently than before, her father shut himself up in his workroom all day with chisels and blocks of marble, and everyone else was far too busy to track Diana's comings and goings. The Emperor and his army were gone, and Marcella with them; Tullia obsessed endlessly about the mud on her floors; Cornelia shut herself up writing letters all day. Diana was free.

She bribed one of her father's slaves to take her every afternoon to the horse farm just outside the city, dashing up the muddy slope on foot so she arrived warm and breathless and soaked. She grinned as she came striding into the stables, slicking her wet hair back from her face with both hands, and Llyn would be waiting to toss her four bridles.

He taught her to drive with a quartet of placid mismatched geldings. "They're slow," Diana objected the first time she saw them.

"You'll graduate up to something faster." Llyn tossed her a battered leather helmet. "If you're any good." It took just one short afternoon before he dropped the courteous "Lady." Cornelia would have been appalled, but Diana didn't mind it. Polite titles weren't necessary with Llyn—his oblique shell already kept everyone at a distance.

"I want to learn how to drive a chariot," she'd told him frankly before he slipped out of the Emperor's box at the games. "Will you teach me?"

"Why do you want to learn?" he'd asked, looking down at her. "You can't race."

"No." Diana had corrected him. "I *won't* race, because women aren't allowed to. But that doesn't mean I *can't*. I'll know I can do it, even if no one else does." She folded her arms across her breasts, peering up at him determinedly. "Look, I'll sleep with you if you'll teach me."

"No need to go that far," he said mildly. "Come tomorrow." She didn't know why he agreed, and she didn't care. She was learning to drive at last, like a proper charioteer.

He taught her how to keep her balance in the low-slung chariot, how to strap the heavy reins about her waist, how to brace her weight against the pull of the horses. She learned how much strength it took to guide a team around a hairpin turn at all, much less keep them close to the *spina*, and was mortified when she careened off the track in a shower of mud on her first try.

"Again," called Llyn. He paced the mud beside the track with his hands clasped behind him, calling instructions as the rain dripped off the ends of his hair and the black dog sat at his feet. He looked exactly the same standing in a pool of mud as he looked standing in the Emperor's box under golden sunlight: calm, contained, aloof. Diana decided she'd be alarmed if his expression ever changed.

"Racing's dangerous," he warned her the first time she crashed a turn, as he impersonally bandaged her scraped arms. "You break your neck, I'll not make excuses to your family."

"Dump my body at the Blues stable," Diana suggested absently, inspecting a bloody scrape on her knee. "With any luck, we could pin a murder on them."

Her elbows and knees turned into patches of scabs, her thighs were chafed red from being crushed against the front of the chariot, and she had a permanent belt of black bruises about her waist from the knotted reins. She stepped down from her chariot at the end of those long afternoons hardly able to stand, her arms trembling under the weight of the harness when she unhitched the geldings and staggered off home.

"Oh, my beauties, I'm getting good," she whispered when she visited her Anemoi at the Reds faction stables. The four stallions pushed their red noses eagerly into her hands, knowing her well by now. "I wish I could drive you in a real race." She dreamed of it sometimes, dreamed of wearing a red tunic embroidered in gold flames about the neck as she stood in a chariot crowned by a fire god's painted head, sending her four red winds streaking ahead to victory. Getting the victory palm, that simple branch that weighed nothing in the hand, but meant everything.

Of course she knew she'd never drive the Anemoi, or have a victory palm. Young men of the patrician class sometimes raced in the circuses, if their families didn't shunt them into the legions or the Senate or anything more exalted—but never a woman, not of any class.

But at least she *could* drive.

"Surely I can handle a faster team by now," she cajoled Llyn.

"You're too small to hold a faster team."

"But I'm strong now. Feel!" She took his hand between hers and squeezed with all her might. Even through the leather gloves, her hands had grown hard as horn. As hard as Llyn's.

"I'll think about it," Llyn allowed with a faint smile. Diana took it with a grain of hope as she led the geldings back to the barn. She put them away one by one and glanced into the next stall. "Pomona's lying down."

"Pomona?" Llyn called from the end of the barn where he was hanging up the harness.

"Just because you don't name your horses doesn't mean I can't. The bay mare with the white face—is she ready to foal already?"

He came in his silent long-legged stride, unlatching the stall and squatting down by the pregnant mare. She flicked her ears at him as he ran a hand over the swollen belly. "Looks like it."

Diana glanced at the sky outside, already darkening toward dusk. She usually went home after her training, but she came to the stall door and folded her arms along the top. "Can I help?"

"Catch her head. She keeps trying to get up."

Diana came into the stall and knelt in the straw, taking hold of the mare's nose. "Sshh," she soothed as Llyn stripped off his tunic and arm rings and felt expertly inside the mare.

"Feels like the foal's turned wrong," he said. "She's always had trouble foaling. Hold her while I straighten things out in here."

"Yes, sir." Diana gave a little salute, and he smiled at her. She settled by the mare, murmuring wordlessly.

"Ah . . ." Another moment of patient fishing. "That should do it. Let's let her push."

He cleaned his arm in a bucket of water and pulled his tunic back over his head. He was marked all over with old scars—a slash across the left arm, a crater on one shoulder, a healed spear thrust marking his brown ribs. Strange to remember he had spent his youth killing Romans and fighting battles as his father's right arm. *I'm glad he got captured—otherwise I'd never have the Anemoi or learn to drive*, Diana reflected. *Better not tell him that, though.*

They waited in comfortable silence, Diana chewing a straw, Llyn with his arms folded across his chest. "You shouldn't be here at night." He glanced at the darkening sky outside the barn door. "Your family wouldn't like it. My father was rumored to eat young maidens for dinner once the sun went down, and now that he's gone I've probably inherited the reputation."

"I'm not worried," she smiled. "How long will it take her to push that foal out?"

"Not long." Llyn ran a hard hand over the mare's nose, outstretched by his leg on the straw. "Maybe you're not worried about your family, but I'd rather not have my house and horses confiscated by an outraged father who claims I ravaged his daughter before feeding her to a Druid."

"My father doesn't get outraged about anything except broken chisels," Diana said. "Anyway, I haven't got any virtue left to ravage."

"Some charioteer, I suppose." He shook his head. "You Roman ladies. Not a real warrior in your whole city, so you fall all over any substitute you can find."

"Give me a little credit, O great leader of rebels," Diana snorted. "It wasn't any charioteer, just some sweaty Praetorian of Otho's. Stank like a brewery and didn't last long enough to boil an egg."

"Ah." A slight pause. "I trust your family had him thrown to the lions?"

"Oh, my family doesn't know. It wasn't their business." She'd gone looking for Piso's head after the Othonian uprising, and a Praetorian guard had somehow ended up with it. She'd had to buy it off him, and he hadn't wanted money. "It was a matter of honor, sort of," Diana temporized, seeing Llyn's glance. She didn't know why she was telling him when no one else in the family knew, but she went on. "My decision. So it didn't concern my family."

They'd only fuss, and why should they? Piso's shade was laid to rest, and Cornelia had her peace of mind back. Well worth it all around. "Do Druids really eat people?" Diana asked.

"With mistletoe sprigs. Look—it's happening."

The foal came slithering into the world, miles of leg and sticky tufts of mane. "That's a fine little colt you've got," Diana said as Llyn rubbed him dry with a wisp of hay. "A chestnut, too. I'll be wanting him for the Reds soon."

"Let him dry off first."

The little colt looked around with wide eyes as his mother nosed him. "This might even be better than the races," Diana said, smiling.

"It's the part I like best." Llyn squatted back on his heels. The little colt struggled, trying to get his legs under him, and the mare nudged him encouragingly. In half an hour he was up, wobbly but standing, and his fluffy coat was drying. "Definitely a chestnut," said Diana.

Llyn rose. "Better leave him to his mother."

They wandered outside, the black dog tagging behind. It was full dark now, and a fine warm night. The stars were finally free of rain clouds, and Llyn tilted his head up to stare at them. Diana wondered if they looked any different from the stars he grew up with.

She touched his arm. "Tomorrow?"

"Tomorrow."

Her father didn't notice how late she was to dinner, but then he never did. Diana supposed he was an odd sort of father, but she reckoned herself for a strange daughter. They were really more like sire and filly than father and daughter—blood ties and a certain fondness, but certainly they would neither have dreamed of interfering in each others' lives. Strange or not, it suited them both.

"There's been a battle," her father said vaguely, his pale hair gray with stone dust after a day in his studio. "Somewhere around Bedriacum, they're saying."

"Really?" Diana said, wondering without much interest where Bedriacum was, and skipped upstairs to count her bruises. She looked in her polished mirror and didn't see the silken Cornelia Quarta of the Cornelii, courted by half of Rome. She saw a girl in an old woolen tunic hacked off at the knee, hair bundled into a careless horse tail down her back, freckles across her nose and bruises up and down her arms. A girl who longed not for a husband but for the grudging praise of a rebel chief turned tamer of horses. She looked in the mirror, and she saw a charioteer.

Eleven

FORTY thousand dead.

However many times Marcella began her account of the battle of Bedriacum, it started with those words. *Forty thousand dead.* Later she learned that the number was nowhere near so high—perhaps ten thousand, but not forty. No one knew for sure. But forty thousand was the number that resounded in her mind, the number that the gasping messenger brought to Emperor Otho.

Forty thousand dead.

She sat quiet in a storm of shouting voices and shrill laughter, reviewing her notes.

Vitellius was not present with his army, still some distance behind with reinforcements. His commanders launched a daybreak attack upon Placentia, where Emperor Otho's commander was camped with three cohorts of Praetorian Guards. The Praetorians fought like madmen and the attack was repulsed.

Like madmen—florid words, not fit for a cool and sober history. But Marcella had seen the Praetorians come like gods of war from the field to report to their Emperor in Bedriacum some miles away. A trio of officers had made the report, giddy and triumphant. One of them was Centurion Drusus Densus.

"The Vitellians are running, Caesar," the chief centurion had crowed. "We sent them off with their tails between their legs—"

"Ha!" Otho slapped the arm of his chair in delight. He had not traveled light on this campaign; in a rude soldier's tent he sat ensconced in his own gilded chair from the Domus Aurea, a silver flagon of his favorite wine to hand, his own barber to shave him twice a day, and his own musicians to provide entertainment. The musicians were silent, fingers twitching on their lyre strings, eager as the rest of Otho's considerable entourage to hear the rest of the Praetorian report. Marcella stood at the back with the few other women who had wheedled their husbands or lovers into taking them along, craning her neck for a better view.

"Our reports say Fabius Valens is some days out, Caesar," Densus said. A slash on one forearm was oozing blood down over his fingers, but he didn't seem to notice it. "He and Caecina Alienus have quarreled in the past—they'll not get along when they join forces."

"Confusion to the enemy, then!" Otho raised his goblet and a storm of shouts and laughter went up—

Emperor Otho removed himself to Brixellum, some miles distant, for sake of safety. He took a substantial reserve force and left several observers to act as messengers and bring him constant news of the battle.

One of the observers was Lucius Aelius Lamia, who had barely spoken to Marcella since they'd left Rome. "It isn't fitting for a woman to witness a battle," he sputtered when she announced her intention of staying at his side to observe the fight.

"I'm sorry," Marcella said blandly. "Did I give you the impression I was asking permission?"

He glared at her in open loathing. "You're making a fool out of me!"

Marcella smiled. "I think you do that all on your own, Lucius."

"You willful bitch—I'll divorce you, see if I don't—"

"Go ahead." Marcella wandered away. "In the meantime, I'll be watching the battle."

Emperor Otho just seemed amused when he heard that. "How valiant," he laughed. "And how fortunate you were born to a Roman clan, Marcella my dear. If you'd been born a Pict, you'd be painting yourself blue and charging into battle with an ax."

"No, Caesar." Marcella bowed. "I'm only the watcher."

"Well, write up my stunning victory in good style, and be sure to give me a copy." He patted her hand. "I'd like to read it." And although Marcella knew he'd forget all about her history as soon as he turned away, his touch was so sincere and his smile so warm that she flushed with pleasure. He went off in great splendor to Brixellum, surrounded by Praetorians, laughing and throwing dice with all the handsome young courtiers who tried so hard to look just like him. Marcella heard later that he went to a play that night as his troops prepared for battle a few miles away, and the whole town marveled at his composure. *I believe that.* He'd have lounged in the tiered seats with his gaudy friends, perfumed and braceleted and perfectly at ease, throwing coins to the actors in their comedy masks.

Otho's generals entered the battle with two legions, another standing in reserve. In the center position was the Praetorian Guard.

She got the names of the legions later, when she had time to put her facts together. At the time it was only a mass of armored men and spear points. The legionaries all looked alike from a distance, but one cohort passed quite close below the hillock where Lucius and the other observers were stationed, and suddenly the armored ants became men again. Fair-skinned Gauls with their skins peeling in the sun, swarthy Spaniards, copper-skinned Egyptians, darker Nubians. Men from all over the Empire, once distinct, now hammered into a fearsome and brutal anonymity.

After some confusion, the Praetorians in the center engaged against the Vitellian legions. No javelins were thrown; only shield against shield.

Marcella knew battle was all confusion on the ground, but she'd thought it would be clearer observed from above. Lucius and the other observers—herself among them, despite Lucius's rage and the disdainful glances of the others—were stationed on a hillock well back from the fray. For a while Marcella could follow the agonizingly slow motion as the two masses of men heaved themselves up the causeway like whales giving birth and marched stolidly into each other. But then the dust from so many marching feet kicked up into the warm spring morning, and all she could see was a dust cloud out of which came fearsome screams. She hadn't known a battle would be so loud. Iron shield bosses grinding together, men grunting as they shoved back and forth in furious swaying lines, swords clashing over the top of the shields, and always the shrieks of wounded men. They'd fall back clutching themselves, bleeding fearsomely, turned from armored ants back to men again, and the next disciplined rank would step forward into the gap, blank-eyed and eager—

On the left flank, the Othonian legion plowed into the Vitellian line and captured their eagle. The Vitellians regrouped and advanced again, surrounding the legionaries on broken ground and slowly cutting them down. The Othonian generals fled, while the Vitellians continued to feed in reinforcements. The central block of the Praetorian Guard was left standing alone.

All pieced together later, of course—from the hillock Marcella could see nothing. That evening she'd found a legionary, one of the few to escape the horror of the right flank's massacre. "A bloody mess," he said, blank eyes fixed somewhere over her head, not knowing or caring who or what she was. "Half of us had friends on their side—we kept lowering our swords and realizing that the one we're fighting was one we used to get drinks with at the Blue Mermaid tavern two months ago. And we'd smile at each other and look sheepish-like, and then we'd have at it again till one of us was dead. A bloody cock-up, Lady, I'll tell you that."

The Praetorians, exposed on both sides, finally broke ranks and fled.

What else could they do? All over the field men fell out of their battle lines and fled, slipping in pools of blood and clambering over fallen bodies. "We go," Lucius hissed, his hand clamped on Marcella's arm. "We're going, it's a rout, have you seen enough for one day, you bloodthirsty bitch?" They clambered into a chariot left waiting and the driver whipped up the horses in a panic toward the road back to Brixellum. Fleeing legionaries crowded all around, dusty, bloody, exhausted. Several put up their hands and cried to be taken along. One

massive aquilifer planted himself screaming in the road, still clutching his ragged standard and hailing them with a clenched fist. Only
it wasn't a fist, it was a ragged stump where some Vitellian had struck
off his hand, and Marcella only saw it for an instant before the horses
trampled him under.

*The Vitellians had no reason to offer quarter to men who could not pay
ransom, so thousands of survivors were slaughtered. Others fled to Brixellum,
joining Otho's reserve force there and hoping for a chance at another battle. The
rest formally surrendered to Vitellius the following morning, among them the
Emperor's brother.*

Lollia's husband, who had cracked his knuckles busily and counseled Otho to launch an immediate attack without waiting for the rest
of the legions to arrive. He'd been allowed to live, for the time being.
Marcella had a moment to reflect that whether he lived or died, Lollia
would soon have a different husband. Her fifth, Fortuna help her, and
she only nineteen.

*A substantial force still remained at Brixellum, bolstered by survivors
from the battle. Several of Emperor Otho's advisers counseled leading a second
attack against the Vitellians.*

Lucius and Marcella were driven at breakneck pace from the bat-
tleground to Brixellum, soon leaving the limping legionaries behind.
They were swept through a vortex of shouting men, stamping horses,
and prowling guards and whisked into Otho's tent. One look at his
taut face told Marcella they were not the first with news of the defeat,
but Lucius bowed and gave his report.

"Thank you, Lucius Aelius Lamia," Otho said, and beckoned a
slave for wine. His hand never shook on the goblet; there was even a
faint smile on his face, but the dark eyes were turned inward like the
blank gaze of a statue. Hours of waiting, then—Marcella knew she
should not have been there, huddled in her corner, but no one thought
to evict her. She saw Centurion Drusus Densus limp in, holding a
wad of rags to a slash on the side of his neck. A final courier fell on
his knees, announcing that forty thousand dead littered the field, and
a tumult of shouting erupted, whirling around the Emperor in his
gilded chair.

Emperor Otho heard all advice calmly before making his decision. Afterward—

There Marcella's account broke off.

D ON'T grieve, friends." Otho spread his hands. "I've made my decision."

They stared at him, dumbstruck: courtiers, generals, messengers, Praetorians, slaves. "Caesar," someone said, but Otho cut him off with one of his perfect careless gestures.

"To expose men of your spirit and courage to further danger I think too high a price to pay for my life," he said. "Vitellius began this civil war by forcing us to fight for the throne. I will end it, by ensuring that we fight no more than once. Let this be how posterity judges me: Others may have reigned longer, but none will relinquish his power so bravely."

His voice rolled around the common soldier's tent as if it were the marble walls of the Senate, and he threw back his head with a brilliant smile. Perfectly groomed, perfectly poised, perfectly in control. A thought drifted through Marcella's head: *How long has he been planning this speech?*

"Caesar," someone said again with half a sob, "we can still fight!"

But Otho raised a hand. "You cannot expect me to allow the flower of Rome's youth, so many splendid legions, to shed their blood a second time. Let me carry away with me the thought that you were ready to die for me, but survive you must." He clapped his hands. "No more delay! I must not endanger your safety, nor you impede my decision. To dwell on one's last moments is a coward's way. The ultimate proof of my determination is that I make no complaints. To find fault with gods or men is the behavior of one who would prefer to go on living."

As one, the men in that room sank to their knees. Marcella was among them. She saw men weeping and couldn't weep herself, but she could feel . . . awe. An emperor was as skilled a performer as any actor; he had to be—and she had just seen a man give the performance of his life.

Nor was it over. He walked among them then, raising every man to his feet, finding a few words for each. He told a weeping Praetor Paetus that he should not gamble so much at dice; he commended Centurion Drusus Densus for his bravery in trying to hold the center line once the flanks collapsed; he joked with Senator Urbinus that now his gambling debts would never have to be paid. One of his commanders tried to argue with him, swearing they could wreak vengeance on Vitellius, but Otho gave a placid smile and told him to offer Vitellius all allegiance. "He is your master now, and Fortuna grant he will be forgiving."

"Fortuna grant," Marcella echoed.

Otho gave Lucius Lamia the same advice, telling him to find a discreet escape back to Rome and offer his loyalty when the time came— and then he came to Marcella. "My dear girl, it appears I will never read that history of yours." He raised her up. "Do me a favor, and write it the way it should have happened? Give me a resounding victory over that tub of lard, and a glorious triumphal procession back to Rome." He leaned in to kiss the corner of her mouth, adding in a whisper, "And write that I dragged you off behind the bushes at least once!"

Her throat thickened then. She nodded, wordless. A tiny pinpoint of panic danced in Otho's eyes, but the hands that clasped hers were steady.

"Ah." Making the circle of the tent, Otho paused at last before the door flap to his bedchamber. A slave stood there with a silver tray, sniffing back tears. On the tray lay two daggers. "This one, I think—" Choosing. "It has a better edge. Good night, everyone."

Marcella didn't see him die.

He slept that night, she knew that much. Several of his friends huddled all night by the door flap, waiting to be called, but he never called them. In the steel-gray dawn came a single cry. The guards rushed into the chamber, but Otho was already dead, a blade in his heart. He died alone.

He must have wanted it that way, Marcella thought. Perhaps he realized the furor that would surround his body afterward: the Praetorians carrying him to a flaming bier so the Vitellians could not despoil his corpse; the weeping as several of his closest friends stabbed themselves rather than serve a new Emperor; the uneasy grumbles from the soldiers; the panic of the remaining courtiers as they struggled to find passage back to Rome. From coronation to funeral, an emperor's life was a circus.

But even an emperor had to die alone.

WHEN she looked back, Marcella could never remember the details of her journey back to Rome. Lucius stayed, anxious to proclaim his undying loyalty to Vitellius once the new Emperor arrived, so she found a cart or a wagon or something with wheels and paid for a place. Jolting roads, silent companions. Just flashes, when she tried to remember it. A journey of a week's duration—two weeks?—and then she was back in the city. She looked about vaguely for a hired litter, something to take her home, but a slave in sumptuous livery recognized her at the city gate and whisked her back to the house in comfort.

"Juno's mercy, you're safe!" Cornelia enveloped her in a violent hug as she alighted on the doorstep. Half the family was arrayed there, but her sister and cousins were at the forefront and Marcella fell into their comforting arms, wondering how she could ever have thought them exasperating. "We had slaves watching every gate in the city for you, ever since we heard the news—"

"You're all right." Lollia was beaming. "I wore down my knees at every temple in Rome—"

"Now you're the crazy one in the family instead of me." Diana flung an oddly bruised arm about Marcella's waist. "Just do what I do, and smile whenever they lecture you. It drives them all mad."

"Good to have you home," Gaius said, smiling.

"Gaius, you aren't condoning this, are you?" Tullia sniffed. "I hope you see the folly of your adventuring, Marcella. You could have been killed."

"I'm sure you're sorry I wasn't," said Marcella. "Then you could redo my room in that sickly pink you've pasted all over the rest of the house."

"She's very tired, dear," Gaius whispered quickly in his wife's ear. "Maybe crazed."

There was a family dinner to celebrate Marcella's return. Cornelia shared her couch, deflecting the family's questions for her while Marcella ate, and Marcella could have cried in gratitude. She gave her sister's hand a fierce squeeze under the cushions, and Cornelia squeezed back.

"So Salvius is alive?" Lollia asked. "I'm glad. He's harmless enough, despite his knuckle cracking. Though this means another divorce for sure." She sighed. "Grandfather is already looking for a Vitellian husband for me."

"You know Vitellius is a Blues fan?" Diana wrinkled her nose. "Well, at least it means more races . . ."

"I'm sorry." Marcella put down her goblet. "But I need to get outside—I need to walk. Can you cover for me?"

"Of course," Cornelia said at once, and headed Tullia off with a complaint about the oysters. Lollia distracted Gaius by letting her dress fall off her shoulders, and Diana tossed Marcella her own cloak.

Marcella's hands were shaking when she climbed into the litter, and despite the fine breeze in the spring twilight she closed the curtains. The slanting sun made rosy shadows through the pink silk, and she lay back on the cushions with the heels of her hands pressed to her eyes as the bearers rose beneath her. "The gardens," Marcella said through her hands, "take me to the nearest gardens." It was a long time before the tremors went away, before she lowered her hands from her face.

When she did, she was smiling.

The bearers stopped, and she climbed out of the litter. A nameless little green patch at the top of the Quirinal Hill; not much of a garden. Just a grassy hillock with a few trees and a stone bench or two, where the pleb boys liked to take their sweethearts on fine evenings— but it did boast a high, wide view of Rome, and Marcella had it all to herself as she strode up the slope on legs still faintly shaky and looked out over the city. Dusk now, the sun falling orange-pink behind purple bands of clouds, the sky on the other side a cool darkening blue.

Torches and lamps lighting the streets below, a sprawling forest of lights. Rome. She'd seen four emperors within the past year—Nero, Galba, Otho, and now Vitellius. Four emperors . . .

Three of them, thought Marcella, *done away by me.*

Partially, anyway.

Nero really had been an accident. "The world would lose a great artist in you, Caesar," Marcella had told him at that private banquet, just trying to soothe his frantic nerves. And instead he'd sobbed into her lap and asked her how he could possibly escape it all, and she'd said he would fall on his sword before the Senate could execute him. All she had wanted was to get out of there and go home . . . but Nero did fall on his sword a week later. He'd even stolen Marcella's words about the death of an artist. Nero never could write a decent line for himself.

Galba . . . well, one could say he was an accident too. Almost. Piso had been declared heir, Marcella jibed at Otho about how he might be declared Emperor yet if the omens weren't favorable, and he had seized the idea, bribing a priest to interpret the omens badly and using the discontent of the soldiers to his own ends. Her little joke hadn't really been a joke—even at the time Marcella had wondered if Otho might take the hint. But she never dreamed he'd go as far as he did. She certainly hadn't wanted Piso dead; hadn't wanted to end up dead herself on the steps of the Temple of Vesta along with her sister and cousins, as had so nearly happened. *That really did get a bit out of hand.*

Otho. That had been more of an experiment. Poor Cornelia was so blind with rage about Piso's death, so burning with hatred for anything Othonian. Marcella couldn't resist dropping her sister a few tidbits of information, wondering what she'd do with them. She'd been much more daring than Marcella would have anticipated—she'd started meeting Vitellius's supporters on her supposed trips to the bathhouse, in fact, to pass along any information that might help defeat Otho. Marcella had been perfectly prepared to meet with the conspirators herself, but with Cornelia being so obliging, all she had to do was feed her sister the necessary information. Movements of legions, supply lines, petty rivalries among Otho's generals—she'd dropped it all into Cornelia's ear or left little jotted notes lying on her desk where they could easily be found. Cornelia had passed it all on for her, every weakness the Vitellians had exploited to defeat Otho at Bedriacum. *Did Otho lose the battle due to my information-passing?* Perhaps not, but it was certainly amusing to think so. Pity Otho had committed suicide, though—Marcella had liked him, very much.

And now, Vitellius.

From what Marcella knew of him, he was just a big, beery, bleary sportsman. Not too clever; surely a pawn in the hands of other ambitious men. What could be done with Vitellius?

She sat down on the worn mossy bench, looking out over the city. Rome. She had written Rome's history in a dozen careful scrolls, but what good were her histories? A woman's writings could never be published, would never be read. She'd written them anyway, thinking there was nothing else to do. Because women didn't *make* history, of course. They could only be the watchers.

But now here she was, Lady Cornelia Secunda known as Marcella, looking down at all Rome with three emperors lying dead at her feet. No one else knew they were there—not the husband who despised her, not the sister who made pained expressions about her writing, not the idiot cousins who cared only for lovers and horses. None of them knew. *But I know.* Marcella laughed aloud, imagining the look on Tullia's face if she knew her hated sister-in-law had brought down three emperors.

Making history was much better than writing it.

"Marcella." A harsh voice behind her. "I went to your house. The slaves said you went out, so I followed your litter."

"Goodness, Domitian." She turned and smiled at the stocky figure coming up the slope toward her. "Such devotion."

"Every day you were gone, I prayed for your safety." His black eyes had never been so intent. "Nessus said you'd be safe, but I didn't believe him till I heard the news."

"Well, you did say your Nessus was never wrong." Domitian . . . younger son to the brilliant and shrewd Vespasian, who was Governor of Judaea and who had the only army in the Empire to match that of

Vitellius. Vespasian had sworn loyalty to Galba, to Otho—would he swear loyalty to Vitellius now? His own men had wanted to make him Emperor after Nero died, or so Marcella had heard . . .

"Thank the gods you're unharmed," Domitian said roughly, and seized her.

"Yes, yes, I'm unharmed." She laughed, pushing him as he began tugging at her skirts, but there was surprising strength in his arms. He dragged her down to the grass, pushing himself inside her before his lips even landed on hers. His eager tongue filled her mouth to gagging, but a savage little tendril uncoiled in Marcella's stomach and suddenly she was ravenous. She locked her thighs around him and began tearing at his tunic, sinking her teeth into his cheek when he tried to kiss her again. He buried his face in her breasts but she slapped him away, panting as she crushed him down into the grass. She raked his chest with her nails, drawing blood as she rode him. He cried out in the falling dusk, spasming, and Marcella bared her teeth at the sky.

"You're mine," he gasped, clutching her. "You're mine."

No, you're the one who belongs to me. She rolled off him, pulling her torn *stola* around herself. *Domitian. Vespasian's son. What can I do with you?*

She'd have to be stealthy, of course. Sneaky, underhanded. But why not? Every time she'd tried to be forthright this year—with her husband, with her brother, with anyone—she'd been ignored, brushed aside, or outright stepped on. Had she *ever* gotten her own way with honesty? Not once. Only by stealth.

The sun had sunk below the horizon now. The stars were out, shining in a blue-purple sky over the torch-lit city. Rome. The city that in this year alone, even though it was only spring, had already seen three emperors.

Marcella wondered idly, *Why not four?*

PART THREE

VITELLIUS

April A.D. 69–December A.D. 69

"Had he lived much longer . . .
the empire would not have been sufficient
for his appetite."

—JOSEPHUS

Twelve

CORNELIA couldn't stop herself from smiling, even when Lollia hurled a hairbrush at the mirror.

"That's it." Lollia scowled as her maids made soothing noises and swept up the fragments. "I'm done. This is the *last wedding*. Vitellius had better hang on to his throne, because three husbands in one year are *enough*."

Lollia kept scowling and muttering as her maids disposed of the broken mirror and began draping her curls with the red bridal veil. Cornelia just lay back on the couch, smiling up at the carved blue marble ceiling and jingling the bangles on her wrist. She'd put on a bright yellow dress for the wedding, stacked gold bracelets on both arms, and gathered her dark hair into a gold circlet dipping low on the forehead. She'd put her black off the minute she heard the news of Otho's death. The minute she knew Piso was avenged.

Cornelia drank a silent toast to that now, emptying her cup of summer-light rose wine in a gulp, and rose restlessly. "Let me fix your hair, Lollia. Those plaits aren't straight in back."

"Have at it. I suppose I should be grateful you're at least talking to me again."

"Well, I've come to see it wasn't your fault," Cornelia said generously, repinning Lollia's unruly plaits. "Supporting Otho, I mean. It wasn't your idea to marry his brother, after all."

"No, it wasn't," Lollia said shortly. "So you'd better not be expecting an apology, because I didn't do anything wrong."

They eyed each other a moment in the looking glass the maids had brought to replace the broken one. Lollia yanked a stray thread out of her sleeve with unnecessary force. Cornelia slid a jeweled pin into the piled red curls. "Will the Emperor be coming to your wedding feast?" she murmured, conciliatory.

"He'd better," Lollia scowled. "Two hundred thousand sesterces my grandfather spent on the feast, all because Vitellius has a taste for delicacies. The cooks are in an uproar."

Cornelia thought of the newest Emperor's pleasant beefy face. Vitellius had taken a slow triumphal procession through Italy after the victory at Bedriacum, stopping in every town to be feted and feasted. Spring had fluttered away into a liquid, molten summer before Vitellius made his entry into Rome: walking along on foot, followed by the proud eagles of the legions, the legionaries in smart formation, the German auxiliaries in their wolf skins. Cornelia had stared eagerly at the new Emperor as he climbed the Capitol to make a sacrifice to Jupiter for his victory: a tall man with a slight limp, massive shouldered and massive bellied, ruddy-faced and beaming. A big, rugged, good-natured sportsman. Not a treacherous perfumed sophisticate like Otho.

"—know if Diana will even come today?" Lollia was grumbling. "She's gotten very strange. Keeps disappearing and coming back with bruises all over. Well, maybe it's better if she doesn't come. Emperor Vitellius is a Blues fan, and we don't want her cursing him to his face." Lollia tilted her head, regarding her rouged cheeks in the mirror. "Will Marcella come, at least?"

"I don't know." Cornelia gave a last pat to Lollia's piled hair, and retreated back to her couch. "She's still very withdrawn—you know, after what happened at Brixellum."

"*Did* anything happen to her at Brixellum?" Lollia sounded tart. "She didn't seem all that terribly scarred to me, when she came back. She still doesn't. 'Oh, poor me, I had to watch a battle.' Just like that incident with Emperor Nero, whatever it was—a convenient excuse to duck everything she doesn't want to do."

Cornelia shifted uncomfortably. It didn't matter if she privately agreed—she still always defended her sister. "You shouldn't say that, Lollia."

"Isn't it true?"

"Of course not." Cornelia thought of Gaius's last dinner party, the most recent set of races at the Circus Maximus, Lollia's last betrothal feast—Marcella had ducked them all. "I can't face it," she said, her eyelids trembling, and everyone was quick to urge her to lie down and rest. Only whenever Cornelia ventured up to her little study, she didn't appear to be resting . . . more like sitting at her desk with a pen in her hand and a gleam in her eyes. "Won't you tell me about Brixellum?" Cornelia said. "I'd understand, you know—I'm not Tullia."

"What's to tell?" Marcella shrugged—a hard shrug, Cornelia thought. "Another emperor died. We're getting rather a lot of that, this year."

"I wouldn't have minded seeing Otho die." Savage satisfaction coiled in Cornelia's stomach. "I wish I'd been with you at Brixellum. So I could have spit on his corpse."

"I don't think you would have." Marcella sounded thoughtful. "He died quite heroically, you know."

"My husband died heroically too!"

Marcella's thoughtfulness had vanished in a smooth blink. "Of course he did."

Cornelia looked at her sister's impassive face. ". . . Should I leave you alone?"

"I'm very tired," Marcella said at once. "Ever since Brixellum . . ."

"Ever since Brixellum, you've been shutting me out!" Cornelia snapped, and stamped off.

Lollia was surveying herself in the mirror, still chattering gloomily. "Rubies," she said to her maid. "I'd better remind Fabius exactly how rich I am. It's all he's interested in, after all." She held out both arms for the ruby cuffs to be shackled about her wrists and tipped her head back for the heavy shoulder-sweeping earrings.

"So, this new husband of yours—does he suit you?" Cornelia dragged her thoughts away from her sister, back to the niceties. For months she'd been so consumed by grief and then by vengeance that she'd had no time for polite conversation—and of course, she had hardly been talking to Lollia anyway. But now all could be forgiven. "Commander Fabius Valens," Cornelia smiled. "Your grandfather certainly didn't waste any time catching him for you."

"Grandfather didn't do a thing. Fabius spent a few days sniffing out the city's richest heiresses and came knocking right on my door. And Grandfather wasn't pleased, I'll have you know—he likes to check all my husbands out thoroughly, make sure they're decent sorts before anyone starts talking wedding plans. But Vitellius gave his generals their pick of any bride in the city as rewards, so Grandfather didn't have any choice in the matter and neither did I." Lollia sighed. "Well, if it wasn't Fabius Valens, it would just be somebody else."

"A man of very little family," Cornelia sniffed, but tolerantly. Fabius Valens might be a common adventurer but he was Vitellius's right-hand man, the winning general of Bedriacum—the man who had defeated Otho.

"Vitellius thinks the world of him." Lollia twisted a massive pearl-and-ruby ring into place. "We're to live in the Domus Aurea for the time being, but Fabius has informed me he'll have a palace of his own by the end of the week. I think he's booting Senator Quintilius out of his huge new place on the Caelian Hill with all the water gardens." She gave a little sigh. "He's already turned some praetor out of a summer villa in Baiae. And he confiscated poor Salvius's house in Brundisium."

"Poor Salvius." In the wake of Otho's death, Cornelia could feel tolerant toward his brother. He'd returned to Rome with a great deal less swagger than he'd left it, small and ordinary without his brother's cloak of power. "Not even cracking his knuckles anymore," Lollia had said rather sadly. Vitellius let him live, at least for the time being, but everyone in Rome avoided his company. Lollia's grandfather had prudently arranged a divorce for his little jewel, reclaiming her dowry down to its last aureus, and not two days later Fabius Valens came along and snapped her up.

"There." Lollia surveyed herself without much joy. The maids clustered around her to add a final dusting of powder or a jeweled hairpin—her cosmetician, her hairdresser, her manicurist, her dresser, her seamstress, and the girl who looked after her skin; all arrayed like centurions with attending slave girls filed behind like legionaries, and all beaming pride in their handiwork. "Don't I look marvelous." Lollia made a face, but she passed out coins freely among all the maids. "Sorry about the mirror. You all go have yourselves a day off. Likely it'll be a better day than mine."

Cornelia flicked her cup aside and followed Lollia out. For three of Lollia's previous weddings, she had acted as bridal escort. But now it was Tullia who stood waiting for Lollia with the rest of the bridal party, fussing with her coral silks and snapping at her four-year-old son Paulinus.

"Well, well." Tullia looked Lollia up and down. "A new husband for the summer. Let's hope you keep this one longer."

"I'm surprised you've kept Gaius as long as you have," Lollia said sweetly. "Marcus Norbanus had the patience of a god for putting up with that voice of yours as long as he did. Like fingernails on slate."

Tullia tossed her false ringlets, ignoring little Paulinus, who was climbing determinedly up onto the rim of the fountain. "Gaius doesn't seem to mind."

"Dear, you haven't let Gaius get a word in edgewise for months. Who's to know what he thinks about anything anymore?"

"So lovely to see little Paulinus again," Cornelia put in quickly, hauling Tullia's son off the fountain's rim. "Has Marcus come too?"

"No, didn't you hear?" Tullia yawned. "Vitellius had him imprisoned for something or other, so I've got Paulinus for the time being. I may send him out of the city for a while. I certainly don't want anyone associating the Norbanus name with *me* anymore."

Poor Marcus. Cornelia had been profoundly shocked when she first heard the news, and still couldn't help a pang of unease every time she thought of it. Marcus Norbanus, imprisoned for the crime of carrying Emperor Augustus's blood in his veins . . . surely Vitellius would release him soon? It was a new era now. Nothing bad could happen now that Otho was dead, nothing.

Well, at the very least, she could see little Paulinus well cared for during his father's imprisonment. Especially since Tullia was about as maternal as a stone. . . . Cornelia had always adored Paulinus, vigorous funny little charmer that he was. "You can chase frogs later," she chided, pulling him back from the fountain again. "Juno's mercy, Paulinus, you need a haircut! I'll do it myself tomorrow, and then I promise I'll play with you all day—"

"Oh, gods." Lollia sent a page to fetch her grandfather from the triclinium, where he was fussing over the banquet arrangements. "Almost time to begin, and where's Fabius?"

Tullia eyed Lollia's rubies—bigger than her own. "Perhaps he got tired of you a little quicker than the others."

"It's my money he wants, Tullia dear, and how does one get tired of money? Certainly you never do." Lollia smiled. "Fortunately, it should take Fabius longer to run through mine than it's taking you to run through Gaius's. You certainly sucked Marcus dry before you divorced him."

"I have other charms besides money to offer *my* husbands," Tullia snapped.

"Like what?" said Lollia. "Rome's driest hump under the sheets?"

Lollia's grandfather appeared then, tugging his wig into place, and glowered at them all. Tullia subsided with a disapproving sniff, and Lollia came forward to kiss little Flavia, who beamed from her great-grandfather's arms with a wreath of festival flowers in her curly hair. *Juno's mercy*, Cornelia thought, *Flavia's the only one smiling*. The wedding procession toiled grimly out the door.

"Would you like to walk with me, Paulinus?" Cornelia asked, since his mother was utterly ignoring him.

"Yes, please," he said sunnily, slipping his hand into hers. "My mama hates weddings."

"Does she?"

"Maybe she just hates Aunt Lollia's weddings." He considered. "Or Aunt Lollia."

"Quando tu Gaius, ego Gaia." Another wedding. Cornelia made a saddle of her hip for Paulinus to sit on, watching Lollia's rubies blink in the sunlight like dozens of crimson eyes, watching the priest look irked as the absence of Lollia's husband-to-be held up the ceremony, watching Fabius Valens bound up the steps at last with a band of his officers and German auxiliaries behind him. What a strange lot they all were, rough provincials with shaggy hair and scarred arms and rough-edged Latin. So different from Galba's entourage of sober toga-clad senators and Otho's crowd of elegant courtiers. Hardly Romans at all—but however rough Fabius Valens might be, he and his men and their accents, they were now the kingmakers of Rome. *Yesterday he was nobody,* Cornelia marveled as Lollia's newest betrothed repeated his vows with a wink at his men. *Just an ordinary legionary commander. Today everyone's bowing and scraping in his presence.* What strange times they lived in.

Fabius Valens was a handsome man at least—Cornelia was glad of that, for Lollia's sake. He stood tall and dark and well-built in the breastplate he had not bothered to remove for his wedding, forty-six years old but as vigorous as a man half his age. His eyes resting appreciatively on Lollia's rubies, he grinned his way through the ceremony. The sacrificial bull panicked on the steps of the altar and required three strokes of the knife before the neck could be opened. A bad omen, but when were any of Lollia's weddings well-omened?

Cornelia felt her sister at her side, silent and indifferent in pale green embroidered with jade beads. "Are you all right?" she whispered.

"Of course," Marcella said, bland. The same look she gave everyone else in the family when they pried, only she used to follow it with a private wicked glance behind their backs that was all for Cornelia. But Cornelia couldn't see any sign of that sisterly gleam now. *Since when did she start lumping me with them? Just another family member to be tolerated?*

"Gaius!" Tullia's hissing whisper came behind them. "Why didn't you buy me those sapphires I wanted? Everyone else is jeweled to the skies!"

Diana came halfway through the ceremony, bringing a momentary
pang of panic to Cornelia's throat. Diana had been late to Lollia's last
wedding too, bringing something unspeakable in a sack, something
with a terrible distorted grimace—"Aunt Cornelia, you're squeezing,"
little Paulinus protested, and she loosened her death grip around his
strong little body as Diana slipped empty-handed into place. "I suppose we should be glad she didn't bring a severed *leg* this time," Tullia
tittered.

Diana turned and eyed her. "Could be arranged."

Lollia and Fabius Valens joined hands; the contracts were signed. A
ripple of applause from the Cornelii; an inarticulate roar from Fabius's
Germans. "Now the feast," Cornelia heard Lollia's grandfather mutter, twisting at his rings. "Dear gods, my cooks—!" But the massive
triclinium was in order when the wedding party returned; the silk
couches perfumed and plumped, the slaves smiling and immaculate,
the statues garlanded with flowers and the fountain outside flowing
Aminean wine in golden streams instead of water. Even the sky above
was an immaculate blue, echoing the blue of the marble columns
circling the triclinium and the cornflowers strewn on the mosaics
underfoot. *Did Lollia's grandfather contract with Apollo for a sunny day?*
Cornelia wondered, fanning herself with one hand as they entered. *I
wouldn't be surprised.*

Paulinus was hot and fretful, drooping against her shoulder. "Tullia, Paulinus is tired. He should have a nap."

"Well, get his nurse!"

"No, I'll tuck him in—" But the nurse was already descending,
bearing Paulinus off with a frown for Cornelia as she tried to take
him up herself. Clearly, in the nurse's view as well as Tullia's, patrician
women should not be allowed to tend their children. Paulinus smiled
sleepily as he was carried off, and Cornelia's heart squeezed. *I dreamed
of having sons like that. Dreamed and prayed and wept, while Tullia—*

But she couldn't think of old dead dreams like that. She would
never have children; she would never marry again. Her life belonged
to Piso, and at least she had avenged him. It would have to be enough.
When Paulinus was grown, and all her nieces and nephews still

unborn, they would whisper about their aunt Cornelia, gray-haired and old, but still in black: "She could have been Empress," they would whisper, awed by her devotion, "but her husband died and now she dedicates her life to his memory. Fifty years and she still wears his wedding ring . . ."

Fabius's Germans descended whooping on the wine fountain, grabbing silver cups from the slaves. Fabius led Lollia to the couch of honor, talking over her head to his officers. Cornelia saw her sister send a poisonous look to the steward when she found herself paired on a dining couch beside Tullia: "Wonderful, why didn't you just seat me in a snake pit?" For herself, Cornelia fared better on a couch with Diana, though she had a moment's surprise when Diana's shawl slipped off her shoulders. "What have you been *doing?*" she exclaimed, eyeing the purple bruises that marched up and down her youngest cousin's arms. "Did your father finally take a belt to you for all your running about?"

"No." Diana shrugged. "I fell out of a chariot."

"You got all that from falling out of a chariot?"

"Well, it rolled on me a little."

The *gustatio* courses entered in a stream: white and black olives, sparrows cooked in spiced egg yolk, grilled sausages and damsons and pomegranate seeds, a ragout of oysters and mussels. Lollia turned to wash her fingers first in a basin of rose water, but Fabius plunged a hand directly into a silver dish of sausages. The rest of his officers followed suit, calling to each other across the couches. Of course, legates who had spent half their career in Germania couldn't be expected to know the niceties.

A trio of flute players entered to play, but sudden trumpets drowned their melodies out. "The Emperor—!" Another flood of men; Praetorians in red and gold, a dozen more Germans in their barbaric trousers, a few brightly painted women, the Emperor himself loud and laughing in a wine-stained synthesis. Lollia's grandfather bustled forward, bowing very low; the couch of honor was brought forward, and Vitellius flung himself on it with a happy roar, waving Fabius Valens to join him. "And the bride—a pretty one, eh!" as the Emperor patted Lollia's cheek. The guests streamed up to offer their smiles, their bows, their desperate hopes that no one would ever find out how brightly they had smiled and how low they had bowed to Otho.

In two more months Otho will be forgotten. Cornelia smiled, watching Gaius and Tullia simper at Vitellius. When news came of Otho's death there had been an hour or two of cautious panic—plebs running through the streets to tip over his statues, smash his busts in the public forums, and hang garlands of flowers about the statues of Vitellius instead. The old statues of Galba had even been brought out and garlanded, since Vitellius had declared himself Galba's avenger. All the friends and acquaintances who had looked past Cornelia during Otho's reign as if she had the pox had come to her door in a stream, pressing her hand and offering their sympathies for Piso's death. "Such a fine man, Lady Cornelia, and he would have made a great Emperor. I was intending to visit you earlier, of course—"

In a week no one will ever admit they supported Otho at all. Cornelia hugged the thought to herself. *And in a month, he'll be written neatly out of every history and every mind in Rome.*

The *fercula* course was brought in: pheasant cooked inside its plumage, roast sow with her roasted litter of piglets around her, an entire eel served on a bed of grilled vegetables. "I'll take the head!" the Emperor called, and the eel's head was brought to him on a silver dish inlaid with garnets. A troop of African dancers came out to entertain, all gilded curls and oiled ebony skin, but the drumbeats of the music could scarce be heard over the appreciative shouts of the Germans.

"My dear Lady Cornelia!" The Imperial steward gushed forward— a supple Greek who had served all three emperors with equal fervor, Cornelia thought with disdain, and would probably serve the next three too. "Have you been introduced to Commander Fabius Valens? He particularly wished to meet you—"

Ushered to the bridal couch with oily introductions, Cornelia bowed low to Lollia's new husband. "Commander, I must congratulate you on your great victory at Bedriacum." Who cared if he had greasy handprints all over his white lawn synthesis, or if his Latin was a trifle rough? He had still crushed Otho's armies and crowned Vitellius. *Fortuna wasn't picky about the tools she chose for her vengeance, and neither was I.*

"So you're Lady Cornelia?" He wiped his hand down his front as he gestured her up. Lollia had gone to the next couch to greet a friend, and he waved Cornelia to sit in her place. "I'm told you're one of the ones to thank for my victory. You kept us well informed as to Otho's movements."

"Yes, Commander." She smiled. "I did what I could for the Emperor."

"*Our* Emperor."

"For me, Commander, Vitellius was the only Emperor."

Fabius smiled, eyes going over her. "You were married to Piso Licinianus, weren't you?"

"Yes."

"You should have been Empress, then. Pity about your husband. We'll have to see what we can do about that."

"I need no reward," Cornelia started to say, but Fabius had already turned away, calling across the room to the Emperor.

A tiny thread of unease curled through her stomach. If she meant to be an unmarried figure of tragedy for the rest of her life, perhaps it would have been better to wear her mourning black tonight . . .

The slaves came staggering out with the next round of courses. Exotic dishes this time: flamingo necks, peacock brains, pike livers, lark tongues, sow's udders, elephant trunks and ears extravagantly frilled with parsley. A dish of red mullet was laid before Cornelia as she returned to her own couch: the fish was still alive, flopping and expiring slowly in a sauce of lamprey milk. Some said a delayed death improved the fish's flavor.

"I find," Marcella observed on the next couch, "that I prefer my food to be dead by the time it reaches my plate." Tullia was exclaiming and tucking in on the next couch, but Cornelia waved the dish away, wrinkling her nose. Of course Lollia's grandfather had gone a little overboard in his urge to impress the new Emperor.

He never went overboard before, a little voice whispered in her head. *He gave Galba severe suppers . . . Otho got exquisite banquets . . . and now for Vitellius, all this excess. Exactly what they each wanted.*

A Greek poet entered to recite an ode dedicated to the new Emperor, but not one word could be heard over the din of the drunken Germans. They were stumbling off their couches toward the gardens, grabbing at the dancers, roaring drinking songs. Two of Fabius's officers quarreled over a wine flagon and grappled drunkenly at each other. Lollia's grandfather had them whisked apart by two burly slaves, but more quarrels were erupting all over the room. Cornelia looked at her empty wine cup, but called for water instead.

"I'm going home," announced Diana. "This is absurd. Not to mention boring." She slid off her couch, ducked around a blond giant from Agrippinensis, plucked his hand off her breast, and disappeared into the hall.

On his couch, the Emperor cast aside the plucked bones of a peacock carcass, wiping his massive greasy hands on the blue silk cushions. "Where's your *vomitorium?*" he called out to Lollia's grandfather, who looked frozen for a moment before pasting on a smile.

"Allow my steward to escort you to the bathhouse, Caesar." Lollia's grandfather could not quite hide the twinge of disgust, and Cornelia couldn't blame him. No one in the Cornelii family *ever* made use of a *vomitorium*. But Emperor Vitellius swayed out of the triclinium, still chewing on a sweet-cooked dormouse.

"I think Diana had the right idea," murmured Marcella. "What an interesting chapter this is going to make for my account of Vitellius."

"Marcella, don't leave me to stand all this by myself!" But her sister had already slid off her couch, sidestepping a weaving German waving an alabaster vase over his head, and disappearing without a backward glance. Cornelia felt a wounded pang somewhere deep in her stomach but kept her place beside Gaius and Tullia, matching their increasingly uneasy smiles.

The Emperor came weaving back, an arm slung around Fabius Valens. The slaves were bringing in the *mensae secundae* course now; goose eggs, pastries stuffed with raisins and nuts, snails in sweet sauces, platters of lustrous perfect fruit. Cornelia waved it all away, so stuffed with food she could hardly move, but the Emperor fell to eating again, sinking his teeth into a fricassee of almonds and jellied roses.

Sprawled on his couch, Fabius knocked his wine goblet all over Lollia. She gave a tight rueful little smile, dabbing at herself with her red veil, but her husband brushed the slaves away when they came forward with clean cloths and basins of water. "Let's get you out of those wet clothes," he grinned, and dragged the white *tunica* off her shoulder. He buried his mouth in her neck, hand fumbling over her breast.

Cornelia caught a look of utter fury on the face of Lollia's grandfather, but Lollia gave a sharp shake of her head at him. "Perhaps we should retire," she said brightly to her new husband.

"We'll see what you look like under those rubies." Fabius grabbed her arm and dragged her off toward the stairs. His officers whooped and cheered. The slaves looked frozen in the hall, already poised with unlit torches for the bridal procession back to her new husband's house, the walnuts prepared in baskets to throw under the bride's feet for luck, the flute players ready to serenade her as she was carried into her new home. Cornelia guessed there would be no bridal procession tonight. Lollia's grandfather turned away, fumbling needlessly with a wine cup, and Cornelia caught his furious mumble.

"—vulgar pigs, spilling wine all over my little jewel like a common whore—not fit to wipe her sandals—"

He stamped away, his chins wobbling helpless fury, and Cornelia looked around the beautiful blue-marbled triclinium. The flowers, the food, the slaves, and the music—all designed as a setting for his little jewel. *My father never called me that*, Cornelia thought. Had he ever called her anything, except *You there, girl*? Of course it was proper that a patrician father maintain a certain decorum even among family . . .

"I need some air," Cornelia said to Gaius, and stumbled off her couch toward the gardens. The sky was already black—had the banquet gone on for more than five hours?—and the gardens were filled with Vitellius's Germans. Two were wrestling, stripped to the waist and surrounded by cheering friends; they barreled into a stone nymph holding an urn of summer violets and sent it tumbling over in a crash of stone chips and crushed blossoms. Another soldier lay under a lilac bush, his hips pumping rhythmically over one of the dancers. The blond giant who had groped at Diana unsheathed

his dagger to dig the ivory eyes out of one of the matched ebony statues that lined the walls. Pools of regurgitated food lay everywhere.
Someone had vomited into the fountain, still splashing streams of
expensive wine.

Lollia's grandfather gave them just what they wanted, Cornelia couldn't
help thinking. *And now they're ruining his beautiful house.*

Well, none of the damage was serious. They were celebrating, that
was all. Of course they were bound to get a little wild—they had
defeated Otho, after all, so now they wanted a little raucous fun. No
harm in that.

Someone threw up all over her shoes.

Lollia's grandfather sighed at Cornelia's shoulder. "Perhaps I'll have
that *vomitorium* installed after all."

W ELL, this is better," Cornelia said aloud, relieved. The Emper-
or's box at the Lucaria races was a cheerful hubbub—shouted
bets, peals of laughter, rough jests—but the noise was merely high-
spirited. She hadn't intended to go to the races at all that day—Lucaria,
coming at the height of summer, was always so hot, and she would
have preferred a book and a cup of cold mulberry infusion in the coolness of the atrium to a sticky afternoon at the circus. But a Praetorian
delivered a scroll that morning with a toneless mumble, and Tullia
had ripped it open to find the Imperial seal.

"Fabius Valens has invited us to the Imperial box at the Circus
Maximus," she said gleeful. "Especially you, Cornelia. Thank goodness
for your connection with Piso and Galba—it was a trifle inconvenient
with Otho on the throne, I admit, but Vitellius seems determined to
honor anyone even remotely connected—"

"Perhaps the Emperor means to marry you to one of his supporters," Gaius broke in, taking the scroll from his wife's hand. "Lollia isn't
the only one who can make an advantageous marriage."

"For once you're right, Gaius." Tullia eyed Cornelia sternly. "I do
hope you'll be sensible."

"Let Marcella make the advantageous marriage." Cornelia folded her hands at her waist to keep them from clenching into fists. "She and Lucius haven't even spoken to each other since Brixellum—he'd happily divorce her. Or Diana—seventeen years old now, it's high time she married—"

"Of course I don't want to force you." Gaius patted her hand. His chin was now covered in patchy stubble in imitation of Vitellius, who unlike Otho was careless about shaving. "But I'd love to see you properly settled again, Cornelia—"

"*Gaius*, don't be stupid!" Tullia cut off her husband. "It's not about happiness these days, it's about connections! You have a connection to Galba, Cornelia, and it's your duty to the family to use that!"

Haven't I done my duty enough? Cornelia went straight up to her bedchamber and put on the deepest mourning black she could find, not even a pair of earrings to offset the severity. "How are you supposed to find a good husband looking like a hired mourner?" Tullia scolded. "You don't have the figure Marcella does, but you could make more of it. *Gaius*, tell her, this will never do!"

"It won't do at all, you know." Marcella looked up from her desk in the cluttered *tablinum*, giving her sister an amused head-to-toe glance. "Though not for the reason Tullia thinks."

"What do you mean?"

"If you want to escape attention, don't wear black. You're rather beautiful in black."

Cornelia looked into the glass at her own reflection. The black dress had turned the coils of her hair to black as well; glossy ebony reflections from silk and hair alike surrounding a pale shield of a face. "I suppose you're not going, Marcella?"

"I have a headache."

"You've been having quite a few of those lately," Cornelia couldn't help saying. "At least whenever it's the races or the games or anything else you think is boring. Imperial dinner parties or Senate discussions, you never have headaches for those."

Marcella smiled, turning her ink pot over in one hand. "Pass me any good gossip you hear at the races, won't you? I've heard that Governor Vespasian is making ominous noises in Judaea."

"Juno's mercy, not another rebellion." Cornelia gave an appalled blink. "Where did you hear *that*?"

"From young Domitian. He's not supposed to correspond with his father, but he does."

"He's not supposed to be spreading rumors like that, either." Cornelia nibbled at her nails, still stripped down to painful nubs. "Is he still in love with you?"

"Madly. He wanted me to know he'd be a prince within the year, once his father becomes Emperor." Marcella gave a small smile, ink-spattered and plain with her hair in a braid over one shoulder. "Should I pass Domitian on to you? If you're going to be married off anyway, it might as well be to another possible prince of Rome."

"You could be more sympathetic, you know," Cornelia snapped. "Your husband's already found favor with Vitellius—and he's gone off to Crete, so you don't even have to deal with him! No one's trying to marry *you* off!"

"No." Marcella stretched head to toe like a languorous cat. "I make sure of that."

"You're very self-satisfied these days, do you know that, Marcella?"

Her sister's chuckle followed her out.

The Emperor's box was a sea of blue when Cornelia arrived: blue banners, blue flowers scattered underfoot, blue plums and blue-black oysters circulating in lapis lazuli bowls, a blue *stola* on every woman and a blue cloak on every man. Fabius Valens wore a sky-blue synthesis, and Lollia's sapphires were larger than those worn by Vitellius's meek little Empress. Vitellius's massive belly stretched under a blue tunic with half a dozen charioteer medallions about his neck, each proclaiming his fabled allegiance to the Blues team. Derricus, the star charioteer for the Blues, had the place of honor at the Emperor's side, preening in his striped blue tunic. Cornelia felt like a crow in a pride of peacocks and gratefully found a seat for herself at the back. But Vitellius, turning to gesture for more wine, caught sight of her and beckoned. She came forward, bowing.

"Lady Cornelia Prima." Up close, the Emperor's ruddy face showed broken veins about the nose, and rolls of fat at the neck from many years of heavy banquets. But he had only a mild smell of wine this afternoon, and the hand that raised her up was steady. "I owe you a debt, my dear."

"I only did my duty, Caesar." She kept her eyes properly lowered.

"Not for passing information. For the loss of your husband." Vitellius dropped his voice. "I am so sorry."

Startled, Cornelia looked up at him. Otho had paid her polished, insincere apologies. Family members had given stilted condolences; her sister and cousins wordless hugs. No one had simply said, *I'm sorry.* A lump rose in her throat, and Vitellius's smile was kind.

"I'll make it up to you," he promised, squeezing her fingers in his massive ones, and Fabius Valens over his shoulder grinned. Cornelia curtsied again and hastily retreated. As long as the Emperor's notion of making it up to her wasn't a new husband . . .

Diana, flopped in her seat at the back, was not hard to find. She sat scowling, ignoring the glances from the Emperor's officers and courtiers—disapproving glances for once, rather than admiring. In a sea of blue she was a spot of bright unapologetic red, a medallion for each of her four favorite horses about her neck, red skirts fluttering and scarlet ribbons braided through her white-gold hair. "I'm not going to put off my colors just because the Emperor roots in opposition," she said to Cornelia's raised eyebrows. "Anyway, I don't see you wearing any of that gaudy Blues trash."

"No," Cornelia agreed, taking her seat. "What *have* you done to your hands?" They were rough as sandstone, callused across the palms.

"Sshh, the parade's beginning."

The horses began their ceremonial parade around the track of raked sand, five teams prancing under a sweltering brass bowl of a sky. The Blues came first, Derricus pointing his whip out at the crowd in the famous gesture that brought screams of adoration. Women cooed and threw flowers; Vitellius let out a whoop and banged a meaty fist against the arm of his chair. Diana hissed, clapping loudly only for the team she had named the Anemoi after the four winds. Cornelia had to admit the horses were beautiful: chestnuts as red as their traces, almost dancing before the chariot in their eagerness to run. Diana let out a whoop as they took their place in line, drowned out by Fabius Valens, who was laying uproarious bets with the Emperor.

"Hello, my loves." Lollia dropped beside them, waving a peacock feather fan against her face. "Gods, it's hot."

"How are you and your husband?" Cornelia asked, since Diana was too rapt on the track for any kind of courtesies.

"He's . . . energetic. Tireless, in fact. Thank the gods he spends half the night dicing and whoring with Vitellius, or I'd never get any sleep." Lollia peered down at the track, where Derricus the Blues charioteer was preening in the gilt-crusted blue chariot. "Goodness, he does look smug." She whispered in Cornelia's ear. "I hope Diana never finds out I had a little fling with Derricus once. She'd never forgive me."

"You slept with a *charioteer*?"

"Yes, and let me tell you a fast finish might be nice on a track but *not* in a bed."

Cornelia caught herself before she could giggle.

The blood bays at the Blues chariot lunged ahead before the scarf dropped and had to be muscled back in line. The crowd groaned at the false start, and to distract them Vitellius tossed a basket of numbered wooden balls one by one into the sea of humanity below, each one to be redeemed with the Imperial stewards for a prize—a prize bullock, a team of horses, even a summer villa. *Our new Emperor certainly is generous.* Groans turned to squeals as the plebs fought over the balls, cheers mounting like waves. Fabius snapped Lollia back to his side, stuffing a blue scarf into the Emperor's hand as the horses drew up to the starting line again. Diana leaned forward, lips parted. Vitellius dropped the scarf, and the horses surged down the track.

At once the crowd surged up, shouting, calling encouragement to the drivers, laying bets. Vitellius leaned over the rail yelling down to the Blues. Diana chewed her lip. The Reds pulled ahead in the first lap after a spectacular scrape of a turn, and hers was the only cheer to go up from the Imperial box. Fabius glared back at her. "I'll cheer whom I like," Diana said, unrepentant. "Gods' wheels, I wish Centurion Densus were here."

Cornelia blinked. She hadn't thought of that name in a long time, not since he walked her home from the Campus Martius before Bedriacum and said such rude things. "Why would you want *him* here?"

"Because he roots for the Reds. He was cheering them on with me, the first races of this year. And any man who could stand off five to one like he did before the Temple of Vesta would have the spine to root out loud, no matter what the Emperor thought."

Diana leaped to her feet swearing as the Greens clipped the *spina*, and Cornelia beckoned a Praetorian standing guard at the back of the box. A new man; she didn't recognize him, but Vitellius had inserted many of his own men into the Praetorian Guard. "Can you tell me what happened to Centurion Drusus Sempronius Densus?" She didn't know why she asked. Surely he had died at Bedriacum, or she would have seen him by now accompanying Vitellius with the other Praetorians.

"There's a warrant for Drusus Densus, Lady. Treason."

"Treason?"

"He survived Bedriacum smart enough, Lady, but Commander Valens winnowed through the Praetorians afterward. Dismissed a batch of them for turning on Galba."

"But if most of them were just dismissed, why was Densus charged with treason?" The crowd was on its feet, shouting at something that had just happened on the track, but Cornelia hardly heard the screams.

"Commander Valens charged he must have sold out Galba and the heir, Lady. Maybe killed the heir, who knows. Valens figured he should be made an example of, since Otho made such a hero of him."

"That's absurd!"

"What's absurd?" a voice intruded, and Cornelia looked up to see Fabius Valens standing at her shoulder, a goblet of blue-blown glass in one hand.

"Centurion Drusus Densus being charged with treason," she said roundly. "He certainly did not have any hand in murdering my husband. I was *there*, I know what happened."

"He failed to save your husband, though." Lollia's new husband dismissed.

"That was hardly his fault." Densus might have been rude on occasion, but he was surely the farthest thing from a traitor. "Has he been executed already?"

"No. Never even arrested—got wind of it somehow and ran. No matter. He'll never serve again."

"But . . ." She trailed off.

Fabius smiled. "Consider your husband avenged."

"I don't need vengeance, Commander." *Not anymore. Not with Otho dead.*

"I'll decide what you need."

Cornelia turned her eyes back to the track again, blindly. "What lap is this?" To Diana.

"The fifth." Diana sat on the very edge of her seat, lips moving silently. The Blues and the Reds had swapped the lead a dozen times.

Fabius spoke very low, his arm grazing Cornelia's. "You need a husband, and one of my friends needs a wife. Caecina Alienus, his name is—"

A howl went up from the crowd as the Whites team tried to slip past the Blues on the inside; the Blues charioteer veered inward, and the Whites were crushed. The chariot disintegrated, a wheel rolling madly across the sand as the screaming horses staggered free. They careened directly across the Reds, and Diana swore horribly as the Reds had to pull up in a violent toss of chestnut forelocks and red leather reins. "Diana," Cornelia scolded, and seized the excuse to ignore Fabius's cozy voice at her elbow and subject her youngest cousin to a crisp lecture on the evils of foul language. A shorter lecture than it would normally have been—Cornelia's own mind was whirling.

Vitellius let out a shout of laughter and pounded the rail in delight as the Blues settled into the lead. Far behind, the Reds disentangled themselves from the mess of the crash and whipped into a gallop again. "They'll never make up the distance," Diana groaned, sinking back in her chair. But her winds put their long noses out in a pounding gallop, red manes streaming flat against their glossy necks, and they began chewing back the gap. Half a lap behind—a third—passing the Greens as if they were standing still. Their hides were more black than red with sweat.

"Do you know Caecina Alienus?" Fabius asked, his lips closer to Cornelia's ear. "Bit of a rough customer, but he'd be a fair enough match. A young widow like you, surely you're wet for a new husband by now."

Cornelia licked her lips, keeping her eyes desperately fixed on the circus. She saw the Blues charioteer look behind him and shake the whip over his blood bays. Both teams screeched around the last turn at white heat.

"*Come on!*" Diana shouted, but the finish line came too soon, the stretching noses of the Reds pulling even with the axle of the Blues chariot. "Oh—" Diana's head dropped, her blue-green eyes glittering with tears. "Oh, my poor winds, it was almost enough."

"You really must not show so much emotion over a race," Cornelia chided, feeling Fabius's hand on her elbow and launching hastily into a longer lecture on proper patrician decorum. Diana sat deaf, drooping in her chair, watching the Blues charioteer take his victory lap as adoring women screamed and the Emperor slapped his cronies on the back. Cornelia hardly heard them, too conscious of Fabius's hand on her arm. *Juno's mercy, he's going to arrange my future for me, and I can't keep ignoring him.*

Derricus the Blues charioteer vaulted up to the Imperial box, dusty and grinning as the Emperor gave him his victory palm. "You'll share my couch at the feast tonight!" the Emperor shouted, ruddy with triumph, dropping an arm around the charioteer's shoulder. "And we'll drink a toast to beating those cowardly bastard Reds—"

A whirl of red silk. Cornelia lunged for Diana's arm, but too late. Vitellius was already looking with surprise down at the slim scarlet girl under his nose.

"Do *not*"—Diana jabbed a finger at the Emperor of Rome—"insult my Reds. They ran a good race. Better than your Blues."

Derricus laughed, looking down at her from under the Emperor's jovial arm. "Lady Diana here is a Reds fan," he grinned. "And a poor loser, but—"

"Shut up," she snapped, and a ripple went around the onlookers. Vitellius's brows beetled. Cornelia froze in her chair. Gaius stopped with his mouth open. Lollia gave a pleading shake of her head, but Diana turned her narrowed blue-green gaze back on the Emperor and kept going.

"The Reds had bad luck, Caesar—the Whites ran them off the track. Plenty of teams would pull up and quit then, but not my Reds. They made a race of it and they nearly beat your Blues, because your precious *Derricus* here was so busy counting his victory palms he'd dropped the pace. Shut up," she said again as the charioteer bristled. "That's bad driving, Caesar, and it's worse than bad luck any day. So don't you be calling my team cowards." Jabbing a finger into the massive chest of the Emperor of Rome. "Because my Reds can beat your precious Blues any day of the *week*."

Complete silence. Diana stood with her scarlet silks fluttering, hair sliding down her back in a tumble of white-molten gold, chin thrust out. The Emperor's ruddy face was immobile, his eyes glittering, and suddenly Cornelia saw the man whom three legions had proclaimed Emperor in Germania.

Diana glared up at the Emperor, unafraid. Derricus stared daggers at her. Cornelia dragged in a frozen breath and prepared to jump in with some bright social nicety.

Suddenly, the Emperor threw his head back and laughed. "You're right," he agreed. "Your Reds ran a good race. I shouldn't have called them cowards." Tossing his arm around her shoulders, he turned to the Imperial steward. "Put the spitfire here on my couch tonight too. We'll talk strategy, Lady, and I'll get you to admit that my Blues are faster than your Reds."

"Are not," said Diana from under his arm, still glaring, and a titter of laughter went around the balcony as Vitellius grinned at her and then turned away, calling for wine. Cornelia laughed too, feeling her knees weaken. *Diana, you mad little fool.* Only Diana could have gotten away with it. Only Diana.

Cornelia heard Fabius murmuring to the steward. "Put Lady Cornelia beside Alienus at the feast tonight, or maybe Suonius—one of the officers who can appreciate a juicy young widow."

First lady of Rome, Cornelia thought, her laughter suddenly withering. *I was first lady of Rome once. And now all I am is a juicy young widow.*

She willed her fingers not to tremble, willed her eyes not to fill or dart or blink. *Be marble*, she remembered telling herself during the bad weeks after Piso's death. *Be ice. See how much juice you can squeeze out of a column of black ice, Fabius Valens.*

Thirteen

～⌒～

"PAULINUS!" Cornelia had hardly put one foot into Lollia's bed-chamber before she whirled around again and sent Tullia's son back the other way. "Why don't you go play in the atrium?"

"Gods' sake, my honey." Silk rustled, and Lollia sounded amused. "No need to hustle him out. It's nothing he won't be doing himself in a few years."

"Paulinus," Cornelia said firmly as he looked interested. "Go find Flavia and play."

"Just don't play like that with *my* daughter," Lollia giggled. "Not yet, anyway."

Cornelia kept her eyes on the mosaics as Paulinus dashed out. "Can I turn around yet?"

"Yes, yes. Though really, Cornelia, you are a prude. Seeing a naked cock isn't going to turn you to stone, you know."

"I'm sorry, I should have knocked." Cornelia did her best not to blush as she turned. "Paulinus has been missing his father terribly and Tullia just ignores him, so I thought I'd bring him to play with Flavia, but—"

"Goodness, you look red." Lollia now sat decorously in an orange silk robe on the bed, her big golden-haired slave waving an ostrich feather fan at her side. His tunic was inside out. When Cornelia had first come into the bedchamber, he'd been on top of Lollia with one of her ankles crooked around his hips and the other twined around his neck.

"Didn't you ever try that one with Piso?" Lollia continued. "One does have to be limber, but it's bliss."

"I don't care to discuss such things." Cornelia wrinkled her nose, nodding at the slave. "You may go."

He looked at Lollia. "Yes," she dimpled, and gave a little giggle as he bowed and dashed gratefully out. "Poor darling, he's been terribly embarrassed this morning. Fabius caught us too, you see."

"Your *husband*?"

"Yes, he walked in early this morning when we were doing the bridge. Did you ever try that one? You get down on all fours and then—"

"What did Fabius do?" Cornelia said hastily, feeling the blush come back. Really, Lollia had no more shame than a cat in heat.

"Oh, he glared a lot and stamped out again." Lollia sashed her robe more tightly around her waist. "Really, I was hoping he'd catch me. It's about time he learned."

"Learned what?"

"Well, Fabius is a pleb, so he has all these ridiculous ideas about how a wife should conduct herself. All of a sudden I'm being expected to concern myself with his favorite dishes and the temperature of his bathwater, *and* behave like a Vestal Virgin. In public, anyway. In private, he wants a whore."

"It's hardly backward and plebeian to expect good behavior from a wife," Cornelia pointed out.

"Of *course* it is, my honey. Do you think Vinius or Salvius or any of my other husbands fussed about Thrax? Of course they didn't. But Fabius has a thing or two to learn about patrician wives." A flicker of hardness went through Lollia's eyes as she rose, surprising Cornelia. Lollia might be flippant, but she had never been hard. "I'm paying the bills, after all. Doesn't that entitle me to something of my own?"

"So where is Fabius?" Privately, Cornelia wasn't sorry to have missed him.

"Off intimidating the Senate. They waffle, and he stalks around reminding them that his sword put Vitellius on the throne. These days it's called politics."

They passed from the bedchamber through the pillared halls to the peristyle. "So this is your new house?" Cornelia asked, looking around the jumbled array of pools and fountains, with banks of jasmine and water lilies and statues all jammed together. "It's very . . . large."

"I think you mean ghastly." Lollia shuddered. "Fabius confiscated it from some Othonian supporter, down to the last slave, statue, and household god, and moved us in wholesale last week. I haven't even figured out where all the rooms are yet, and he wants me to host a betrothal party."

"Who's getting married?"

Lollia settled into a scrolled silver couch beside a mossy urn and beckoned for fruit and barley water. "You, of course."

"*What?*" Cornelia froze halfway down into her chair.

"Fabius said . . ." Lollia trailed off.

"What did Fabius say?" Cornelia felt suddenly cold, despite the sunlight pouring through the open roof of the atrium. "He hinted something to me at the races, but—"

"Oh, darling. Fabius doesn't hint. He just gives orders." Lollia waved away the flagon of barley water before it could be set down. "Wine instead, Phoebe. We're going to need it." She poured a cup as soon as the flagon arrived and pushed it into Cornelia's hand without even bothering to water it down. "Drink up. Fabius, well, he wants you for one of his friends, I'm not even sure which. He's handing out rewards to all of them. Money, estates, wives—"

"He has no legal authority over me!"

"Things have changed, Cornelia. This isn't *Rome* anymore, not the Rome we know. The kingmakers rule this Rome. Fabius laughs every time his friends grope me at their parties, and he helps himself to any little knickknack from Grandfather's house that takes his fancy, and he likes me to walk around the bedroom dressed in nothing but jewels . . ." Lollia massaged her head under her hair, dislodging reddish curls. "He makes me tired."

"I will not be given away to some victorious soldier like a sack of loot!"

"Now you know how I feel, don't you?" said Lollia. "One gets used to it."

". . . How?" Cornelia whispered.

"One husband at a time."

They were both silent for a while at that. Cornelia thought of Fabius's smug smile and smugger voice: *A young widow like you, surely you're wet for a new husband.* She shivered.

Lollia had turned her face away, talking in a brittle voice of something else. Diana. Of course, everyone talked about Diana these days. With an enormous effort, Cornelia forced herself to hear what Lollia was saying. "—hear the new epigram about her from Martial? *'The huntress in her chaste flight, bagged at last by Imperial might.'*"

"Surely Diana wouldn't . . ." Cornelia couldn't help but make a face, thinking of the Emperor of Rome's red face and food-swollen body. "Not with Vitellius?"

"Oh, I doubt it. You know Diana—she'd tell an emperor *no* if she felt like it. And she isn't really mistress material, is she?" Lollia dandled her fingers in the spray of a silver wall fountain beside the couch. "If any man took her to bed, she'd lie there looking up at him with those gorgeous eyes until he was finished, and then she'd ask him what he thought of the Reds' chances at Saturnalia. Bit of a flattener."

Cornelia thought of the Imperial banquet after the races last week, where she'd watched her youngest cousin sit cross-legged on a dining couch beside Vitellius, waving a goose leg and arguing race tactics with him until dawn. He seemed to find his new little pet very amusing, and now the rest of his entourage did too; a trickle of courtiers soon followed Diana wherever she went, murmuring about the word or two she might drop in the Emperor's ear on their behalf. "Unless it's to do with horses," Cornelia heard Diana say bluntly to these requests, "go away."

"You know, I used to worry about Diana's reputation," Cornelia said. "But now I think she's too odd to be wanton. It would be too commonplace for her, somehow. Of course Tullia goes on and on about Diana being the Emperor's whore—"

"Tullia's the whore," Lollia snorted, pouring herself a goblet of wine and taking a generous gulp. "Not that she'd ever break *her* vows, oh no. But she'd shove any one of us into the Emperor's bed if it would benefit her. Is she carping at Diana to get Gaius made a legate yet?"

"A governor."

"See?" Lollia gave a disgusted shrug. "I may like a tumble with my body slave, but I'm better than Tullia. At least I'm no hypocrite."

Cornelia surprised herself with a laugh. "No, you aren't."

Little Flavia and Paulinus ran in then, and Lollia promptly swept them both into her lap and blew loud kisses everywhere. Cornelia watched wistfully as Flavia giggled and Paulinus yelled objections.

"Flavia, your aunt Cornelia needs cheering up," Lollia consulted her daughter gravely. "What do you say? Shall we all dress up and take ourselves out somewhere fancy? To the theatre, perhaps, or the Campus Martius?"

"Circus," Paulinus said at once.

"Uncle Paris," Flavia said.

"I wouldn't call Uncle Paris fancy, exactly—"

"Uncle *Paris*, 'cause he said he'd make me a little statue of a *dog*!"

"Well, that settles it."

"Why does *she* get to decide?" Paulinus scowled.

"Because she's a girl, and girls always get their way. Your future wife will thank me, Paulinus, if I pound that into you young. Uncle Paris's house it is."

Cornelia watched in some surprise as Lollia swept off to dress Flavia herself rather than calling the nursemaid, tethering Paulinus capably with her other hand. "—yes, we'll call for Aunt Marcella too," Lollia was promising her daughter as they returned ten minutes later in matching rose-colored gowns. "It will be just like old times."

"Don't bother stopping for Marcella," Cornelia advised. "She'll be too busy scribbling in her *tablinum* to make time for us."

"Scribbling about what?"

"Who knows?"

Trying to find words for this new Rome, perhaps? Cornelia certainly found it a stranger place every time she went outside. Rome in summer was usually such a sleepy place; slaves moving languidly through their errands, oxen and mules dozing somnolent under a brass coin of a sun, plebs sweltering in hot stinking rooms. Everyone who could escaped to their summer villas in Baiae or Brundisium or Tivoli, sitting on sea terraces eating grapes and being cooled by ocean breezes, not returning to the city until Volturnalia at the earliest. But now . . .

Cornelia climbed into the litter, tugging Paulinus into her lap, and the city pressed in on them through the rose silk curtains as the bearers began their trot toward Uncle Paris's small house on the farthest slope of the Palatine Hill. Rome was *full*—that was one disquieting thing. None of the patricians left that summer for their summer villas. First everyone was too petrified by news of Otho's defeat to move, lest it be construed as flight. And when Vitellius arrived in the city he stayed despite the heat, consolidating his position, and everyone stayed with him. So the summer games that saw the arena seats only half full in normal years were packed to the sky, the Circus Maximus was filled to bursting for every race, and the Domus Aurea spilled over every night with parties. Not Galba's dour dinners with their sour wine and droning discussions of Rome's economy; not Otho's elegant gatherings of beautiful people saying witty things. Parties where common soldiers drank side by side with senators and the senators strove to drink like common soldiers; where an Emperor boasted that he wasn't too proud to curry horses for the Blues; where a common legionary commander like Lollia's husband had become a kingmaker. It was summer, it sweltered and burned, and the world was upside-down. A new Rome, just as Lollia had said . . . and Cornelia didn't like it at all.

"Juno's mercy—" She gazed in disapproval at the entry hall as they all came into Uncle Paris's house. Scraps of marble and chisels lying everywhere, dust on everything else, and the slaves idling in corners chattering to each other and not even pretending to look busy. "Uncle Paris," Cornelia scolded as Lollia threw open the door of his studio. "Doesn't Diana do anything to keep the house in order?"

"She's busy," Uncle Paris said absently, working at a scrap of marble with a polishing cloth, white-blond hair falling in his eyes. Faces surrounded him, faces in marble and stone and clay; everyone from slaves to senators to family members. "Some savage from Britannia is teaching her to drive a chariot. I saw him once; wonderful face. I've got to carve it. "

Lollia giggled, but Cornelia sighed. "Uncle Paris, you should stop her."

He blinked. "Who stops Diana doing anything?"

"But she could be doing something very unwise. I doubt it's just driving a chariot."

"So do I," Lollia laughed. "I just hope it's fun too."

"Little ones," Uncle Paris regarded Flavia and Paulinus, who both stood gazing up with round eyes. "Who do you belong to? Never mind, just keep your hands off my mallets. Didn't I promise one of you a carved dog? Let me see . . ."

Cornelia wandered the shelves, crammed with carvings old and new: rough studies of nymphs and veiled maidens, Vitellius's hearty double-chinned face, what looked like a carving of Lollia's Gaul with the arrows and quiver of Apollo . . . "These four here on the table, Uncle Paris—did you carve us again?"

"Yes, as various goddesses." Diana's father wandered over to the worktable littered with marble chips and stone dust, where four busts stood in a row. "Took some thinking, really, to find the right one for each of you."

"Of course Diana is Diana the Huntress." Lollia smiled at their youngest cousin as the virgin goddess of the moon and the hunt, her exquisite cheekbones chiseled in fine white marble, her eyes sleepy and proud, a crescent moon crowning her disheveled hair. "What about me?"

"Ceres. Goddess of the earth and the harvest." Lollia's carved face had a lush mouth carved in a gentle smile, and tiny ears of corn woven into her marble curls.

"Not Venus?" Cornelia smiled. "Surely Lollia is goddess of love."

"Oh, no," said Uncle Paris. "Goddesses of love are jealous fickle things. Our Lollia's as warm as the earth. And like Ceres, she has a daughter she loves above anything."

"Mama, Mama, you're blushing!"

"I am not." Lollia tucked Flavia closer against her side. "I couldn't be Venus anyway, with my fat chin. What about Cornelia? I suppose she's Juno?"

Cornelia looked at her marble-carved self and frowned. No Imperial crown on her marble hair; just a simple veil surrounding her face.

"Vesta," said Uncle Paris. "Goddess of hearth and home. Since you won't ever be Empress, now."

"Uncle, really—" Lollia began.

"No, he's right." Cornelia gave a bitter little one-sided smile.

"Is this Marcella?" Lollia looked quizzical, gazing at the last bust. The carved eyes were blank and ferocious, and instead of hair she had a writhing nest of snakes.

"That's Marcella," Cornelia said slowly. "But as . . . what?"

"Eris," said Uncle Paris.

The goddess of discord and chaos, causing trouble wherever she went? Cornelia cocked her head, puzzled, but Uncle Paris just wandered off again.

"Goodness," Lollia whispered. "He's mad, sometimes."

Cornelia busied herself wrapping up the bust of Lollia as Ceres and had a slave lug it out to the litter. She didn't want to think about the statue of herself as Vesta. Goddess of hearth and home. *What good is that, with no husband, no hearth, and no home?*

L OLLIA heard a sharp cracking noise as she reentered the house that might as well have been her own prison. Flavia dozed on her hip, and Lollia wished she could sleep so easily. A nice tense evening was doubtless awaiting her tonight, what with Fabius glaring murder over catching her in bed with Thrax. "Down you go, Flavia, let's tuck you into bed for a nap if you're sleepy—"

Another crack. Lollia looked around, but nothing had fallen off its pedestal or gone crashing to the floor. She summoned a slave, ordering the marble bust to be brought in and placed in a spare niche in the entrance hall. Perhaps it would make the house feel more like home . . .

The sharp crack came again, and what sounded like a muffled cry. "What's that?" Lollia asked. The slave girl looked at the floor. "Tell me!"

"It's Dominus," she mumbled.

Suddenly Lollia felt cold. "Fabius? Where is he? What is he doing?"

"In the atrium—please, Domina, we couldn't—"

Another crack. This time Lollia heard a scream. She picked up her skirt and ran, Flavia trotting at her heels. *No, no, it can't be*—but it was.

It was Thrax.

He stood naked against a pillar in the atrium, his arms jerked up high and lashed around the column. For a moment Lollia thought he was wearing a red cloak, but of course he wasn't. His back was in ribbons, crossed by lashes, streaming blood in a dozen places. Blood runneled down his legs, dripping on his feet. As she stopped, appalled, Fabius brought the whip down across his back again.

Thrax gave a muffled cry through clenched teeth, and it loosened Lollia's feet. She flew across the atrium, seizing Fabius's arm as he drew the whip back again. "No, no, what are you *doing*, you can't—"

Fabius sent her spinning with a shove. She crashed into an ornamental stone bench and fell to her knees. He snarled, teeth bared, but he was smiling too and it filled her bones with horror. "No one beds my wife but me," he said, and he turned and brought the whip down across Thrax's shoulders.

Thrax screamed. Lollia struggled to her feet, grabbing for the whip as Fabius drew back again. He hit her in the throat, hard and accurately, and she collapsed, gagging. Fabius seized her hair and hauled her back up, his eyes blazing a bare inch away.

"I catch you in another man's bed again," he whispered, "and it'll be you under the lash. You understand me?"

"Yes," Lollia whimpered. She could hear Thrax gulping in long breaths that sounded like sobs. "Yes, I understand."

"Good." He studied her another long moment, hand still wrapped in her hair, and then he staggered. Flavia had thrown herself against his side, pounding with her little fists as high as she could reach. He knocked her aside with one slap, and she crashed into a stone urn of lilies.

"*Flavia!*" Lollia lunged for her daughter, but the hand in her hair snapped her up short. Fabius held her a moment longer, the whip still dangling from his hand, and then he threw her away. Lollia crashed to her knees on the tiles and crawled to her child, who lay huddled and quietly crying.

Fabius threw the whip aside with a soft rattle. Dimly Lollia saw him surveying Thrax, a bloody mess against the column. "Get rid of this filth," he ordered, and then she heard boots retreating down the long pillared hall.

She scrambled to her feet as soon as he fell out of earshot, still holding Flavia. "I need to put you down, my honey, let me go a moment." But her daughter clung even harder, limpetlike, and Lollia had to undo Thrax's knotted cords one-handed. She could hear the other slaves rustling behind her, but none came forward to help—of course they wouldn't; Fabius Valens was their master and his will was law now. The knots took a long time, and Thrax dragged his forehead off the column and stared at her in mute gratitude. His gaze stabbed like a knife. *If I hadn't kept him with me—if I hadn't just assumed Fabius wouldn't care enough to touch him . . .*

"*Someday you'll realize what a slut you are,*" Lollia remembered Cornelia telling her once during a snarling fight.

Now she knew.

The last knot came loose under her shaking fingers, and Thrax collapsed. It wasn't just his back that was in ribbons—both eyes were puffed and black, and his nose was smashed. All his golden beauty was in ruins, but Lollia had no time to grieve for it. "Thrax—Thrax, please, you have to get up. Can you walk a few steps? Just a few."

He took her hand, slowly staggering upright. "Domina," he mumbled. One bloody hand brushed her throat, where Fabius's fist had already left a bruise. "Sorry—Domina—"

"Sshh. Come with me." Still holding Flavia on her hip, Lollia led Thrax by the hand through the pillared hall. She felt the slaves staring from behind the corners, but Fabius's ferocity had scared them all into silence. Thrax left bloody footprints on the beautiful mosaics, and the busts of the house's previous owners stared down in blind accusation. *If I live here a hundred years, this place will never be my home.*

She summoned the litter, easing Thrax into it face down. His back was still bleeding freely, and she threw her fine rose wool *palla* over it, settling the cloth with gentle pats to absorb the blood. Not enough, but it would have to do for the moment. Flavia whimpered as her arms were detached, but Lollia pried her away ruthlessly and settled her in the corner of the litter. "Don't cry, my honey," Lollia said, crying. "And don't jostle Thrax. He's sick."

"Where to, Domina?" the litter-bearer asked.

"My grandfather's house," Lollia choked. "Tell him the slave needs a doctor, the best there is. Tell him I'll be sending Flavia's nurse and her things."

"How long will they be staying, Domina?"

"For good." Lollia turned away, wiping her eyes. "I won't have either of them in this cursed house."

She wore her emeralds to the Domus Aurea that night, because the necklace covered the blue bruise on her throat. She walked into the vast triclinium on her husband's arm, smile stretched wide for a hundred guests as the Emperor shouted a greeting and gestured them in with the crispy-feathered neck of a flamingo. She lay on the dining couch beside Fabius, laughed at his jokes, ate peacock breast and drank wine. Lollia did her duty.

For now, she thought, watching her husband over the rim of her goblet. *Just you wait.*

Fourteen

❧

"TELL him I'm out," Cornelia pleaded. "Tell him I'm sick."

"Nonsense." Tullia dismissed that with a flick. "Perhaps you should change. The blue dress? No, there isn't time. Pin that black thing in front with a brooch; show a little breast. Your new husband will want to see what he's buying."

"I can't go down, I can't—"

"Don't be absurd. You're lucky to be getting such a chance. It's a great thing for our family." After yanking Cornelia's neckline downward, Tullia rummaged in the jewel chest for a pair of gold-and-ebony earrings, and twisted them into Cornelia's ears. *Piso gave me those earrings,* she thought with a wrench in her stomach, *and now they're making me pretty for a new husband.*

"Gaius is waiting to give his official consent, so just give the slave a signal," Tullia ordered. "I imagine there will be a betrothal feast for you and your husband—"

Cornelia felt her head whirling. "I can't."

"Of course you can." Tullia's little varnished fingernails dug painfully as she seized Cornelia's arm. "It's your duty. You will *not* disappoint me. Living in my house, eating my food—"

"Did I have a choice? My house was confiscated!"

"—you owe it to me to make a good marriage!" Tullia took her arm, towed her from the bedchamber and down the stairs. At the foot of the steps, Gaius shuffled nervously from foot to foot as Tullia yanked his sister past.

"Gaius—" Cornelia wrenched her arm out of Tullia's grip, turning to her brother. They had never been close growing up, but surely— "I'm your sister, Gaius. Please—"

But Gaius just gave her a guilty smile as Tullia grabbed her by the wrist again and towed her past. "Pinch your cheeks," Tullia told her. "You're pale as a corpse. Go out to the garden, they're waiting by the fountain."

"Tullia, I will *not*—"

Cornelia rocked back as her sister-in-law's ringed hand flashed out and slapped her, first one cheek and then the other, so hard tears sprang to her eyes. "At least that gives you some color," Tullia said, and shoved Cornelia out toward the garden. "Now *smile!*"

Two officers in breastplates and greaves turned at the sound of footsteps. "Lady Cornelia," Fabius Valens smiled, and they both bowed. The other man's face was just a blur in her eyes. She forced back the tears that had come to her eyes, hearing Tullia click away behind her. Ahead, the fountain threw its spray high in the air behind her prospective suitor, glittering in the sunlight; a dazzling aureole behind his head. The moss was soft and green underfoot, every bush was exploding into bloom, and the smell of jasmine hung on the air. *A garden full of flowers, a perfect summer day, a waiting suitor,* Cornelia thought distantly. *A thousand poems begin like this.* She descended the two marble steps into the garden but couldn't feel the ground under her feet.

Fabius took possession of her elbow. Her skin crawled at his touch, but he was all smiles today. "You know Caecina Alienus, of course?"

The man bowed—her next husband—and Cornelia saw the thin handsome face through a haze. Alienus, another of Vitellius's most trusted advisers, a Roman who had been in Germania so long that he wore shaggy hair and trousers like a tribesman and drank German mead at banquets until he was soddenly unconscious. He grinned, his eyes crawling over her body, and contempt warred in her stomach with nausea.

"—Emperor will give a wedding feast for you, of course. He's always valued you, Alienus—"

Alienus tipped his head back, half-turning Cornelia for a look at her haunches, and rage choked her throat—rage at Tullia and her brother. *I was the wife of Lucius Calpurnius Piso Licinianus, Imperial heir, descendant of Crassus and Pompey Magnus. And now they sell me to a man like this.*

"—don't mind if you take her to Baiae after the wedding, Alienus. If you want to try out your wife for a few days, I can handle matters here—"

It had been winter when Piso came to ask for Cornelia's hand. He'd gone to her father first, as was proper, and afterward they had been allowed a few moments to walk in the frozen garden, breath steaming white on the air. She had been too excited to feel the cold.

"—give you a house on the Aventine, the one with the pink marble columns. It's got a spectacular view over the Tiber—"

"I know that house," Cornelia managed to say. "Doesn't it belong to Senator Septimus Fulvius?"

Fabius smiled. "Now it belongs to your new husband."

Cornelia wanted her own house back, the one where she'd spent eight years of married life. The mosaics with their twining vines and buds, the frescoes of acanthus leaves and bunches of grapes, the statues she'd chosen herself for each niche. Long since confiscated, and doubtless now belonging to some other opportunistic thug.

"—do a great deal of entertaining, of course. The Emperor expects a feast every time he comes to dine, sixty courses at least, but you'll manage. You'll do a damned sight better than that stupid slut I married."

Cornelia rallied. "You will not call my cousin—"

"I suppose I should settle matters with your brother." Fabius overrode her, rising businesslike from the fountain's edge. "The dowry and so forth. It won't take long. Gives you two a chance to know each other."

"My dowry isn't much," Cornelia managed to say, looking past Fabius to the shaggy Alienus. "You could find a much richer wife than me, sir."

"I want you." The first words he had spoken. He had a guttural voice like a German.

"I'm barren," she said desperately. "Eight years I was married to my last husband, and no sign of a child—surely you want a wife who can give you sons?"

"If I want sons," he grinned, "I'll just get another wife. Keep you for a concubine."

Fabius guffawed, and Cornelia looked at him. *He's enjoying himself even more than Alienus.* She wondered how long Fabius Valens had looked at patrician girls like her, aloof untouchable girls he could never have. *He can have us all now, either to take for his own or dispose of as he likes. We're all his, and we hate it. He likes that.*

"I'm busy with the new Praetorian Prefects all afternoon," Fabius was saying, "but you'll both dine with me tonight. Dusk—no, better make it an hour after."

It's your duty, Cornelia reminded herself. *Your duty.*

She nodded, and Alienus's hard fingers closed on hers.

"Your betrothed's a pretty one, Alienus." Fabius's fingers brushed along her arm. "Maybe she and I should dine alone tonight instead. I'll try her out for you."

His fingers brushed along her breast, closing on the nipple. Cornelia sank her teeth into the inside of her lip. *Duty. Duty.*

His smile broadened, fingers stroking her as he looked at the grinning Alienus. She could smell his hair pomade. "I'll see she's wet for your wedding."

Cornelia threw his hand away and slapped his grinning face, as she would have slapped an insolent slave. "Go to Hades, you sticky little pleb." She jerked her hand from Alienus's. "And take your German thug with you."

She turned and stalked away, past the fountain with its sparkling spray, past the slave who stood ready with a congratulatory flagon of wine, past Gaius where he waited to give his formal consent to the betrothal. "Cornelia?" he said, puzzled, but she walked straight past him to the stairs, to her bedchamber, and shut the door. It was quiet inside, cooling the blood that thundered in her ears. Probably the last quiet she would get in quite some time. Cornelia sat on the bed, waiting. Didn't have to wait long.

"*Why, WHY?*" Tullia shrieked, banging through the door. "You told the Emperor's right-hand man to go to *Hades*—you selfish, selfish, inconsiderate—"

"In future, Tullia," Cornelia said coldly, "I would rather you didn't eavesdrop on my marriage proposals."

"*Gaius—!*"

"Now, now, I'm sure there's no harm done." Gaius tried a coaxing tone. "A man like Fabius Valens isn't one to be put off by a flighty woman. He'll be back, and with a proper apology Cornelia can still—"

"No apology," Cornelia said. "No marriage. No arguments. I will not marry any of Fabius Valens's thugs, and if he comes back I'll tell him so again."

"But you must!" Gaius turned red to match Tullia's purple. "You know what he said to me on the way out? 'Keep your women in better order, Senator—'"

"You think a man like that won't be vindictive?" Tullia screeched. "He could cook up charges against us, have our property confiscated—"

"With Diana in such favor with the Emperor, I doubt it," Cornelia said. But Gaius rode over her.

"You want to ruin this family, Cornelia? These are different times! It's for me to say who you will marry—"

"Yes, and if you made a proper match for me, I'd consider it!" Cornelia flashed back. "But you're just shoving me into the bed of some German savage for an Imperial favor or two—no, don't look at her!" As his eyes crept to Tullia. "I know this was all her idea. But you're master here, Gaius, not her. Grow a *spine!*"

"This is all your fault, Gaius!" Tullia rounded on him. "If you hadn't indulged her in everything she wanted, her and all the rest of your cousins—"

"What's all the shouting?" Marcella blinked from the doorway, still holding a pen.

"Your sister has refused to marry Fabius Valens's friend!" Tullia screamed. *"Refused!"*

Marcella looked at her sister a moment. "Not very wise," she said at last. "Though I wouldn't want to marry any of his friends either." She wrinkled her nose in sympathy and went away again, tucking her pen behind her ear, and Cornelia spared a split second in all the chaos to choke on a wave of pure fury at her sister. She could have used Marcella's support in all this screaming abuse, Marcella's comforting arm at her waist and Marcella's voice backing up hers. Once, Marcella wouldn't have left her to face it alone—it would have been the two of them, shoulder to shoulder against the storm. *But now, if it takes her away from her writing and scheming, it's too much to ask.*

Cornelia staggered then as Tullia flew across the room and began raining slaps wildly down around her head. "Selfish slut—you need a *husband*; one of Fabius's favorites could protect this family—we're all on a precipice with emperors changing every month! Who do you think you are? *Who do you think you are?*"

"I'm not you," Cornelia managed to say, warding off the slaps. "I'm not a whore."

Tullia began to choke and weep, her face the color of a pomegranate, and Gaius pulled her off. The slaves rushed in making soothing noises, and Cornelia put her hands over her ears and walked out of the room. She went down the stairs again, past the staring slaves, past little Paulinus who with his father in prison was still trailing forlornly about the house. "Aunt Cornelia?" he said hopefully around his thumb, but though she would usually pick him up and fuss over him and spend an afternoon playing games with him, Cornelia just dropped a kiss on his forehead and kept walking, out the front door.

She walked past the bathhouse where she had so often met with Vitellius's supporters, passing the information that helped put Vitellius on the throne and bring Fabius Valens to power. *How stupid I was.*

An acquaintance called out from the bathhouse gate, a matron in a blue *stola*, and Cornelia turned in the opposite direction, down a narrow little street with cramped houses.

Maybe I'll be exiled. She felt very calm and cold. Tullia was right; a man like Fabius Valens would be vindictive if Cornelia kept refusing him, would want revenge even if their family was in favor with the Emperor. Exile—a little island covered in sea grass, perhaps. At least it would be quiet. All Cornelia wanted was quiet. She heard the raucous voices of a forum somewhere up ahead and turned down another dim little side street.

If they make me marry that thug, I'll kill myself on the wedding day. Diana can bring my head out to the ceremony, and he can kiss it if he wants, but that's all he'll get of me.

Cornelia halted, looking around. How long had she been walking? It wasn't a quarter of town she knew. Not a quarter of town she wanted to know either—tenements leaning crookedly overhead, the smell of sewage leaking along the gutters. A stray dog bared its teeth, slinking by, and a crowd of naked children ran past, shouting and chasing one another. Two ragged women in a low doorway whispered behind their hands, and Cornelia was suddenly conscious of her fine linen, her tooled sandals, her gold-and-ebony earrings. *Perhaps I'll be robbed and murdered before Fabius can even order my execution.* She reversed her steps, looking for the turn that had taken her from the Palatine Hill into the slums, but found only more tenements, more dim streets, more foul smells. A cluster of manure-stained mule drovers staggered past, stinking of wine, whooping. Cornelia put up her chin, forcing herself not to hurry. She'd have to ask for directions . . . there was a man on a stool, leaning against a dingy tenement wall and looking up the street. At least he appeared sober.

"Excuse me," she said, approaching, and halted as he looked up. ". . . Centurion?"

"Not Centurion," said Drusus Sempronius Densus. "I was thrown out of the Praetorian Guard, Lady. Or didn't you know?"

". . . I heard. It was very unjust."

He shrugged, very different now from the proud soldier in his breastplate and red plumes. Just a stockily built man in a rough tunic, sitting against the wall of a slum tenement. His eyes were flat and unfriendly.

"I'm lost." Cornelia felt foolish.

"Thought you must be." The old tone of dogged courtesy had utterly gone. "Don't usually see patrician ladies in the slums otherwise."

"Can you show me the way out?"

"Give me those earrings of yours, and I will."

Cornelia's hand flew up to the gold-and-ebony drops swinging by her throat. "My earrings—"

"I don't draw my centurion's pay anymore, Lady. I need money."

She pulled off the earrings Piso had given her and dropped them into Drusus Densus's callused hand. He came up off his stool in one swift movement, gesturing to the doorway behind him. "I should tell the madam I'll be gone."

"The madam—?"

"Wait inside. You'll be robbed if you stand out here alone."

Gingerly, Cornelia followed him through the low doorway. A dark hall beyond, ragged strips of cloth curtaining off niches. There was a perch for cloaks by the first door, but she came closer and saw that it was a crude little statue of the god Priapus with his leer and his huge jutting phallus. Then she got a look at the fading frescoes that lined the walls and felt herself turning red.

"Room at the end, Lady," said Densus curtly. "Wait there unless you want to be taken for the new girl."

He disappeared into one of the curtained alcoves, and Cornelia fled down the passage. She heard moans from behind the thin curtains, panting, rhythmic thumping. A man brushed past, adjusting his belt, and Cornelia fell gratefully into the last room and shut the door. *You're no innocent girl*, she reminded herself. *You know what a whorehouse is.* But she still felt herself blushing, and looked hastily around the empty room.

It was small, painfully neat, chokingly hot. There was a narrow bed that sagged in the middle, a stool, an unlit lamp. A niche in the wall with two crude figurines. She picked them up. Mars and Minerva, gods of war and strategy. A soldier's gods.

The door banged as Densus came in. Cornelia turned, still holding the little statues. "You *live* here."

"Shocked, Lady?" He rummaged under the thin mattress.

". . . No."

"I throw out the customers if they get rough on the girls. In return, the madam lets me have the room." He retrieved his short *gladius* from under the mattress.

"You kept that?"

"I earned it. Twelve years in the Praetorian Guards." He scowled at the edge, rummaged under the mattress again, and came up with a whetstone.

She gestured at the little room around them. "You don't decorate much, do you?" Striving for a little lightness.

"Keep anything here but the household gods and the bed, and it'll get stolen." He rasped the whetstone down the short blade. "The whores lift anything that isn't nailed down."

Cornelia sat on the rickety little stool. "Maybe you shouldn't take me home. My family knows what you look like, and the slaves—someone might turn you in."

"*You* could turn me in, Lady." He tossed the whetstone aside.

"I won't. And even if I did, I don't think anyone would listen to me. I'm very unpopular with the Vitellians right now. At least some of them."

"Are you a traitor too?" He turned his back on her, rummaging for his cloak.

"Maybe. Commander Valens wants me to marry one of his officers, you see."

"That's not treason."

"It might be if you tell him to go to Hades." Cornelia smiled, feeling very light inside somehow. "Maybe I'll be arrested when I go home."

"You can't be arrested for refusing a marriage proposal, Lady."

"You can now." She shrugged. "You can be arrested for anything the Vitellians don't like. So maybe you'd better steer clear."

"I'm not giving your earrings back either way, so I might as well take you." Densus turned, a rough brown cloak over one arm. "Let's go."

Cornelia looked up at him from the stool. "My sister was at Bedriacum. She said you fought very bravely."

"It doesn't matter. Let's go."

"They never should have accused you of treason." Rising. "I know you didn't sell Galba and Piso—"

"Generous of you, Lady." His chestnut eyes stared into hers. "Am I supposed to thank you for that?"

"I'm just trying to—"

"You're glad I was booted out of the guard, aren't you? You think I deserved it. I didn't save Senator Piso, did I, so I'm not worthy to be a Praetorian."

"No." She fell back a step under his rage.

"You think I'll bow and feel grateful, because you're telling me I'm not a traitor? Think I'll apologize again for getting your precious husband killed?" Densus hurled his cloak down. "Piss on that, Lady. I did my best to save him. It wasn't good enough, but I did my best. I'm *done* apologizing."

He turned away, his breath coming harsh and fast in the little room. Cornelia saw his hand opening and closing on the hilt of the *gladius* and addressed the tense knotted back. "I never thought you should have been thrown out of the Praetorians. You're the best of them. Better than the Prefects who give you your orders—"

"The ones you let suck on your neck behind closed curtains?" Densus swung around again, jaw clamped. "Not much of a compliment."

"I wanted information," she said miserably. "The Prefect gave me information, and I passed it on to the Vitellians. I just wanted Otho dead—"

"Well, it worked. You like the results?" Densus flung the sheathed *gladius* across the room. It crashed into the little niche, and the figurines of Mars and Minerva tumbled over with a tinny rattle. "All you meddling patrician bitches, playing with lives—"

"I didn't mean—"

"You never do. You never do." Densus dropped down on the narrow bed, clasping his square hands between his knees. His fingers were shaking. "Get out, Lady. Find your own bloody way home."

Cornelia crossed the room, all of two steps. She opened her mouth, but her mind had never been so blank, wiped clean by his rage. She just stood awkwardly before him, wishing she knew what to do. She could only see the top of his head, dropped level to his heaving shoulders.

"Go home," Densus repeated thickly. "Marry some Vitellian thug and lie there thinking about your duty while he's mounting you. You patricians are all so good at doing your duty."

"Not always." Cornelia reached out and touched his cheek. He flinched, but she stepped closer, pulling his head against her waist. His arms closed around her, bruisingly hard, and Cornelia ran her fingers through his curly hair as his shoulders heaved. Through the thin door panels she could hear the moans of a woman down the hall, a man's grunting. *A whorehouse in the slums, a fetid summer day, an accused traitor,* she thought distantly. *There are no poems that begin like this.*

Cornelia kissed him first, leaning down to take his face between her hands. He looked up at her, startled, and all she could do was shake her head silently and press her lips to his again. His rough jaw scratched her skin as he rose, sinking his hands into her hair. He pulled the dress off her shoulders, burying his face in her breasts, and she sank down on the narrow bed as she helped tug the tunic over his head. *So strange,* she thought remotely as she pulled him down beside her, rubbing her cheek against his rough shoulder. The only other man's body she'd ever known was Piso's. Densus was broader, browner, harder. So different from Piso's lean height. Cornelia tried to close her eyes against the strangeness of it, but Densus cradled her face between his hands. "No," he said, "no," and he kissed her eyes open as he moved inside her, so slowly. She clutched him, crying out, and Piso disappeared.

THEY lay on the narrow bed, hands clasped between them on the ragged pillow. The room was stifling. He ran a hand slowly over the curve of her hip, sheened with sweat. "Cornelia," he said.

"What?"

"Nothing." His face was serious, drained of rage, the chestnut eyes steady over their linked hands. "Weeks I spent following you around on guard duty, dreaming about calling you by name. Cornelia."

"Drusus." She said his name shyly. They had made love half the afternoon in the ferocious heat, and only now did she feel shy.

Fifteen

～∽

S HE said *what?*"

Marcella mimicked Diana's flat matter-of-fact voice. " 'Get yourself a whore. I'll never marry a Blues fan.' "

Cornelia winced. "That sounds like her. Which one of Vitellius's officers was it?"

"The same German thug who proposed to you." Marcella smiled. "Two rejections in a row! I'll leave you to imagine the scene that ensued. Tullia said—"

Marcella lifted her feather fan to hide their whispering. The Theatre of Marcellus was full for once with the Emperor in attendance in his box rather than at the races, and the air was swelteringly close. The actors sweated under their masks and paint on stage as they declaimed through the lines of some turgid drama, and fans waved listlessly through the packed tiers of the audience—feather for the patricians, paper for the plebs below. No one from the Emperor on down appeared to be paying much attention to the play.

Marcella kept whispering. "At least now we know—Vitellius doesn't want Diana for himself, or his officers wouldn't dare set their caps at her. I think that's what maddened Tullia the most. She had such a touching little dream of Vitellius divorcing that meek wife of his and making Diana Empress instead." Marcella glanced at the Emperor, ruddy-faced and roaring with laughter in the Imperial box just one row away, surrounded by his officers. Properly men and women sat apart at the theater, but Diana had the stool at his feet as she always did these days, and Vitellius's heavy drink-reddened face was tilted down toward the little blond head. "I could have told Tullia he wasn't interested in Diana that way. He might pat her hips now and then when he's drunk—but since when is a man like Vitellius really interested in anything besides eating, throwing up, and watching the Blues win?" Marcella cast her eyes up to the heavens. "And that's our Emperor."

Cornelia just nodded absently, and Marcella suppressed a sigh. She'd dragged her sister out to the theater that afternoon, hoping to give her a treat—Gaius and Tullia were still barely speaking to her, after all—and all Cornelia could do was twitch in her seat, fingers beating a restless tattoo on the ivory handle of her fan. It wasn't like her, but everyone in Rome seemed overheated and distracted these days. Summer rolled toward September, scorching hot, bringing swirls of dust on the slightest breeze. Everyone groaned about the heat, spent hours in the *natatio* pools of the bathhouses, bemoaned their cool river villas in Toscana or Tivoli.

Everyone but me. Marcella felt cool as ice in all the heat, and she wouldn't have left this boiling, bubbling, scheming city for all the gold in Egypt.

Her eyes drifted speculatively over to Vitellius again. She could hear his bull voice clearly over the declaiming of the actors—and even if he'd whispered, she thought she would have heard him. *My ears can pick up every whisper in Rome*, she sometimes thought.

"—those chestnut stallions of yours, the ones named after winds," Vitellius was saying down to the little blond head at his side. "You're afraid to stack them against my Blues!"

"Caesar," Diana shot back, "your Blues are spavined cow-hocked mules compared to my Anemoi." The other guests in the Imperial box exchanged glances—Marcella knew they couldn't believe how freely

Diana spoke her mind to the ruler of Rome. But Vitellius had spent a good many years as governor in rough places like Germania and Africa: he liked plain speaking, and he liked Diana. He roared laughter, and his friends were quick to laugh with him.

"You might think he'd be more worried," Marcella mused aloud. "What with the news from Judaea . . ."

Cornelia blinked, drawn out of her reverie again. "Oh, that."

"Aren't you even *interested* that Vespasian's been proclaimed Emperor?" Marcella didn't understand her sister. What an exciting time they were all living through, and all Cornelia could do was mope around taking endless trips to the bathhouse! "Surely you realize this means war."

Cornelia pushed a strand of hair behind her ears. "We've had war all year."

"But Vespasian has the eastern legions! The Tenth, the Fourth, the Twelfth, and the Fifteenth—" Marcella ticked them off with satisfaction. "He'll march on Rome, and Vitellius will have to muster an army to beat him. And I wonder . . ." She trailed off, thoughtful.

"I ever tell you how I got this limp, girl?" Up in the Imperial box, Vitellius heaved his bulk out of his carved chair.

"A battle in Africa, wasn't it?" Diana took his arm as he swayed. "Gods' wheels, you're drunk. Lean on me, Caesar."

"I tell everyone it was a battle. But the truth? A horse kicked me." Vitellius grinned down at Diana. "Don't tell."

"See this, Caesar?" Diana lifted the hem of her red silk dress, showing an ankle Marcella couldn't see. "I told my family I tripped getting out of a litter, but really—" She stood on tiptoe to whisper in his ear.

"Really?" A laugh. "What a devil you are."

"Don't tell, Caesar?"

"Not if you won't." He ruffled her hair. "What a pair of frauds we are, eh?"

His smile had a bluff kind of charm, Marcella conceded. Despite his grosser habits, Vitellius had a certain direct appeal: he laughed when he was amused, ate when he was hungry, drank when he was thirsty, and rarely got angry at anyone. Refreshing after so many subtle politicians with wheels spinning in their heads and plots behind their backs—but would such easy simplicity be enough to hold the loyalty of his generals? *They're a shifty bunch.* If more legions went over to Vespasian, the rats might just start wondering which ship was about to sink . . .

The play halted momentarily as the Emperor left the box to go relieve himself, and a buzz of halfhearted overheated gossip rose. "Where's Lollia?" Diana was asking Fabius, flopping back onto her stool. "She likes the theater."

"The bitch says the heat's giving her headaches," Lollia's husband complained.

"You're very stupid to treat her so badly," Diana told Fabius calmly. "But ambitious little toads like you are usually stupid."

Fabius looked at Diana with loathing. "You won't always be the Emperor's pet, girl."

"Poor Lollia," Cornelia said, overhearing. "She's been crying all week, since Fabius flogged her slave. And I'm not sure he doesn't beat Lollia too—she's got marks she keeps trying to cover up with powder and bracelets, and she's avoiding her grandfather. I suppose she doesn't want him to see the bruises. He didn't want the marriage to happen in the first place, and he'll just be miserable he can't do anything about it now."

Marcella eyed Fabius thoughtfully as the Emperor reappeared in the box, hitching at his toga. Vitellius would raise an army soon against Vespasian, and he'd count on Fabius to do it. What kind of army could he raise? Those eastern legions were hard, seasoned troops—German savages and palace guards wouldn't be enough . . .

The Emperor settled back into his chair, waving an irritable hand, and the perspiring actors hitched their masks into place. "Damned long play," Vitellius complained loudly to Diana, splashing more wine into his cup. The actors onstage looked rather resigned as they resumed trudging through their verses, the Emperor's strident voice bulling over their own. "I'd rather have a good race any day. No sulks from you when my Blues win at Vinalia, now—losers should wear a smile."

"Did that mean you were smiling all last year, Caesar?" Diana said sweetly. "When the Blues came in last of all the factions?"

"You've got a tart tongue, girl. Your father didn't beat you enough growing up."

Marcella only half-listened to Vitellius and Diana's wrangling, still pondering the possible loyalty of the Emperor's generals. "If they're shifty sorts, I wonder what Vespasian's generals are like? Domitian might know. Of course he'll be boring and try to get me into bed, but if I can't wheedle a little information out of an eighteen-year-old boy . . ."

There was a rustle at her side, and Cornelia rose abruptly. "I'm going home."

"Are you all right?" Marcella looked up, blinking her thoughts away.

"A headache—I hate this hot weather." Cornelia looked more distracted than ever, pushing a damp tendril of hair off her neck. "Excuse me—" and off she rushed.

Marcella wondered for a moment if she should go with her sister—offer to take her to the bathhouse where they could cool down in the *frigidarium* and have a good gossip like they used to in the old days. But a moping sister just wasn't much amusement compared to everything else going on. *I'll spend more time with her later,* Marcella thought vaguely, *when things have calmed down. Will they ever calm down?*

She listened to a few more verses from the lackadaisical actors, thoroughly overridden now by the Emperor's bull voice and Diana's strident one as they argued horses, and then someone claimed the seat beside her.

"You shouldn't sit here." Marcella waved her fan, languid.

"The Emperor doesn't care about the rules." Domitian's hand settled on her knee, moist and warm. "So why should I?"

Marcella smiled and deftly shifted away. "Behave, now."

"Why?" he breathed. "You weren't always so well-behaved."

"That was a mistake. I was very distressed after what I'd seen in Bedriacum." Ever since that swift ferocious coupling in the garden overlooking the city, Marcella had been careful not to allow Domitian any further intimacies. He worked so much harder for her when he was frustrated . . . and he was so easily frustrated. Sulky, he flopped back in his seat and started to mutter the latest news from his father in Judaea, but Marcella only listened with half an ear. Her eyes had settled on one discontented face in the crowd below, a face she had noted before.

"Excuse me," she murmured to Domitian, rising and pulling the pale-green veil over her hair. "I won't be a moment—

"Caecina Alienus!" Marcella smiled, sinking into the seat beside the man both her sister and Diana had turned down. "I did not know you were such a devotee of the theater."

"A soldier can make time for the arts, Lady." His German-accented bass was surly—he could hardly be pleased to see another member of the Cornelii, after what happened with the first two—but he gave Marcella a curt nod before turning his attention back to the stage. Several of his officers diced beside him, bored.

"Isn't Fabius at the Senate now?" she asked innocently. "Surely you're his little shadow."

Alienus scowled—a man of considerable power, Marcella knew, but not as high in Vitellius's favor as Fabius Valens. And no doubt smarting from being rejected—publicly—by two patrician brides in a row.

"What good taste you have," Marcella said, fanning herself. "Theater is for subtle men—wasted on these straightforward sorts like Fabius. Vitellius too, really."

"Mmm." Alienus glowered at the stage.

"I think more things are wasted on Vitellius besides theater," Marcella continued. "Good men like yourself, for example."

A fleeting glance from below thick brows.

"I should like to tell you something, Commander." She dropped her voice. "Of course we all know that the eastern legions proclaimed Governor Vespasian as Emperor some weeks ago. You probably don't know that the Moesian legions have declared for him as well, five days back."

"What?" She had Alienus's full attention now, the dark eyes narrowed. "Five days—how could you possibly know that?"

"Vespasian's younger son Domitian. He's mad for me." Marcella smiled, keeping up the fan's placid movement. "So you see, I *do* know what I'm talking about. Vespasian has four legions in Judaea, but it's a long time before they can get here, isn't it? However, the legate of the Moesian legions has persuaded his men to march at once on Rome . . . and they are much closer."

"I don't believe you."

"Why should you?" Marcella tilted a shoulder. "I'm just a woman whispering rumors during a play. You'll receive confirmation of the rumors in a few days' time, however, and perhaps then you should come see me." She rose.

"Why would I do that?" Alienus challenged.

"Why?" Marcella looked back over her shoulder. "Because unlike Vitellius, Vespasian isn't the Emperor to overlook good men. Maybe you should consider that."

She drifted back to her seat, where a scowling Domitian took possession of her hand. "What kept you so long?"

"Nothing unimportant." She put an arm about him, stroking the back of his neck openly, and he dove forward to bury his lips between her breasts. She looked over his shoulder at Alienus, watching her with narrowed eyes, and lifted an eyebrow. *See, you ambitious little man? I do have sources.*

"Domitian," she murmured, pushing him back a little. "You may want to drop a word in Caecina Alienus's ear sometime soon."

"Alienus?" Domitian lifted his head from where he'd been nibbling along the line of her shoulder. "Why are you talking about him? If you're bedding that thug in breeches—"

"You don't have a rival, you silly boy." Flicking the tip of his nose. "I just know an opportunity when I see one. Alienus is a powerful man—and lately he's been humiliated by two proposed brides, edged out by Fabius Valens, and neglected by the Emperor. I think he's feeling . . . restless."

"So?" Domitian scowled.

"So, that could be exploited. Why don't you and your uncle host a dinner party, and invite him. Put him next to me, and I'll drop a few words in his ear about your father. How generously he rewards his supporters. Then you can chime in with convincing details."

Domitian's black eyes began to gleam.

"Maybe bring your pet astrologer," Marcella suggested. "He must be hard up these days; Vitellius doesn't like astrologers. He could say a few encouraging words about the fates of all those who serve your father . . ."

"You're a goddess," Domitian breathed.

Marcella smiled. "Perhaps I am."

CORNELIA remembered the days back at the beginning of this strange year when she'd been meeting with Vitellius's brother to pass on information about Otho; how easily she had managed to come and go unnoticed from her brother's house for those clandestine gatherings. *I could be bedding half of Rome and my family would be the last to know*, she'd thought at the time, and scoffed inside at the patrician matrons who bemoaned the difficulties of meeting with their lovers.

She knew what they were moaning about now.

"My family thinks I'm at the theater with my sister," Cornelia said breathlessly, coming through the rickety door of the whorehouse and landing in Drusus's arms.

"Good." He pinned her against the wall of his room, pushing the veil off her hair, kissing her throat. "How long?"

"An hour—" she murmured between kisses. "Maybe two—"

But two hours wasn't enough, and Cornelia found herself running back through the streets, heart hammering in her throat, slipping through the slaves' gate and hoping no one had noticed how long she'd been gone. Two hours here, three hours there—it was never long enough.

"Don't take any risks," Drusus urged. "You've got more to lose than me."

"You've got your life to lose." She twisted her head on the pillow to look at him.

"That's already lost," he shrugged. "They just haven't collected payment yet." He cupped a hand around Cornelia's cheek, and she shivered at his touch. "You be careful. At least—"

"What?"

He reddened, but his chestnut eyes were steady. "You are taking care, aren't you?" His rough fingers brushed her belly mutely. "The madam, she said patrician women knew what to do . . ."

"No need for that." Cornelia shook her head. "I'm barren." Still a painful word to speak, but she forced it out matter-of-factly. "It makes things easy now, though, doesn't it? Otherwise I'd have to ask my cousin Lollia for those Egyptian tricks that keep her out of trouble, and Lollia can't keep a secret to save her life."

"Be careful about everything else, too." He kissed the tip of Cornelia's nose.

"I'm a fine patrician lady—I know how to sneak!"

But somehow she couldn't manage to be careful.

For four days the following week, Tullia fancied herself ill and dumped the house's supervision on Cornelia. Meals had to be planned, the slaves supervised, little Paulinus tended, and there was no time to spare for the squalid whorehouse in the Subura slums. Cornelia ran there all the way the following morning when Tullia finally pronounced herself well again, and when she saw the smile that split Drusus's face she seized his hand and dragged him back through the narrow stinking hallway toward his room, shrugging down the shoulders of her gown before the flimsy door was even closed. "Gods, I missed you," he groaned against her mouth, and they didn't even make it to the bed. Four days was too long, three days was too long. Cornelia came every other day, dry-mouthed, every inch of her skin burning. "They think I'm at the bathhouse—they think I'm at the races—they think I went to bed early." Any excuse she could find.

"You should go." Drusus ran a hand down the curve of her back at the end of a long hot afternoon. "Most people don't take five-hour baths."

"Mmm. No." But she nestled against his hard shoulder, drowsing another half hour in the baking heat instead of getting up. "Oh,

Juno's mercy, is it twilight?" she exclaimed, looking at the slant of light through his narrow slit of a window. "Where's my gown?"

"And they say patrician women take hours to get dressed." Drusus grinned, watching her fly around the little room. Cornelia made a face at him, twisting her hair into a knot at the back of her neck, hopping on one foot to lace her sandal.

"Tomorrow—" She collected her *palla*, holding one hand out for a quick squeeze. "I'll be back tomorrow; I've begged off a family banquet."

"Tomorrow." His fingers squeezed hers, warm and hard. Cornelia looked at him, sitting on the edge of the bed with his chestnut hair mussed, his eyes warm and steady, and she dropped her *palla* on the floor and climbed into his lap and made love to him again, fierce and silent, before running back to the Palatine Hill and coming home far later than she had any right to be. She looked in the glass that night, hastily tidying herself, and didn't know her own face. These flushed cheeks and over-bright eyes and wild hair couldn't possibly belong to the cool and elegant Cornelia Prima, the impeccable matron who never did anything unseemly or incorrect, who would have wrinkled her nose at the very idea of taking a common soldier for a lover. This was someone else entirely.

They'll notice, she thought in dread. *Juno's mercy, someone's bound to notice.* But to her astonishment, no one noticed. Gaius was out from dawn until dusk trying to curry favor with Vitellius or at least keep up with his frantic pace of feasting. Marcella was obsessed with Vespasian's whispered march on Rome. Lollia could normally be counted on to pick up the slightest hint of any love affair; Cornelia waited with an inward wince for her laughing wink and her whispered, "Well, who is he?" But even Lollia seemed wrapped in her own somber thoughts. The rest of the family, Tullia in the lead, were so diverted by Diana's new status as the Emperor's pet that they had no time for anything else.

"If Diana could get a provincial governorship for Gaius," Tullia breathed. "Lower Germania—the Emperor did say he would need a new governor there . . ."

"I don't know if I really want to govern Lower Germania," Gaius ventured. "Nasty cold place."

"*Gaius*, don't be ridiculous! Of course you want to! Or maybe Pannonia . . ."

"No one has time for me in all this fuss over Diana," Cornelia told Drusus. "The family's after her day and night to get Imperial posts and appointments and favors out of Vitellius for them. Even more, they want her to marry someone very grand. But she keeps turning down all the suitors, and the family keeps going into spasms."

"Turning them down?"

"She turned down Fabius's chief commander Alienus; that wasn't pretty. And not a week later one of his German officers caught her after the races and tried to drag her off by force—she broke a driving whip over his head, and said she'd stab him if he tried again."

Drusus blinked. "How does a little thing like that know how to stab anyone?"

"We all do." Cornelia demonstrated. "Under the breast into the heart, fast and clean. All patrician women know how to die."

"You people are savages." He curled a hand protectively around the threatened breast.

"Diana's certainly a savage," Cornelia admitted. "Thank the gods Vitellius is too amused by her to be offended. He just keeps saying there are some fillies that won't ever be saddled."

"What about you?" Drusus grinned.

"I am a woman of Cornelii," Cornelia said primly. "I certainly refuse to be saddled."

"What about worshipped?" As he tipped her over on her back.

"You have a peculiar notion of worship, Drusus . . ."

Cornelia bribed the doorkeeper. She bribed the steward. She bribed her maid. They pretended not to smirk when she came back to the house disheveled and yawning, and still no one put the signs together. "Are you happier these days?" Marcella asked one night, idly.

"What do you mean?" Cornelia tried to keep the edge out of her voice.

"You always bite your nails when you're wretched. And look at them now, all smooth again for the first time in months. So you must be happy."

"Well, I'm happy I escaped marrying that German thug," Cornelia said lightly, and braced herself for one of Marcella's knowing smiles. She could never hide secrets for long, not from her little sister—but Marcella just wandered away with a yawn. It wasn't like her, to drop a clue where it lay instead of pursuing it—but Cornelia didn't question her luck. She was far better off if Marcella's observant eyes weren't fixed on her.

Fool, she told herself harshly in the quiet dark of her bedchamber. *You know what will happen if anyone finds out.* A dalliance with a man of her own class was one thing. Gaius might glare and Tullia might say cutting things about loose-moraled widows, but Lollia would be the first to wink and bid her good luck, and plenty of others would do the same as long as Cornelia was discreet. But a common soldier who rousted drunks out of a whorehouse in the slums . . . a man accused of treason, sentenced to death for failing to protect her own husband . . .

I'd have to leave Rome, if the scandal got out. Every night Cornelia made herself dwell on it: the whispers, the snickers, the disgrace. *My family would be humiliated. Gaius would disown me.* And Drusus would likely be caught, arrested, executed on the warrant that had never been brought to charge. *He'd die, because of me.*

Every night Cornelia made herself think of it, every grinding detail of humiliation and disgrace and death, until she dropped off to an exhausted sleep. *I'll come to my senses in the morning. I'll realize what a fool I'm being.* But then morning came and a slave brought a plate of breakfast fruit and eggs, and before Cornelia even rose from her bed she was planning how soon she could get out of the house to see Drusus.

"Coming every day now, Lady?" The raddled madam of the Subura whorehouse raised her painted eyebrows as Cornelia slipped into the hall. "My, my. That boy must be doing something right. You make more noise than any of my whores."

Cornelia drew herself up with a freezing glare, but the madam chuckled unafraid. "Don't play the great lady with me. You're here for the same thing *they* are." She gestured at the men who slipped in and out of the little curtained niches, grabbing at the whores, hitching their belts. "Only difference is, that boy back there is too addled to make you pay for it."

"Now there's an idea," said Drusus when Cornelia reported this in sputtering rage. "Should I start charging you, Lady? How much?"

"Maybe I should charge you!" Cornelia wriggled away from him, but he flung her back down on the bed. She struggled but he pinned her easily, grinning. "At least you could pay for all those hired litters I have to take getting down here," she informed him.

"Can't I pay you in services rendered?" He pried her arms apart, setting his mouth at the base of her throat.

"Not on my neck!" Cornelia broke down laughing. "I'm getting marks—Lollia's bound to notice soon."

"Lollia's the one who loves horses?"

"No, that's Diana. She wouldn't notice a mark on anyone's neck, unless it was one of her precious Anemoi. But Lollia's got sharp eyes."

"So I'll stay away from your neck for a while," Drusus murmured against her waist. "Too bad, it's such a pretty neck . . ."

He knew all about her family now. Sweating, too hot in the airless little room even for a sheet, they lay naked on the narrow bed that sank in the middle and talked. "What about your family?" Cornelia asked, propping her chin on her hand.

"I grew up in Toscana." He linked his hands behind his head on the pillow. "My father ran a wine shop. A good wine shop," Drusus added rather defensively. "He was able to buy entrance to the equestrian class three years ago."

"Equestrian class?" Cornelia smiled. "Oh, good."

"Better than bedding a pleb?" He pinched her hip gently.

"Well, if you were a pleb, then these meetings of ours wouldn't be just ill-advised, they would be illegal." She began to enumerate the various laws forbidding congress between plebeians and patricians, but Drusus stopped her mouth with a kiss.

"Snob. But I'll forgive you, just for those dimples." He kissed them too, one by one. "You know how often I tried to make you smile, following you around on guard duty, just so I could see those dimples? I could put my thumb in them up to the knuckle . . ."

"Your family?" Cornelia prompted after a while.

"Yes, my family. My mother has a house with an atrium now—she's very proud of it. And my younger sister will make a good marriage; we're all proud of that. I've got an older brother in the legions, doing his tour somewhere in Dacia. He might make *optio*, but he doesn't care much. He just likes the life."

"So you're the pride and joy of the family?" Cornelia ran a hand through his hair. "Centurion in the Praetorian Guard by thirty-four! They must be proud."

"They were." His smile disappeared. "I've kept away from them this year. Don't want to drag them down with me."

Cornelia kissed him silently. Hiding in a whorehouse when once he'd guarded emperors at a palace—even with her here, she knew he still felt the shame of his demotion. "So your sister will be married soon?" she said, changing the subject. "Does she have a sweetheart, or are your parents arranging a proper match?"

"There's a boy she wants." He smiled again. "Son of another local shopkeeper. My father would rather see her married to a magistrate, but likely she'll get her way."

"Your father should arrange a marriage for her," Cornelia decreed. "Young girls don't have the sense to pick out a dress, much less a husband. And it's not just young girls, either—does anyone pick sensibly for themselves? Lollia's current choice is a slave from Gaul, Diana would rather marry a horse than any man—"

"And my choice is you." Drusus lifted Cornelia's sweat-damp hair off her neck, coiling it around his hand. "My family would be appalled at me. Aspiring to one of the Cornelii? You're right, no one picks well for themselves."

"No." She settled against his arm. "I let my father choose for me, and I was very happy."

"Senator Piso?"

Cornelia nodded. The first time either of them had brought up that name. Drusus's hand slowed in her hair.

"Do you—think of him often?"

"Not here." She drew a finger over Drusus's chest. "It's just us in here."

"This room's too small for anyone else. Even a flea."

"There's always room for fleas! My maid keeps finding them in my clothes and complaining—one more thing to bribe her to keep quiet about—"

Drusus laughed, pulling Cornelia over him. But she thought about Piso on the way home, as the hired bearers trudged back toward the house. That seemed to be where he seeped into her mind, almost unobtrusively.

Eight months dead. If Otho's coup had failed, Galba might have died naturally by now and Piso would be Emperor. Emperor Lucius Calpurnius Piso Licinianus, attending the Senate, hailing the crowds. Certainly never making love to his wife in the middle of the day; it wasn't seemly and anyway there would never be time. Frowning if he saw his wife with her hair disheveled, but a Caesar's wife would never have disheveled hair anyway. She would be Empress of Rome, riding jeweled and applauded through the streets rather than furtively sneaking through back alleys, never thinking of the sturdy centurion at her back as anything but a bodyguard.

I'm sorry, Cornelia thought toward her husband, *I'm sorry*—but she hardly knew what she was sorry for. He'd been gone so much longer than eight months, surely. She could still call his dark handsome face perfectly to mind, his lean body that looked so well in the pleats and folds of a toga, his beautifully kept hands and his half-smile. *He'd be shocked to see me now.* His cool immaculate wife who had always modestly pulled the sheet over herself after making love, eternally calm, eternally in order; now rushing off like a madwoman at all hours of the day into the arms of the man who had once been his bodyguard, lying naked and sweating and unashamed afterward in a narrow little bed that smelled of mold.

Piso wouldn't approve of me now, Cornelia thought with a twist. *He'd think I was behaving like Lollia, like a light woman.*

But Piso would have been even more shocked at the events of this year, had he lived to see them. Emperor succeeding emperor succeeding emperor, every patrician family in Rome running madly to keep up and keep in favor, men of ancient lineage and unstained service like

Senator Marcus Norbanus thrown in prison to rot while swaggering
jumped-up plebs like Fabius Valens preened like princes. *That* would
have shocked Piso profoundly. So maybe, with the whole world going
mad, he would have forgiven his wife. *Even if he were shocked, maybe he
would be glad to see me happy.*

September, now. Marcella reported that the Moesian legions had
declared for Vespasian; that Vitellius would have no choice but to
fight. Vitellius still caroused in the Domus Aurea every night and
insisted he could lick Vespasian in one battle, but Rome worried—
Rome worried a great deal as Fabius Valens began to assemble an
army. Everyone worried except Cornelia . . . and one other person, she
realized one sweltering afternoon.

"I saw you yesterday," Cornelia said abruptly to Diana one evening
as they waited to go to an Imperial banquet. Marcella had appeared,
unjeweled as always, and Lollia declared she looked too plain and
dragged her off to be fitted with earrings and brooches. Diana and
Cornelia had been left alone. "I know your secret."

"Do you?" Diana twirled one of the charioteer medallions around
her neck.

"Your father says you've been sneaking out in the afternoons to
meet some charioteer from Britannia. And yesterday on the Campus
Martius, I saw you with him."

Cornelia had been hurrying to Drusus, taking a shortcut. The
Campus Martius had been quite empty in the fierce heat of the
afternoon—empty except for one chariot and a team of tired horses,
with two figures flanking it. Cornelia's little fair-haired cousin, and
another figure much taller.

"I usually go to his villa to drive," Diana said, unembarrassed. "But
no one else uses the Campus Martius in this heat, so he took me to the
city to practice on a real track."

"Just practicing?" Cornelia asked gently. She'd seen them only
from a distance, but there had been such ease between Diana's little
figure and the tall one, whoever he was. Diana had playfully squeezed
half a water skin over the back of his neck, and he'd smiled and picked

her up quite unselfconsciously to toss her into the chariot. "You looked very—well, close."

Diana smiled.

"I won't tell," Cornelia sighed. "I should, but I won't."

"Good. Because I'm not stopping."

Cornelia looked at her youngest cousin, so little and so brave, sneaking off to meet her charioteer. *I know I should disapprove but I can't. Juno's mercy, I can't.*

"Cornelia?" Drusus was a dim shape in the darkness, sitting up in bed, reaching in reflex for his sword. "You've never come at night before—how long can you stay?"

"All night," Cornelia whispered, crawling naked into bed beside him in the hot little room, half drunk with her own daring. "All night, Drusus. Every night." She kissed him, twining her arms around his neck as the sounds of moans and grunts came through the thin walls on either side—and realized she was happy.

She hoped Piso would have been a little glad.

Sixteen

ᔕᓄ

"F LAVIA!"
Cornelia smiled as Lollia picked up her daughter and whirled her in a circle. "Or *is* it Flavia?" Lollia continued. "We dropped a giggling little girl off to stay with her great-grandfather, and you are a beautiful young lady. Where's Flavia?"

Lollia pretended to look around, and Flavia giggled. "Four years old," Lollia said softly. "What a big girl you are. Did you like your party?"

"Great-grandfather gave me a *pony*! And a pearl necklace an' a fan an' little jade *animals*—"

"It was a beautiful party," Cornelia said. "She had a lovely time." Little Flavia had been the center of a heap of gifts; riding her proud great-grandfather's shoulders, scrambling on and off various laps, harnessing Diana with a ribbon and driving her around the garden. Lollia had been unable to go; Fabius wanted her at an Imperial banquet. "She was too busy to miss you, Lollia."

"Not much comfort," Lollia said, as Flavia grabbed her mother and her aunt by the hands and tugged them through the tiled atrium. "I should have been there."

"You didn't feel much guilt missing her first three birthdays! First you were in Baiae visiting a new summer villa, then you were on a pleasure boat somewhere off Crete with a poet, and after that—"

Lollia made a face. "Seems like a lifetime ago."

"Can't you bring Flavia back to live with you again?" Cornelia ventured. "You could keep her well away from Fabius."

"I don't dare. He's suspicious of anything connected with Vespasian these days, and Flavia *is* Vespasian's granddaughter. Not that he's ever set eyes on her," Lollia added. "I don't think I ever met Vespasian myself above twice in my life. I remember him congratulating Titus and me at our wedding in the thickest provincial accent you ever heard. A nice man. He and my grandfather got along like anything—both shrewd traders, you know."

"You think Fabius would consider *Flavia* a threat?" Cornelia blinked. "A little girl—"

"How do I know what he'd think?" Lollia's tone was tight. "Titus has another daughter, from his second marriage, and her family's taking no chances with her safety. Just whisked her off to the country in hiding the moment Vespasian started making trouble for Vitellius. A little girl even younger than Flavia, and someone thought *she* might be a threat!"

"Come see the fish!" Flavia crowed, dragging them to the little private garden with its splashing fountain that led off from her pink-frilled bedchamber. "Great-grandfather put gold *rings* on them!" She sat Lollia and Cornelia down on the fountain's edge, breathlessly telling them about the king fish and the queen fish and all the princess fish in the fountain, her fair curls bouncing on her shoulders and her doting great-grandfather's pearls gleaming around her neck.

"Goodness," Cornelia said. "Do fish really have such dramatic lives?"

"They do, they do, an' if you take off your sandals they'll nibble your *toes!*"

"That sounds too good to pass up." Lollia unlaced her silver sandals and put her feet in the fountain next to Flavia's little plump toes. "Come on, Cornelia! Don't be a prig."

But Cornelia was already unlacing her sandals. Long iridescent fish slid languidly around her ankles, gold rings gleaming through their fins. "Did your grandfather really put those rings on them, just for Flavia?"

"Yes. Apparently he's going to get little gold crowns made for the king and queen fish. Light ones, you know, so they can still swim."

"He spoils her."

"Someone should." Lollia tipped her head back to the lace-leaved trees overhead. *I used to wish she'd take her responsibilities seriously*, Cornelia remembered, watching the cousin who had always annoyed her the most out of all of them . . . but now Cornelia found she didn't like this downcast version of Lollia at all. Her cousin's wide generous mouth wasn't made to droop so sadly.

"You look tired," Cornelia said at last.

"So do you, my honey. Are you sleeping?"

"Of course." Quickly. "I don't have nearly the social life you do these days. Mornings in the Senate—"

"Listening to Fabius bully Vitellius's latest vague directive through; very exciting."

"Afternoons at the Campus Martius—"

"Watching Fabius complain that the army isn't assembling fast enough. At least my vocabulary of swear words is expanding."

"Evenings at one banquet after another—"

"More like competitive vomiting. Meals that cost half a million sesterces each, just splashed all over the floor of a *vomitorium*. The most appalling waste you ever saw."

"I never knew you had such an economical streak." Cornelia smiled.

"I never knew I did either. Every gown I have smells like vomit, my head aches all the time like Vulcan's anvil, and every night Fabius has me dress up in my jewels and parade around the bedroom naked, telling him he's history's greatest kingmaker . . ." Lollia broke off. "Oh well."

Cornelia cast about for a lighter topic of conversation. "Where is your grandfather this afternoon?"

"Cutting deals with the grain factors. The Prefect of Egypt just declared for Vespasian, so grain may come in short supply. At least *our* tenants will be well fed."

"You should be careful, saying such things." Cornelia splashed gently at Flavia, who was trying to catch the fish and whispering some game to herself. "Fabius might . . ."

"Arrest me? He's arresting anyone else who says Vespasian's on the way. Even though everyone knows Vespasian's on the way."

"Well, the Emperor says there's nothing to worry about." Cornelia trailed her toes through the dappled water. "I could hardly hear the last play at the theater, he was reassuring everybody so loudly."

"Vitellius is riding a tiger and doesn't dare look down." Lollia snorted. "Diana says that's why he gets drunk instead, so he can pretend everything is all right. She's quite sensible when she's not raving about horses, isn't she?"

A long iridescent fish nibbled at Cornelia's toes. "Vitellius will have to send his armies north soon, though." She felt a shaft of relief that this time, Drusus could not march with them. "Do you know if he'll send Fabius?"

"If the gods are good." Lollia stared at the mossy green nymph in the middle of the fountain, tossing up the water with her cupped stone hands. Little Flavia perched humming on the nymph's stone feet, but Lollia didn't smile. "If the gods are *very* good, he won't come back."

"Even if he does come back, he won't last long," Cornelia found herself saying. A year ago she would have thought it improper to make such a remark even to a cousin, but a year ago everything had been different. "Men like Fabius Valens fall from favor. And after that, your grandfather will find you someone better."

"Or maybe I could just stay divorced for a while. I'm so *tired* of weddings."

A shriek of delight—Flavia lost her footing and fell with a splash into the fountain. She came up giggling, her dress soaked through. "I'm wet," she said gleefully.

"I see you are." Lollia rose and waded toward her, but a voice sounded from behind.

"Out of the fountain, Mistress Flavia. We get you dry."

A big golden Gaul in a knee-length kilt loped out into the little garden with a towel, and Flavia scrambled out and held up her arms to be rubbed dry. As the slave turned, Cornelia saw the vivid purple lash marks half healed across his back.

"I'm glad he didn't die of his beating," she said to Lollia, who had lifted her feet self-consciously out of the fountain.

"Yes, I made sure Grandfather got him the best care." Lollia became absorbed in relacing her sandals. "He's Flavia's body slave now. She adores him."

"I can see that." Cornelia watched as Thrax enveloped Flavia in a towel, flicking a drop of water from the tip of her small nose. "Pity about the scars, though. His value will go down, with his looks spoiled like that."

"I don't think they're spoiled at all," Lollia said. "I like a few scars on a man."

"He's just a slave," Cornelia said automatically. But she saw the way Flavia clung to him when he picked her up, the way he smoothed her wet curls out of her eyes.

"Inside, little one," he said in his deep Gaul-accented voice. "You take your bath like a good girl, and I tell you a story."

"The one about the fishes and the loaves!" Flavia played with the rough little wooden cross about his neck. "I looked for loaves in the fountain next to the fishes, but there aren't any."

"You want loaves, you have to really believe." Thrax's eyes flicked across Lollia's as he bowed, and then he carried Flavia inside.

"Is he teaching that child some strange religion?" Cornelia wondered. "Loaves and fishes—"

"Just stories," Lollia said defensively. "All about a carpenter in Judaea who turns into a god, or maybe a god who turns into a carpenter. But at least they're nice stories, all about healing lepers and walking across rivers. Better than those ghastly ghost stories we used to get from our nurses, that scared us out of our wits." Lollia's voice was brittle, and she rushed on before Cornelia could say anything. "So, did you hear about Vitellius's new edict? Gods forbid he do anything to straighten out the financial mess we're in, but he's found time to forbid patrician boys from driving chariots in the Circus Maximus! So ridiculous, but—"

She burst into tears.

Cornelia put an arm around her, tugging Lollia's head against her shoulder. *Just a few months ago I was picking quarrels with her for being a gadabout and a careless mother, and now here she is crying into my shoulder like a little girl.* Lollia cried a long time, and an answering lump rose in Cornelia's throat.

"Oh, gods." Lollia sat up at last, scrubbing at her wet red cheeks. "I hate crying. What good does it do? I'm not even one of those women who get all misty and pretty when they cry. I just turn into a blotchy mess. So what's the point of it all?"

"Not much," Cornelia agreed.

Lollia gave a long quivering breath, looking at the doorway where the golden slave named Thrax had vanished. "Those scars are my fault, you know. All my fault. I die of shame every time I look at him now."

Cornelia stared at her own feet, still dunked in the fountain and turning all green and wrinkled, and supposed she should be shocked. Not that it was shocking that Lollia had taken a slave to her bed . . . just shocking that she had so clearly developed feelings for one. But somehow the shock came to Cornelia distant and blunted, as if it were underwater along with her feet. "I'm having an affair with a soldier," she found herself saying abruptly.

Lollia's swollen eyes widened. "Oh, Cornelia—"

"You can't tell anyone. Not a soul."

"What do you take me for, the old Lollia?" Recovering a little sparkle. "Who is he?"

"No one."

"Tell me!"

Cornelia gave a firm shake of her head. "I'd put him in danger if I did. And don't ask why."

"Have it your way, then." Lollia scrubbed at her eyes again. "I hope he's fun, at least."

Cornelia smiled involuntarily.

"Ha, he is. Good for you, my honey. I must say, I never thought I'd see the day. You of all people!"

"We've all lost our heads this year." Cornelia trailed one finger through the water. "First you, then me—and according to Uncle Paris, Diana is sneaking off to meet some charioteer . . ."

"We're just prizes up for grabs, all of us." Lollia shrugged. "So we might as well grab what we want while we can."

"Your logic is very backward," Cornelia sighed. "But I'm too tired to figure it out."

"Of course you are, my love! You haven't been getting any sleep lately, and for good reason. Now, about your soldier—can he get away for a few days?"

"What?"

"Well, if he can get away, then find some excuse to get out of the city and have yourselves a proper idyll." Lollia stood up, dusting off her hands. "Diana's clearly managing to see her man without any trouble, whoever he is. Uncle Paris wouldn't notice if she moved a charioteer into her bedchamber—horses, chariot, and all. But you must be having quite a time of it sneaking out under Tullia's eagle eye. Get yourself a holiday if you can."

"How will I do that?" Cornelia looked up at her cousin.

"You'll manage. Clearly you've gotten quite good at sneaking." Lollia pulled Cornelia to her feet. "Yes, a vacation. It will give you something nice to remember when everything goes to Hades."

"Will it go to Hades?"

"Oh, my honey. It always does."

D ON'T—I can't, you know that—"

"Come on, just let me—"

"I can't." Marcella pushed Domitian's hand away before it could slide up her thigh. "Why do you make it difficult for me?"

"For you?" He buried his face in her throat. "You're killing me."

"I'm the wife of Lucius Aelius Lamia—"

"Barely!" Domitian bristled. "And he's in Crete now—you could divorce him—"

"My family wouldn't allow it. And until the day they do, I'm a Roman matron. Not a courtesan to be tumbled in a litter." Marcella pulled away, tidying her hair, and let Domitian see a flash of thigh as she rearranged her skirts. He groaned and fell back on his side of the litter, and Marcella felt the bearers shift below as they turned a corner.

"Some day," Domitian said, his eyes unreadable, "I'll have you all to myself."

"Perhaps." She smiled. "Until then—? I thought we were here to discuss the army." With the Moesian legions crossing into Italy now, even Vitellius couldn't pretend everything was all right. His troops had been hastily assembled and finally marched north.

"The army's at Hostilia, sure enough," Domitian was saying. "They're dug in, and negotiating. Negotiating! You swore they'd change sides!"

"They will. Just wait. Didn't your precious Nessus tell you all would be well?"

"I'll believe it when I see it." Domitian folded his arms across his stocky chest, drumming his fingers on the cushions. "What about Fabius Valens? He's still loyal to Vitellius."

"And he's still in bed recovering from food poisoning." From a dish of red mullet at a banquet; not enough to kill him, just enough to keep him in bed here in Rome instead of marching north in command of Vitellius's army.

"Who wouldn't get food poisoning, trying to keep up with Vitellius at a banquet?" Lollia had said. "Though he's not too sick to demand I join him in bed. These days, I just don't seem to have any luck at all."

Because all the luck these days is coming to me, Marcella thought. With Fabius sweating off his dish of red mullet in bed, Vitellius's army had been led north by . . . Caecina Alienus.

Really, it couldn't have worked out better. Marcella wished she could have joined Alienus and the army, to be in at the battle as she'd been at Bedriacum to see Otho's end, but there was no mortal way to manage it this time. And anyway, things were still quite exciting enough here in the city.

Domitian's voice was accusing again. "I don't see why you're so sure of Alienus. He never *said* he'd turn for my father's side."

"Not in so many words," said Marcella. "But he's got the army stalled now, doesn't he?"

"If he's going to turn, then why is he negotiating?"

"Because he wants the strongest position possible before he turns his troops over." She stroked a finger down Domitian's wrist. "Trust me. He'll turn. Wasn't it lucky *he* ended up in command of Vitellius's army, and not Fabius? If your father ever takes the purple, he could owe it all to a bad dish of seafood."

"Or to you." Domitian's black eyes assessed her. "Did you have anything to do with that bout of food poisoning?"

"Really," Marcella rebuked. "All I do is pass on whispers. You think I would poison a man?"

"You're the cleverest woman I know," said Domitian. "I don't like clever women, usually." He wrapped a hand around her ankle, sliding up her leg again. Marcella brushed him away, but not too fast.

"You'd better go. My bearers have marched five times around the Forum now—someone's bound to notice."

He got out, sulky, and Marcella leaned down and kissed him loosely at the corner of the mouth. His lips dove after hers, hungry.

"Don't put your tongue in my mouth," Marcella advised. "I'll see you when I hear more."

She retreated back into the litter, snapping the silk curtains shut with a soundless laugh. Who would ever have guessed that an eighteen-year-old boy with a hopeless case of puppy love could be so useful? Domitian was all on fire with anticipation now that the two armies were approaching each other: one minute crowing that he'd be made prince when his father was crowned Emperor, the next minute envisioning the brutal defeat of all his father's hopes. For herself, Marcella felt quite calm. She had nothing invested in either side, after all. *I just want to see what will happen.*

Though if she'd been one to bet, she'd put her coin on Alienus turning traitor . . . Marcella had met with him five or six times before his march, and he'd been wary of her at first, but she'd introduced him to Domitian, passed on two or three rumors about the northern troop movements that proved true, and slowly Alienus had begun to listen when she spoke of Vespasian's need for clever men and the rewards that would be his to give out if he became Emperor. "It's all up to you now, isn't it?" she'd whispered when Alienus was named commander of Vitellius's armies over the bedridden Fabius. "You could be Vespasian's kingmaker. He wouldn't forget that. Not like Vitellius has already forgotten you."

"He didn't forget me. He gave me his army—"

"Only when his right-hand man was unavailable. Don't you want to be the right-hand man for a change?"

Alienus hadn't committed himself when he left Rome with his army, but Marcella knew. *He'll turn,* she thought. *He'll hesitate, but in the end he'll turn—and he'll take the army with him.*

She looked down at her hands, trembling in her lap. Not fear, though: intoxication. She hadn't known that the terror and the excitement would war so fiercely in her stomach, that her palms would be sweaty, that she'd have to fight to keep her voice level. And she hadn't known what a wave, what a *surge* of satisfaction would sweep through her tingling body when she saw the thoughtful glitter in Alienus's eyes.

Of course, anything might still go wrong. Battles were unpredictable things. But *if* Alienus turned, *if* he managed to turn his army over to Vitellius's rival, *if* Vespasian took the purple because of it . . . well, Alienus wouldn't be the kingmaker. That title would belong to Cornelia Secunda, known as Marcella!

She still looked at her histories from time to time, but the words all seemed lifeless on the page. Why had she ever slaved over those flat, dead accounts? *I'm working on something much better than a scroll now.*

Marcella patted her hair, refreshed, and pulled back the curtains of the litter. Perhaps a little shopping in the Forum before the heat of the day settled in? As she stepped down, she saw a familiar head of pale hair in the throng of housewives and shopkeepers. "Diana!"

Diana waved, loping over with two slaves trotting behind, and Marcella smiled in greeting. She no longer felt irritated by Diana, or even envious of her. *All the freedom you want, and you use it to make horses run in circles,* Marcella thought tolerantly. *I make emperors run in circles.*

"Shopping?" Marcella greeted her. "I didn't think you knew what shopping was."

"Father wants a new block of marble from Carrara." Diana pushed a stray lock of hair behind one ear. "I said I'd order it for him. Who was the boy getting out of your litter?"

"What boy?" Marcella said vaguely.

"Just now. Dark hair. Vespasian's son?"

"Oh, him." Marcella laughed, carefully careless. "He's been in love with me all year, didn't you know? Wants me to divorce Lucius and run away to a life of eternal bliss."

"Mmm." Diana paused to finger a little stone carving of a horse, and Marcella let out a breath. Diana might be stupid, but she was observant. *Best not to forget that.* "Oh, look at these." Marcella tugged her cousin toward a stall with polished brass bowls and figurines. "I suppose you're off to the circus next?" she asked brightly, fingering a gleaming platter.

"What's the use of going to the races these days?" Diana demanded savagely.

"You're not still angry with the Blues for taking all the races at Volcanalia, are you?" Volcanalia had been quite a celebration this year—fish from the Tiber had been ceremonially thrown onto a fire to appease Vulcan, god of fire and forges, and Vitellius had needed no excuse to turn the festival into a citywide fish bake. Everybody had enjoyed themselves but Diana, who had been spitting curses as she watched the Blues win every heat in the day's races. "You can't win them all, you know."

"You can if you're the Blues." Diana glared at her own reflection in a polished copper pan, her mirrored face distorted and savage. "Did you know that damned Fabius Valens is having all the races fixed just to keep Vitellius happy?"

"So?" Marcella shrugged. "As long as racing has existed, there have been fixed races."

"Oh, a race here and there gets thrown," Diana snarled. "But not all the races. Not *every single one!*"

"So, tell the Emperor."

"He just laughs and says I hate eating mud now that his Blues are winning." Diana folded her arms across her breasts, callused fingers drumming. "It's not just bribes to keep the other factions losing. A charioteer for the Whites died last week—he dared beat the Blues, and Fabius had the Praetorians beat him to death. As an object lesson to the rest."

"It won't be forever," Marcella said, amused.

"And what happens to my Anemoi in the meantime?" Diana whirled. "They don't know who's Emperor, or that they race for the wrong faction. They just want to win. You know what happens when you teach horses how to lose? Their hearts *break*." She shook her head, furious. "And I tell you, I'm not putting up with it!"

"What are you going to do?" Marcella laughed, but all she saw was the whisk of Diana's fair hair like a horse's tail whipping around a corner as she stamped to the next booth. Marcella caught up, impulsively slipping her arm through her cousin's.

"It'll be better soon, you'll see." If Vespasian toppled Vitellius, surely no one would be bothering to fix chariot races anymore. "I promise."

"Let's hope," Diana scowled, and they walked arm in arm back to Uncle Paris's house, where Marcella marveled over the latest batch of carvings.

"Though why on earth does this bust of me have snakes for hair, Uncle Paris?"

He surveyed her with those cloudy blue-green eyes so like his daughter's. "You tell me."

"How should I know what's going on in your head?" Marcella laughed.

"I wonder if anyone knows what's going on in *yours*."

Marcella laughed again and took herself home. There were a few discreet letters she could write, pushing one or two indecisive men in Vitellius's entourage toward a change of heart . . .

Seventeen

ᔕ◠ᔓ

"Pull the Reds out of the races today." Diana paced to the other end of the small faction office. "Xerxes, you have to!"

"I tried." The Reds faction director flung down his stylus. "For a big day like today, we've all been ordered to run."

"Then at least jog them at the back! Make it into a training run—"

"No, we're to make a good show of it. Right till the end, when everyone leans on the reins and lets the Blues scamper off in front." Xerxes shook his head, disgusted.

Diana nibbled her thumbnail. "I can't watch them dump one more race."

"Well, you'll have to. We all have to." Xerxes heaved his hard bulk out of the chair. "It's a different world, Lady. We'll do as we're told."

"Isn't there one charioteer who would risk trying to win?" she burst out.

"After what happened to that boy who drove for the Whites? It's hard enough finding a driver who won't pull up after three laps just to make sure."

"This isn't happening." Diana closed her eyes. "This is not happening."

"Well, it is. And I've got work to do, Lady, so if you'll pardon me—"

"How long do you think we'll have an audience for this puppet show, if no one does anything? We have to—"

"*We?* You might be the Emperor's pet, Lady, but you're not one of us." Normally Xerxes tolerated Diana well enough, but now his face looked like a stone as he jerked his slab of a chin at the door. "Get out, Lady. You don't belong here."

Speechless, Diana wandered out into the faction courtyard, where grooms and page boys rushed back and forth. It was autumn now, the air crisp and cool—and the rumors flying. There had been a battle up north. A victory, a loss, no one knew. Not even Marcella, who knew everything these days. But Vitellius had decided it was a victory, that his armies had crushed the Moesian legions, and the Circus Maximus was aggressively decorated to celebrate. Colorful banners flapped at every post, the *spina* was draped in flowers, and a flood of plebs in their holiday best and patricians in their finest silks jammed the tiered seats high. There would be smaller races all through the early afternoon, but the winner of the final crowning race would accept the victory palm from the Emperor's own hand and take away the largest purse in the history of the Circus Maximus.

On such a day Diana should have been excited, flying everywhere in a fever of anticipation. On such a day the grooms should have been boasting and laying bets, the stable boys careening around in such excitement that they had to be smacked half a dozen times before they settled to work, and the charioteers should have alternately been bragging and praying as they waited their instructions. But all she could think of was the Volcanalia races, when she'd watched her Anemoi take the lead only to be muscled down in the last lap so the Blues could breeze ahead. Diana had escaped the Emperor's box and run home all the way, weeping tears of pure rage. It had even sucked some of the pleasure out of her lessons with Llyn. "What's the point of learning to drive a tight turn?" she'd burst out at him when he criticized her hold on the reins. "Nowadays, all any charioteer in Rome knows how to do is lose!"

He'd looked at her calmly. "You learn to drive a tight turn on my track, or you go home."

"Easy for you to say." Diana glared back. "You don't care if the races are rigged."

"No," he said. "I don't care who wins what race, or even who's Emperor. But when I teach anyone to do something, they'll learn to do it right."

Diana knew she'd regret it, but found herself wandering to the faction yard for the Blues. Plenty of swagger there—the grooms were already half drunk as they passed the harness back and forth, and the famous blood bays were tossing their heads in excitement. Derricus stood impatiently, already wearing his leather breastplate and striped blue cloak pinned to the shoulders with gold horse-head pins.

"Yes, yes." He was barely listening as the faction director gave him his instructions. "I won't tire them out. Why bother?"

He dropped his blue-plumed helmet and caught sight of Diana as he leaned forward to pick it up. In this yard full of blue, she was conspicuous in her red silks. "Lady Diana!" he grinned. "Come to wish me luck?"

"You don't need it," she said coldly. "Not to win a race like this one."

"Don't be sharp, Lady. Let's have a smile."

"Aren't you ashamed of yourself?" she glared. "A charioteer of your stature, driving in *fixed* races?"

His smile disappeared. "Maybe I don't like it much, Lady, but a win's a win. A purse is a purse. And some of us do this for a living, not just dabbling in between banquets."

If she stayed a moment longer she'd fly at him, so she stamped out of the Blues yard. She was shaking with too much fury to go up to the Emperor's box yet, or she'd fly at Fabius Valens too. He'd recovered from his bout of food poisoning and was conducting Vitellius's business in Rome, though he made noises about going north to take over the army now that there were so many rumors flying about a battle. Diana hoped he left soon and she hoped he died, but for today he was here, dragging Lollia with him. Everyone else would be there too: Marcella, Gaius and Tullia, even Cornelia, who hadn't been to a public function in weeks. Diana couldn't bear to face them, and she trailed back to the Reds yard to watch the Anemoi being harnessed.

They were being led out one by one, her four winds. Zephyrus, dancing on his toes with excitement, outside runner and fastest of them all, named for the fleet West Wind . . . Eurus, running just inside Zephyrus, nearly as fast but not so wild and named for the ever-constant East Wind . . . Notus, second inside runner, steady as the strong-blowing South Wind . . . and Boreas, the implacable North Wind, her favorite. Diana curved an arm around Boreas's stocky neck, crooning wordlessly. He was the oldest of them, the innermost runner, scarred and savage-tempered and solid as a rock around a turn. He didn't bite Diana quite as often as he bit everyone else, which she counted for affection.

Her Anemoi were gazing about with pricked ears and bright eyes, stamping restlessly as the grooms bustled about with the harness, Boreas swiping his teeth at any groom who got too close. Like any good team they knew it was race day; they knew what harness and bustle and cheering meant, and they chuffed through flared nostrils as they were harnessed to the chariot. Diana could hardly bear to look at them. They hadn't learned yet that their speed wasn't required; they didn't know they were supposed to lose for an emperor's pleasure.

Xerxes stood scowling to one side with the charioteer, a lean Greek named Siculus. "Keep them in front till the end." The directions came halfheartedly. "Ease them off gradual, though. That Boreas gets the bit in his teeth if you're not careful."

"Of course."

"Ah, damn it." Xerxes stumped off. "Just get it over with. I'm going to get drunk."

"Hey, you." Siculus collared a groom, pressing a purse into his hand. "Take this to the bettor under the statue of Nero and put it all on the Blues, will you?"

"Blues?" The groom blinked.

"Why not? They're making me money hand over fist, and I don't even have to drive for it."

The groom gave Siculus a disgusted look, and two more traded glances behind his back. "Get on with it," Siculus ordered, and that was when Diana snapped.

"Lady Diana." The charioteer bowed as she approached, looking surprised when she stood on tiptoe to whisper in his ear.

"Siculus," she breathed, "I will hump you silly if you win this race."

He pulled back. "Lady, the orders . . . Fabius Valens said—"

"Fabius Valens is leaving Rome soon, and the Emperor is so drunk and happy today, no one will retaliate. Win this race," she repeated, "and you can have me any way you want. Backward, sideways, upside-down—"

Siculus looked to the side, gnawing his lip. "I don't know, Lady—" He'd looked at her in the past; Diana knew that. Plenty of the drivers did.

"Want something in advance? Come with me." She took his hand and led him back to the small shed where they kept the chariots. It was empty now—the chariots had already been rolled out—and Diana was already dragging his head down to kiss him before they reached the shadows inside. "Just close that door," she breathed against his mouth as he started fumbling at her dress. He turned to bar it, and she picked up one of the heavy blocks they wedged under the chariot wheels to keep them from rolling and banged him over the head with it. Siculus went down like an ox on an altar; she banged him one more time to make sure he wouldn't wake up for a while and then got to work. There wasn't much time.

She stripped off his leather shin guards and buckled them around her own legs, kilting her red dress up to the knees. Another few moments dragging at the limp limbs and she had the leather breast-plate off—too big for her but that was good; it would hide the shape of her breasts. She had her own gauntlets with her and pulled them on as she reached down for the red-plumed helmet. She crammed her hair under it, wishing the helmet hid more of her face, but it would have to do. Siculus was slim and lightly built, like most charioteers; the height difference wasn't too bad. Anyone who took a close look would realize something was wrong, but she didn't plan on giving anyone a close look.

"Where's that bloody Siculus?" A groom's voice came from outside, annoyed. "They're rolling out!"

Diana waited as they looked for him. Waited.

"Drat it, the Greens and Whites just went—look in the yard."

She came running out of the chariot shed at the last minute, dropping the bar on the door in case Siculus woke up, and dashed to where the grooms were waiting with the Anemoi. Her four winds, bright-eyed and flame-bright, eager to run with the light chariot behind them crowned by its flaming fire god. "Sorry," she said as gruffly as possible, and vaulted up into the chariot.

"You're late," the groom said, handing her the red leather reins to knot around her waist. "You'll be last, but—" He paused, and Diana pulled feverishly at the knots. If she could just get out to the track before he raised the alarm—

"Siculus," the groom said finally. "You shrank." He handed her the red-beaded driving whip. "Fortuna be with you."

Diana was already urging her team forward, toward the track.

W ATCH it," the Greens charioteer hissed at her, and she edged the Anemoi back in line. Quite a trick, keeping the four teams exactly even as they paraded in their preparatory lap around the track before the race. On the turn, the inside team had to nearly step in place and the outside team had to speed to a trot in order to keep all sixteen noses exactly in line. Taking a turn at a walk wasn't something Diana had ever practiced, and she'd drawn the outside position. Her hands were already sweating inside their gauntlets, and she could feel the tug of the knotted reins against her waist. Her mouth was tinder-dry, and somewhere inside she could hear her family shrieking in dismay and even her own voice telling her she would crash the team and kill the Anemoi, and then she'd never forgive herself. But the voice she heard most clearly was Llyn's, and he sounded as mild as ever.

You're a fool, he told her as the four teams reached the final turn. *If I'd led my first attack against Rome when I was as green a leader as you are a driver, then I'd never have lived long enough for us to meet.*

"No," she gritted out between concentration-clenched teeth.

You'll lose, you know.

"But at least I'll lose honestly," she said aloud. The Anemoi deserved a charioteer, however poor, who would at least try. She managed the last turn quite neatly, and the four teams began lining up. Somewhere overhead was the Imperial box, where Vitellius sat watching, doubtless pouring wine from his second flagon of the day and wondering where his little pet was.

Don't try to do too much for your horses. They know their job. Trust them to do it.

"Yes." She could sense the Anemoi stretching on the other end of the reins, feeling her out. An unfamiliar pair of hands, and they were cautious. But they wanted to run, and that would take over once the signal came.

The four teams were poised to start. Adoring women still shrieked in the stands for Derricus. Through the slit of her helmet, Diana saw a figure in purple step forward in the Imperial box.

Good luck, said Llyn inside her head, and that was it. He was gone, and she was alone. Diana pulled a Reds medallion out from under her breastplate and kissed it for luck.

A scrap of cloth fluttered, caught the autumn breeze, drifted down . . . and sixteen horses surged off the line.

THE Reds lunge off the drop a second late, trailing last before the wheels are even in motion. But Diana doesn't mind that. She doesn't want to get caught in the jockeying for the inside space against the *spina*; she doesn't have the experience to bull her way through a crush. All she has is the raw speed of her four winds. The chariot rocks under her feet, the air blurs her eyes through the slit in her helmet, the reins are taut sawing lines in her hands, and oh gods, she never dreamed that even the four winds could run so fast. She braces her arms, adjusts her weight against the front of the chariot, tucks her chin into her chest to cant the streaming airflow away from her eyes; minuscule adjustments that are second nature now after months of Llyn's nitpicking, and she realizes that under the helmet she's grinning like a fiend. "Slowly, beauties," she sings out to the Anemoi, who are fighting her grip. "Slowly."

They're fourth and last coming into the turn, but Diana doesn't want to rush. Her first turn in the Circus Maximus—gods' wheels, if she clips it wrong out of nerves she'll wreck the chariot and likely kill the horses. She grips her lip in her teeth, heart hammering as she gathers the reins on the inside—and Boreas lowers his head into the harness like a bull and the chariot wheels around neat as a pin and they're thundering into the straightaway again. One more turn, pretty as the one before, and the first lap is done. In a flash of gold overhead she sees the dolphin tilt its carved nose down.

That wasn't so hard.

She hears a dull roar somewhere behind the rush of wind in her ears, and knows the crowd is shouting. The Greens have the lead, the Blues on the rail behind, the Whites somewhere on the outside. If she were watching from her usual place in the stands she'd be screaming now, begging the charioteer to pick up the pace, but she wants another lap or two to feel out her team. After months of watching from the stands she knows them inside and out—knows exactly how much speed Zephyrus can produce in the stretch, knows how Eurus and Notus can match their strides so perfectly they look like one eight-legged horse, knows how Boreas can lean nearly horizontal into a turn to bring a chariot around—but she's never driven them before, and she has exactly six laps left to get to know them. No, four laps—two more have come and gone in a flash, and maybe seven laps isn't so long as all that, because the race is almost half done.

Time to move up.

She lets an inch of rein through her fingers, and the Anemoi leap ahead. They're terrifyingly strong, much stronger than the placid geldings she usually drives under Llyn, and the reins are already cutting into her waist where she stands braced against the pull, but she leans

back and only gives them an inch. Just enough, they're moving up—
she steers them wide to pass the Whites, and it takes a whole lap, but
when the next gold dolphin tips down, the Reds are in third.

The Blues have settled into the lead, a nose ahead of the Greens,
who will pretend for another lap or two to make a fight of it. Diana
settles behind them, and the Anemoi hate her for it; they want to run
and as they fight for their heads she can feel her hands blistering inside
the gauntlets, but it isn't time yet. "Not yet!" she shouts to them,
words whipped away on the wind. Her arms are screaming pain, and
she remembers Marcella saying once—scornfully—that Diana is too
small to hold four horses.

Fifth lap. The Greens drop back. Diana can see the charioteer leaning on the reins, holding his team in. For a while they run side by side,
then the Greens are behind her and only the Blues block the view in
front. Derricus is whipping up his bays, sending them easily ahead as
the dolphin drops. He takes a moment as he flashes past the Imperial
box to flourish his beaded driving whip, and Diana brings the reins
down in a crack.

The Anemoi lunge forward so hard her vision slips, slamming her
forward against the front of the chariot. Her whip flies out of her hand,
gone in a flash, and she clutches the reins as the Reds come lunging
out from behind the Blues and into the middle of the track. Three
long strides and the straining chestnut noses pull even with the blue-
enameled wheels. Derricus looks back and sees her; he gives his whip
a casual crack over the heads of his blood bays.

I could win. The thought comes suddenly, and her hands tighten
on the reins, blistered and fiery inside her gauntlets. Of course she'd
wanted to win the minute she stepped into the chariot, but she hadn't
thought it would be possible. Raw charioteers never win their first
race . . . but Derricus still thinks the Reds will pull up at the end.
He's barely stirring his team, and the Greens and the Whites have
already given up.

I could win.

Sixth lap. Diana lets the reins through her fingers another few precious inches and the Anemoi respond like a sixteen-legged machine,

flying up alongside the Blues. Eight horses, nose to nose, and then Diana abandons all caution and opens them up. They flick past the Blues in an instant, and before Derricus can stir up his own team the turn is on them. The Blues are hugging the *spina* and have to slow down or crash, but Diana takes the turn at reckless speed in the middle of the track, sawing ruthlessly on Boreas, and he hunches his broad neck and scrabbles almost horizontally at the sand to give her the speed she wants. She loses ground on the turn but the Reds are still ahead by a nose as they flash past the Imperial box, the blood bays in their blue harness clawing grimly on the inside.

Last lap.

Derricus pulls even, shouting something, but Diana never looks at him. All she can see are the four red noses stretched ahead of her, the smooth red bands of rein spinning back into her blistered hands, which are now breaking open inside her gauntlets. Her waist is a circle of pain from the knotted reins, the horses are cutting her in half and her arms are on fire holding them, but she's laughing behind her helmet as she at last gives the Anemoi their heads.

The Blues keep up for a moment, and Diana can see Derricus's startled black hole of a mouth. *Does he know who I am now?* Maybe he does, but then the first turn comes and Boreas digs savagely into it and drags the others with him, and as they pull onto the straightaway they settle in next to the *spina* because the Blues are gone and it's just the Reds in front, the Reds all the way to the finish, and nothing will ever catch them. Diana knows she should pull them up, try to conserve their speed—they keep running like this, they won't be fit to race again for months. But they have the bits in their teeth; she couldn't stop them even if she wanted to. And she doesn't want to. She wants them to run forever, to run the Blues into a ruined oblivion. She steers them into the final turn, neat and tight against the *spina* as Llyn taught her, and then she leans forward and snaps the reins against their backs. Boreas stumbles, tiring, but fleet Zephyrus jumps out against his harness on the outside, pulling the others along, and they streak down the final stretch all alone, four red winds flying to eternity.

The last dolphin drops. The Blues come in five long seconds after, the Greens and the Whites trailing at the end, and by that time the Reds are halfway around the track again on their victory lap. They pull Diana's blistered hands to ribbons before she can get them to walk. They keep breaking into a trot, throwing their heads up, preening, and for the first time Diana hears the screams of adulation raining down from the stands, the rose petals drifting down on her head. Red rose petals. She puts her hand out, dazed, and catches a handful as two hundred fifty thousand people scream their delight. *"Reds! Reds! Reds!"* The plebs are overflowing the stands now and flooding into the track, running after her, scooping handfuls of sand for souvenirs, stretching for a hair from Zephyrus's tail or a chip of paint from the chariot's axles. Hands brush at her tunic, and her ears are ringing from the shouts. *"Reds! Reds! Reds!"* The world comes slowly back into joint as she realizes it.

She's won a race at the Circus Maximus.

DIANA pulled the chariot up at the finish line, where a mob of jubilant grooms in red tunics waited. She dropped the reins as they rushed forward to seize the bridles and realized her hands were trembling. The tug of the horses had pulled the reins so tight around her waist the knots were almost fused, and she had to cut herself free. She staggered as she stepped down from the chariot, and the world tilted dizzily overhead, but the grooms were surging around her, shouting gleefully. "Lady! Lady!" They all seemed to know she wasn't Siculus.

She stripped off her gauntlets, seeing the huge blisters that had broken open across her hands. She was shaking all over now, not just her hands, but she staggered around the chariot to where the Anemoi were being unharnessed. They were trembling too, knees vibrating, noses drooping toward the sand. No horses should ever run the way they had just run; they tapped every reserve of strength and speed and then went deeper when she asked it. They wouldn't be fit to race again for weeks, maybe months, but that was all right. If it was months before they were asked to lose to the Blues again, then it wasn't too long. They won today and that was enough. They won today and they knew it, her brave four winds.

Diana couldn't breathe inside her helmet and she flung it away, not caring about the murmur that went up when the crowd outside the Red faction saw her face and her long sweaty hair. She cradled Zephyrus's nose against her cheek and thanked him for picking them all up in the last turn; she tugged Notus's ears and crooned that he could have beat the sun horses across the sky; she moved Eurus's braided forelock out of his eyes and whispered that he'd never been so sure-footed—and then finally she flung her arms around Boreas's knotted neck and sobbed into his sweat-foamed shoulder.

"Fortuna, girl," a voice growled, and she looked up to see Xerxes's scowling face. "I realized it was you in the second lap. Don't you ever get behind one of my teams again!"

"No." She wiped her eyes, smiling radiantly.

"You'll tell the Emperor that I had no part in this little stunt?"

"Yes."

People were lifting her up now, carrying her toward the steps that led to the Emperor's box, and she trailed her blistered fingertips across Boreas's nose one last time before she let them usher her up. She caught a bare glimpse of Derricus, standing by his blood bays, and his face was tight and furious.

She barely had the strength for the steps toward the Emperor's box. She would have crawled up on all fours like a dog if her hands hadn't hurt as much as her legs. A bare glimpse of the Emperor in his purple robe, dim and hazy on his carved chair with a wine cup in hand, and then a whirl of silk and perfume descended on her.

"Diana, you *idiot*—"

"Juno's mercy, what possessed you—"

"We didn't even realize it was you until the race was over—we'd have been wrecks if we'd known—"

It was her cousins. Lollia wrung her hands, Marcella mussed her hair, Cornelia hugged her from behind, and Diana started laughing shakily. All of a sudden they were laughing with her, and she realized how long it had been since they had all laughed together. They stood there swaying, giggling like hyenas and getting smeared with Diana's sweat as everyone gazed in disapproval, and finally Diana pushed free.

"Caesar—" Another mild bout of cackles seized her as she bowed before him. "It was all my idea, so don't blame the Reds faction."

Fabius Valens was staring at her. If looks could kill she'd have been dead on the tiles—but a patrician girl couldn't be murdered in an alley like that poor Whites charioteer who had dared to win over the Blues.

"Girl," rumbled Vitellius, "you know I passed an edict, forbidding patricians to drive?"

"I know." She pushed her sweat-matted hair off her neck. "But the edict didn't say anything about patrician *girls*, Caesar."

"By Jove, I overlooked that." The Emperor's face split in a reluctant grin as he slapped the victory palm into her hand. "Promise me you'll leave the racing to the professionals from now on, and I'll forgive you."

"Oh, I promise," Diana beamed, and the cousins were there to catch her when her legs gave out.

"Your hands," Cornelia mourned. "They're in absolute shreds—"

"You should have seen the look on Tullia's face," Marcella crowed. "The Emperor might forgive you, but she never will!"

Diana didn't hear them. She just stared down at the branch in her hand. A simple cutting of palm, curling a little at the edges. By tomorrow it would be a dried husk, lighter than air. Her palm, for her first and only race.

"Come on, girl." Vitellius swung his bulk up out of his chair. "I've a mind to go down to the stables. Only so much perfume a man can take before he wants a sniff of good honest hay. What did you name those horses of yours?"

"After the four winds, Caesar." Hurting everywhere, still clutching her palm, Diana staggered after the Emperor. Derricus fell in behind her, still unsmiling, and in this giddy mood she couldn't hate him. She waved everyone into the Reds faction stables, where an impromptu party had clearly broken out among the grooms. They hid the wine jugs when the Emperor and his party trailed in, but no one could hide their grins.

"Ah, very nice." Vitellius paused in appreciation before the Anemoi, unharnessed now and being curried. Rose petals still caught here and there in their manes, but the grinning grooms left those alone. "From what stud?"

"From the stables of Llyn ap Caradoc." Diana rattled off the lineage of each horse, heaving up a bucket for Eurus. The horses were cool enough to drink now without cramping, and Eurus slurped the whole bucket down in a few swallows. She laughed and filled another, moving to Notus, who slobbered on her shoulder as he drank.

"Yes, I like them." Vitellius ran a hand down Zephyrus's neck. All horses loved Vitellius; even bad-tempered Boreas nuzzled at the Emperor's rough horseman's hands. Behind Vitellius, his German officers swaggered and placed bets while the senators stood around gingerly pretending they didn't mind getting manure on their sandals. "Let's see what they'll do with a real driver, eh? Not that you didn't drive a decent race today, girl, but you know it was half luck."

"Oh, I know." Diana was radiant.

"Good." Vitellius turned to Xerxes, who stood beaming with a wine cup next to the unharnessed chariot. "See that these horses get turned over to the Blues faction."

"What?" Diana turned back from giving Boreas his drink, swinging an empty bucket from one torn hand, still smiling.

"Can't wait to see what they do for Derricus!" the Emperor said in high good humor, and he chucked Diana's chin hard enough to snap her head back. "A good race, girl. What a wicked one you are!" He chuckled as he moved away, a little glint showing hard in his eye, and his entourage melted with him. Behind him silence rippled outward in little frozen waves. The grooms stood uncertainly, wine jugs in hand, and Xerxes looked like he'd been turned to stone. Derricus leaned against the stable wall, arms folded across his chest, smirking. Only the horses moved, still drinking thirstily.

Finally, Xerxes spoke. "Aulus," he called to one of the grooms through lips that barely moved. "Lead these horses over to the Blues faction stables."

"No!" Diana lurched in front of Boreas. "You can't do that—no one can do that, they belong to *us*—"

"He's the Emperor. He can do what he likes." Xerxes rounded on her, snarling. "And if you hadn't interfered, Lady—"

But his voice trailed away. Word had already spread somehow to the Blues; their faction director was waddling down to see for himself, all smiles. "Well," he beamed, running a hand over Boreas's haunch.

Someone—she didn't know who—latched a hand onto Diana's elbow before she leaped forward and tried to kill him.

Her Anemoi. The Blues. Her Anemoi.

Derricus looked at the victory palm in Diana's hand, and he laughed.

The Blues.

Diana watched in numb misery as one by one, her four winds were draped in blue horse blankets and led away.

S HE didn't know how she got to Llyn's villa. A hired litter maybe, or a wagon, or maybe she ran the whole way. She just found herself stumbling up the slope, shivering violently. Her blistered fingers throbbed, her waist was a belt of pain from the knotted reins, her legs barely worked anymore, but all she could feel was the frozen place inside.

Llyn was striding out of the stables with a broken bridle, unknotting the stitching on the reins, when he saw her. He paused. "Lady?"

Diana stopped, shivering in great waves. She realized she was still clutching her victory palm.

"Lady?" Llyn came another step closer, and she blundered forward into his broad chest.

"My horses," she mumbled against his rough tunic, and the frozen place finally cracked inside her. "They took my *horses*."

"They took my everything," said Llyn.

He stood like a pillar, holding her as Diana finally began to weep.

Eighteen

∽つの?

"I s it true the horses lifted off the ground and flew in the last lap?"

"No." Cornelia smiled. "Well, not quite. Almost. I can see how *that* rumor got started—they were a full quarter lap ahead when they crossed the line. A new record for the Circus Maximus, I believe."

"I'd have liked to see that." Drusus looked envious for a moment, but he looked down at Cornelia's head in the crook of his shoulder and grinned. "Is it true your cousin was glowing silver when she stepped down from the chariot?"

"Glowing *silver*? How on earth—"

"From the divine blessing of Diana the Huntress," Drusus intoned solemnly. "It's well known around the Forum."

"Juno's mercy, my cousin does not glow. As a matter of fact, she had so much dust on her face after that race that she looked like a Nubian, and her hair was plastered flat with sweat, and she could hardly stand. But she was grinning like a fiend." Cornelia looked up at the ceiling, considering. "You know, I think the family might just have to give up on the idea of getting her married? Men look at Diana, and all they see is her looks. But the real Diana is the dirty grinning fiend who came staggering out of that chariot."

"Is it true she spat in the Emperor's face, after he gave those horses to the Blues? That's all over the Forum, too."

"No," Cornelia sighed. She'd seen her youngest cousin plead with the Emperor these past weeks—at banquets, at races, not caring about the snickers that rose behind her, but he wouldn't listen. "All's fair in victory, girl! You won your race, well, now we'll see how those horses do for my Blues. Not that they'll be fit to run for weeks, the way you drove 'em—"

"*Fair?*" Diana had demanded. "You think the races these days have anything to do with *fair?*"

"My Blues have won twelve straight since yours, haven't they?" Vitellius had grinned, but the grin was a spasm in his flushed face, and Cornelia had seen the sudden flick of fear in his eyes. She found herself thinking of Marcella's prediction that Vitellius's generals would sell him out. Vitellius always laughed at such rumors, but that day Cornelia saw something small and shivering in his gaze.

As long as Vitellius is drunk and his belly is full and the Blues are winning, the world is blessed and Vespasian can't touch him. Such a fragile fantasy, even a lost horse race could set it rocking. And Cornelia felt sorry for him, almost as sorry as she felt for her littlest cousin, whose brash sparkle had all been extinguished.

"Cornelia, you know all about the gods." Diana came to her almost in tears, looking suddenly ten years old. "Which one do you think would listen, if I prayed to get my horses back? I've already been to a handful of fortune-tellers, but they just tell you what you want to hear—even that pet astrologer of Domitian's just said, 'Don't you worry, dear, you'll drive those horses again and for much bigger stakes—'"

"Never mind astrologers," Cornelia told her gently. "Pray to Diana the Huntress. She has horses too, you know—moon-white mares she drives across the sky, and she loves them. And you're her namesake, so she'll listen to you."

"You think so?" Diana dashed at her eyes with a grubby hand.

"I know so."

"—retaliation?" Drusus was saying, and Cornelia blinked.

"What?"

"I said, keep some guards around that little cousin of yours. Emperor's favorite or no, a lot of unsavory people lost money when she won against orders. Someone might be angry enough to try for revenge."

"Oh, she's untouchable—too much of a heroine." Cornelia couldn't help a smile, nestling closer against Drusus's chest. "All those young tribunes who race up and down the Campus Martius worship her now. There's been a whole new spate of marriage proposals. Tullia doesn't know what to think—she was preparing a great scene, shrieking about the disgrace Diana brought on the family, and she was just working up to full volume when a cluster of the finest bachelors in Rome appeared on the doorstep with flowers. Quite took the wind from her sails. She's retired to bed from the strain of it all."

"What about you?" Drusus grinned.

"Oh, I've retired to bed from the strain of it all, too." Kissing him. "Hadn't you noticed?"

October now. The days were still warm, but the nights cooled quickly. Normally October was a festival time in Rome, when the last patrician families returned from their summer villas and prepared for the fall round of parties and gladiatorial games. But the city this fall was curiously quiet. Fabius Valens had finally gone north with the last of the troops, hurrying to join Alienus and his army against the Moesian legions and leaving Lollia behind on a high tide of bliss. "He's gone, he's gone, he's gone," she sang, and all but skipped back to her grandfather's house to play all day with Flavia. The Emperor had retired to a little villa just outside Rome, declaring himself unwell . . . or maybe fleeing the whispers that the battle up north had not been a victory at all, but a hideous loss.

"If only we'd get some news!" Marcella groaned over and over, feverish to know what was happening, but Cornelia didn't care. *Lovers are selfish*, she couldn't help thinking. *All Rome waiting to see if the Moesian legions are coming to murder us in our beds, and all I can think is how easy it's been to see Drusus.* She'd been sneaking out to him every night for weeks now, and no one in the household seemed to suspect a thing. Not Tullia; not sharp-eyed Marcella, who still hadn't noticed that her sister could barely stay awake through dinner these days.

"At least it's quiet family suppers again," Tullia said that night as they ate. "Not all those dreadful hundred-course affairs at the Domus Aurea."

"When were you last invited to the Domus Aurea, Tullia?" Marcella said sweetly. "A month? Vitellius hates scolds."

Tullia sniffed. "He's welcome to keep his invitations. If I never see another pike liver or elephant ear or peacock brain on my plate again, it won't be too soon—"

"Yes." Cornelia took a sip of wine, fighting to keep her lashes from drooping. She hadn't returned from Drusus's bed until dawn. At her side, Marcella picked restlessly through a dish of grapes.

"Lovely fish," Gaius offered. "Delicious, my dear."

"Yes, from our pond at the villa in Tarracina." Tullia ate in critical little bites. "I had them salted and sent here, since we never managed to get to Tarracina this year. *Paulinus*, don't play with your food! Fortuna only knows what condition the house is in. The steward sent me word that the hypocaust in the bathhouse is broken, but I suppose repairs will have to wait until next spring. You can't trust builders to work without supervision, but I don't dare leave the city now to oversee everything—"

"Why don't I go?" Cornelia looked up from her own plate, carefully idle. "I have so little to do these days, I can certainly travel down to Tarracina to put the house right."

"Travel *alone*—"

"The steward will see to my needs there." Cornelia kept her voice nonchalant, but felt her palms begin to sweat. "And I certainly shan't be entertaining in Tarracina. I'll just put the hypocaust to rights and return in ten days. Best not let a bathhouse go during the winter— pipes freeze, and that's a much costlier fix."

Tullia looked suspicious. Cornelia glanced down, fiddling with the fringe on the couch cushion.

"Fortuna's sake, Tullia, let her go," Marcella snapped. "You're always complaining about having the two of us underfoot."

"Of course I won't go if Tullia thinks it's improper," Cornelia said quickly. "A widow in my position, after all . . . you could ask Lollia to tend to the hypocaust. Her grandfather has a house in Tarracina, so she could easily send the steward to look in on the repairs. I'm sure she'd be happy to do you a favor."

"I'd never ask *her*," Tullia bristled. "You'll go at once, Cornelia. *Paulinus*, if you can't stop playing legions with your food—"

Cornelia ran into Drusus's airless little chamber that night and covered his face with kisses. "Can you get away for ten days?"

"What?" He caught her up with a laugh.

"We're taking a holiday."

Find some excuse to get out of the city, Lollia had advised, *and have yourselves a proper idyll*. Cornelia thought it might be the first time in her life she'd ever taken Lollia's advice.

She kept herself calm in the days before—packing a few things, arranging a comfortable traveling wagon—but Marcella gave her a long look as she closed the trunk. "Cornelia," she said thoughtfully, "do you have a secret?"

"Of course not." Though Cornelia sometimes wondered why she had told Lollia about Drusus, and not Marcella. Marcella was her sister, Marcella had a lock instead of a mouth, Marcella knew everything anyway . . . but somehow, she'd spilled her burden to Lollia instead, and felt no impulse to spill it again now. Marcella wasn't the only one who could keep her sister shut out of her business. "I don't believe in secrets, and I certainly don't have any. Do you?"

"Many." Marcella stretched her pale arms overhead. "That's how I know the look."

"Ridiculous." Cornelia brushed her off, climbing into her wagon for Tarracina, knowing Drusus would be a day behind on a mule drover's train. Tarracina, beautiful jewel-blue Tarracina, where a white marble villa waited on a cliff top.

"Domina." The steward bowed when she arrived. "I have prepared

the house for you, on Lady Tullia's instructions. The slaves are prepared to—"

"No slaves, please. I'll tend to everything myself."

"Domina?"

"Thank you, you may go." Cornelia kicked off her sandals as she
prowled through the empty villa. A gift from Lollia's grandfather
when Gaius entered the Senate, and as beautiful as any of his houses.
Every niche graced with some work of art in marble or silver or ivory,
every tile and column and piece of furniture chosen to adorn and not
just to serve. *How did I ever think Lollia's grandfather was vulgar?* Freedman or no, he had more good taste in one finger than Tullia did in her
whole patrician-born body.

"You're sure this is the right place?" Drusus said when he arrived,
looking around the airy porticoed halls. "Surely a disgraced ex-soldier
like me isn't allowed in a house like this. Disgraced *filthy* ex-soldier," he
added, looking down at his travel stains as Cornelia dragged him inside.

"I'll only have you thrown out if you don't carry me to bed." Cornelia tugged him toward the bedchamber. "Right *now.*"

"Is it safe?" he asked, shedding his travel-dusty cloak.

"No one here but us." She tossed back the bed's airy white curtains,
spinning a happy circle. "I left my maid behind, dismissed the slaves,
and got rid of the steward. No one but us for ten days."

Days and days in a wide bed that smelled of lilac, broad windows
open to a horizon of blue sea framed by billowing curtains so that they
slept nearly afloat in the sky. Days and days of home-cooked breakfasts
on the circular terrace—or so Cornelia imagined, until she tried to
make bread and it refused to rise.

"I don't understand it." She contemplated the sullen lump of dough
on the slab. "I used to supervise the baking every week in my household. I was known for my bread!"

"Ahh." Drusus rubbed his jaw. "And did you actually bake the
bread yourself, or did you just watch the slaves do it?"

"Well, of course the slaves did the actual mixing and kneading,
but I know how it's done." She poked at the grimy lump of dough.
"How hard could it be?"

The bread never rose, and the fish Cornelia purchased for their dinner proved difficult to bone. "I can cook," she said defensively as Drusus grinned at the raw flayed mess that had once been a salmon. "I set one of the best tables in Rome! My husband always praised me for my sauces!"

"My love"—Drusus kissed her eyebrow—"I'm sure you're perfect in every other way. But you're useless in the kitchen."

After that he tugged on his tunic and sandals in the mornings and padded down to the street vendors for bread and sausage, fresh fruit, and slabs of fish. They ate on the terrace every day, watching the galleys pass by in the harbor below with their oar banks flashing in the sun.

"What's that?" Drusus asked as Cornelia surveyed a lengthy scroll.

"A list of household tasks Tullia wants me to see to. First there was just the broken hypocaust, but she thought of a few other little things." Producing a second scroll.

"Well, I can help if you need—"

"No need." Cornelia tossed both scrolls off the balcony into the sea. The bathhouse never did get fixed. They bathed every day in the gentle waves, where a small rocky crescent of beach kept them private from spying eyes. Cornelia shrieked in dismay, looking in the glass afterward. "As if a snub nose weren't bad enough. Now it's a *freckled* snub nose!"

Drusus took to padding about the cliff-top garden in a decrepit old tunic, redesigning the flower beds. "All you've got here is flowers," he complained. "Don't you want grapevines, a few nut trees—something useful?"

"Flowers are useful. They're beautiful to look at." Cornelia sat cross-legged on a marble bench in one of Drusus's old tunics, hair loose down her back, eating a pear. "Isn't beauty useful?"

"You shouldn't even be growing lilies up so high on a cliff," Drusus said critically. "The soil's too sandy."

"You're a gardener now?" she teased.

"My grandfather owned a vineyard. I wouldn't mind having a vineyard." He looked around the garden as if seeing rows of orderly vines.

"Making my own wine, tending the vines, watching the women climb into tubs full of grapes at pressing time—"

"Children running up and down the rows," Cornelia said. Easy to imagine them, little girls with dirty feet and little boys throwing grapes at each other . . . A painful thought, and she put down the pear.

"Cornelia—" Drusus picked up her hand, straddling the bench.

"No, I'm all right." She looked out over the terrace. "I just always assumed I'd have children, running all over a house just like this. But I assumed I'd be Empress too, and look how that turned out."

He looked as if he wanted to say more, but he just leaned forward and folded her in his arms. Cornelia looked over his shoulder at the blue sea beyond the terrace, blinking a little.

She managed to stretch ten days into two weeks, sending Tullia complaint-filled messages of dawdling workmen and chipped tiles. Two weeks of sunlight and blue water and lovemaking as October slipped past—and then it was over.

Drusus had the news first, from a gibbering fruit seller when he went down to buy breakfast: Caecina Alienus had turned traitor and joined the Moesian legions. His men were disorganized, slaughtered on the field after ten hours of battle. The city of Cremona had been sacked and destroyed . . . and now the victorious legions were marching on Rome.

"I wonder how many men Vitellius can muster to protect the city?" Cornelia asked without curiosity, standing on the terrace with her arms wrapped around her own waist. "My sister will be sure to know."

Drusus picked up her hand, lacing his fingers through hers. "We can't stay here. A place so isolated, no guards—if the army came to Tarracina—"

"Yes." She forced a smile. "My family will expect me to come back, anyway. Though they might not stay long in the city, themselves."

"Only wise." Drusus forced a little cheer into his voice. "Get out of the city altogether, somewhere safe. Where would you all go?"

"Brundisium, maybe. We have a villa there, and it's sure to be a long way from the fighting . . ."

"Brundisium," said Drusus. "That's—far." Hundreds of miles to the south.

They stood on the circular white-marbled terrace, the shadows stretching over the cushioned couches, the sea washing violet below, the sky a deepening twilight blue. Dinner cooled on a tray. Cornelia felt sick, remembering the other half of what Lollia had said when she urged a vacation:

It will give you something nice to remember when everything goes to Hades.

Will it go to Hades? Cornelia had asked.

Oh, my honey. It always does.

Well, Lollia knew these things. She'd had lovers before, after all. She'd know how to say good-bye with flair, how to end things with humor and dignity and compassion. All Cornelia could do was wrap herself around Drusus, clutching him desperately close through the night. "Not yet," she whispered to herself the following morning, as she climbed into the litter and left him for their separate journeys back to Rome. "Oh, not yet!"

PART FOUR

VESPASIAN

December A.D. 69–June A.D. 79

*"He was the first emperor whose character
actually improved after he attained the throne."*

—TACITUS

Nineteen

ᔓᲦᲦ

"CORNELIA?" Marcella called as soon as she entered the atrium, shedding her ice-white *palla*. "Gaius, Tullia—you'll never believe what I heard at the Forum. Cornelia?"

Sounds of a shriek from the triclinium. "Fortuna's sake," Marcella grumbled. With news like this, one might think she'd have an attentive audience for once. But of course not. Marcella caught sight of the slaves, clustered round-eyed and eavesdropping outside the triclinium, and shooed them off. "Gaius, Cornelia, I have such news—" Marcella began as she swept in, but no one was listening. Cornelia sat rigid on a stool, Gaius leaned against a couch nibbling his nails, and Tullia was storming up and down shrieking.

"—saw you, actually saw you sneaking out of the house at night! How many others saw you, you loose-kneed whore—"

"Now, now," Gaius said nervously.

"Tullia." Marcella greeted her sister-in-law. "I have news, but clearly it can wait. What's going on?"

Tullia whirled around, curls vibrating over a reddened face. "Did you know about this?"

"About what?"

"About your *sister*!" Tullia screamed. "About your sister spreading her knees for a *soldier*!"

Marcella's eyes flew to her sister, gazing straight ahead at the frieze on the wall. Cornelia was as white as the frieze, and she spoke through stiff lips. "Marcella didn't know anything, Tullia. No one knew."

"Don't you *dare* speak to me!" Tullia rounded on her.

"Now, dear—" Gaius began.

Marcella raised an eyebrow and sank onto the nearest couch. "What *is* all this?"

"I questioned Cornelia's maid yesterday." Tullia stalked back and forth across the mosaics, coral-colored silks swishing. "I wanted to know why Cornelia's been so quiet lately—I thought she might be ill! Fine thanks for my thoughtfulness! Her maid was evasive, and after a good beating she finally admitted that Cornelia has been leaving this house every night for *months*. To spend her nights with some *legionary*!"

Marcella glanced at her sister, expecting an explosion. Color flared in Cornelia's cheeks, but she was silent. Marcella thought of her odd sleepiness the past few months—her long walks—her extended trips to the bathhouse . . .

"Cornelia," she said admiringly, "I didn't think you had it in you!"

A flick of a smile from her sister, but it was doused fast enough as Tullia began shrieking again.

"A widow in your position, once wed to an emperor's heir, taking a lover from the *slums*? Who is he?"

"It doesn't matter," said Cornelia. "It's over now."

"I suppose he wasn't the only one, was he! As long as they're rough and common, you don't care who they are, do you? I always knew that perfect front of yours was a sham—you're nothing but a common *slut*—"

"Now, now," Gaius said again.

"—and how long have you been disgracing this family? How long have you been making a fool out of me?"

Cornelia looked at her scornfully. "Tullia," she said, "you were easy to fool. The next time a woman tells you she spent five hours at the bathhouse, rest assured she was not taking a *bath*."

Tullia inhaled for a scream of rage, but Gaius put a hasty hand on her arm. "Dear, allow me. Cornelia—"

"I know what you're going to say, Gaius." Cornelia sounded tired. "Yes, I've been discreet. No one else knows but us."

"And about twenty-two slaves," Marcella added. "All eavesdropping as hard as they can."

"This—*soldier*." Gaius could barely pronounce the word. "Will he make trouble?"

Cornelia turned her head away. "No."

"*Whore*," Tullia hissed.

"Really, Cornelia." Gaius looked reproving. "I would not have thought it of you. Have you no respect for our family name, our position, our reputation—to say nothing of your own—"

"Perhaps that can wait a moment." Marcella rose. "Fascinating as Cornelia's clandestine lover is, and I *am* fascinated, I've learned something else of interest this afternoon. Fabius Valens was captured and executed in Urvinum, and his troops have surrendered."

Utter silence. Gaius swung around, and Tullia paused midway through another stream of insults. Cornelia stared blindly into her lap.

"The Emperor and his advisers know by now, and the news is leaking through the Senate," Marcella continued.

Cornelia looked at her. "How do you know these things?"

"Domitian," Marcella shrugged.

"The Emperor—" Gaius's voice came out in a squeak; he cleared his throat. "The Emperor will deploy another army—"

"He doesn't have another army. And the Moesian legions are marching on Rome. They're camped about fifty miles north."

Another frozen silence. All through November, Marcella thought, everyone had been so sure something would come to save Rome. Fabius Valens, or loyal legions in the south—or maybe the gods. Anyone or anything.

"Oh, no." Tullia resumed her pacing, back and forth across the mosaics. "Oh no, oh no. Oh no. We can't stay, Gaius, we can't stay. Barbarians knocking at the gates, all those legionaries from Dacia and Germania—"

"Might I recommend Tarracina?" Color was coming back into Cornelia's face now. "I spent two weeks there with my soldier from the slums. I admit I never got around to fixing the hypocaust, but the weather is lovely this time of year."

But Tullia wasn't listening anymore. She ran out into the atrium, calling for the steward, calling for little Paulinus, calling for the slaves, who all hastily started polishing things to prove they hadn't been eavesdropping and then started running in circles when they realized their mistress was in hysterics. Gaius rushed upstairs toward his *tablinum*, and Cornelia and Marcella were left sitting in the atrium. Cornelia was staring at the mosaics, as if trying to imagine those savage advancing legionaries marching over them.

"So—" Marcella looked at her sister. "Who is this lover of yours?"

"Does it matter?" Cornelia blinked hard, her dark hair gleaming and her hands motionless in her lap. "It's over now. I won't drag him into trouble with Tullia and Gaius."

"Lollia and her slave," Marcella said, amused. "You and your soldier. Diana and her charioteer. All the Cornelias are being scandalous this year."

"Except you." Cornelia managed a watery smile.

"Marcella, Cornelia—" Gaius rushed back downstairs, a case exploding with scrolls under one arm. "Surely you should pack a few things. Brundisium, that's far enough away—"

"I'm not going," said Cornelia.

"Why?" Gaius glared. "Refusing to leave your pleb lover, are you?"

"No." She looked at him coldly. "Perhaps I have some idea of patrician duty, Gaius."

He reddened. "Marcella, talk to her."

"I'm not leaving either," Marcella said. "I want to see what happens."

Gaius reddened even further, scuffing a sandal across a loose tile in the mosaics. He opened his mouth, but then something shattered in the hall and a slave burst into tears and Tullia called *"Gaius!"* and he bustled away.

Cornelia picked up her *palla*, moving as slowly as if she were underwater. "I'd better go to Lollia. She should know she's been widowed again."

"I'm sure she'll be delighted." Marcella picked up her own *palla*. Cornelia looked back over one shoulder. "Where are you going?" Marcella spread her arms. "To tell the *world*."

L EAVE my house?"

Lollia watched her grandfather gaze around the atrium—his pride and joy, still blooming with banks of bronze crocuses in late November, every column imported fluted and perfect from Corinth, every niche adorned with a life-sized ebony statue with carved ivory eyes. A wealth of rooms beyond the atrium, each one spacious and perfect, the mosaics worth a fortune, every vase and statue lovingly chosen from the best the world had to offer. The house he had spent a lifetime assembling for himself piece by piece; the house Lollia knew he had dreamed of when he was a slave boy polishing other people's possessions.

"The legions won't get inside Rome," she promised her grandfather. "Vespasian's men will set up camp outside the gates, the Senate will flutter, then we'll surrender and Fortuna knows what will happen to Vitellius. But the house will be safe."

"Then why leave it?" He fingered a little carved nymph in rosy marble.

"Because I want my daughter out of Rome," Lollia said grimly.

"The house in Ostia," her grandfather relented after another hour of browbeating. "Is that far enough for you, my jewel? We'll leave in two days—"

"No, you go tomorrow. Take Flavia. I'll go with Cornelia and Marcella and Uncle Paris when they leave for Brundisium."

"Aren't they going with Gaius and Tullia?" Lollia's grandfather winced. "That woman has a voice like a cart over flagstones."

"I'm sure I can put up with it for a few days."

Lies, of course. Lollia had no intention of going with Gaius and Tullia to Brundisium, and she knew Cornelia and Marcella didn't either. They would stay together in Rome, and Lollia couldn't help wondering why. Well, Cornelia would stay because of patrician duty, and Marcella would stay because of boundless curiosity. *But why me?* Why didn't she feel the urge to pack her jewels and her daughter and go with her grandfather to Ostia? A few weeks on his sunlit terrace overlooking the sea—playing with Flavia, celebrating her widowhood now that Fabius was dead, and waiting for the trouble in Rome to be over. Half the patricians in Rome were making discreet and speedy exits. *Why not me?*

Lollia didn't know. Most of the time she prided herself on being practical, like her grandfather with his slave good sense . . . but she'd had a patrician father, and sometimes patrician duty bit her too.

She made soothing noises and set her grandfather to packing before he could change his mind. For herself, Lollia retired down to one of the storerooms to hide as many of his beautiful things as she could. His collection of African ivories, the lacquered bowls from India, the white and green jade figurines, the rare books in their inlaid cases . . . She had just filled one of his many hidden caches when she heard footsteps on the stairs.

"Domina?"

"Hello, Thrax." Lollia picked up a malachite gaming board imported from Crete and packed it carefully away into another little paneled cupboard cut into the wall. She heard Thrax descending the last step, coming into the dim coolness of the storeroom.

"The steward—he says you won't go to Ostia, Domina?"

"No, I won't." She looked at a marble nymph—too tall for the cupboard. "Shouldn't you be helping Flavia pack, Thrax? Make sure she takes her jade menagerie animals and her pearls. They're her favorite things."

He ignored that, coming closer. Lollia had never seen him agitated before, but now his hands were clenching at his sides. "Domina, you won't be safe here."

"Oh, I won't be here in Rome. I'll be leaving for Brundisium with my cousins—"

Thrax gave a sharp shake of his head. "Lie. I know you, Domina."

"It appears you do," Lollia said wryly. "Well, don't worry about me. No one will dare sack Rome."

"Then why have the little one taken away?"

"Better safe than sorry." The second cupboard was full, and Lollia closed it up. If looters did break into the house, at least some of her grandfather's favorite pieces would be saved.

"You should have guards, Domina." Thrax sounded stubborn.

"I'll hire some."

He hesitated. "Let me stay with you."

"No. You need to stay with Flavia." His face was stormy. "*Please*, Thrax."

He looked away. Lollia drank in the sight of his fair hair, his wide shoulders, his broad Gallic face and blue eyes, memorizing everything. They hadn't touched or spoken alone since she'd transferred him to her grandfather's house with his back a sheet of lash marks . . .

"Let me ask you something, Thrax." She looked down at an ivory bowl, turning it over in her hands. "Fabius got sick, just before he was supposed to march north."

"Yes, Domina?" He looked suddenly cautious.

"Food poisoning, everyone said. From that banquet my grandfather threw in this house for Vitellius. And really, who wouldn't get food poisoning, eating fifty courses and throwing them up and eating fifty more? But Fabius has—had—a stomach like an ox. He never got sick before, eating red mullet."

Thrax wouldn't meet her eyes.

"You tried to poison him, didn't you?"

A long silence.

"I won't tell," she sighed. "I just want to know."

"The first time I see him since you sent me away," Thrax said softly. "And he's laughing. And you look so sad next to him, the sad with your eyes and not your mouth. And—and I just go to the cupboard where the cook keeps nightshade to kill rats . . . but he didn't get enough, not with the way they all throw up their food between courses. Not enough." A sigh. "I wasn't thinking. I should not have tried—my Lord, he doesn't like murder."

"I think he'd have forgiven you, Thrax." But Lollia shivered, thinking of the penalties for slaves who attacked their masters. Public execution in the Forum, disembowelment in the arena—no punishment was too harsh. He'd risked the lives of the other slaves too, who would have been put to death for his crime, and even the life of her grandfather, who had lived in panic of being accused of killing the Emperor's right-hand man. "Gods, Thrax, *why*? Why did you risk it? Because he had you flogged?"

Thrax blinked, surprised. "Because he hurt you." Fingers brushed her throat, light as butterflies where Fabius had struck her after she came to Thrax's defense.

"But I'm not worth it!" she cried. "I'm a stupid girl who gets married too much and drinks more wine than she should and spends too much money—"

"You were kind to me," he said.

"Was I? It's my fault you were flogged, Thrax, all my fault—I should have known Fabius would hurt you if he found out—"

"You were *kind* to me," Thrax repeated stubbornly. His accent was stronger now as he struggled for words. "Always kind. You asked my name. Asked about my family—my sister. Said 'Thank you' when I got you things."

"What does that matter?"

"Owners, they—I've had three, since I was ten. All three, they bought me for prettiness, but—" He gave an awkward shrug. "They used me, hard. You were kind. *Are* kind."

Lollia could hardly bear to meet his eyes, they were so full of light.

"I didn't look out for you, with Fabius," she managed to say. "But I'm doing it now, Thrax. You'll take Flavia now, and you'll get to safety."

"Domina—"

"There's no one else I trust my daughter to, Thrax." Lollia looked up at him. "Please—take care of her."

"Like she's mine," he said simply. "Sometimes I pretend she *is* mine."

Lollia reached up and cupped his cheek in her hand. "When this is over, I will find your sister and I will buy her, and any other family you still have, and I will bring them all here for you."

He turned his face against her hand, kissing the palm. Lollia hesitated for a moment, thinking of Fabius and his whip and the blood flying in sprays across a flower-filled atrium—but Fabius was dead now, beheaded in Urvinum, and for what he'd done to Thrax, Lollia hoped the headsman had been drunk and taken at least ten messy strokes to get Fabius's foul screaming head off his neck. A hundred strokes. But fast death or slow, he *was* dead; she was a widow twice in one year—and for once this wasn't adultery. So Lollia put her hands on Thrax's shoulders and stood on tiptoe to kiss him, and pushed him to sit on a barrel of salted herring as she climbed into his lap. He knew a hundred different ways to please her by now, but this time she wanted to please him, and she pushed his hands away. She moved slowly, slowly as she could, and he gripped her hard and the words he muttered into her hair were in his own language. She knew the last word, though. *"Lollia,"* he gasped against her throat, shuddering, and Lollia held him a moment longer. *The first time he ever called me by name.*

"We'd better go," she said softly.

He disentangled himself, and for a moment Lollia thought he'd just throw her across one shoulder and carry her out of Rome kicking and screaming rather than abandon her here. But his habit of obedience was still strong, and so instead he just helped her move a gold-inlaid wine service into another of her grandfather's hidden cubbyholes. She brushed a cobweb out of Thrax's fair hair, and he took the little wooden cross from his neck and slipped it over her head. "For God to protect you." He reached for her hand, gripping it for a long desperate moment, and then he went back up the stairs.

Lollia watched her grandfather leave for Ostia the following morning, taking with him Thrax and Flavia and his cash box and most of his slaves. Flavia had a tantrum at the last moment, wanting her mother to come along, but Thrax fixed her with a stern look and she subsided, waving over his shoulder as he carried her into the wagon. Lollia waved back with a happy smile, waved until they were just specks in the road. Afterward she went back inside and sat in the deserted atrium and had a good cry, clutching Thrax's little wooden cross and surrounded by ivory-eyed ebony statues. *Me crying,* she thought. *Lollia the scandalous.* This time, scandalwise, she'd really surpassed herself. What would the other Cornelias say if they knew she'd done the worst—worse than taking lovers, worse than marrying five times by the age of twenty, and three of those marriages in one year?

She'd gone and fallen in love with a slave.

* * *

I think I've seen enough," said Diana.

"Enough?" Marcella's heart was pounding. *He's finished; Vitellius is done.* There would be no escape now, no mercy—and she'd seen it all. "You want to leave already?"

"Don't you?" Diana looked down the long hall of the Domus Aurea, curiously empty though the streets outside resounded with uproar.

"I thought you'd be glad to see it," Marcella said. "You've been furious at Vitellius since your race, after all."

"I don't like seeing a horse stagger along with a broken leg," Diana said tightly. "Still alive, but not knowing it's dead."

"Oh, I think Vitellius knows. And it won't be long before someone comes to knock him on the head and put him out of his misery."

"I hope I don't have to see it, that's all." Diana looked as lovely as ever in a blue cloak pinned at the shoulder with a round silver brooch from Britannia, but there were shadows under her eyes. "Let's go before the streets get worse."

Reluctantly, Marcella let herself be tugged along. Seeing history being made close at hand might be exciting, but she had no desire to get killed in a mob. That was a little *too* close at hand.

A moon was rising in the frosty purple sky by the time they fought their way out into the streets. Rough and jubilant crowds shouted on every street corner and in every forum, and Marcella was glad of the guards Vitellius had distractedly assigned to escort them home. *Anything for his little pet, even now.*

"Wait." Diana stiffened for a moment, craning her neck, then slipped out from behind a pair of Praetorians. "What are you doing here?"

A man paused, looking down at her. Iron-gray hair, a bronze torc, breeches—yes, the rebel's son, Llyn ap Caradoc. Marcella remembered how resentful she'd felt at the games earlier this spring when he'd ignored her questions about his father's rebellion in Britannia. *Why was I so interested?* she wondered. *A failed rebellion twenty years ago certainly isn't as interesting as a simmering rebellion under my nose. Especially when I've done so much to help it simmer!*

"You shouldn't be out in the streets, Lady," he was telling Diana. "I heard there was killing before the Capitol."

"There was." Diana rubbed the back of her neck tiredly. "Vitellius tried to abdicate. He didn't know how to do it, really—there's never been an emperor who abdicated before. So he offered his dagger to the crowd and made a speech, but he was drunk and it didn't go over very well."

Marcella thought of Vitellius's bravado as he went out to make his abdication speech, his terrified eyes over a wide smile as the crowd roared his name. "Well," he said, coming back inside and spreading his rough horseman's hands, "I suppose I'm still Emperor. They seem to want me." There had been a mix of horror and courage in that reddened, food-bloated face.

Llyn's eyes gleamed like two pieces of steel. "Is he dead?"

"No," said Diana, "but his soldiers ran wild. They went looking for Vespasian's son to kill, but they couldn't find him. So they found some inoffensive brother of Vespasian's and tore him to bits instead."

Marcella wondered absently if Domitian would survive the next few days. The Moesian legions who supported his father's claim were rumored to be camped just ten miles away . . . still, Domitian wouldn't live to see their arrival unless he found a very safe place to wait out the danger. *I'm certainly not going to hide him under the bed if he comes crawling to my door.*

Diana was looking at Llyn critically now, and her eyes came to rest on the long sword he wore strapped against one breech-clad leg. "I'm quite certain you're not supposed to have that."

"Are you?" Amused.

"That's no Roman sword," Marcella interjected, interested despite herself. "Too long for a gladius. Surely it isn't the sword you had in Britannia? They'd have disarmed you and your father the minute you were captured."

He shrugged. "You should both go home."

"So should you," said Diana.

"I have business here."

"Business? With who?"

"Vitellius."

Diana smiled coolly. "Don't pretend he's the Emperor who imprisoned you here, Llyn."

He balanced one foot on a curbstone, graying hair stirring in the twilight breeze. "I never pretend anything."

Their eyes drilled each other. Marcella tilted her head, watching.

"Vitellius is a dead man still walking," Diana said at last. "What does he matter to you?"

Llyn smiled at her, the last gleam of daylight catching the torc at his neck and the rings on his arms. Prizes won in battle against another Emperor of Rome, long ago. "I am a dead man too, Lady."

"You still have a remarkable ability to make all other men in Rome look small," Diana remarked. "I wish I had met you in Britannia."

He laughed at that. "I'd have made a warrior out of you."

"You made me a charioteer instead. Good enough."

"Diana?" Marcella raised her eyebrows. "Are you done yet? It's nearly dark, and you were the one to warn me about mobs."

Diana turned, signaling the guards as she moved past Llyn, but her blue cloak fluttered back and his hand caught her bare arm.

"If anything happens to me," he said, "my horses are yours."

"Did you have to do that?" Diana glared at him. "Now I have to decide which I want more—your safety, or your horses. And you have *very* good horses."

He smiled again, released her arm, and moved noiselessly into the milling crowds. "What was that about?" Marcella asked as they hastened on. "Don't tell me that's your lover. He's a complete savage."

"Oh, gods' wheels," Diana said disgustedly. "Let's go home before we get invaded."

Twenty

ｰｰｯﾞﾞﾞ

CORNELIA had always loved Saturnalia.

Everything about it. The cleaning first, scouring her house top to bottom for the new year. Then the traditional feast, where for once the slaves reclined on the couches and the masters served them. Piso hadn't enjoyed that part—he said it wasn't dignified—but Cornelia never minded going around the couches with a wine flagon while her slaves grinned at her self-consciously. What harm did it do to switch places once a year? *It keeps us all humble.* And then after that the more usual festivities: Diana fretting herself into a fever over the Saturnalia races, Gaius so self-conscious as he led the traditional revelries, Lollia getting tipsy and shrieking *"Io Saturnalia!"* and Marcella sitting there, eternally amused by all the antics. Saturnalia: the year-end festival.

This year Cornelia didn't think there would be any festivities. No gifts. No merriment. This year there would only be death.

"Domina!" A wide-eyed maid clutched at her arm. "I heard there is fighting at the Milvian Bridge!"

"I'm sure there is, Zoe." Cornelia made a mark on her wax tablet, pushing back the nausea that had assailed her all morning. "Have you finished counting those linens?"

"No, but—"

"Count them, Zoe." No banquets and games, but at least Cornelia could see that the house was given its Saturnalia cleaning before it was sacked. She was pleased to discover that Tullia wasn't a terribly good housekeeper, for all her bustling with keys and menus. Clearly her sister-in-law was more interested in making sure the slaves weren't stealing food or making love in the spare bedrooms than in keeping her corners clean.

Cornelia gave the shivering maid a gentle push toward the linen cupboards. "Busy yourself, Zoe. It will make the time pass faster."

She made her way down to the *culina*. "Has the week's supply of bread been baked?"

"No—but Domina, the doorkeeper says he saw troops advancing toward the Colline Gate—"

"The bread must be baked. See to it." Cornelia's eye caught a cluster of little boys craning round eyes through the window shutters. "And put the potboys to work cleaning all the glass."

"Yes, Domina." The slaves were tense, resentful, and frightened, but Cornelia lashed them into work. If they worked, they would not panic. If *she* worked, *she* would not panic. Easier to inspect the mosaics in the atrium and decide if they needed retiling than to think about the envoys Emperor Vitellius had sent that morning with peace terms to the army now camped on Rome's doorstep. Easier to evaluate the cloth stores and make notes for the new year's weaving than think of the rumors that the Moesian legions had rejected all terms and come pouring into the city.

"They're advancing in three columns," Marcella had reported breathlessly a few hours ago. "The main body is advancing down the Flaminian Way across the Milvian Bridge, but there's a second column coming toward the Aurelian Gate and a third force along the Salarian Way."

"Where are you going?" Cornelia noted her sister's pink cheeks and bright eyes. "You can't go out in this madness!"

"I want to see what happens."

"*Cella*—" But Marcella tore out of her grip and dashed out of the house, as eagerly as another woman might have dashed to a lover. *As eagerly as I dashed to a lover, anyway.* Cornelia looked after her sister a moment, uttering a prayer to Juno—Minerva—anyone who might be listening—and then set herself back to cleaning. Surely the fighting would cease once Vitellius's forces were defeated. Then the troops would be taken in hand.

"Domina," the understeward moaned, "legionaries are storming through the Gardens of Asiaticus—we must flee—"

"We will not flee." Cornelia borrowed a little of Drusus's crisp centurion snap. "Do as you're told, and we will be safe."

Drusus. In the slums, he'd be safe enough—fighting would surely be concentrated around the Forum, the half-burned Capitol, the Campus Martius, and the city gates. Cornelia had sent him a note the day Gaius and Tullia left Rome. *They found out*, she wrote, and then added a disjointed *Be safe—please be safe. Don't reply, and don't come for me.*

"Where is Zoe?" Cornelia asked, looking around for her maid.

The steward's eyes shifted sideways. "I don't know, Domina."

"Find someone else to dust those cobwebs, then."

By midmorning Cornelia started to hear distant crashes, muffled shouting. She summoned the litter-bearers to carry a note to Lollia— surely she would rather wait it all out here than alone in her grandfather's massive cave of a house—but the litter-bearers had all gone missing, and no note could be sent. By midday all the male slaves were gone. By midafternoon, Cornelia didn't have enough maids left to lift a massive feather bolster for its yearly turn.

"Well." She sat down rather suddenly on the feather bed. "That's it, I suppose."

"Domina," one of the slave girls whispered. "There is fighting in Forum Julium—by the Circus Maximus—by the Temple of Minerva—"

"Is there?" Cornelia pushed back the surge of nausea again. "Then you may as well flee if you want to."

They scattered without another word. Cornelia lay back on the bolster, curling into a ball. Perhaps Lollia would come, even without a note, and bring Diana with her. They had to be frightened, alone in Lollia's great cave of a house. Or Marcella would come back . . . oh, why had she gone out? Why? Cornelia wanted her sister's hand over her own, her sister's cool voice explaining all the logical reasons why the world would come right again.

Maybe the world wasn't going to come right again.

The sound of a banging door downstairs sent Cornelia bolt upright. Heavy footsteps up the stairs—surely the fighting hadn't spread as far as the Palatine Hill, *surely*—she looked around her for a weapon, frantic, but then a familiar voice shouted *"Cornelia!"* She flew across the room and fell into Drusus's arms almost before he burst through the door.

"Gods—" He gripped her with violent relief, his voice thick against her hair. "I thought you'd have left the city by now—why didn't you leave?"

"Why didn't you?" Cornelia said against the rough wool of his tunic. "I told you not to come—"

"You thought I'd *listen?*"

"But if someone here recognized you, the treason warrant—"

"Everyone's got more important things to worry about today than minor traitors." Drusus pulled back, eyes sweeping her anxiously. "Don't you have any guards? Slaves with cudgels, even—"

"All fled."

"Then we should flee too. The fighting around the Campus Martius is bad, and it's worse by the Colline Gate. We'll get out now, back to the slums—no one will bother bringing the fighting to the slums—"

"I can't." She shook her head. "My brother fled, but my sister and cousins are all here in the city. If they need to flee, they might come here—"

"Then we barricade ourselves in." He went through the house like a one-man legion, barring doors, curtaining windows, dragging heavy shelves and barrels before the gate.

Cornelia watched him. "Drusus . . ."

"What?" He pushed his sweat-damp hair off his broad forehead. He was bare-armed in a rough tunic, his *gladius* belted at his waist again.

She smiled. "Nothing." Let him barricade; it gave him something to do.

He dropped down on the couch at her side, taking her fingers and plaiting them with his own. "Your note—you said your brother found out? Is that why he refused to take you? I'll flog him around the city, abandoning his sister like that—"

"No, I refused to go. But he did find out. Not about you, but that I've been—" A shrug. "Disgracing myself, he put it."

"I'm sorry—" Drusus began, but Cornelia laid a finger over his mouth.

"Sshh. I'm glad you're here."

"I won't leave you till it's safe." He wrapped her in his arms, hugging her close against the warmth of his chest, and the words trembled on her lips again. *Drusus, I should have had my bleeding when we came back from Tarracina two months ago, but I didn't. Drusus, I never used any of Lollia's Egyptian tricks because I thought I was barren. Drusus, I was married eight years without any sign of a child, but now—now I think I am pregnant.*

She felt the pressure of his sword against her side and bit the words back. It was too late to tell, too late to flee—too late to do anything, this violent Saturnalia afternoon, but wait.

PULLING her *palla* up over her hair, Diana shifted into a swift jog. She'd seen Llyn move like a wolf in a ground-eating lope, and she certainly couldn't match him, but she was still fast and fit after so many months of driving his horses. Just a quick scout through the streets and she'd go back for Lollia, who sat stitching halfheartedly on a bit of embroidery in the big empty atrium of her grandfather's house and trying to keep calm. All morning they'd waited in restless silence, thinking the city gates couldn't possibly be breached. But by noon the Milvian Gate had broken, and the Colline Gate, and enemy troops were forcing their way in.

Lollia had looked up with white all around her eyes, like a horse ready to bolt. "Let's get the guards," Diana had said. "We'll go wait with Cornelia and Marcella—they're farther up the hill from the fighting."

But every guard Lollia had hired to protect her had fled.

Diana stuck to the back streets, scouting with watchful eyes. Women stood in doorways, hard-faced and wary, thrusting their children behind them. A tavern still stood open for business, drunken shouts rising from within. A row of vendor stalls—a few were open and Diana watched a housewife calmly feeling through a basket of apples before handing over a few coppers for the least-bruised fruit. A child tugged at her skirts, looking up at Diana with no sign of fear as she skidded to a halt.

They could make their way through, she and Lollia. If they skirted the Forum, and Lollia left off all her jewels . . .

Diana looked down the slope of the street, in the direction of the broken gates. Distantly she heard a roar—she'd think it was thunder, if she didn't know it was bloodshed.

It wasn't so far to the faction stables from here.

Diana hesitated only a moment.

I'll just see if the horses have been moved to safety. That was all she wanted to know. The Reds faction director fled the city a week ago, taking his teams with him, but she didn't know about the Blues. Were they stupid enough to think Vitellius would be able to shield them?

She took a detour around the Forum, circling through a maze of back streets. Normally she wouldn't walk alone in such places, but the small streets were empty today, the windows shuttered, eyes glittering through cracks in doors. Two men darted past carrying bulging sacks, a mad beggar crouched mumbling in a vestibule, and over everything hung a strange silence.

Diana picked up her jog again. *The Anemoi.* She wouldn't stay long. Just a quick look into the Blues stables to make sure the horses were safe, and then she'd go back home and take Lollia to safety. By morning everything would be done one way or another. Gods only knew where Vitellius was now—she heard some rumor he'd fled to his family home on the Aventine and barricaded himself inside, but who knew what was true?

Diana halted in the entrance of the Blues stables, putting her hands to her knees and panting. *"Bassus!"* she called the Blues faction director, but her voice echoed unanswered. A broken length of blue-dyed rein was trampled forgotten in the straw, and a bucket rolled disconsolately by the water troughs. She saw a guard or two, Praetorians by their armor, and a few souls wandering at the end of the passage, but no one halted Diana. Just refugees looking for a place to hide from the rampaging soldiers. The Blues director and the horses were clearly long gone, and Diana's heart eased. The Anemoi were safe. She came to the first set of blue-painted stalls where they had been installed with such hateful pomp, looking over the first gate—and froze. Her fleet-footed Zephyrus was there, looking at her through his red forelock with a calm liquid eye. Notus put his head over the next stall, and in two more steps she saw that Eurus and her savage Boreas were there too, and beyond them the famous team of blood bays. The Blues had fled in panic, and they'd left all their horses behind.

"Oh, you bastards," she gritted out and spun toward the shed where they kept the harness. Another few hours and the horses would all be gone, claimed by grinning legionaries who knew what a good horse was worth. The blood bays would be split up and led off by four new owners, sold or traded a dozen times by morning, never to race together again. But that wouldn't happen to her Anemoi. "You, help me," she called to one of the slaves she saw edging about at the end of the passage, but he just stared at her.

She dived into the harness shed, coming out with a pair of bridles thrown over each shoulder, and swung into Boreas's stall first. "Come with me and no biting," she started to say, but then she halted and the first bridle fell into the straw at her feet.

"Hello, girl," Emperor Vitellius said softly.

He sat in the corner of Boreas's stall, arms resting limp over his massive belly. Manure stained his purple robe, and he picked at it idly. A wineskin lay flat and empty at his side. A guard stood in the corner, nervously fingering his *gladius* as he looked at Diana, but

Vitellius jerked his double chin and the guard edged around Boreas and tramped out of the stall.

"Caesar," Diana said. "Gods' wheels, what are you doing here?"

"I was going to my family's home on the Aventine, but—" Vitellius shrugged. "There's fighting around there. You know there's fighting?"

Diana stepped closer. "Why aren't you in the palace?"

"Oh—" A restless movement set his heavy jowls wobbling. "Never liked that palace. Everyone's getting ready to bolt. Don't think I don't know it! Alienus betrayed me, and now all my own guards are looking to do the same. I liked Alienus . . ."

He subsided, muttering, but then he reached out and ran a heavy ringed hand down Boreas's scarred foreleg. Boreas pawed the straw, but didn't kick. "Horses don't betray you," Vitellius said, wistful.

"They've been abandoned." Diana picked up the bridle that had fallen out of her surprised hand. "The faction director, he just left them all—"

"Yes, I filled their haynets when I got here," said the Emperor of Rome. "They were hungry."

Diana pulled the bridle between her hands. Vitellius picked up the wineskin, squeezed a reluctant drop into his mouth, tossed it aside again. His eyes were bloodshot, moving everywhere, but the massive bloated body was still. "You should flee, Caesar," Diana said. "You could hide, maybe even get out of the city. You could abdicate for Vespasian."

"Tried that. Didn't go so well." He picked up a piece of straw and twirled it between his fingers. "Anyway, an emperor doesn't flee."

"An emperor doesn't hide in a stable either!" Diana couldn't help but feel a flash of disgust. Galba had been an old man, but he died on his feet barking orders. Otho had taken his own life with flair and grace once his cause was lost. "An emperor faces his enemies head-on!"

Vitellius's bloodshot eyes moved tiredly across hers. "Well, I'm not much of an emperor."

She had no words for that.

"I ever tell you I curried horses for the Blues once? Proud to do it, too." Vitellius lumbered upright, heaving his bulk out of the straw. He held out his big hands and Boreas came to him, nuzzling the Emperor of Rome for treats. "Gods," Vitellius said, stroking the heavy head. "I do love horses. And I love my Blues."

Diana looked away.

"Take them." Vitellius gave Boreas a last pat. "I shouldn't have taken them from you. That race you drove—girl, on the last lap they lifted off the ground and flew. What a thing to see! They won't run like that for me. Maybe not for anyone."

"Caesar—"

"Take them!" He pushed roughly past her out of the stall, gathering the purple folds of his robe. "There's a mob that wants me, and I want to be drunk when they get here."

"But Caesar—" She was running after him, trying to find the words to rouse him, when a tall figure came through the stable doors in a few long strides.

"Hey, you, get away from here." One of Vitellius's remaining Praetorians drew his *gladius*, gesturing the man back, but a long sword came hissing out of its scabbard and buried itself in the Praetorian's neck. His eyes sprang open whitely, and he folded like an unironed tunic. Vitellius halted in the straw-covered passageway, his mouth wobbling as Llyn ap Caradoc calmly booted the body off his blade.

"Get back from the Emperor!" The other Praetorian dived at Llyn, swinging his *gladius* in a massive slash, but the Briton moved with molten ease, sliding out of reach and then back in with a short brutal chop at the man's face. His eyes disappeared in a sudden gout of blood, and suddenly the third Praetorian and the last nervously lingering hangers-on were all fleeing and stumbling out of the stables.

"Llyn?" Diana whispered. "No, you can't—"

He finished off the second guard and moved forward, his gaze fixed on the Emperor. The rage in his dark eyes was bottomless, far outstripping fat trembling Vitellius and his pathetic little sins. It was a rage big enough for all Rome, and any protests on Vitellius's tongue died visibly.

"Well," he said dully, "whoever you are, get on with it."

"Caesar—" Diana began.

"Leave me!" Vitellius roared, and in that moment at least he looked like an emperor.

She found herself kneeling, her hands still full of harness.

Vitellius's rough hand touched her hair. When she looked up, Llyn was dragging him down the passage by the neck, stumbling and panting.

"Better get out of here," Llyn called to her, not looking back. They were suddenly gone, the tall figure and the fat one, gone at the end of the passage into the last of the empty horse stalls, and Diana lingered frozen for a moment. But there was a surge of shouting close by, a sudden wave of noise, and it jerked her back into motion.

She scrambled up and went to Boreas, dragging a bridle over his ears, and then got the others one by one and led them out to be harnessed. The racing chariot was too conspicuous with its crusting of gilt and bright blue paint, but there were plain practice chariots in the back shed, and she hitched the Anemoi to one of those. She'd never harnessed a team so fast. She looked toward the last stall once or twice, but no one came out, and she dragged a grubby hand across her eyes.

The Anemoi stood ready, necks curved, noses flared, looking eagerly about them as they smelled excitement. *A different kind of excitement today, my loves*, Diana thought as she fetched a driving whip and scrambled into the chariot. *You won't smell rose petals today, or palm branches. Just blood.*

She whipped them up, taking them out the broad entrance gate rather than the gate to the arena, but it was too late. She saw torches there, and soldiers pressing in a relentless armored mass toward the palace, and another crush of soldiers spreading toward the fine houses on the Palatine Hill, and all she could do was whip the Anemoi into a gallop. It was too late to do anything but run.

W*HAT are you DOING?"* Lollia shrieked.

"Climb in." Diana had steered the Anemoi off the circular drive to the house, over a bed of winter lilies and into the entrance hall. The axles grated on the door frame, but the chariot just fit through the doors. "It isn't safe here anymore. The fighting's getting closer. I barely outran a mob getting here."

Lollia didn't need to be told twice. She slung a bundle under one arm and hopped up into the chariot. "You're utterly mad. You went to fetch your *horses?*"

"Good thing I did, because we're going to need them. They're the only things that can get us to Cornelia and Marcella in time." Diana leaned back on the reins, clicking her tongue at the horses. Tiles crunched as a priceless mosaic was destroyed underfoot.

"You'll never get them turned around in this space—"

"Yes, I will." Diana leaned back, tendons cording all down her arms, and somehow she got the horses wrenched around and wedged back through the entrance gate. "Hold on."

Lollia whimpered as she saw the lights at the foot of the slope, and suddenly there were men whooping everywhere, flashes of bright breastplates and torches brandished overhead. "Hey, my pretties, slow down—!" But they scattered as the Reds barreled through the gates, and Diana lashed the chariot straight down the street.

"Oh gods, they're coming to loot." Lollia jerked, looking back at the torches weaving giddily through her grandfather's front gates. "Why don't their commanders stop them? This is *Rome*, not some barbarian citadel! They can't just tear it to pieces!"

"Maybe their commanders can't stop them. Or maybe they just don't care it's Rome." Diana slowed the Reds to a trot again, and their hooves clashed resoundingly loud along the empty street. Only it didn't feel empty now. The shadows were lengthening with the onset of night, and Diana didn't need to see the eyes to know they were there. Lollia clutched the rail of the chariot, teeth crashing together at every bump, but she didn't complain.

"You're marvelous," she said through her shivering. "You're mad, and you're marvelous, and you've likely saved my life—" Diana barely listened, all her attention spinning down through the reins in her hands. The horses were close to panic, and as they drove past the Forum Romanum she saw why.

"Oh, gods," Lollia moaned. There were twisted crumpled things lying still on the stones, things that had to be bodies, dark pools that had to be blood. Shadows darted in and out of the temples—a soldier in a plumed helmet staggered down the steps of Jupiter's temple under the weight of a silver urn, behind him an ordinary shopkeeper who had joined the looting troops and was now trundling away a barrow full of prizes. A stray dog lapped at a rivulet of blood leaking down the gutter, and the horses threw up their heads as they caught the stench of it. Diana yanked the chariot around a corner into a darkened side street, and the blood-crawling Forum disappeared from sight.

"Faster!" Lollia tugged at Diana's arm. "Can you go faster?"

Two soldiers staggered out of a tavern, whooping drunkenly. Diana cracked her whip at them and they flinched back. Another side street, another, another—"What's taking so long?" Lollia groaned.

"The direct route isn't safe. I saw soldiers spilling out of the palace earlier."

"The *palace*? But the Emperor—"

Diana set her lips in a line. "Vitellius is dead."

The houses of the Palatine, flashing by—Diana saw a shrieking patrician woman running from her doorway with an armload of clothes, a slave behind her with a jewel box. Somewhere a man was shouting. Lollia nearly spilled out of the chariot on a sharp turn, but one more block passed and they were pulling up before the family house. Zephyrus reared, white showing all around his eyes and sparks striking on the stones under his hooves, and Notus plunged against the reins. "Get down," Diana shouted at Lollia, fighting them. "Get down and fetch Cornelia and Marcella, I don't dare let go of the horses!"

"Cornelia and Marcella—but can't we—"

"We can't stay here, it's not safe!" Diana heard a roar somewhere behind and Lollia tumbled out of the chariot, stumbling up the pink marble steps to hammer at the door. *"Cornelia! CORNELIA!"* The door flew open to reveal a legionary with drawn sword, a snarl cutting his face in half, and Lollia screamed.

"No, Lollia—" Cornelia pushed around the legionary, her hair wild down her back. "No, he's with me—"

"Cornelia, get in." Lollia yanked her frantically toward the chariot, where Diana had managed to fight the horses down to a bursting standstill. "We have to run—get Marcella—"

"Marcella isn't here."

"Not here? Oh, gods—*Marcella*—"

"No time," the soldier snapped, jamming his short sword back into its scabbard. His gaze flicked over the trembling horses. "You can hold them?" he barked up at Diana.

She nodded curtly. "I can." How long she could keep on holding them was another matter. Her hands were tough as cured leather, but she had no gloves and her palms were already a mass of dark blisters.

"Aim for the Aurelian Gate," Cornelia's soldier said. "That should be deserted by now. If they went for the Emperor, the fighting will be concentrated up at the palace instead." He grabbed Cornelia's arm, hauling her toward the chariot. "Get in, love."

"No, not without you, you have to come too—" Cornelia clutched him, but he cut her off.

"Won't fit me." The chariot was built for one; it would barely hold three girls jammed together, much less a stockily built soldier. "Get in."

"*No*," Cornelia wept. But there was a roar of voices and a sound of breaking timbers from the street beyond.

"Hurry up," said Diana. Her arms were burning now as she held the Anemoi, plunging and bucking against their harness, screaming up at her through the reins.

"Cornelia," Lollia shouted, scrambling into the chariot, "*get in!*"

Cornelia shook her head, still clinging to her soldier, but he took her face between his hands and shook her. "I'll slip out through the back," he said. "I'll blend in—the soldiers will think I'm one of them. Won't work for you, love. Up you go."

He bundled her in, and she was hardly clear of the wheel before the Reds were plunging madly down the street. Cornelia twisted her head to look back, tear tracks marking her white face, and Diana saw the soldier running up the street with his *gladius* drawn.

"Marcella," Lollia was shouting, "*where is Marcella?*" But Cornelia could only shake her head helplessly. Marcella was gone.

The Reds careened down the slope of the Palatine Hill, houses and streets a nightmarish blur on their way toward the Campus Martius and the Aurelian Gate. The shouting grew louder, and suddenly it was on them. "Oh gods," Lollia gulped, gripping the little cross her slave had given her, and Cornelia whispered "Juno's mercy," and started reciting the names of her ancestors as if she were preparing the litany for death.

The Campus Martius had vanished. Usually patricians strolled there to see and be seen; young sparks raced their horses and plebs gathered to gawk at whatever famous face they could find, but now it had all disappeared into an ocean of slaughter. The rampant soldiers had come squeezing in through the Aurelian Gate, but Vitellius's last troops led charge after charge against them, and Diana could see the tidemarks of the charges in the fallen bodies. Looters were already scurrying among the wounded, scrabbling for valuables, and more people stood in vestibules watching and making bets as they would at a race. A temple was ablaze, flames writhing up to the twilight sky, and the firelight cast mad leaping shadows across the broken writhing men. The legionaries howled and capered, hauling sacks of loot, waving wineskins, dragging their bloodied swords. Diana saw a man run up to a cluster of soldiers, pointing at a doorway and shrieking "Vitellian, Vitellian!" and the legionaries swaggered over to kick down the door. A heartbeat more and a woman began screaming inside. The pleb pocketed a few coins and ran chuckling to another group of soldiers, pointing to a different door.

"Straight through," Diana said. "No other way." She cracked her whip and the Anemoi leaped forward into the madness.

A legionary looked up, staggering with wine, but they'd already flashed past by the time he stretched out a hand. A wounded man screamed, and Diana heard the thump as his leg was trampled under the rim of the wheel. Two plebs darted for safety, a plumed officer held up a spear to halt the chariot, but they were just blurs. The Anemoi were running wild, ears pinned flat against their heads, mad with the smell of the blood under their hooves and the blood in their veins that told them to go faster, faster, and they yanked Diana half over the side of the chariot as she fought to hold them. A cluster of legionaries hailed her with shouts, drawing their short blades and pointing at the horses, but Diana slashed at them with her whip and saw one stagger with blood oozing in a sharp line from his snarling face before they all slid back into the whirling madness. A tremendous lunge past the fountain where a dozen wounded men were screaming and trying to reach the water, and the chariot was through. Somewhere ahead was the Aurelian Gate, beyond that was a road, and somewhere beyond that was a world that was still sane.

"Marcella!" Cornelia screamed. *"Marcella!"* She hauled Diana's taut arm, pointing, and Diana looked up to see her cousin. *She's dead, surely she's dead*—but Marcella was alive, and gods only knew how Cornelia managed to catch sight of her in this maelstrom. Their cousin stood in her pale-blue *stola* beside the altar of Mars, her hair whipping about her calm face: a column of ice watching the slaughter. There were a score of plebs around her, cheering various struggling combatants and slapping down coins in bets, but she stood quite still.

"Marcella!" Lollia added her voice to Cornelia's, shouting, and finally Marcella heard. Her head turned and Diana saw the calm carved face, the watchful eyes, and then she was running toward the chariot.

"Diana, stop the horses, you have to stop them—"

"—Can't—" she gritted through bared teeth, her blistered palms weeping blood, but she threw her whole body back on the reins and the Anemoi pulled up in a thrash of hooves, dripping foam, shrieking like the wounded men in the fountain. The chariot tilted perilously on one wheel and they all clutched at the rail, but it righted itself and the horses gathered to run again, and this time they tore the reins through Diana's hands in a blaze of agony. She knew she'd never hold them now, but Marcella was close, and Lollia and Cornelia put out their hands and brought her flying up into the chariot as the Reds lunged into a crazed gallop. A legionary tried to grab for Boreas's reins but recoiled screaming as the old stallion swiped foam-flecked teeth at him and took off his ear and half his cheek. Diana fumbled whitely for the reins, every finger sawed open and bleeding, but Marcella was clinging safe to the chariot rail, squashed up against Lollia with Cornelia on her other side. There was barely room for the four of them and Marcella hung perilously off the back, but her eyes were gleaming. "Where are we going?" she shouted, but Diana was fighting the horses and had no breath left to answer.

The Aurelian Gate was open, littered by half a dozen prowling guards. They stepped into the path at the sound of hooves, holding their spears up to halt the chariot, but the Anemoi ran them down without a blink. Diana felt the bodies bump under the wheels and Cornelia nearly slipped off the back of the chariot, but Lollia flung an arm around her waist and hauled her back in. They clung to each other, the four Cornelias crammed close behind four runaway horses, and first Diana looked up at the sky and saw that night had fallen, and then she looked back and realized they'd left the city behind.

Twenty-one

⌒⌒⌒

"WHAT is this place?" Marcella blinked sleepily in the dawn light, looking up at the dusty rafters overhead.

"It belongs to Llyn ap Caradoc." Diana yawned, stretching her arms overhead as Marcella looked around the hay bales, the harness hooks, the rows of stalls. "He usually has a steward and a few slaves, but they must have fled. Still, I knew Llyn wouldn't mind if we borrowed his barn."

"Couldn't we have borrowed his house?" Marcella shivered in the morning chill, rubbing her bare arms.

"Oh, no. Britons take guest-right very seriously. You don't ever just invite yourself into a Briton's house."

"You know the oddest things, Diana."

Still, Marcella thought, a haystack was better than nothing. Even if they'd trotted half the night to get to it. The villa wasn't far outside city walls, Diana had explained at some point last night during the long dark drive, but it was a good distance around from the Aurelian Gate, where they'd had to make their escape. She'd pulled up the horses in the yard well past midnight, and Marcella had been only too happy to pile off the chariot in Lollia and Cornelia's wake, stagger into the barn, and collapse without a further word into the haystack.

Lollia was still asleep, curled into a ball in the hay and looking no older than Flavia, but Cornelia was just starting to stir. Marcella yawned again, and Diana put her hands to the small of her back and grimaced as she stretched. "Gods' wheels, I've never hurt so much in my life," she groaned. "Not even after my Circus Maximus race."

She held up her hands in the gray dawn light and Marcella saw that blood had spiraled down from her blistered, sawed-open palms and dried around her wrists in brown ribbons. "Those horses pulled your hands to pieces, didn't they?"

"I don't mind." Diana tugged affectionately at the old stallion's drooping ears. "They ran like gods." The Anemoi looked as exhausted as Diana, still standing harnessed to the chariot with their noses hanging at their knees. They'd galloped half the night and trotted the other half once they ran themselves tired, and even when Diana pulled them up in the barn she said she didn't dare unharness them. "What if a stray raiding party comes along? We might need to make another fast escape." The last thing Marcella had seen before her eyes snapped shut in sleep had been Diana curled up against the old stallion's legs, stroking the heavy nose that dropped on her shoulder and gazing at the road below in search of further danger.

"I think we can unharness them now." Marcella rubbed her bare arms again. "I doubt we'll see any marauding legionaries this morning. They'll all be too busy sleeping off their hangovers and guarding their loot." She gestured at the horses. "Can I help?"

"Fetch them some water? There's a well outside."

Marcella lugged four buckets over, two at a time, as Diana began unbuckling straps and traces. The first stallion shook himself in relief as the bridle slid over his ears, and Diana murmured loving nonsense at him.

"You really were splendid, Diana." Marcella heaved up a bucket for the horse to drink. "Lollia says you saved her and Cornelia, and I don't doubt it."

"You were the one in real danger." Diana unbuckled the breastplate from the old stallion's heavy chest, looking at Marcella. "What were you doing down there in the Campus Martius?"

Marcella shrugged. "I wanted to see what would happen."

"You could have died."

"Oh, I don't think so." She smiled. "You saved me, didn't you?"

"Maybe." Diana rubbed the second stallion's silky nose as he started eagerly for the water bucket. "We might all be dead if Vitellius hadn't given me the horses."

"*Vitellius?*"

"He was hiding in the Blues stable." She hauled an armload of harness to one side. "I spoke with him. He was . . ."

"What?" Marcella asked eagerly. "Tell me!"

Diana looked at her. "Nothing. He gave me the horses. I suppose he's dead now."

"Do you have to be so close-mouthed?" Marcella said, exasperated.

"There's nothing to tell." Diana looped ropes about two of the arched chestnut necks, and the stallions followed her docile as ponies to their stalls. Marcella rolled her eyes. But by the time Diana put up all four horses with hay and more fond words, Lollia and Cornelia were awake and there was no more privacy to press Diana for her secrets. *The one time she knows anything interesting*, Marcella thought, *is the one time she keeps her mouth shut!*

"Juno's mercy, whenever did you find time to pack?" Cornelia was asking as Lollia rummaged in her satchel and triumphantly produced a packet of bread and cheese.

"Well, I resigned myself to a noble death as was proper." Lollia began parceling the bread out among them. "But I thought that just in *case* we had to do the sensible thing and flee instead of the patrician thing and die, it would be nice to have some food and perhaps a little money and an extra *palla* or two . . ." She produced coins, cloaks, and more food like a conjurer.

Cornelia laughed, but the laughter died away quickly and she looked out the wide barn doors toward the city. "Worried for your soldier?" Diana said, rummaging about the barn for rags to tie up her blood-crusted hands.

"Soldier?" Lollia dug to the bottom of the pack.

"You didn't know about Cornelia's lover?" Marcella spread her *palla* out on the hay to catch the breadcrumbs from Lollia's bread. "Tullia screamed loud enough to be heard in Gaul."

"Of course I knew about Cornelia's lover, and long before you did! So that was him, the soldier at the house? Of course it was. He came to protect you, how romantic! Who is he? You have to tell us now, my honey."

"Centurion Drusus Sempronius Densus." Cornelia took a chunk of cheese and started to nibble. Even if Cornelia were starving, Marcella thought in amusement, she'd never wolf her food. "Formerly of the Praetorian Guard."

"So *that's* where I knew him." Lollia sounded satisfied. "Your old bodyguard. I always used to think he had an eye for you—"

"How long did it go on?" Marcella wondered. "You never did tell me."

"Over four months," Cornelia said, composed. "And that's all I'm going to say about it."

"Do you suppose we could return to the city today?" Marcella broke a chunk of bread in half as she gazed out at the road, letting her own eyes drift out toward the city. "Just think what must be happening . . ."

"If you're that curious, you can go alone." Diana was bandaging up her bloody hands. "We stay here a few days until things calm down."

"Who are you to give orders?" Marcella said, nettled.

Diana looked back at her calmly. "I'm the only one who can drive a chariot, that's who I am. Unless you plan on walking back to the city? Because the horses are staying here, and so should all four of us until things settle down."

Marcella glared. Cornelia didn't look happy either—still worrying for her soldier—but Lollia flopped back into the straw with a groan of contentment.

"A few days to sleep in this delightful hay—bliss, even if it is scratchy. I don't think I'd even care if some legionary raped me at this point, as long as he didn't wake me up. I could even sleep through sex with Fabius, and that's saying something. Gods, I hope he really is dead. Pass the cheese?"

They slept a great deal over the next day. Lollia made friends with the nameless black dog who haunted the barn, as well as the horses who had saved their lives—even the savage old stallion succumbed to her cooing and let her put braids in his mane. "It appears," Marcella observed, "that no male of any species can resist Lollia." Marcella spent a good deal of time staring down the road toward the city, calculating a dozen different possibilities for Rome's outcome. *Vespasian is Emperor? Vitellius is prisoner? Vitellius is dead . . .*

It wasn't till sunset that the villa's owner returned. Marcella saw him first from the door of the barn, a lone figure striding up the long slope of the hill toward the barn. Her muscles tensed before she realized it was only one man. His sword was out, but he strode far too unhurriedly to be looking for a fight. "Diana," Marcella called, "is that our, ah, host?"

Diana swung off the fence railing where she'd been watching the Anemoi frisk in the long grass, her pale hair gleaming in the fading sun. She looked down the slope a moment, then turned swiftly and jogged to meet the approaching figure. She met him a short distance from the barn's entrance, and Marcella could hear them without straining. "I wondered if you'd be back, Llyn."

"I'm back." He looked her over, and Marcella wondered if he'd start feeling her legs up and down like he'd check a horse for spavins. "I see you came out unscathed."

"Me and my three cousins." Diana gestured behind her, and Marcella gave a vague wave from the door of the barn and retreated a little into the door's shadow as if she were out of earshot. "I put them up in your barn—we didn't have anywhere else safe. Don't worry," Diana added, though Marcella didn't see the Briton's face move. "We didn't enter your house. I wouldn't violate guest-right. Though I did borrow your tunic," she added, plucking at the coarse cloth. It hung to her shins, and she'd belted it around her waist with a spare length of rein. "My dress was all bloody, and I found this hanging on a nail in the barn. I figured guest-right didn't extend to old clothes."

"It does not," he said formally. "And I welcome you and your cousins to my hall, as guests—though you can probably return to the city if you wish."

"Why?" Diana tilted her head at him. A stray lock of hair curved over her forehead like a little crescent moon: Diana the Huntress more than ever, Marcella thought. "Is the city quiet?"

"Yes. The legionaries are under control now." The black dog padded out, tail wagging, and Llyn bent to scratch his ears. "An emergency meeting of the Senate is soon to be convened. They will undoubtedly confirm Vespasian as Emperor. They're already hailing his son Domitian at the Domus Aurea."

So Domitian survived. Marcella was mildly surprised at that. And the Senate was confirming Vespasian already? She drew in a breath, praying the Briton would go on.

"Another emperor." Diana put her bandaged hands at the small of her back, stretching. "There will always be one, you know, no matter how many times you take matters into your own hands. I hope you realize that."

The Briton smiled, tilting his long sword up across one shoulder—and Marcella suddenly saw that the blade was dark.

"He wasn't worth it," said Diana. "I hope you realize that, too."

"Perhaps not."

"Then why?"

The Briton paused, fingering the hilt of the blade still tilted across one shoulder. "Eighteen years I've been in Rome," he said finally. "And every morning when I wake up, I think for a moment that I'm in Britannia. Sometimes it's my friends pounding at the door, shouting at me to go hunting with them. Sometimes it's my father, planning a raid on a Roman fort and wanting me to lead my scouts for a diversion. But for a moment or two, it's real. More real than any of this." His arm encompasses the hill, the horses, the city below. "More real than you."

"And?"

"Emperor Claudius made us swear oaths we'd never leave Rome. I wanted to kill him for that. My father kept the oath, but my father's dead now. Dead of captivity. I'd go ahead and kill Claudius, if he were still alive, but—" Llyn shrugged. "Another emperor will do just as well."

Diana gestured at his sword. "Better hide that." The Briton paused, looking up at her as he squatted down to shove the sword under a pile of harness at the corner of the yard, and Marcella wondered if she'd ever get the full story.

I S it over?"

Marcella could hear the question being asked everywhere as the blood was cleared away and people came creeping back to their daily lives. "Is it over?" Not just a matter of the bloodshed being over, or Vitellius's reign being over. *Is it* all *over?*

Rome was silent. Plebs scurried hastily back to their bolted homes, blood dried in the gutters, slaves who had fled their masters in panic crept shamefacedly back. The Cornelii family home was a wreck, the furniture smashed or stolen, half the statues broken, the doors gaping wide. The house of Lollia's grandfather had fared better—his wine cellar was empty, but the task of emptying it had clearly distracted the looting soldiers, who had otherwise left the house untouched except for a few broken statues, sundry small stolen valuables, and a wrecked mosaic in the entrance hall. "And the mosaic," Lollia said affectionately, "can be blamed on Diana the Huntress here. You must all stay with me until everything else is put in order, of course—"

"Not me," said Cornelia. She was still pale with the nausea she couldn't quite seem to shake off, but she threw her *palla* over her head and started resolutely for the door. "I'm going to find Drusus."

"What's wrong with her?" Marcella wondered, then blinked as her cousins both turned and eyed her a little oddly. "What?"

"You didn't guess?" Lollia raised her eyebrows. "It's plain as the nose on Cornelia's face."

"*What* is?"

"She's pregnant." Diana said. "Mares get that same look. Edgy."

"Why didn't she tell me?" Marcella complained.

"You never tell anybody anything," Lollia pointed out. "Why should we?"

"But she's my sister!" Marcella accosted Cornelia as soon as she returned the following day, her eyes soft and shining. "You could have told me your news, Cornelia."

Cornelia looked puzzled. "Why?" But Marcella forgot to be annoyed with her when Cornelia relayed some different news: Vitellius, beyond all shadow of a doubt, was dead. "No one seems to know quite how it happened," Cornelia winced. "He hid in the stables and a mob tore him to pieces, or he was paraded out on the palace steps and beheaded—but however he died, they threw his body down the Gemonian Stairs. Drusus saw it."

Marcella saw Diana bow her head. And later, she went out with a black veil over her hair and came back with a somber face. "What have you been doing?"

"I bought a little medallion for the Blues," said Diana, "and I buried it at the foot of the Gemonian Stairs. Vitellius would have liked that." She scrubbed her hands down the front of her dress. "He'd better appreciate it—that's the first and last time I ever buy a Blues medallion. Maybe we'll race our teams together in the afterlife."

"So what *did* Vitellius say to you before he died?" Marcella urged.

Diana gave her a long contemptuous look.

"I'll just get it from someone else, you know."

"Not from me," said Diana, yanking the black veil off her hair and stamping off.

Vitellius gone, Marcella thought. He'd lasted the longest of all three emperors that year, and now there was a fourth. The Senate had certainly wasted no time acclaiming Vespasian, and all the provinces were united behind him. His brilliant elder son, little Flavia's father Titus, was marching to take control of the chastened eastern legions, and Vespasian himself was supposedly only weeks behind. Domitian was already being feted as a prince of Rome at the Domus Aurea. Marcella saw him two days after returning to the city, striding like a conqueror through Lollia's atrium with six Praetorians marching smartly behind.

"I heard you were back." His eyes flew past the slaves, whom Marcella had been supervising as they swept up the broken tiles of the mosaic. "I had my guards watching for you."

"As you can see, I'm safe." Marcella waved the slaves away, giving

Domitian a curved smile. "And so are you." He'd survived, she heard, by skulking in the Temple of Isis among the worshipers until the violence was over. Not terribly brave, perhaps, but prudent.

"I'm prince of Rome now—did you hear?" He had the Imperial purple stripe on his tunic already. "I told you I'd be prince someday."

"Well, you're not Rome's only prince," Marcella said lightly. "When does your brother arrive with his armies? I suppose your father will pronounce him heir . . ."

"Don't count on it," Domitian scowled, and, trapping Marcella in his arms, he kissed her. She let him plaster kisses on her neck for a while, wondering how long this obsession of his was going to last now that he was a member of the Imperial family and could have any woman he wanted. *I might have the best breasts in Rome, but now he has* all *the breasts in Rome to choose from.* Well, Domitian had had his uses, but Marcella thought she wouldn't be entirely sorry when his eye wandered on to someone new. Perhaps she could find another man to nurture along in some interesting new direction. Someone older than Domitian, more intelligent and promising . . .

Vespasian's older son, Titus, arrived a week later with the first of the eastern legions and proceeded to restore order, efficiently preparing the celebrations that would welcome his father to Rome in another few weeks. Titus: Marcella's mental pen sketched him thoughtfully. Perhaps ten years older than Domitian, black-eyed and ruddy-faced like his brother but with a constant smile instead of his brother's scowl.

"Titus was always the nicest of my husbands." Lollia wrinkled her nose affectionately at Titus's stocky figure as he strode into the Senate house in the armor he wore like a second skin. "I hardly ever saw him, but he was always kind. He's already sent me a message, saying of course he won't take Flavia away from me to raise now that he's back in Rome. He just wants me to bring her for a visit soon, so she can meet his other daughter. Julia, I think her name is. I'm sure they'll be great friends, just like all of us. Sisters need each other. But wasn't that nice of Titus to take a moment to put my mind at ease with everything else he has going on? He was always splendid, but never too grand to be kind. Not like Domitian—royal or not he's just a pimply black-eyed thug." She shuddered. "Always sneaking into the bathhouse when he was younger, trying to watch me bathing. Is he still in love with you, Marcella?"

"Not for long, I'm sure."

Titus declared the formal resumption of trade in Rome, and with such reassurances Lollia's grandfather was back in a trice from Ostia. He was ordering new mosaics and new wine barrels before he even got through the door, and within two days he hosted a lavish banquet to cultivate every contact he had with the new Emperor. The guest of honor was little Flavia. "She's a person of importance now," Lollia's grandfather said happily the following day, watching his great-granddaughter drive Diana around his atrium on all fours, lashing a long-stemmed lily for a driving whip. "Granddaughter to the Emperor! Lollia, my jewel, there's not an ambitious man in Rome who doesn't want to be Flavia's newest stepfather. I've had inquiries already for your hand, and vetted every suitor—not a man among them to lay a hand on you! You could have your pick, and we might arrange a wedding in the new year—"

"No one ever offered me my pick of suitors," Marcella complained. "It was just 'Here's a husband for you; I hope you have a dress; be ready in a week.'"

But Lollia wasn't listening, just giving a deep dreamy smile as Thrax came into the atrium, scooping up Flavia and scolding her softly.

"Thanks." Diana sat back on her heels, spitting out the ribbon Flavia had strung between her teeth for a bridle. "I've got more sympathy for my team now."

Diana was back with her father, who had returned to the city lugging a just-begun bust of the new Emperor. Gaius and Tullia were slower to return, so slow Cornelia had the house entirely tidied by the time they came back. Small thanks she got for it, Marcella thought, since Tullia embarked at once on the rant over Cornelia's ruined morals that had been so inconveniently interrupted by the invasion of Rome.

"I'm afraid that will have to wait, Tullia." Cornelia fixed Gaius with a stern gaze. "Brother, I need to speak with you." Doors closed firmly behind them.

"And I should inspect the house!" Tullia clicked off down the hall. "Though what condition it's in, I don't like to think—if that slut

Cornelia can't keep her own morals in order, I shudder to think what she's made of my spare rooms."

"Actually, everything looks perfect," Marcella said as Tullia bustled upstairs. "Though doubtless you'll still find something to complain about."

"Just wait till I tell Gaius!" Tullia's voice floated down the stairs. "Not two minutes home, and you're picking quarrels!"

"Only with you, Tullia. Only with you."

They had a guest within the day: Senator Marcus Norbanus, released from prison now and come to collect little Paulinus. "Marcus!" Marcella greeted him gaily. "Delightful to see you again."

"Delightful to see anything that isn't a stone cell." He looked around the atrium with its square of winter sunlight and glassy pool. His hair, only threaded with gray at the beginning of the year, had gone entirely iron-colored, and he had a bracket of harsh lines about his mouth. "Are you hurt?" Marcella asked, noticing him limp as she waved him to a bench.

"A broken shoulder from my arrest," he said briefly, releasing Paulinus's plump little hand and pushing him gently to go play. "The guards weren't gentle. It was never set properly, and now I find it pulls me off-balance."

"I'm sorry, Marcus."

"It would have been far worse without that doctor your cousin Lollia smuggled in for me." Marcus rotated the crooked shoulder, smiling wryly.

"Lollia sent you a doctor?" Marcella blinked.

"Yes, along with food baskets and jugs of good wine. I hate to think what it must have cost her in bribes. Your sister was also kind enough to visit a few times, to give me news about Paulinus." Marcus smiled again, fond. "And your mad little cousin Diana came every week, smuggling just about every book I owned under her dress, just to keep my mind from rotting away with boredom"

I suppose I should have thought to visit myself, Marcella thought. Dethroning an emperor had been so time-consuming. Perhaps she could do something for Marcus now, since he was out of prison. He really looked very distinguished in his toga—the crooked shoulder could hardly be seen, and his eyes were as penetrating and intelligent as ever. *Senator Marcus Norbanus, descendant of Emperor Augustus . . .* such an intelligent man, so respected in the Senate, with a consulship already to his credit at the age of thirty-three. Respected enough that three successive emperors this year had feared his influence. Surely he was bitter about the misfortunes they'd inflicted on him.

I wonder if you have ambitions, Marcus. To be something beyond a senator.

"So everything seems to have gone back to normal," she remarked brightly. "I wonder if it really has."

Marcus watched his son, splashing his hands in the atrium's pool. "One hopes."

"Four emperors! Fortuna, I wonder what Vespasian will be like." Marcella fanned herself, artless. "None of them could hold a candle to you, in my opinion."

"Really?" His eyes still followed little Paulinus.

"Yes, and I'm not the only one to think you might have made a fine Emperor. Certainly Galba and Otho and Vitellius were worried about the prospect. Isn't it a pity that—"

"Stop," said Marcus.

"What?" Marcella smiled. "Stop what?"

"I don't know. But stop it." Marcus looked at her, and his eyes were cool and measuring. "I've always admired you, Marcella—you're an intelligent woman, after all, and I like intelligent women. But I find I don't like you anymore, and I don't precisely know why. Perhaps it's just my feeling that you're a schemer."

Marcella's lips parted, but for once she couldn't think of a thing to say.

"Good day to you." Marcus rose, holding out a hand, and little Paulinus came running to his side. "Don't visit."

Twenty-two

ᔕᓯᔓ

"THANK the gods the bathhouses are open again," Lollia said. "I need a really good sweat to wake up my skin. All this emperor-swapping is just *terrible* for the complexion."

"Not to mention all your husband-swapping." Cornelia couldn't help a laugh as she put her arm through Lollia's, and Lollia giggled back. They threaded their way across the *caldarium*, around the splashing fountain in the center, past the busy bathhouse attendants and the clusters of flushed women in towels toward a pair of marble massage slabs. Marcella had gone to the *natatio* pool in the next chamber for a swim, and Diana had announced her desire for a little exercise and loped lean and naked over to the gymnasium. But Cornelia felt happy and lazy and only wanted a massage.

"Look at all those old cats hissing away." Lollia stretched her pink naked self in the billows of steam, making a face across the *caldarium* at a trio of plump avid-eyed matrons whispering behind their hands. "Rumor-mongering bitches."

"Let them talk." Cornelia smiled as she stretched out face up on the massage slab, unable to stop her hand from stealing down to caress her waist through the towel. *Pregnant. Me, pregnant at last at twenty-five.*

"You're sure?" Drusus had said when she told him, that first long night back in Rome. He'd all but crushed her in his relief when she came tumbling through the narrow door of the whorehouse—though the relief had faded away soon enough to a stricken guilt. "Oh, gods," he said, appalled. "I'm sorry—I should have taken care, I should have—"

"Sshh." Cornelia laid a finger over his lips. "I know what to do."

"You mean—" He looked at her belly. ". . . you'll wash it out?"

"No." Not the child she was already envisioning: a sturdy little boy, compact and brave, or a girl with chestnut curls and maybe her mother's dimples. "I won't do that."

"But your family, they'll—"

"I can handle them. I'll have to marry, but—" She had to turn her eyes away from the stricken look that reappeared on his face.

"Aye," Drusus jerked. "I suppose you will."

Cornelia kept that look before her when she'd marched her brother into his study. "Gaius," she'd said without preamble, before her courage could fail, "you should make preparations for a wedding feast early next week. I am going to marry Centurion Drusus Sempronius Densus, and it would be better to have the wedding soon, since I am going to have his child."

Gaius's mouth, which had just closed after hearing the word *wedding*, dropped open again.

"It's not a grand match, but it is respectable," Cornelia continued as serenely as she could, though her heart was thumping loud in her own ears. "Drusus's family is solid equestrian class in Toscana. No, Gaius, don't interrupt me. Drusus's record as a Praetorian has been distinguished, and the treason charge laid against him by the Vitellians has been lifted. Gaius, I told you not to interrupt. Drusus will be calling on you this afternoon to discuss details."

She'd been halfway across the *tablinum* before Gaius whimpered, "What am I going to tell Tullia?"

"Gaius." Cornelia turned, giving her brother an exasperated look. "Tullia isn't the paterfamilias of the Cornelii. You are. *Act* like it!"

That had been that. In a week's time the family would see yet another wedding—but for once, not Lollia's. Cornelia wriggled pleasurably under the masseuse's fingers at the thought.

"What are all those old bags over there hissing about?" Diana padded naked into the steam of the *caldarium*, toweling her sweat-damp hair. "They're nearly making the sign of the evil eye at us."

"Oh, just our scandalous Cornelia," Lollia said airily.

"I am not either scandalous." Cornelia couldn't help the defensive edge in her own voice. Not that she was ashamed of Drusus, or herself . . . but she'd never been an object of salacious gossip in her life. "It's a perfectly respectable wedding."

"Respectable?" Diana snorted, stretching her arms out so the bathhouse attendant could scrape the sweat off with a strigil. "You're dropping a foal in six months."

"Well, we thought we'd make our home outside Rome." Cornelia propped chin on hand as the masseuse moved from her shoulders to her back. "Then no one will know how long we've been married . . ."

Drusus would be at the palace today, cooling his heels in a hall full of petitioners as he waited to see if he could possibly be reinstated to the Praetorian Guard. "Don't know if I want palace duty again," he'd confided. "But I'd like to train the young soldiers, maybe down in Tarracina at the training camp. Get some loyalty pounded into them young, so they don't go wrong like this batch did when the bribes and the emperors started flying." He'd made several inquiries about being reinstated, but heard nothing yet. Surely any commanding officer worth his salt would be proud to have a man like Cornelia's future husband in his ranks . . . *Husband—Juno's mercy, I love that word* . . .

"Well, I hope the baby's a girl," Diana was saying around a groan as the strigil scraped over a bruise on her shoulder. "So I can teach her to drive a chariot too, and have someone to race against. Go on, keep scraping—"

"You are not making my daughter into a charioteer!" Cornelia protested. By now everyone in Rome had heard the latest story about Diana: how the Blues faction director had come puffing up to the hillside villa to reclaim the Anemoi, how the tall Briton had wordlessly handed Diana a knife—some said a sword—and how she had run the faction director off at bladepoint . . .

"So let's have the truth now, Diana." Lollia rubbed rose oil into her dimpled knees. "You're madly in love with that imposing Briton, aren't you!"

"I did wonder for a while," Diana mused. "But I don't think so."

"Admit it, my honey! We're all scandalous here—I'm bedding my daughter's body slave, Cornelia's marrying a pleb—"

"He's not a pleb!"

"—so the least you can do to keep us company is fall in love with a savage!"

"I don't think I'm very good at falling in love." Diana shook her damp hair out of her eyes. "Not with anything that has less than four legs, anyway. Boreas, now—he's the love of my life."

They all giggled, and then Cornelia slid off the massage slab and wrapped herself modestly in a towel, and Lollia tipped the bathhouse attendants. They filed through the steam toward the *tepidarium*, and Cornelia heard smothered whispers as they passed the avid little cluster of gossiping matrons.

"—true she met him in a *whorehouse?*"

"Oh, he's not the only lover she met there! Half the Praetorian barracks trooped in and out of her bed—"

"Before her husband was even dead! Poor Piso, if he'd known half her antics—"

Cornelia's eyes dropped to the floor a moment, but she lifted her chin and gave a blind, bright smile. "Juno's mercy," she said, trying to laugh, "I'll be glad when they move on to some new scandal."

"Sooner than you think." Diana turned on her heel, marched up to the loudest of the whisperers, grabbed a handful of the woman's bobbing ringlets, and gave a swift yank. The woman squeaked, making a vain grab for her wig as Diana wound her arm like a discus thrower. The mass of false curls landed in the fountain with a splash, and Diana aimed a glare around the suddenly silent *caldarium*. "One more nasty word about my cousin from any of you," she warned, "and you go into the fountain after that wig. Head first."

Lollia giggled. Cornelia blushed and ducked out of the *caldarium*, but she pressed Diana's hand in wordless thanks as her little cousin sauntered after. The door swung shut on the bald matron's shriek.

"Well, that was amusing," Lollia said as more bathhouse attendants came forward with perfumes and powders and wine. "Yes, a face mask for me, please—nail varnish for Cornelia here, maybe red to match the bridal veil? And something to take the calluses off Diana's hands. No, a pumice stone isn't going to do the job. Maybe a chisel . . ."

Marcella came through the door wrapped in a towel, flushed pink from her swim. "I didn't mean to be so long. The water was wonderful." She shook her wet hair around her neck as she joined them on the long marble benches, but not fast enough. Lollia pointed triumphantly as the slaves began fluttering around them.

"Someone's been putting marks on your neck! Don't tell me our slimy little junior prince of Rome finally wore down your defenses?"

"*Domitian?*" Cornelia wrinkled her nose as she stretched her toes into a slave girl's lap for filing and varnishing. Somehow, she'd have rather had Diana tumbling that tall Briton than see her sister in bed with that mean-tempered little thug.

"He's very tiresome sometimes." Marcella leaned her head back as a slave girl moved in with combs and scented pomades. "But he has his uses."

"A source for your next history?" Diana asked. Two bathhouse attendants had captured her hands and were moaning over the calluses.

"Oh, I've given up writing histories." Marcella closed her eyes as the comb stroked through her wet hair. "No one will ever read them, and anyway it's far more interesting seeing what happens in real life."

"Is it," said Diana.

"Lollia, you look like a ghost," Cornelia laughed. A slave girl was applying a bread paste all over Lollia's face and neck to whiten and tighten the skin.

"'I want to see what happens.'" Diana's spear-straight gaze was still narrowed on Marcella. "That's another favorite phrase of yours, this year."

"I do want to see what happens." Marcella opened her eyes, blinking. "It's been an interesting year."

"Not the word I'd use." Diana brushed away the slave girls and took a step forward, hair falling down her naked back. "You say you've given up writing histories. But you're always writing—up in your *tablinum*, at dinner parties on napkins, at the races on parchment scraps. What are you writing, Marcella?"

She smiled: Cornelia's tall sister wrapped in her white towel, wet hair combed sleekly down her back, her face carved and cool. "Nothing important."

Diana looked at the bathhouse attendants. "Leave us."

"What's this about?" Cornelia asked as the slave girls filed out. Lollia's puzzled eyes peered out from her stiff white mask of bread paste.

"When you're not writing, Marcella, you're whispering all over town," Diana continued as if Cornelia hadn't spoken. A few matrons glanced over from the opposite corner, but no one was close enough to hear. "I see you meeting with Domitian in the Forum, and it doesn't look like any lover's assignation. I see you sitting next to Caecina Alienus at a play, and neither of you is paying attention to the play. I see you at one of Otho's parties, whispering into the ear of Vitellius's brother. And at Galba's parties months and months ago, I see you whispering to Otho."

Cornelia looked at her sister, who sat quite still with a comb in her hand and a faint smile playing on her lips.

"All that whispering," Diana continued. "To senators who went over from Vitellius to Vespasian. To praetors who went over from Otho to Vitellius. To governors who went from Galba to Otho. And now there's Domitian in your bed."

"Diana," Cornelia began, "what are you—"

"You really don't write histories anymore, do you?" Diana's blue-green gaze never wavered from Marcella. "Too pointless, just like you said. You've started writing *history*."

"Goodness," Marcella said mildly. "I just do a little whispering now and then. No harm in that."

"Isn't there?"

"Will someone tell me what you're both gabbling on about?" Lollia interrupted. Her masked face was beginning to flake.

"I'll tell you." Diana crossed the room in two lithe steps. Diana the Huntress they all called her teasingly—but now she *was* the huntress, stalking her prey. "Marcella got bored writing histories, and decided she'd start meddling in the real thing. A comment to Otho, maybe; something he hatched into a rebellion. Then Vitellius declared himself Emperor up in Germania, and she wondered *what would happen* if she passed on information about Otho's troops."

"Marcella didn't do that." Cornelia flushed. "I did. I was so crazed after Piso died, I just wanted Otho dead—"

"And where did you get all those little gems of information, Cornelia? You wouldn't know where to begin, but a historian knows what information is valuable. She dropped it all in your ear, everything Vitellius's commanders needed to defeat Otho, and you passed it along for her." Diana looked back at Marcella, now running a finger over the teeth of the comb in her hand. "Otho's army lost, maybe because of her. And she even went along so she could watch the battle. So she could watch Otho die."

"You think I'm a prophetess?" Marcella protested. "I never dreamed he'd commit suicide. I just went along because—"

"You wanted to see what would happen," Cornelia echoed.

"And you came back," Diana continued. "And Vespasian declared himself Emperor, and you thought you might start whispering in Alienus's ear and others too, to see if they'd turn traitor. And enough of them did, and Vitellius lost his army because of it, and Rome tore itself to bits. And now we have a new Emperor and a bit of peace, and the first thing you do is take Domitian to bed and start whispering about—what? How he'd make a better Emperor than his brother?" Diana looked around, to Cornelia frozen in her towel, to Lollia bewildered and white-masked. "From all that *what might happen*, something did happen. Four emperors have ruled Rome this year. And our Marcella had her hand in the fall of three of them."

"Well, four if you count last year too," Cornelia's sister confessed. There was a little flush on her cheeks . . . could it possibly be pride? "There was that little incident with Emperor Nero. But that was just a whisper, really, and I had no idea he'd follow my advice and actually commit suicide. What?" She looked around at them. "Why are you looking at me like that?"

They stared at her as if she had snakes for hair.

"You're all making too much out of this." Marcella put down the comb. "So I meddled a little. No more than a hundred other scheming senators were doing, for their own advancement. But you lay the blame for all three Imperial coups at *my* door?"

"You didn't meddle for your own advancement," Diana said, implacable. "Or for your own protection. I could understand that. You meddled for *fun.*"

Cornelia forced the words out through stiff lips. "And my husband died."

"I didn't know that would happen. No one could." Marcella looked around at them. "You think I wanted harm to come to any of us?"

"But it could have." Lollia grabbed a towel and hugged it about herself as if she'd suddenly gone cold. "It nearly did. Piso dead—and I had to marry that pig Fabius—and all of us were nearly killed, first before the Temple of Vesta and then by the mob when Vitellius was overthrown. And you just standing there on the Campus Martius, *watching*—"

Watching with flushed cheeks and shining eyes—Cornelia remembered that, very clearly. She'd thought it was shock, or disbelief . . . now she wondered if it had been pleasure.

"It's not so much what you did." Diana pronounced sentence. "It's that you enjoyed it. You don't feel sorry. And you don't feel one straw's worth of guilt."

"Why should I?" Marcella picked up the comb again, stroking it through her damp hair. "Everything turned out all right."

Cornelia spread her hands in her lap, looking down at the newly varnished nails that were no longer bitten to ragged nubs, and spoke politely. She didn't look up—she didn't think she could bear to see her sister's face. "I don't want you at my wedding."

"Cornelia!" Marcella looked hurt. "You can't do that. After what happened with Piso, I was so happy you found your centurion, you have no idea."

"Yes, I'm very happy. And Drusus might join the Praetorians again, guarding the new Emperor, and if you prod Domitian into making trouble for his father, then Drusus might get killed too." Cornelia looked up. "So I don't want you at the wedding, wishing us happiness."

Marcella looked from face to face, smiling her customary faint smile. Marcella the historian, the watcher.

"Oh, dear," she sighed. She put the comb down, discarded the towel wrapped around her, and walked back toward the *caldarium*. For a moment the billows of steam surrounded her tall naked body, and then she disappeared from view.

Y OU'RE thinking again," Domitian observed.
"I tend to do that, Lord," Marcella smiled. He liked to be called Lord, but now he just scowled.

"I don't like women who think so much."

"Then why do you like me?"

"I don't know." He seized Marcella's bare leg, pressing his mouth against her ankle. "You're beautiful."

He kissed his way up her leg, pushing the sheets aside, and Marcella lay back against the silk pillows. A blank-eyed slave stood at the head of the bed waving a peacock feather fan over her head, and another slave stood ready at the door with wine and sweetmeats in case she was hungry. *Nothing but the best for a prince of Rome*, Marcella thought. *And for his mistress.*

She hadn't planned on that—in fact, she'd been convinced Domitian would drop her altogether now that so many other women would be competing for his Imperial favors. But Domitian hadn't looked at anyone else yet. And when Marcus Norbanus had been so rude to her, so utterly shriveling . . . well, Domitian had looked like a more appealing prospect. *Better to have a lover I can control than one with a mind of his own.*

Domitian wasn't Rome's only prince, though. Marcella thought about that as Domitian pinned her down across the pillows and began kissing her breasts. "Have you met with your brother yet?" she murmured, arching back into his mouth.

"When he arrived."

"He's terribly popular," Marcella said artlessly as Domitian wound his hands through her hair. "You should have heard the cheers in the Forum yesterday. When will your father formally announce him as heir?"

Domitian scowled, rearing back. "Titus might be named heir, but Nessus says he'll never have any sons. So it'll be me who gets the crown, and they'll call me Lord and God. They'll call *you* Lady and Goddess."

"Fortuna, how grand." Marcella looked at the gray light coming through the window. "Can it be dawn already?"

Domitian had swept her away for a week at one of his newly acquired Imperial villas in Aricia—and really, his timing could not have been better. Marcella knew her three fellow Cornelias were quite put out with her; it would be better to give their tempers time to cool. Later she might visit her sister and cajole her back into good humor. Cornelia was surely too swamped in wedding bliss to hold grudges, and anyway they'd never had a serious fight about anything in their entire lives, since the days they were children squabbling over dolls. Lollia, well, she was too flighty to stay angry with anyone, and Diana too dense to remember any quarrel past the next Reds win. They'd all forgive her soon enough. But in the meantime, Marcella told Gaius she was visiting a friend, ignored his sputtering, and went to Aricia with Domitian.

She'd never had anyone so mad for her. Quite diverting, really. There were whole days Domitian wouldn't let her out of bed, and even outside lovemaking he always had a possessive hand on her arm or the nape of her neck. He gave her jewels and then threatened to take them back, he mocked her writing and then begged forgiveness, he grew furious when she wandered out for an hour's walk and accused her of meeting another lover, then dragged her to bed swearing he'd make it all up to her. Marcella quite enjoyed it. And she talked a little, here and there, about Titus.

So popular, so charming, so dynamic. A much better prospect than reticent Marcus Norbanus. *I might have made him an emperor, but now he'll never amount to anything past a modest career in the Senate.* But Titus, according to all reports, had the ambition and dash for an Imperial crown. Might the younger brother be a bridge to the older?

"Where are you going?" Domitian demanded as she slid out of bed.

"It's time I went home. My sister's wedding is very soon, you know." Marcella held her arms out, and two obedient slaves came forward and started looping her *stola* about her shoulders.

"You're staying with me!" Domitian sat up in bed.

"I can't. I'll be missed."

"You won't have to worry about your family anymore." Domitian tossed the bedclothes aside, rising. "Gather your things. We're leaving."

"What are you up to, Lord?"

"Nothing that concerns you, yet." He pulled his tunic over his head.

"Yet?"

"I'll tell you when you need telling."

"And until then I'm to know nothing?"

"Correct."

He stalked out of the room and was waiting impatiently in the litter when Marcella gathered her few things and went to join him. Her hair was still hanging loose down her back as he liked it, but he hardly gave her a glance as she climbed into the litter. *Tiring of me, perhaps?* Well, she'd known it couldn't last long at this heat. And really, who would want it to? One needed such stamina, dealing with jealous boys.

Domitian didn't speak on the journey back from Aricia, and Marcella prepared to be left unceremoniously at her doorstep. But the litter-bearers kept their steady jog past the Cornelii house with its repaired pediments, and she raised her eyebrows. "Where—?"

"Sshh," Domitian snapped, and the litter soon pulled up before the Domus Aurea.

"You might have told me you were taking me back to the palace," Marcella said. "One more time in bed before sending me home?"

"You are home."

"What do you mean?"

He locked his hand about Marcella's wrist, jerking her from the litter. Before she could catch her breath he was hurrying up a flight of shallow marble steps, past a pair of curious slaves, down one pillared hall and up another as they left the public entertaining rooms behind for the private Imperial quarters. At last he flung open a set of doors, and Marcella saw an airy green-marbled chamber with an inlaid pool set in the floor, and a high corniced archway to a vista of other rooms.

"Your new quarters," said Domitian. "Do you like them?"

"I can hardly live here," Marcella said, amused.

"Yes, you can." Domitian's downy lip was beaded in sweat. "Your husband was informed this morning that you are no longer his wife."

Marcella burst out laughing. *"What?"*

"Don't laugh at me," Domitian scowled. "You're my wife now. We'll have the ceremony tomorrow morning."

"Your father will never allow it!" She'd be divorced again within the week, once Vespasian or Titus found out. Or perhaps they'd let him have his way, counting on him to call for divorce himself once his passion cooled.

Domitian began dragging Marcella through the other rooms of her new quarters, talking too loudly. A private bathhouse, a bed-chamber with a vast sleeping couch . . . and a huge spacious *tablinum* with arched windows and a whole wall of shelves filled with scrolls. Marcella ran her hand along the smooth surface of the desk, already stocked with blank rolls of parchment, wax tablets, fresh pens . . .

Perhaps it wouldn't be so bad, being a prince's wife for a few weeks or months. As Lucius's wife, she certainly had all the disadvantages of being a girl and none of the advantages of being a matron. *And after Domitian tires of me, perhaps I won't remarry at all.*

Cornelia Secunda, known as Marcella, a prince's wife. Who would have thought it?

"See?" Domitian muttered into her neck, pulling her down on the huge bed. "I said I'd have you."

"How impetuous you are," Marcella murmured between kisses. "Your brother will be furious, you know."

"Who cares what he thinks?" Tugging at her skirts.

"He's the heir, darling—he can do whatever he wants."

At first she didn't feel the pain. Only the shock, as Domitian slapped her across the face.

"Don't play me," he said calmly.

For an instant she thought she was back in the sunny atrium while Marcus Norbanus looked at her with such dispassionate dislike . . . back in the bathhouse where Diana regarded her with such utter contempt. ". . . I don't play you," Marcella managed to say.

"Yes, you do." He was inside her now, his weight heavy on her breasts, but his thick body stilled for a moment as he looked down into her eyes. "You play everyone, Marcella. You're very clever at it. I don't like clever women, but I can put up with your cleverness. Just don't use it on me. No more little whispers about Titus. He doesn't concern you, and neither does my father. Your only concern now is *me*."

"Of course." Marcella reached placating arms around his neck, but Domitian slapped them away.

"You'll keep my house," he said, and one of his heavy hands dropped across her throat. "You'll warm my bed." Fingers sinking into her neck. "You'll bear me children." Tighter. "Those are your duties, Marcella. The duties of a proper Roman matron. Nothing more."

She tried to speak, but his hand was an anvil across her throat. Black spots danced across her vision as he began to move inside her, his eyes two brilliant points of light spearing her down, and not until he finished in utter silence did his hand shift from her throat.

"Excellent," he said cheerfully, getting up. Marcella heaved herself upright, gasping for air. "I'll send one of my stewards to inform your family and collect your things. We'll have this whole wing of the Domus Aurea to ourselves. I'll introduce you to my brother tonight at dinner." Domitian regarded Marcella in faint surprise as she coughed painfully. "Titus won't oppose the marriage, if that worries you. He's got no wish to remarry himself and neither does our father, so it will suit them if I have a wife to take on the tiresome social duties. And as daughter of General Gnaeus Corbulo, you're a fit wife for a prince. Even an emperor."

Marcella wheezed, still dragging in breath after painful breath. Her hands were shaking, and she felt a freezing hollow in her stomach. She could still feel Domitian's hand on her throat, see his strangely blank eyes—the eyes of a far different creature than the cheerful ruddy-faced boy who now stood tidying himself and chattering.

"I will be Emperor someday, you know. Nessus has seen it. He says I'll be Lord and God of Rome, and you'll be Lady and Goddess. You'd like that, wouldn't you?" He brushed a lock of hair off Marcella's forehead and she flinched, but he didn't notice. "Of course, even the Lady and Goddess of Rome is a wife first. You will concern yourself with maintaining my family and household, not with matters of state. I never take a woman's advice."

He clapped his hands, and a cluster of slave girls entered. They bowed very low to Marcella. *Dear Fortuna, did they know before I did that Domitian meant to make me his wife?*

"Your new maids," Domitian was saying. "Dress for dinner, but don't wear green. I dislike green. Oh," he added as an afterthought, "and no more of your scribbling. You won't have time for that now, and it isn't seemly in a prince's wife. Your desk is for writing letters only. Naturally I'll read them before they're delivered."

Marcella's breath came in little pants. *No, no, no*—the word pounded through her head in mindless repetition, but when she parted her lips to speak, her breath froze behind her teeth.

Another slave woman entered, holding a little girl by the hand. A year or two younger than little Flavia, but much more solemn, regarding Marcella somberly through a curtain of straight blond hair.

"This is my brother's second daughter, Julia Flavia," Domitian said casually. "He's long divorced her mother, just like he divorced that stupid slut Lollia. You can take over Julia's care now. It will do you well enough until we have our own. As much as I've plowed you, you'll have started one already."

"No," Marcella muttered, "*no*," but Domitian brushed that aside.

"My brother will be wanting me. Arrange your wedding clothes for tomorrow. I'll see you at dinner." He dropped a casual kiss on her cheek. "You know, I dislike the name Marcella. We'll have to change it."

He was gone. Marcella stared after him, so filled with shock she felt rooted to the spot.

"Domina," the nurse said respectfully, thrusting Domitian's niece forward. Marcella brushed her away, wailing inside. *No, no, I don't want this. Not a life filled with children and Imperial dinner parties, dress fittings and running the palace household. Not for me. Not for Marcella the historian, not for the girl who brought down four emperors.*

But already there were Praetorians closing in around her door to protect her and spy on her, and curious courtiers bustling outside in the pillared hall. A wall of people to close her in, to make sure she was never alone again.

I'm going to be Empress, if Domitian has his way, Marcella thought in utter horror. *And I will not have the power to bring down anyone.*

No. Surely not. Surely Domitian would get tired of her long before that. He'd demand a divorce, and everything would go back to the way it was. *Oh, Fortuna, just make that happen and I swear I will never meddle in the affairs of emperors again—*

"Lady." A wary voice broke through her panicked thoughts. "Welcome to the Imperial household. We've met before, a few times—I am Nessus."

"Nessus?" Hardly hearing him.

"My lord Domitian has been good enough to appoint me as Imperial astrologer." A chubby little man bowed before her—already balding despite his youth, swaddled in a new robe embroidered all over with astrological symbols.

"You told him I'd be his wife, didn't you?" Marcella's hand shot out, catching the little astrologer's sleeve. "Well, undo it! Tell him I won't make a good wife, tell him I won't bear him any children—"

"You won't be a good wife," Nessus said. "And you won't bear him any children either, but that doesn't have anything to do with me. Good-bye."

He tugged at his sleeve, but Marcella's fingers latched into the cloth. She could see the slaves staring, feel the baby hand of little Julia tugging at her dress, but she ignored them all. "What do you mean?"

"Oh, why didn't I just open a wine shop?" Nessus mumbled. He drew himself to his full height, but avoided her eyes. "I can't help you, Lady. I'm sorry."

"Then at least read my stars! Or my hand, if that's faster—" *You don't believe in astrology*, something inside Marcella mocked her, *or in charlatans who read palms*. But she shoved her hand at Nessus anyway. "Read my hand and tell Domitian he's destined to divorce me in a month—"

"Oh no." Nessus put his hands behind his back. "I read your hand once before, and that was enough. I was drunk for a week, and I nearly quit this business. No, thank you, Lady. You can figure out the future on your own."

Marcella stared at him. "So why did you tell Domitian I was destined to be his Empress? Why?"

"Because you are," Nessus said wearily, and turned away toward the atrium.

"That's ridiculous!" Marcella started after him. Slaves fell away on each side, openly whispering now, and little Julia toddled along behind, trying to keep up. "You're just telling Domitian what he wants to hear. You're flattering him to keep your post, you're a fake—"

"Yes, and I was happy that way." Nessus rounded on her in the middle of the green-tiled atrium. "Telling people what they want to hear—it might not be noble, but it pays the bills and lets me sleep at night. Or it did. Then I ran across that blood-filled little hand of yours, and now it all comes true! All of it! Do you have any idea how inconvenient that is?"

"So read my hand again!" Marcella screamed. *"Make something else come true!"*

"I'm sorry, Lady, but it doesn't work that way. You're going to be Domitian's wife, and you're going to be Empress of Rome, and there's nothing you or I or anybody else can do about it."

Marcella's lips parted, dry as parchment. Her mind was one great whirling blank. Little Julia caught up with her, twining pudgy baby fingers into her dress. Nessus looked down at the little girl and flinched.

"Look after that one," he said tiredly. "If somebody doesn't, her life is going to be as wretched as yours."

He turned and stalked away, pushing past the crowd of petitioners who already waited in the atrium for a chance to see the prince of Rome's new wife.

Marcella sat down suddenly in the middle of the tiled floor. "He's lying. He's lying."

Little Julia climbed into her lap, cuddling against her stone-still shoulder. Marcella barely felt her. She was trying too desperately to believe her own lies.

Twenty-three

ꙥ

THE first day of the new year belonged to Janus, god of doorways, god of beginnings, and as always Cornelia and her cousins
exchanged coins stamped with Janus's double-faced profile. One face
looked forward and the other back, and on the first day of *this* year,
it couldn't have been more appropriate. Cornelia was looking ahead
to the future along with the rest of Rome, looking ahead to Emperor
Vespasian as he made his triumphal entry into the city . . . but she
couldn't help looking back too, and she felt a twinge as she remembered an emperor who was torn to pieces in the Forum and an emperor
who marched north to defeat and suicide and an emperor who died
alone and terrified in a stable. Three dead emperors, and the thousands
who had died supporting them.

Emperor Vespasian entered the city today, on the first day of the
year, and later Cornelia heard how loudly he had been cheered. But she
hadn't been there to cheer for him. She had other words to say, more
important words.

"*Quando tu Gaius, ego Gaia . . .*" Drusus's hands squeezed hers
fiercely as she recited the ritual vows, and even through the red haze

of the bridal veil she could see the tears in his eyes. Just a small wedding, only family and friends gathered around the public shrine—Lollia bouncing up and down on her toes, Diana slipping in late as always, Drusus's parents and sister clustered together proud and a little shy. Marcella wasn't there—even a prince's wife apparently knew better than to come where she was so bluntly unwanted. Cornelia was grateful.

Drusus's hand squeezed hers again as the priest brought a white goat forward for the matrimonial sacrifice, and Cornelia looked up at the marble statue of Juno that gazed down on her. *Is she smiling at me?* Perhaps.

The goat escaped the priest's knife and ran bleating down the street. Cornelia couldn't suppress a giggle as the priest began to swear, and Drusus was so convulsed with laughter he could hardly speak. "Let it go," Lollia called from the circle of guests. "Some woman in the slums will be the richer for a nice milking goat by evening. That's a better wedding omen than goat blood on our shoes!"

Cornelia couldn't have agreed more.

The wedding party broke up amicably, streaming back up the street toward the house of Lollia's grandfather, who had offered to host the feast. Drusus snugged Cornelia close against his side, pushing her veil back so he could kiss her. "All mine now," he whispered, and his hand brushed her stomach, which had just barely begun to round.

"All yours," she whispered back. He looked so imposing in his formal red and gold—a centurion of the Praetorian Guard once again, thanks to Emperor Vespasian. *Was I so happy the first time I married?* Cornelia didn't know. Maybe that was a question that didn't need an answer. Maybe it was enough that if she'd had to marry twice, it had been to two such good men.

"Juno's mercy," Cornelia exclaimed as they led the way through the vast double doors into the atrium. The columns had been twined with garlands of myrtle and jasmine, the fountain flowed with Falernian wine, soft music filled the air, the smells of a hundred savory dishes tantalized the nose . . . "Lollia, you shouldn't have!"

"This wedding might be a bit on the hasty side, my honey, but no one will say it wasn't done up properly. My grandfather did the *works*, let me tell you." Lollia gazed around with satisfaction. "It's such fun to plan a wedding that isn't mine."

"Nothing but the best for you, m'dear." Lollia's grandfather pinched Cornelia's cheek affectionately. "My jewel tells me how much you comforted her when she was married to that vicious bastard Fabius Valens."

Cornelia looked at the plump face of Lollia's grandfather, beaming and happy again, and flung her arms around his neck. She remembered her own father, who hadn't even attended her first wedding and could barely tell her apart from her sister. "You've done more for me than my father ever did," she said, and kissed Lollia's grandfather on both cheeks.

He beamed at her again, and then took Drusus by the arm and bore him off to the other side of the atrium. "You come with me, my lad! Plenty of guests here want to meet our brave soldier. Let's see what we can do to make you a commander down in Tarracina, eh?"

The wedding guests were flooding in now, exclaiming over the flowers and the wine, and Cornelia looped an arm about Lollia's waist. "I suppose there will be another wedding for you soon?"

"Yes, to some cousin of Vespasian's," Lollia said unconcernedly. She wore a sunny yellow dress with an embroidered sash, simpler than the elaborate silks she used to wear, and scarlet poppies in her hair instead of rubies. And Cornelia rather thought the hair itself had been dyed a gentler shade of red. "I think his name is Gnaeus Flavius. Or was it Publius Flavius? Well, I'll find out soon enough . . ."

"Domina." A familiar golden Gaul bowed at Lollia's side. "The steward, he wants to know if the musicians should begin."

"Gods, yes, Thrax. And get the wine flowing, please." Lollia turned back to Cornelia, beaming. "I have to say *please*, since Thrax is a freedman now. Freed last week! So if I'm not *very* polite to him, he might leave me."

"Somehow I doubt that." Cornelia smiled. The slave—freedman— stood quietly as Lollia tucked her hand into his arm, but his fingers caressed hers in silence. "Is that a new ring, Lollia?"

"Yes." Lollia admired the plain iron band on the fourth finger of her left hand. "Isn't it nice? Thrax gave it to me when I freed him."

"What happens when your next husband puts a ring on that finger?" Cornelia said, amused.

"Oh, it can go on top. This one isn't coming off."

Diana sauntered up in a gold silk gown, draped high in front and baring her back nearly to the base of the spine. Her arm was looped companionably through that of a graying stoop-shouldered man in a toga, and it took Cornelia a moment to recognize Marcus Norbanus. "Marcus," she exclaimed as he bowed over her hand. Prison had not been kind to him—Cornelia resolved at once to find him a nice wife. Now that she was married herself again, she wanted the whole world just as happy. "We'll see you married next," she told him.

"Oh, I think not. I seem to have bad luck with wives. That Nessus fellow everyone's talking about ever since Domitian appointed him Imperial astrologer—he told me it would be a very bad idea to marry again. I don't normally put much trust in astrologers, but . . ." Marcus's gaze drifted to Tullia, pecking away at Gaius's shoulder with a sharp-lacquered nail. "I think I won't push my luck."

"Nonsense, Marcus," Cornelia chided. *Maybe Diana will do for him* . . . they strolled off companionably, Diana chattering about something and Marcus looking down at her with cautious amusement. As if she were some interesting natural phenomenon, like a freak storm or a two-headed calf.

Lollia clapped her hands for the drummers to begin playing as the guests took their places, and the wedding banquet took no time at all to get into full swing. Definitely the best wedding of the year, as many of them as there had been! Even the slaves looked happy, laughing and talking among themselves as they brought in the wine, the silver bowls heaped with fruit, the roast suckling piglet with fried sage leaves and garlic. Drusus and Cornelia took the couch of honor; he began fussing with her wine, watering it anxiously to the exact degree she liked now that she was pregnant. Cornelia laughed and pelted him with a grape. Lollia had little Flavia on her lap and was tickling her with a peacock feather, Thrax hovering discreet and smiling behind them.

Lollia's grandfather perched a laurel wreath rakishly over his wig and was already talking with a shrewd-eyed man in Imperial dress, likely making another fortune. Drusus's parents had the couch beside their son, and Cornelia promptly dragged them off it and introduced them around the room until they began to lose their awkward stiffness. "Your cousins all have such pretty dresses," Drusus's young sister said shyly, and Cornelia made up her mind to get the girl a new wardrobe at once.

Diana stood leaning against a pillar, tossing grapes into the air one by one and catching them unerringly between her teeth, and Cornelia made sure to spoil her aim with a hug from behind. "You were late to my wedding!" she said accusingly. "How were the races?"

"The Reds won. Seven of eight." Diana hugged her back, but gingerly, avoiding her stomach.

"I'm not made of glass just because I'm pregnant, Diana."

"I know what to do for pregnant mares, but not pregnant cousins," Diana complained. "I can hardly feed you a hot oat mash or wrap your hooves in warm wool."

Cornelia giggled. "Before I get to be the size of a house, we'll have to go to the races—you and me and Drusus. There should be time before we leave for Tarracina." Drusus had been posted to the training camp there—and Gaius had rather unexpectedly given them the villa as a wedding gift, despite Tullia's protests. The same villa where they'd snatched a happy fortnight and dreamed of children running through vineyards. "You know, Drusus and I are thinking we might acquire a few horses ourselves?" Cornelia went on happily. "And a vineyard; Drusus is determined to make the best wine in the region—" She could see Diana stifling a yawn but couldn't stop herself, telling all about the room she'd already had readied for the coming baby, which would of course be named Drusilla if it was a girl and Drusus if a boy . . .

"Oh, gods." Lollia came up in her sunny dress, scowling. "Guess who just arrived to ruin the fun."

"She wouldn't dare," Diana said ominously.

"She's married to a prince of Rome now, my honey. She can dare anything she likes."

They looked across the room as a fanfare of applause started up. Cornelia hadn't even laid eyes on Marcella since she had walked away naked into the steam of the bathhouse—just heard her name, as the news of her unexpected marriage flashed through the city on the wings of gossip. It took Cornelia a moment now to recognize her sister, standing in the entrance hall with her jeweled hand tucked into Domitian's arm as Lollia's grandfather came forward to greet them. A ripple of bows crossed the room—and the buzz of whispered voices rose like soft thunder as Domitian led his new bride into the room.

"I still say it isn't fair," Cornelia couldn't help bursting out. "Vespasian doesn't have a wife, and neither does Titus, so Marcella's Imperial hostess now. After everything she's done, she gets to be *first lady of Rome*."

"And maybe Empress one day," Diana said. "If Domitian ever takes the purple."

"Well, he won't," Lollia snorted. "What did we all learn from this year? No one in line to the throne ever gets there. Marcella will only be Empress if she bumps Vespasian *and* Titus out of the way."

"This is Marcella we're talking about," Diana pointed out. "Look at her win-loss record so far."

They all looked at each other. They looked at Marcella, whose jeweled hand was being kissed by half the room.

"She's in purple," Lollia said a little sadly. "We all used to dress in the same color for parties."

The four dashing cousins of the Cornelii, always dressed in harmony. Lollia and Diana had worn various shades of yellow and gold today, to match Cornelia's saffron bridal cloak, but not Marcella. Cornelia remembered that day at the races little more than a year ago, when they had all put on red with such high hopes of the future. She'd made herself as severe as possible, hoping to look like an empress; Lollia had looked her garish and outrageous self; Marcella had been restrained and unjeweled. But now it was Lollia who looked soft and womanly, Cornelia could feel her own hair coming down in tendrils—and Marcella across the room was stiffly wrapped in heavy silks, her hair prisoned in rigid curls, so many jewels shackled about her neck that she could hardly move. She looked across the room at Cornelia,

and Cornelia looked back, but then Domitian's hand descended pos-
sessively on Marcella's arm. Cornelia saw how her sister dropped her
eyes to the floor as she trailed in his wake.

"What are we going to do about her?" Lollia asked, somber.

"I will *never* speak to her again," Cornelia said under her breath,
but she couldn't help looking across the triclinium where Domitian
and Marcella, after a rapid reshuffling of guests, had been given the
couch of honor. Cornelia had accompanied her sister to a hundred banquets; Marcella always lounged on one elbow with an untouched wine
cup in her hand, watching the other guests and smiling faintly. But
now she lay at Domitian's side, lashes covering her eyes as she drank
deep from her goblet. Utterly still. Utterly silent.

"I'm not sure," Diana said at length, "that we have to do anything."

"What do you mean?" Cornelia blinked.

"I have just had the *most* interesting chat with Marcella!" Tullia
bustled up, her embroidered flounces fluttering. "So good to see her
at last! One might have thought she'd have invited us to the palace
by now, but I daresay she's been busy with her new duties. Really, she
and Domitian could have managed their wedding with a trifle less
sensation, but these impetuous young men!" Tullia addressed herself
mostly to Lollia, since she could still not approve of Cornelia's marriage, and could never bring herself to speak directly to Diana. "Just
think, an emperor's son for our Marcella!"

"You hate Marcella," Diana observed.

"—so, she's looking after Titus's daughter Julia now, such excellent
practice for her when she has her own babies, and she's even asked my
advice about planning a menu for an Imperial banquet next week.
Oh, and she's quite given up writing those wretched histories! I always
knew she'd settle into a proper wife if she had a husband who took a
firm hand with her—"

"Cornelia, I must congratulate you on your wedding," a quiet voice
said behind Tullia. "I'm so happy for you."

Marcella, marble-carved and bejeweled, looked nothing like herself. Up close, Cornelia could see that her heavy bracelets had been
stacked to hide a bruise on her wrist.

"I brought you a wedding gift," Marcella continued, holding out a scroll bound up with ribbon. "I had Nessus draw up your horoscope— he says the baby will be a girl, and you'll have two more girls and a pair of sons too . . . of course Nessus just tells people what they want to hear, but it's a nice fortune for all that."

Cornelia made no move to take the scroll. Marcella finally handed it off to a hovering slave.

"I thought perhaps you might call on me at the Domus Aurea," she said, chin rising as Cornelia just stood looking at her. "Domitian doesn't—that is, it isn't suitable for me to pay visits outside the palace."

"I fear I am quite busy," Cornelia said coldly.

"So am I," said Lollia.

"Cornelia—" Marcella reached out a hand. "Please won't you come visit? We'll put our feet up and have a good gossip. Remember when we used to sneak cakes into our bed when we were little, and talk about who we'd marry when we grew up?"

Cornelia saw Piso lying in his own blood on the steps of the Temple of Vesta. She saw Drusus, a knife in his side, brought to his knees but still trying to protect her. She felt her sister's jeweled fingers twine through her own.

"Please," said Marcella. "I want my sister back."

Cornelia pulled her hand away. "What sister?"

Marcella stared at her.

"I shall call on you," Tullia beamed, oblivious. "Tell me, is little Julia over her cough? I have a very good cough remedy for children—"

Marcella gave a desperate look over her shoulder as she was borne off, but Cornelia turned away.

"I don't think we need to do anything about Marcella," Diana said at last. "She's being punished enough."

"Punished?" Cornelia said bitterly. "She's all but an empress!"

"And she's powerless." Diana's eyes were on Domitian, and Cornelia looked too. Just a stocky boy drinking wine on a couch, being charm- ing to Drusus—everyone knew Domitian liked soldiers, determined as he was to outstrip his brother as a general—but his black eyes were unreadable behind the charm. "He reminds me of those charioteers who claw their way up out of the worst slums," Diana said. "Even when they reach the top—palms and fame and hundreds of victories piled at their feet—they still have that hungry look. Like nothing in the world will ever fill them up."

"That's fanciful," Lollia scoffed. "He's just a boy."

Marcella returned to her new husband's side, passive and jewel-wrapped, and Domitian's hand at once claimed her elbow. He broke off midconversation to kiss her—no, to *devour* her.

"I don't think her life is going to be worth much now," Diana said. "Just—menus and slaves and other people's children. And she'll be utterly alone."

"Maybe she was always alone." Cornelia looked at her sister again. "Even when we thought she was one of us." Domitian had slipped off his couch, dragging Marcella with him as he went to accost Lollia's grandfather about something, so Cornelia returned to Drusus's side and nestled under his arm.

He looked down at her as she pressed her cheek against his shoulder. "What is it?"

"Nothing," she said. "I love you."

"Is it your sister?" He knew her so well.

Cornelia hesitated. "It's not that I'm jealous. I certainly don't grudge Marcella the husband—I'd rather have you any day than Domitian."

"Thank you," Drusus said wryly.

"But *I* was supposed to be Empress!" Cornelia burst out. "Not my *little sister!*"

"Um, you're the empress of my heart," Drusus offered.

"That's not the same thing!"

Drusus burst out laughing and pulled her close, kissing her temple. A reluctant smile tugged at Cornelia's lips, and she let him pour her some more watered wine.

Domitian stayed an hour longer, and rose to leave as abruptly as he'd entered. "But we've just arrived," Marcella protested.

"Correct. And now we're leaving. Did I mention to you all?" he added to the room at large. "I've changed my wife's name. I don't like the name Marcella, so from now on she'll be called Domitia. After me."

"Domitia," everyone echoed, applause rippling. Cornelia saw her sister's eyes hunt around the room, panicky, and finally felt a twinge of pity. But Marcella was gone, back to the Imperial palace and the life she'd somehow earned for herself with her scheming, and Cornelia didn't know her at all. This Marcella was a thousand years removed from the little girl who had nibbled cakes under a quilt with her big sister and giggled about the future. Just as well she had a new name. Marcella—*her* Marcella—might as well be dead.

The sun had started its descent now toward the atrium roof, and the wedding guests sprawled on their couches in happy idleness. Lollia had disappeared somewhere after taking little Flavia upstairs for a nap. Lollia's grandfather was tipsy, in love with the whole world, the laurel wreath slipping more and more rakishly over his ear. A troop of dancers glided out to entertain everyone before the sweets course was brought in, and Cornelia just closed her eyes and leaned against Drusus's shoulder, half asleep and entirely content. Something fluttered in her stomach—could the baby be starting to move already?

Then an earsplitting shriek tore the room in half.

The music died away. Cornelia opened her eyes, and they all looked around. Tullia was clutching the edge of the door leading toward the *culina*. Normally only slaves passed back and forth through that passage, but the slaves were all occupied with the sweet courses. Except for one freedman, tall and golden and quite familiar by now, who had Lollia pinned up against the wall and was kissing her passionately. Lollia's hand twined through his hair, the plain ring gleaming on her fourth finger.

"Really, Tullia," Lollia drawled over Thrax's broad and suddenly immobile shoulder. "Don't you knock?" She dragged the freedman's head down for another kiss, and suddenly half the room was swept in giggles. Cornelia felt a bubble of laughter rising in her throat and clapped a hand hastily over her mouth. Drusus's lips were twitching.

Tullia banged the door shut. "Dear," Gaius said nervously, but she whipped up a hand to quiet the triclinium that was now astir with whispers and giggles. Cornelia clamped harder on the bubble in her throat, trying her best to be appalled. *Shocking of Lollia. I am furious. Just furious.* She coughed.

"That's enough," Tullia said, not shrieking but whispering. "I've tried my best. I've tried to bring morals to this family, but I've failed. Failed! I don't think Juno herself could succeed. You're all degenerates"—her bulging eyes swept Lollia's grandfather with his tipsy laurel wreath— "and plebs"—glaring at Drusus—"and *sluts*"—looking at Diana.

"Why am I a slut?" Diana wondered.

"Now, now," Gaius said, placating, but Tullia rounded on him.

"And you! I'm done with you! You and your degenerate uncontrollable family!" She yanked off her wedding ring and flung it at his feet, bosom heaving. *"Done!"*

Gaius opened his mouth. He closed it again. He turned scarlet. Wordlessly Cornelia handed him her cup of wine, and he drained it in one swallow.

"Well?" Tullia shrieked.

Gaius pointed at the door. "Get out," he whispered.

Someone tittered. Tullia turned the color of a plum, and suddenly the whole room was roaring with laughter.

"Ohh—" Tullia's mouth opened in a soundless shriek. She whirled and ran out of the room, gone forever if the gods were good, and Lollia's grandfather was chortling and Diana was clapping, and Cornelia dropped her head against her new husband's shoulder and laughed until her eyes watered.

"Here, brother." Drusus refilled Gaius's wine cup. "Have another."

"Gods, yes," said Gaius, and grabbed the whole decanter.

IT was near dusk by the time Diana could get away. The party was clearly going to run late and wild. Lollia and her freedman had long since disappeared; Cornelia lay with her head in Drusus's lap as he ran a hand over her stomach and tried to feel the baby, which she insisted was moving; and Nessus the Imperial astrologer had managed to stay behind when Domitian's entourage left and was happily telling fortunes. "No, no," he clucked over the pink palm of Lollia's grandfather, "don't invest in Egyptian grain, they're going to have some bad flooding next year. Silver mines in Gaul, that's the thing—" The rest of the revelers, those still standing, were being led by Gaius, who had not gotten so drunk since becoming the dignified and responsible paterfamilias of the Cornelii.

"Diana," he said vaguely, waving a wine cup at her as she took her leave. "Y're very pretty, you know—always thought so—drive a chariot like a man, but v'ry pretty for all that. More wine! Stay and have a cup?" He patted the cushions beside him. "I might marry you, y'know—you wouldn't fuss and scream at a chap, would you?"

"No," said Diana, amused. "But I think you've had bad enough luck with wives without taking me on, Gaius."

"I'll take care of him." Drusus grinned, rescuing Gaius's wine cup just in time. "Duck out of here if you want, girl."

A festival mood still ruled in the streets as Diana left the house and climbed into her litter. Every tavern spilled over with happy drinkers, and children ran waving bright ribbons in their fists and tossing each other Janus-headed coins. The Year of the Four Emperors, they were already calling it. Who knew if this new year might be the Year of Six Emperors, or Three Emperors—or maybe just One?

Emperor Vespasian was no doubt returning to the Domus Aurea even now for an Imperial banquet, just as tired and victorious as any winning team in the Circus Maximus. Diana wished Vespasian well. He'd entered the city behind his immaculate legions, wearing his armor like a second skin and driving a two-horse chariot with a skill Diana appreciated. His shrewd ruddy face was already familiar; she saw it every day in marble on her father's worktable as he chiseled painstakingly at his bust of the new Emperor. "Still working on that one?" Diana had asked her father after the parade. He had carved his busts of Galba and Otho and Vitellius much more quickly.

"I can take my time with this one," Paris said, his chisel making minute taps over Vespasian's cheerful carved face. "Years, if necessary. This Emperor is going to last."

"How do you know that?" Diana sat on the end of his worktable, swinging her feet.

"It's all in the face. Humorous, you know, and an emperor needs humor." A moment's thought. "And a lot of legions."

"If you say so." She couldn't help feeling a sad twinge for fat, drunk, convivial Vitellius, who had rooted for his team so uproariously . . . though he wouldn't have been cheering today, watching the Anemoi win seven of eight heats and the Blues come in dead last every time. Their famous blood bays had been lost in the riots, and now they had only nags. Diana cackled with glee every time she thought of it.

The litter lurched to a halt after an interminable hour, and Diana climbed down. Her charioteer medallions caught a glint from the last rays of the sun—the Reds faction had struck a medallion in her own image after her Circus Maximus win, bearing the date and her profile, but she'd never wear that. It had pride of place over her bed, right beside her victory palm.

"I suppose you'll never be happy watching the races now," her cousins had teased her, not understanding. "Not now you've driven a race yourself!"

"Oh no," Diana said serenely. She'd driven her four winds to victory once, and that was enough. No one laughed at her now when she trailed down to the stables in her silks; no one scoffed when the Anemoi pushed their red noses eagerly into her hands as if to say, *Remember when we flew together?* She had a withered palm branch in her bedchamber; she was a charioteer; and though the Anemoi would run hundreds more races, they would never run for any other driver the way they ran for her. Horses ran like that only once in a lifetime . . . or maybe twice. She smiled, thinking of how they'd flown under her hands during the riots. Maybe she *had* gotten to drive them for two races, at that. Nessus had been right after all.

So . . . now what?

She kilted her skirt through her girdle, trotting up the long slope to Llyn's villa and coming automatically to the stables. Normally he would be bedding the horses down by this time in the evening, but she didn't find him among the stalls. "Llyn?" She came into the yard, shading her eyes against the sun and looking at the rail where he so often sat looking west toward Britannia. But he wasn't there tonight.

She came up to the villa then, putting her head around the door and calling his name again. No answer. She hesitated a moment, thinking of the laws of guest-right, but finally entered. The villa was a sprawling pillared place, untidy but friendly. The black dog looked up at her entrance and then put his nose down again.

"Llyn?"

Two slaves stared at her but returned silently to their work. Diana passed them, coming to the atrium at the center of the house. No urns or columns, just a square of grass—and a stone in the middle instead of the usual pool. Some dark foreign stone, rough-hewn, flattened like an altar. From Britannia? Somehow she was sure of it.

Something rested on top, and she picked it up. One of Llyn's bronze arm rings, carved with twining leaves and laughing faces. "Seems rather cheerful for you," she'd said once, looking at the sinuous bronze curves. They'd been in the hayloft, sweat drying on naked skin, lying identically with hands clasped behind their heads. "I'd have expected swords and skulls."

"It was my father's," he'd said. "He was lord of all chiefs, appointed by the Druids. Lord of war. Lord of death. A Druid gave him that"—touching the laughing, time-smoothed bronze faces—"to remind him he was lord of life, too. He gave it to me last year, when he died."

The arm ring was still warm in her hands. Something lay under it, sitting on the rock—a wax-covered tablet; signed, notarized, quite official. "If anything happens to me," Llyn had once told her, "my horses are yours." But he'd lived in Rome long enough to appreciate the importance of the legalities, so he'd gone ahead and made it official. The horses, the barn, the house, the slaves—everything now belonged to her.

"Do you ever think of fleeing Rome?" Diana had asked him once in the hayloft, tracing an old puckered scar along his broad chest. "Going back to Britannia?"

"Yes." A restless movement of the shoulder under her head. "But I took that oath. Emperor Claudius forced it out through my teeth, but I said the words."

"Wouldn't that be an oath worth breaking? Rather than putting a knife in your own heart a few years down the line."

He stirred the ends of her hair with his fingers—long fingers, blunt-tipped and callused. "Oaths are the only thing that make men different from beasts."

Diana sat down on the rough-hewn rock in the atrium, turning the bronze arm ring over. It lay heavy in her hands, and it smelled like him. "You smell like bronze," she'd informed him the first time they'd ended up in the loft. "And hay."

"You smell like horse," he'd retorted, one of his big hands exploring the bare arc of her spine. He'd looked bemused, as if she still weren't quite real to him—but he'd smiled too, ruefully, as if he couldn't figure out how he'd ended up in a hayloft with a girl who wasn't quite real, either.

It had been quite easy. They'd boosted each other into chariots and lifted each other out of crashes; they'd bandaged each other's scrapes and massaged each other's wrenched muscles; they'd drunk wine and shoveled manure and argued horse breeding. At some point lovemaking had slipped into the mix as well, with no more fuss than the rest of it.

The black dog came padding into the atrium, and Diana scratched behind his ears. "It's been quite a year," she said aloud. "Quite a year." She'd said as much to Llyn last week, feeling the hay prickle against her bare legs and watching the sunlight coming in brilliant fingers through the cracks in the hayloft's roof.

"A bad year." He'd looked so sober that Diana leaned down and brushed her mouth lightly across his.

"I never met anyone who could brood like you," she said. "Come on. We've got horses to feed." He'd laughed, then—really laughed for the first time since she'd known him as they disentangled their tunics from the hay and helped each other dress. He'd put his hands around her waist and lifted her down from the sparkling dark of the loft, same as always, and with their shoulders brushing easily they went to feed the horses, arguing about whether a colt should be broken to a chariot at age three or age four.

That one raucous full-throated laugh . . . she'd remember that best, now that he was gone.

Diana looked up through the open roof of the atrium. The sky was a deep Imperial purple overhead, but toward the west—toward Britannia—there was still an orange streak of sun. She imagined him walking toward it, long strides eating up the ground, sword swinging beside one breech-clad leg. She wondered if he'd find Britannia unbearably changed; she wondered if he'd gone back to continue his father's fight or only to die in peace—then she smiled a little and picked up the wax tablet again. Cornelia had a home and husband again; Lollia had peace and love; Marcella had power, though it had proved to be a two-edged sword. And Diana?

"I'm going to breed the best horses in Rome," she said aloud, and it felt right. She'd had some thought of having Llyn at her side for that, but now it looked like it would just be Diana. That felt all right, too.

She rose, sliding the bronze ring with its laughing faces over her arm above the elbow. The black dog padded silently from the hall, falling in at her heels as she headed back out to the stables.

Epilogue

ഗറ

IT was the first time in years that they all matched, Cornelia thought. The four Cornelias, all dressed alike again—but the whole city matched, because Emperor Titus was dead and every citizen in Rome wore black.

"Oh dear," Cornelia murmured at the massive public funeral. "I had such high hopes of Titus." So cheerful and energetic, so intelligent and forthright—and dead, after only two years of rule.

Cornelia's youngest daughter leaned against her side, not quite sure what it was all about but needing comfort, and Cornelia leaned a cheek against her smooth chestnut hair. Drusus held the boys, one on each arm, and they persisted in waving at the Praetorians as if it was a parade.

"Everybody had high hopes of Titus." Lollia shifted her baby to her other hip and craned for a better view. Little Flavia stood at her side—fifteen years old! Where did the time go? She was betrothed to the new Emperor's cousin now, and a person of much importance, but she wasn't too grand to carry the first of her golden-haired little half-brothers on her shoulders. Thrax stood behind, as always. Lollia's husbands still tended to come and go—she'd racked up seven by the time her grandfather died, and after that declared she was on hiatus— but Thrax was as permanent as the weather. Roman society had long since stopped being shocked. "And now," Lollia concluded gloomily, "we've got Domitian."

Cheering through the crowds mounted like a wave. Domitian himself was approaching on a gray horse, armored like a general, a wreath tipped back over his head. Burlier now than the boy of nineteen who had carried off Marcella, but the deep-set black gaze was as inscrutable as ever as he smiled and waved to his new subjects. Every year that passed, people whispered more and more of his depravities.

"Isn't anyone going to say it?" Diana looked back and forth between her cousins. She looked more exotic than ever now, face tanned dark gold against her pale hair after so many hours training her young colts under the midday sun. Distinguished men still turned up at her door, hoping that she'd marry one of them, but Cornelia had long since given up trying to push suitors at her. "We're all thinking it, aren't we? Marcella finally did it. She's an empress."

"God help us all." Lollia touched the little gold cross hanging from her neck, a twin to the wooden one at Thrax's throat. "There she is."

Cornelia felt her throat tighten as she looked past Emperor Domitian to the woman in the gold litter. Marcella waved to the crowd with a cool hand, her smile empty and unchanging. *My little sister.* Though there was nothing of her little sister in that perfect marble-carved effigy. In twelve years, Cornelia hadn't traded one word with Marcella beyond the required empty courtesies.

Cornelia reached for Drusus's hand, and he gave it a comforting squeeze. Domitian passed out of sight with his Empress behind him, cheers following like a rumble of thunder. Eleventh Emperor of Rome.

His massive entourage followed. Cornelia's eyes picked out the Imperial astrologer in his star-embroidered robes— his horoscope had predicted three girls and two boys for her and Drusus, which meant she had one daughter still to come. Well, if you believed in horoscopes . . . Diana waved irrepressibly at Marcus Norbanus, consul again this year. No one else could make a limp so distinguished.

"I wonder," Drusus began, but fell silent. Cornelia didn't ask him what he was wondering, and neither did her cousins—more her sisters now than the sister she had been born with. They were all wondering the same thing. They had all four of them stood together before the Temple of Vesta while a city tore itself apart, and it had left its mark. Ten peaceful years under Vespasian, two more peaceful years under Titus, but none of them could help thinking it when a new emperor came to power.

Will it last?

Diana shrugged her angular shoulders. "Come to the races today," she suggested. "The Reds are forever."

Unlike emperors.

Historical Note

Historically, Emperor Vespasian did not enter Rome until late in the year following his coup—but I couldn't resist the temptation of letting the readers see the face of the man who finally ended the madness of the Year of the Four Emperors. Vespasian was shrewd, humorous, sensible, and intelligent, and his reign ushered in an era of much-needed peace for Rome. He was followed by his brilliant son Titus and eventually his second son, Domitian, who proved less popular—but that is a story for another book, one titled *Mistress of Rome*.

Most of this book's main events—Galba's death, Piso's murder at the Temple of Vesta, Otho's speech and suicide after the battle of Bedriacum, Vitellius's love of food and of the Blues, the riots in Rome, Domitian's elopement with a married woman—are true to history, and so are many of the characters in *Daughters of Rome*. Domitia, daughter of the famous historical general Gnaeus Corbulo and renamed here as Marcella, will go on after her scandalous elopement to a grim two decades as Domitian's wife; he eventually came to hate her, but never relinquished his hold on Marcella/Domitia. Her sister Cornelia, Corbulo's elder daughter (also called Domitia, and renamed by me for clarity), is only a shadowy figure in history and disappears into domestic anonymity. Her marriage to Piso Licinianus is my own invention, though the historical Piso did exist and was murdered by Praetorians, who took his head to show the new Emperor and later sold it back to Piso's family. Centurion Densus of the Praetorian Guard also existed, though history records that he died the night of Galba's assassination in a fruitless attempt to save Piso's life. It seemed an unfair end for a brave and loyal soldier, so I let him survive in *Daughters of Rome* to attain a happier ending.

Lollia is a fictional character, but her husbands were real to history—Titus Flavius as Vespasian's splendid soldier son, Senator Vinius as Galba's right-hand man, Salvius Titianus as Emperor Otho's inoffensive brother, and Fabius Valens as Vitellius's ruthless king-maker were all real men and had the fates described here. Valens's counterpart Caecina Alienus is a historical figure as well; he did turn traitor after being appointed commander of Vitellius's armies when a temporary illness laid Fabius Valens low. He was rewarded for his treachery but was eventually executed some years later for trying to betray yet another emperor. Lollia's daughter Flavia Domitilla was also a real figure, though historically she was Titus's niece rather than his daughter. Both Flavia and Titus's daughter Julia grew up to endure tragedy and adventure under the reign of their uncle Domitian.

Diana is also a fictional character, but Llyn ap Caradoc was possibly real. His father, Caradoc, or Caratacus, was a formidable warrior in Britain whose rebellion against Rome is well documented. He was eventually captured along with his family (some accounts mention daughters; some mention a son possibly named Linus or Llyen or Llyn), and they were all taken to Rome and pardoned. They disappear from history at that point, but I always wondered what happened to Caratacus and his family. His son, if he had one, would have been a vigorous young warrior forced to live most of his life among enemies he hated. The historical Caratacus never escaped captivity—history would have recorded that—but *Daughters of Rome* allowed me to hope that at least his son might have one day returned home.

The Roman chariot races that take up so much of Diana and Llyn's time are depicted as accurately as possible. Successful charioteers attained celebrity status in ancient Rome, and many young patrician men drove in the great circuses—though never any women, to my knowledge. The rivalry between the four racing factions was vicious: think Red Sox/Yankees.

The Year of Four Emperors proved cataclysmic to the Roman people. There had been coups before, but always with at least a pretense of legality. The year 69 was the first time the Empire went up for grabs to any usurper with an army, profoundly shocking a nation that had existed many centuries as a Republic. A period of relative stability would follow with Vespasian and his heirs, but Rome would never be quite so secure again from ambitious usurpers. A new era had dawned.

Characters

The Family Cornelii

Gaius Cornelius, paterfamilias
Tullia, his wife

Senator *Marcus Norbanus,* cousin to the *Cornelii, Tullia*'s first husband
  *Paulinus, son of *Tullia* and *Marcus*

*Cornelia *Prima, Gaius*'s eldest sister

  *Piso Licinianus, her husband

*Cornelia Secunda, called **Marcella,** *Gaius*'s second sister

  *Lucius Aelius Lamia, her husband

Cornelia Tertia, called **Lollia,** a first cousin

  Lollia's grandfather, freedman and wealthy trader
  *Titus Flavius, Lollia's first husband, eldest son of *Vespasian*
    *Flavia Domitilla, their daughter
  *Senator Flaccus Vinius, Lollia's third husband, consul and advisor to
    Emperor *Galba*
  *Salvius Otho, Lollia's fourth husband, brother to Emperor Otho
  *Fabius Valens, Lollia's fifth husband, general and advisor to Emperor
    Vitellius

Thrax, a slave

Cornelia Quarta, called **Diana,** a first cousin

Paris, her father
*Llyn ap Caradoc, horse trainer and former rebel
Xerxes, faction director for the Reds
Bassus, faction director for the Blues
Derricus, star charioteer for the Blues
Siculus, charioteer for the Reds
The Anemoi (Boreas, Notus, Eurus, Zephyrus), chariot horses for the Reds

EMPERORS

*Servius Sulpicius **Galba**

*Senator Vinius, consul and adviser, Lollia's third husband
*Centurion Drusus Sempronius Densus, a centurion in his Praetorian Guard

*Marcus Salvius **Otho**

*Salvius, Otho's brother, Lollia's fourth husband
*Proculus, his Praetorian Prefect

*Aulus **Vitellius**

*Fabius Valens, his adviser, Lollia's fifth husband
*Caecina Alienus, his adviser
*Lucius Vitellius, his brother

*Titus Flavius **Vespasian**

*Titus, his eldest son, Lollia's first husband
    *Julia Flavia, his daughter by his second wife
*Domitian, his youngest son
Nessus, Domitian's astrologer

Turn the page for an excerpt from

Mistress of Rome

Available in paperback from Berkley Books

THEA
ROME, SEPTEMBER, A.D. 81

I opened my wrist with one firm stroke of the knife, watching with interest as the blood leaped out of the vein. My wrists were latticed with knife scars, but I still found the sight of my own blood fascinating. There was always the element of danger: After so many years, would I finally get careless and cut too deep? Would this be the day I watched my young life stream away into the blue pottery bowl with the nice frieze of nymphs on the side? The thought much brightened a life of minimum excitement.

But this time it was not to be. The first leap of blood slowed to a trickle, and I settled back against the mosaic pillar in the atrium, blue bowl in my lap. Soon a pleasant haze would descend over my eyes and the world would take on an agreeably distant hue. I needed that haze today. I would be accompanying my new mistress to the Colosseum, to see the gladiatorial games for the accession of the new Emperor. And from what I'd heard about the games . . .

"Thea!"

My mistress's voice. I muttered something rude in a combination of Greek, Hebrew, and gutter Latin, none of which she understood.

The blue bowl held a shallow cup of my blood. I wrapped my wrist in a strip of linen, tying off the knot with my teeth, then emptied the bowl into the atrium fountain. I took care not to drip on my brown wool tunic. My mistress's eagle eyes would spot a bloodstain in half a second, and I would not care to explain to her exactly why, once or twice a month, I took a blue bowl with a nice frieze of nymphs on the side and filled it with my own blood. However, fairly speaking, there was very little that I would care to tell my mistress at all. She hadn't owned me long, but I already knew *that*.

"Thea!"

I turned too quickly, and had to lean against the pillars of the atrium. Maybe I'd overdone it. Drain too much blood, and nausea set in. Surely not good on a day when I would have to watch thousands of animals and men get slaughtered.

"Thea, quit dawdling." My mistress poked her pretty head out the bedroom door, her annoyed features agreeably hazy to my eyes. "Father's waiting, and you still have to dress me."

I drifted obediently after her, my feet seeming to float several inches above the floor. A tasteless floor with a mosaic scene of gladiators fighting it out with tridents, blood splashing copiously in square red tiles. Tasteless but appropriate: My mistress's father, Quintus Pollio, was one of several organizers of the Imperial gladiatorial games.

"The blue gown, Thea. With the pearl pins at the shoulders."

"Yes, my lady."

Lady Lepida Pollia. I had been purchased for her several months ago when she turned fourteen: a maid of her own age to do her hair and carry her fan now that she was so nearly a woman. As a gift I didn't rank as high as the pearl necklace and the silver bangles and the half-dozen silk gowns she'd also received from her doting father, but she certainly liked having her own personal shadow.

"Cut yourself at dinner again, Thea?" She caught sight of my bandaged wrist at once. "You really are a fumble-fingers. Just don't drop my jewel box, or I'll be very cross. Now, I want the gold bands in my hair, in the Greek style. I'll be a Greek for the day . . . just like you, Thea."

She knew I was no Greek, despite the name bestowed on me by the Athenian merchant who was my first owner. "Yes, my lady," I murmured in my purest Greek. A frown flickered between her fine black brows. I was better educated than my mistress, and it annoyed her no end. I tried to remind her at least once a week.

"Don't go giving yourself airs, Thea. You're just another little Jew slave. Remember that."

"Yes, my lady." Meekly I coiled and pinned her curls. She was already chattering on.

". . . Father says that Belleraphon will fight this afternoon. Really, I know he's our best gladiator, but that flat face! He may dress like a dandy, but all the perfume in the world won't turn him into an Apollo. Of course he is wonderfully graceful, even when he's sticking someone right through the throat—ouch! You pricked me!"

"Sorry, my lady."

"You certainly look green. There's no reason to get sick over the games, you know. Gladiators and slaves and prisoners—they'd all die anyway. At least this way we get some fun out of it."

"Maybe it's my Jewish blood," I suggested. "We don't usually find death amusing."

"Maybe that's it." Lepida examined her varnished nails. "At least the games are bound to be thrilling today. What with the Emperor getting sick and dying in the middle of the season, we haven't had a good show for months."

"Inconsiderate of him," I agreed.

"At least the new Emperor is supposed to love the games. Emperor Domitian. Titus Flavius Domitianus . . . I wonder what he'll be like? Father went to no end of trouble arranging the best bouts for him. Pearl earrings, Thea."

"Yes, my lady."

"And the musk perfume. There." Lepida surveyed herself in the polished steel mirror. She was very young—fourteen, same as me—and too young, really, for the rich silk gown, the pearls, the rouge. But she had no mother and Quintus Pollio, so shrewd in dealing with slave merchants and *lanistae*, was clay in the hands of his only child. Besides, there was no doubt that she cut a dash. Her beauty was not in the peacock-blue eyes or even the yard of silky black hair that was her pride and joy. It was in her Olympian poise. On the basis of that poise, Lady Lepida Pollia aimed to catch a distinguished husband, a patrician who would raise the family Pollii at last into the highest ranks of Roman society.

She beckoned me closer, peacock fan languidly stirring her sculpted curls. In the mirror behind her I was a dark-brown shadow: lanky where she was luscious, sunburned where she was white-skinned, drab where she was brilliant. Very flattering, at least for her.

"Most effective," she announced, mirroring my thoughts. "But you really do need a new dress, Thea. You look like a tall dead tree. Come along, Father's waiting."

Father was indeed waiting. But his impatience softened as Lepida dimpled at him and pirouetted girlishly. "Yes, you look very pretty. Be sure to smile at Aemilius Graccus today; that's a very important family, and he's got an eye for pretty girls."

I could have told him that it wasn't pretty *girls* Aemilius Graccus had an eye for, but he didn't ask me. Maybe he should have. Slaves heard everything.

Most Romans had to get up at daybreak to get a good seat in the Colosseum. But the Pollio seats were reserved, so we tripped out just fashionably late enough to nod at all the great families. Lepida sparkled at Aemilius Graccus, at a party of patrician officers lounging on the street corner, at anyone with a purple-bordered toga and an old name. Her father importantly exchanged gossip with any patrician who favored him with an obligatory smile.

". . . I heard Emperor Domitian's planning a campaign in Germania next season! Wants to pick up where his brother left off, eh? No doubting Emperor Titus cut those barbarians down to size, we'll see if Domitian can do any better . . ."

"Quintus Pollio," I overheard a patrician voice drawl. "Really, his perfume alone—!"

"But he does his job so well. What's a smile now and then if it keeps him working hard?"

So Quintus Pollio went on bowing and smirking. He would have sold thirty years of his life for the honor of carrying the family name of the Julii, the Gracchi, or the Sulpicii. So would my mistress, for that matter.

I amused myself by peering into the vendors' stalls that crowded the streets. Souvenirs of dead gladiators, the blood of this or that great fighter preserved in sand, little wooden medallions painted with the face of the famous Belleraphon. These last weren't selling very well, since not even the artists could give Belleraphon a pretty face. Portraits of a handsome Thracian trident fighter did much better.

"He's so beautiful!" Out of the corner of my eye I saw a cluster of girls mooning over a medallion. "I sleep with his picture under my pillow every night—"

I smiled. We Jewish girls, we liked our men to be fighters, too—but we liked them real and we liked them long-lived. The kind who take the head off a legionnaire in the morning and come home at night to preside over the Sabbath table. Only Roman girls mooned over crude garish portraits of men they'd never met, men who would probably be dead before the year was out. On the other hand, perhaps a short-lived man was better for daydreaming about. He'd never be old, he'd never lose his looks, and if you tired of him he'd soon be gone.

The crowds grew thicker around the Colosseum. I'd walked often enough in its vast marble shadow as I ran errands for my mistress, but this was my first time inside and I struggled not to gape. So huge, so many marble arches, so many statues staring arrogantly from their plinths, so many seats. Fifty thousand eager spectators could cram inside, so they said. An arena fit for the gods, begun by the late Emperor Vespasian, finished by his son the late Emperor Titus, opened today in celebration for Titus's younger brother who had just donned the Imperial purple as Emperor Domitian.

So much marble for a charnel house. I'd have preferred a theatre, but then I would rather hear music than watch men die. I imagined singing for a crowd as large as this one, a real audience, instead of the frogs in the conservatorium when I scrubbed the tiles . . .

"Keep that fan moving, Thea." Lepida settled into her velvet cushions, waving like an Empress at the crowds who had a small cheer for her father. Men and women usually sat separately to watch the games, but Quintus Pollio as organizer of the games could sit with his daughter if he liked. "Faster than that, Thea. It's going to be gruesomely hot. Really, why won't it cool down? It's supposed to be *fall*."

Obediently I waved the fan back and forth. The games would last all day, which meant that I had a good six hours of feather-waving in front of me. Oh, my arms were going to ache.

Trumpets blared brassily. Even my heart skipped a beat at that thrilling fanfare. The new Emperor stepped out into the Imperial box, raising his hand to the crowd, and I stretched on my toes for a look at him. Domitian, third Emperor of the Flavian dynasty: tall, ruddy-cheeked, dazzling the eye in his purple cloak and golden circlet.

"Father." Lepida tugged on her father's sleeve. "Is the Emperor *really* a man of secret vices? At the bathhouse yesterday, I heard—"

I could have told her that all Emperors were rumored to be men of secret vices. Emperor Tiberius and his little slave boys, Emperor Caligula who slept with his sisters, Emperor Titus and his mistresses—what was the point of having an Emperor if you couldn't cook up spicy rumors about him?

Domitian's Empress, now, was less gossipworthy. Tall, statuesque, lovely as she stepped forward beside her Imperial husband to wave at the roaring crowds—but disappointed reports had it that the Empress was an impeccable wife. Still, her green silk *stola* and emeralds caused a certain buzz of feminine admiration. Green, no doubt, would become *the* color of the season.

"Father." Lepida tugged at her father's arm again. "You know I'm always so admired in green. An emerald necklace like the Empress's—"

Various other Imperial cousins filed after the Emperor—there was a niece, Emperor Titus's younger daughter Lady Julia, who had supposedly petitioned to join the Vestal Virgins but had been refused. Otherwise, a dull lot. I was disappointed. My first sight of the Imperial family, and they looked like any other clutch of languid patricians.

The Emperor came forward, raising his arm, and shouted the introduction of the games. Secret vices or not, he had a fine reverberating voice.

The other slaves had explained the games to me many times, incredulous at my ignorance. Duels between wild beasts always opened the morning festivities; first on the list today was a battle between an elephant and a rhinoceros. The rhinoceros put out the elephant's eye with its tusk. I could have happily lived my entire life without knowing what an elephant's scream sounded like.

"Marvelous!" Pollio threw a few coins into the arena. Lepida picked through a plate of honeyed dates. I concentrated on the peacock fan. *Swish, swish, swish.*

A bull and a bear battled next, then a lion and a leopard. Tidbits to whet the appetite, as it were. The bear was sullen, and three handlers with sharp rods had to goad its flanks bloody before it attacked the bull, but the lion and the leopard screamed and flew at each other the moment the chains were released. The crowd cheered and chattered, sighed and settled back. Pomp and spectacle came next, dazzling the eye after the crowd's attention was honed: tame cheetahs in silver harnesses padding round the arena, white bulls with little golden boys capering on their backs, jeweled and tasseled elephants lumbering in stately dance steps accompanied by Nubian flute players . . .

"Father, can't I have a Nubian slave?" Lepida plucked at her father's arm. "Two, even. A matched pair to carry my packages when I go shopping—"

Comic acts next. A tame tiger was released into the arena after a dozen sprinting hares, bounding in a flash of stripes to collect them one by one in his jaws and return them unharmed to the trainer. Rather nice, really. I enjoyed it, but there were scattered boos through the stands. Fans of the Colosseum didn't come for games; they came for blood.

"The Emperor," Quintus Pollio was droning, "is especially fond of the goddess Minerva. He has built a new shrine to her in his palace. Perhaps we should make a few large public offerings—"

The tame tiger and his handler padded out, replaced by a hundred white deer and a hundred long-necked ostriches who were released galloping into the arena and shot down one by one by archers on high. Lepida saw some acquaintance in a neighboring box and cooed greetings through most of the blood.

More animal fights. Spearmen against lions, against buffaloes, against bulls. The buffaloes went down bewildered and mooing, the bulls ran maddened onto the spears that gouged their chests open, but the lions snarled and stalked and took a spearman with them before they were chased down and gutted. Such wonderful fun. *Swish, swish, swish.*

"Oh, the gladiators." Lepida cast the plate of dates aside and sat up. "Fine specimens, Father."

"Nothing but the best for the Emperor." He chucked his daughter's chin. "And for my little one who loves the games! The Emperor wanted a battle today, not just the usual duels. Something big and special before the midday executions—"

In purple cloaks the gladiators filed out of the gates, making a slow circle of the arena as the fans cheered. Some strutted proudly; some stalked ahead without looking right or left. The handsome Thracian trident fighter blew kisses to the crowd and was showered with roses by adoring women. Fifty gladiators, paired off to fight to the death. Twenty-five would exit in triumph through the arena's Gate of Life. Twenty-five would be dragged out through the Gate of Death on iron hooks.

"*Hail, Emperor!*" As one they roared out toward the Imperial box. "*We salute you from death's shadow!*"

The clank of sharpened weapons. The scrape of plated armor. The crunch of many feet on sand as they spread out in their pairs. A few mock combats first with wooden weapons, and then the Emperor dropped his hand.

The blades crashed. The audience surged forward, straining against the marble barriers, shouting encouragement to the favorites, cursing the clumsy. Waving, wagering, shrieking.

Don't look. Swish, swish, went the fan. *Don't look.*

"Thea," Lepida said sweetly. "What do you think of that German?"

I looked. "Unlucky," I said as the man died howling on his opponent's trident. In the next box, a senator threw down a handful of coins in disgust.

The arena was a raging sea of fighters. Already the sand was patched with blood.

"The Gaul over there wants mercy." Pollio peered out, sipping at his wine cup. "Poor show, he dropped his shield. *Iugula!*"

Iugula—"Kill him." There was also *Mitte*—"spare him"—but you didn't hear that nearly so often. As I was to find out, it took an extraordinary show of courage to move the Colosseum to mercy. They wanted heroism, they wanted blood, they wanted death. Not scared men. Not mercy.

It was over quite quickly. The victors strutted before the Imperial box, where the Emperor tossed coins to those who had fought well. The losers lay crumpled and silent on the sand, waiting to be raked away by the arena attendants. One or two men still writhed in their death throes, shrieking as they tried to stuff the guts back into their own bellies. Laughing tribunes and giggling girls laid bets on how long it would take them to die.

Swish, swish, swish. My arms ached.

"Fruit, Dominus?" A slave came to Pollio's elbow with a tray of grapes and figs. Lepida gestured for more wine, and all through the patrician boxes I saw people sitting back to chatter. In the tiers above, plebs fanned themselves and looked for the hawkers who darted with bread and beer for sale. In his Imperial box the Emperor leaned back on one elbow, rolling dice with his guards. The morning had flown. For some, dragged.

For the midday break, business was attended to inside the arena. The dead gladiators had all been carted away, the patches of blood raked over, and now the arena guards led out a shuffling line of shackled figures. Slaves, criminals, prisoners; all sentenced for execution.

"Father, can't I have more wine? It's a special occasion!"

Down in the arena, the man at the head of the shackled line blinked as a blunt sword was shoved into his hands. He stared at it, dull-eyed and bent-backed, and the arena guard prodded him. He turned wearily and hacked at the chained man behind him. A dull blade, because it took a great deal of hacking. I could hardly hear the man's screams over the chatter in the stands. No one seemed to be paying attention to the arena at all.

The arena guards disarmed the first slave roughly, passing the sword to the next in line. A woman. She killed the man, roughly cutting his throat; was disarmed, killed in turn by the next who tried vainly to stab her through the heart. It took a dozen strokes of the dull sword.

I looked down the chained line. Perhaps twenty prisoners. Old and young, men and women, identical in their bent shoulders and shuffling feet. Only one stood straight, a big man gazing around him with blank eyes. Even from the stands I could see the whip marks latticing his bare back.

"Father, when does Belleraphon's bout come up? I'm dying to see what he can do against that Thracian—"

The guards gave the blunt sword to the man with the scars. He hefted it a moment in his shackled hands, gave it a swing. No hacking for him; he killed the man who had gone before him in one efficient thrust. I winced.

The arena guard reached for the sword and the big scarred man fell a step back, holding the blade up between them. The guard gestured, holding out an impatient hand, and then it all went to hell.

H AND it over," the guard said.

He stood spraddle-legged on the hot sand, heaving air into his parched lungs. The sun scorched down on his naked shoulders and he could feel every separate grain beneath his bare, hardened feet. Sweat stung his wrists and ankles under the rusty cuffs of his chains. His hands had welded around the sword hilt.

"Hand over that sword," the guard ordered. "You're holding up the show."

He stared back glassy-eyed.

"Hand—over—that—sword." Extending an imperious hand.

He cut it off.

The guard screamed. The slick of blood gleamed bright in the mid-day sun. The other guards rushed.

He had not held a sword in over ten years. Much too long, he would have said, to remember anything. But it came back. Fueled by rage it came back fast—the sweet weight of the hilt in his hand, the bite of blade into bone, the black demon's fury that filmed the eyes and whispered in the ear.

Kill them, it said. *Kill them all.*

He met the first guard in a savage joyful rush, swords meeting with a dull screech. He bore down with every muscle, feeling his body arch like a good bow, and saw the sudden leap of fear in the guard's eyes as he felt the strength on the other end of the blade. These Romans with their plumes and pride and shiny breastplates, they didn't think a slave could be strong. In two more thrusts he reduced the guard to a heap of twitching meat on the sand.

More Romans, bright blurs in their feathered crests. A guard fell writhing as dull iron chewed through his hamstrings. A liquid scream.

He savored it. Lunged for another bronze breastplate. The blade slid neatly through the armhole. Another shield falling, another scream.

Not enough, the demon voice whispered. *Not enough.*

He felt distant pain along his back as a blade cut deep, and smiled, turning to chop down savagely. A slave's toughest flesh was on his back, but they didn't know that—these men whose vineyards were tended by captive warriors from Gaul and their beds warmed by sullen Thracian slave girls. They didn't know anything. He cut the guard down, tasting blood in his rough beard.

Not enough.

The sky whirled and turned white as something struck the back of his head. He staggered, turned, raised his blade, felt his entire arm go numb as a guard smashed an iron shield boss against his elbow. Distantly he watched the sword drop from his fingers, falling to hands and knees as a sword hilt crashed against his skull. Sweat trickled into his eyes. Acid, bitter. He sighed as the armored boots buffeted his sides, as the black demon in his head turned back in on itself like a snake devouring its own tail. A familiar road. One he had trodden all his years under whips and chains. With a sword in his hand, everything had been so simple.

Not enough. Never enough.

Over the sound of his own cracking bones, he heard a roar. A vast, impersonal roar like the crashing of the sea. For the first time he turned his eyes outward and saw them: spectators, packed tier upon tier in their thousands. Senators in purple-bordered togas. Matrons in bright silk *stolas*. Priests in white robes. So many . . . did the world hold so many people? He saw a boy's face leap out at him from the front tier, crazily distinct, a boy in a fine toga shouting through a mouthful of figs—and clapping.

They were all clapping. The great arena resounded with applause.

Through dimming eyes, he made out the Imperial balcony. He was close enough to see a fair-haired girl with a white appalled face, one of the Imperial nieces . . . close enough to see the Emperor, his ruddy cheeks, his purple cloak, his amused gaze . . . close enough to see the Imperial hand rise carelessly.

Holding out a hand in the sign of mercy.

Why? he thought. *Why?*

Then the world disappeared.

L EPIDA chattered on as I undressed her for bed that night—not about the games, of course; all that death and blood was old news. Her father had mentioned a certain senator, a man who might be a possible husband for her, and that was all she could talk about. "Senator Marcus Norbanus, his name is, and he's *terribly* old—" I hardly heard a word.

The slave with the scarred back. A Briton, a Gaul? He had fought so savagely, swinging his sword like Goliath, ignoring his own wounds. He'd been snarling even when they brought him down, not caring if he lived or died as long as he took a few with him.

"Thea, be careful with those pearls. They're worth three of you."

I'd seen a hundred slaves like him, served beside them and avoided them. They drank too much, they scowled at their masters and were flogged for troublemakers and did as little work as they could get away with. Men to avoid in quiet corners of the house, if no one was near enough to hear you struggling. Thugs.

So why did I weep suddenly when they brought him down in the arena? I hadn't wept when I was sold to Lepida. I hadn't even wept when I watched the gladiators and the poor bewildered animals slaughtered before my eyes. Why had I wept for a thug?

I didn't even know his name.

"Well, I don't think Emperor Domitian is terribly handsome, but it's hard to tell from a distance, isn't it?" Lepida frowned at a chipped nail. "I do wish we could have some handsome dashing Emperor instead of these stolid middle-aged men."

The Emperor. Why had he bothered to save a half-dead slave? The crowd had clapped for his death as much as for the show he put on. Why save him?

"Go away, Thea. I don't want you anymore. You're quite stupid tonight."

"As you wish," I said in Greek, blowing out her lamp. "You cheap, snide little shrew."

I weaved my way down the hall, leaning against the shadowed pillars for balance, trying not to think of my blue bowl. Not good to bleed myself twice in one day, but oh, I wanted to.

"Ah, Thea. Just what I need."

I stared blurrily at the two Quintus Pollios who beckoned me into the bedchamber and onto the silver sleeping couch. I closed my eyes, stifling a yawn and hoping I wouldn't fall asleep in the middle of his huffing and puffing. Slave girls aren't expected to be enthusiastic, but they are expected to be cheerful. I patted his shoulder as he labored over me. His lips peeled back from his teeth like a mule's during the act of . . . well, whatever you want to call it.

"What a good girl you are, Thea." Sleepily patting my flank. "Run along, now."

I shook down my tunic and slipped out the door. Likely tomorrow he'd slip me a copper.

PART ONE

JULIA

In the Temple of Vesta

Yesterday, Titus Flavius Domitianus was just my brusque and rather strange uncle. Today he is Lord and God, Pontifex Maximus, Emperor of Rome. Like my father and grandfather before him, he is master of the world. And I am afraid.

But he has been kind to me. He says I will marry my cousin Gaius soon, and he promised me splendid games for the celebration. I couldn't tell him that I hate the games. He means to be kind. He says his Empress will fit me for my wedding gown. She is very beautiful in her green silk and emeralds, and they whisper that he's mad with love for her. They also whisper that she hates him—but people like to whisper.

I stare at the flame until there are two flames.

I'm afraid. I'm always afraid. Shadows under the bed, shapes in the dark, voices in the air.

My uncle watched a thousand men die in the arena today—and he saved just one. He hates the rest of the family—but is kind to me.

What does my uncle want? Does anyone know?

Vesta, goddess of hearth and home, watch over me. I need you, now.

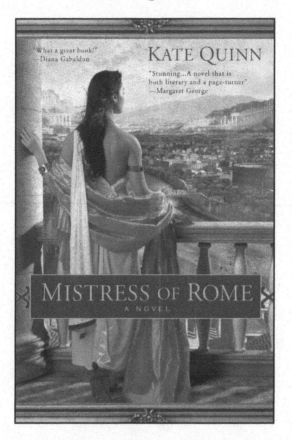